DRIFT

DRIFT

JON MCGORAN

A Tom Doherty Associates Book

New York

DRIFT

Copyright © 2013 by Jon McGoran

A Forge Book
Published by Tom Doherty Associates, LLC
175 Fifth Avenue
New York, NY 10010

www.tor-forge.com

Forge® is a registered trademark of Tom Doherty Associates, LLC.

ISBN 978-0-7653-3470-1 (hardcover)
ISBN 978-1-4668-1524-7 (e-book)

Forge books may be purchased for educational, business, or promotional use. For information on bulk purchases, please contact Macmillan Corporate and Premium Sales Department at 1-800-221-7945 extension 5442 or write specialmarkets@macmillan.com.

First Edition: July 2013

Printed in the United States of America

0 9 8 7 6 5 4 3 2 1

For Elizabeth, and for Will

ACKNOWLEDGMENTS

Writing is often called a solitary pursuit, but by the time a book is finished, and even before it is started, there is a long list of people whose contributions have made that book possible. At the top of my list are my wonderful wife, Elizabeth, whose love and support sustain me; my son, Will, who fills my life with laughter and joy (among other things); and my mom and dad and my siblings—Maeve, Alison, and Hugh—who allowed me to grow up believing I had something worth saying.

I am fortunate to be part of an amazing community of writers, and I would have been lost without the boundless support and friendship of Jonathan Maberry, Dennis Tafoya, Don Lafferty, Greg Frost, and the entire Liars Club: Merry Jones, Ed Pettit, Solomon Jones, Marie Lamba, Kelly Simmons, Keith Strunk, Chuck Wendig, Stephen Susco, Keith DeCandido, and, of course, Leslie Banks, who is with us always. That community also includes the Mystery Writers of America, the International Thriller Writers, and the folks at Bouchercon, Thrillerfest, NoirCon, and the Liars Club's Writers Coffeehouse.

Others who have been indispensible include Anne Dubuisson, for her help with *Drift*, but even more so for her invaluable advice, support, and friendship over the years. Special thanks from my characters go to beta reader extraordinaire Tanya Rotenberg, for making sure they are eating right (and for everything else), and to Robb Bettiker, for helping me make sure they are dying right. Thanks also to Lincoln Brower, Bill Johnson, Bruce Castor, Adam Silverman, and Irv Rotman, and to the Academy of Natural Sciences in Philadelphia, for help and support, and for being a very cool place with crazy big dinosaur skeletons and an amazing butterfly exhibit.

Massive big thanks to my incredible agent, Stacia Decker, at the Donald Maass Literary Agency (*GO TEAM DECKER!*); and to my excellent editor, Kristin Sevick; publisher, Tom Doherty; and everyone else at Tor/Forge.

Finally, I'd like to thank the communities of Weavers Way Co-op, CreekSide Co-op, and food co-ops everywhere, as well as groups like Just Label It, the Non-GMO Project, the Center for Science in the Public Interest, Food Democracy Now, the Center for Food Safety, and the Union of Concerned Scientists. These groups don't agree on everything, but they all advocate for more research, better regulation, and labeling of Genetically Modified Foods. They know, as do more than 90 percent of the American public, that if you are what you eat, it's important to know what it is you are eating.

This book is a work of fiction, but much of what happens in it is only slightly exaggerated. These are interesting times, as they say, and for better or for worse, we now have access to powerful technologies that are often not fully understood. We are in the midst of a food revolution that offers great promise, but while it's important not to be reflexively resistant to new technology, it's also important to understand the potential for far-reaching consequences that, once realized, cannot be undone.

DRIFT

PROLOGUE

The pain was everywhere—in his eyes, his throat, his chest, his head. His hands and feet were shreds. All Renaldo could remember was running and trying to breathe. And pain. He didn't know what he was running from. It was not the pain. It was something worse.

The sun was hot and so bright he could barely see. Stumbling across the field, he came upon a figure, small and frail, wearing pale purple, like jacarandas, and carrying a handful of books. He closed a hand on her arm and she pulled away. His fingers left a green smudge. He tried to ask for help, but he could only cough, a deep cough with no breath in between, just the gray-green taste of dirt and decay and death from the inside out. He followed her, a tiny speck of purple hope getting smaller and smaller. When the coughing finally stopped, she was gone.

He tried to find her, tried to keep going. But after a while, he found himself lying on the ground, and he knew he would never get up again. A rock dug into his back, but he was too weak to move. There was little of him left.

An orange blur fluttered in the air, and he knew it was important, but he couldn't remember why. Then it was gone, too. He closed his eyes, and when he opened them, he was no longer alone. A figure stood over him, massive, blocking out the sun. It had no features at first, no face. Then he saw sunlight glinting off the metal on its brow and its lips, and a darker light glowing in those gray eyes.

This was what he was running from.

The man with the metal face smiled. "Where did you think you were going?" He shook his head, looking back the way Renaldo had come. "Was a good chase," he said, looking almost sad. "But long. Much to clean up."

The man pulled the magazine out of his weapon, his lips moving slightly as he counted the bullets, then he looked at his watch before sliding the magazine back into place. "Guess we have time for a little more fun," he said, smiling as he raised the gun.

Renaldo knew the smile meant pain, but ultimately it also meant salvation. He closed his eyes and turned his face to the white-hot sky, praying to a god he could no longer remember. And when the final bullet came, he welcomed it.

1

The surveillance van smelled of old cheeseburgers, coffee, and me. Parked in front of a vacant storefront in North Philly, I was watching on a little screen as my partner, Danny Tennison, made a buy from a scumbag named Dwayne Rowan just around the corner.

We'd been trying to nab Rowan's supplier, see if we could swim upstream and get the next guy up the chain or the guy above him.

Rowan was almost out of stock, and Danny was trying to find out about the re-up. Rowan didn't have the faintest idea Danny was a cop, and he wasn't trying to be discreet, either. He was just a dumbass.

"So, you getting any more of this?" Danny asked him.

"Yeah, this stuff or something else."

"Same guy, or you got somebody new?"

"Nah, always the same guy."

"Oh yeah? When's that going to be?" Danny asked, keeping it casual.

That's when my phone rang. The whole thing was being recorded, but I still needed to be paying attention. No chance in hell a guy like Rowan was going to start trouble, but I was still Danny's backup.

The call was from Frank, my mom's husband. She was pretty sick by then, between the cancer and the chemo and the infections. I'd been trying to wrap up the case so I could visit her, but things were conspiring to keep me in Philly. Things like this asshole Rowan.

I'd only seen her twice since the diagnosis, but my guilt was tinged with annoyance at her and Frank for moving so far out in the sticks.

"Oh, you know, like, in a couple days," Rowan told Danny.

"So what, you mean like Tuesday?" Danny asked, without a trace of the exasperation I was feeling. "Or like Wednesday?"

"Yeah, that's it," Rowan replied.

"What is it, Frank?" I said, answering the phone in an exaggerated whisper so he'd know this was not a good time.

"Well, which is it?" Danny asked. "Tuesday or Wednesday?"

"Wait," Rowan said. "What day is it today?"

"Monday," Danny told him.

"Right . . . so probably later, then."

"It's your mother," Frank said, his voice strained.

"You mean, like Wednesday or like Thursday?" Danny said, finally revealing a hint of aggravation.

"What about her, Frank?"

"It's another infection. A bad one. She's back in the hospital. . . . I think this is it." His voice cracked, and I thought I heard him sob. He cleared his throat. "If you're going to come up, you need to come up now."

Rowan was babbling on in the background, sounding suddenly far away. "Could still be Tuesday, man. I forget. What night is the wrestling on?"

As the phone fell away from my face, I thought: My mom is going to die while this fuck-head tries to get his days straight. I don't remember thinking much after that. I got out of the van, a cardinal sin in the middle of surveillance, and I walked around the corner, straight up to where Danny and Rowan were standing.

Danny's eyes widened, then his face fell back into the same heavy-lidded suspicious gaze as Rowan's. We'd been working pretty hard the past few days, so I looked rough enough to pass for someone making a buy. As Rowan looked over at me, ready to take my order, Danny flashed me one last glare to remind me how much time and energy he'd invested in his cover.

The first thing I did when I came up to them, I planted a left in Danny's face. I didn't pull it, either—I popped him and dropped him. If I was going to pull something, it had to look real.

Rowan yelped like I'd stepped on his tail. He tugged a gun from the back of his pants, but he couldn't seem to get a grip on it, bobbling it like some half-assed juggler until I snatched it out of the air between his hands and pressed it against his temple.

"When's the re-up?" I asked quietly.

"Tuesday," he said with great certainty. "Um . . . six o'clock."

I was about to ask him where when he said, "In the parking lot behind Charlie B's."

I figured, what the fuck: "Who's your supplier?"

He didn't even pause. "Marcus Draper."

First chance he got, Danny Tennison drilled a right to the side of my head that left my ears ringing. But he was okay after that. Danny was cool that way. He didn't always approve, but he understood.

I got a couple of uniforms to take Rowan in, then I got in my car and drove.

Twenty minutes later, I got a call from Lieutenant Suarez, screaming at me that I was on admin duty, pending an investigation.

Normally, I would have screamed back, but I just said, "Whatever."

Ten minutes after that, I got another call from Frank. I could barely hear him, but it wasn't the phone breaking up, it was him.

"We lost her, Doyle," he said when he could speak. "Your mother's dead."

2

In the end, it hadn't worked out so bad, except for me. Danny got the bust, and it was a good one. Marcus Draper had gone down before, but not like this: money, drugs, guns, and lots of all three.

Dwayne Rowan filed suit, of course: mental anguish due to the excessive force of my implied threat to blow his brains out. No surprise there. He was pretty excited about a big pay-off until they told him the videotape of him giving up Marcus Draper would be the main attraction at the trial. Maybe they'd call Draper as a witness, just to make sure he saw it.

By the time I got back to Philly after my mom's funeral, Rowan had dropped his lawsuit and given his full cooperation in exchange for immunity, discretion, and the goodwill of the Philadelphia police department.

Three weeks later, I was sitting on a hard wooden bench outside a hearing room wearing my best suit and my three-hour shoes, waiting to find out if I was still a cop.

I tried not to blame the shoes for the pain I was in; they were three-hour shoes, and for three hours they'd been fine. But I'd been out there waiting for five hours, and between the shoes and my athlete's foot, I was wondering if I'd ever walk again.

Danny Tennison was sitting next to me, looking like hell. For the past three weeks he'd been my drinking buddy and my babysitter. We'd been out the night before, but I suspected his rough appearance may have had more to do with the reception he got at home afterward than the booze and lack of sleep.

Danny testified before I did, and I knew he told it exactly how it happened. He'd slant it as hard as he could in my favor, but he wasn't going to change the facts.

Shifting uncomfortably, I wondered if the people considering my fate knew how my feet felt, and if that was part of my punishment. I was seriously considering taking off my shoes when my cell phone went off.

The caller ID said "St. Luke's," the hospital that had treated my mom. I figured it was probably about billing or something, but I answered it anyway. Not like I had anything else to do.

The voice on the phone was warm and soothing. "Hello, is this Doyle Carrick?"

"Yes, it is," I replied, thinking this was the nicest collection call I had ever received.

"I'm calling from St. Luke's Hospital in Dunston. I'm afraid I have some bad news."

"What is it?" I asked the nice lady on the phone.

"I'm afraid it's about your father."

My father had been dead for twenty-five years. "You mean Frank?" I said. "What is it?"

"He's had a massive heart attack. We did everything we could, but we couldn't save him."

"Frank Menlow?" In the fraction of a second before the news sank in, I almost laughed, because I totally didn't see that one coming. Before I could say, "There has to be a mistake," the voice on the phone continued.

"Yes. I'm afraid Mr. Menlow is dead."

Frank had called the night before, left a message wishing me luck, asked me to call back to go over a few things. We'd gone over a lot of things the past few weeks. I figured I'd call him back after the hearing, once I knew the result. Save myself a call.

Danny looked over at me and said, "What's that about?"

"It's Frank."

Danny rolled his eyes. "Again?"

I tried to explain but my throat seemed to have swollen shut. Before I could say anything, the door to the hearing room opened and Suarez walked out. "Twenty days, Carrick," he said, not even looking at me. "Suspended without pay, and a recommendation for anger management training, which I hope you will take seriously." He dropped a fat manila envelope onto my lap. "You got three weeks to get your shit together."

3

Twenty days was about what I'd expected, but the recommendation for anger management pissed me off. As with so many things, I tried not to think about it. It seemed to be a theme, and I tried not to think about that, either.

My mom's death hurt me deep, and I had tried to put it away for later. If time heals all wounds, I was more than willing to let time take care of this one. But without the job to distract me, it had been getting harder and harder to avoid thinking about it. With Frank dying, too, it was hopeless, like the box I was packing it away in wasn't big enough for all the stuff I wasn't ready to deal with.

Driving west on seventy-eight, I was so distracted, so deep in nonthought, I had to slam my brakes and swerve hard to avoid missing my exit. Even three years after my mom and Frank moved out to Dunston, exit thirty-five still caught me by surprise. I swallowed hard against a twinge of guilt that threatened to become a wave of emotion as I struggled to remember my way to a place I should have known by heart.

I took a moment to get my bearings, but ten minutes later, driving through cornfields patrolled by tractors and tomato fields swarming with migrant workers, the farmland that should have accompanied me the rest of the way there had been replaced by thick woods. I turned onto a street called Burberry Lane and by the time I realized it was not the road I was looking for, the trees were so tight on either side I didn't have enough room to turn around.

After another quarter mile, it started getting dark, but the sun wasn't setting; it was just disappearing behind a steep hill as I descended into a wooded valley. As I approached a deeply rutted driveway, I noticed a familiar smell, the acrid mixture of ammonia and acetone and burned house. Weathered strips of crime-scene tape hung from pine trees on either side of the driveway. Beyond them was a small clearing surrounded by blackened branches burnt back like they were recoiling from the scene. I recoiled a bit myself, goose bumps rising on my arms. I'd had a thing about fires, ever since I was a kid. But I had a thing about crime scenes, too, and as I drove up the driveway, I felt my pulse quicken the way it did almost every day on the job.

I slowed to a stop, looking for a house, but all that remained was a blackened rectangle of cinder blocks, maybe twenty feet by thirty, in the center of the clearing. The cinder blocks only came up about a foot and a half, and the charred rubble inside barely rose that high. A blackened toilet slouched in the corner, cracked in two, the exposed porcelain gleaming white against all that black. The remains of several cots sat in the opposite corner, the metal twisted and collapsed.

Nothing else was recognizable, except that smell, the classic bouquet of eau de meth fire. Looked like a bad one, too. The foundation was uninterrupted on three sides; there might have been windows, but there was only one door. Meth fires can start with a bang and spread fast and hot. The fumes don't help, either. I couldn't help picturing it, and I suppressed a shudder. Not a good way to go.

Above me, the sliver of sky visible through the dense trees was losing light for real now. It seemed very far away. Closing my window against the smell, I doubled back the way I'd come.

The scene left me feeling even more somber. But even as I was thinking that a few weeks away from the job might not be so bad, my hand had my phone out, calling Danny Tennison.

"Jesus, Doyle," he said. "You been gone one day. You miss me that much?"

"What are you doing?"

"What do you mean what am I doing?"

"I mean what are you doing? I'm stuck out here in America. Tell me what's happening in the big city."

He laughed. "You're pathetic."

"Come on, what are you doing? Tell me."

"I'm at Target, standing outside the dressing room while Laura is helping Julia and Becca try on back-to-school clothes. That make you feel any better?"

"Are you holding a handbag?"

"Two of them. One has pink ponies on it."

"Then, yes, I do feel better. Hey, you know anything about any meth activity out here?"

"Meth in rural America? Well, gee, I suppose it's possible."

"Fuck you, I'm serious. Just came across a burned-out meth lab. Wondering what's up with that."

"Well, a lot of it has to do with the disintegration of the American family, deteriorating moral standards, a lack of opportunity for young people."

"Danny, seriously."

"Sorry, Doyle, but what does it matter? You're on suspension, remember?"

"Danny. Don't fuck with me. You know anything about it or not?"
I recognized a barn with a Pennsylvania Dutch hex sign, a white
disk with red tulips and birds, and I made a left, back on track.

"Dude, you're suspended."

"Danny, I'm just curious, that's all. Like a tourist."

He sighed. "I don't know. Stan Bowers could probably tell you.
He's working out near there now."

Stan Bowers was with DEA. We had worked with him on a few
task-force cases. He was loud and obnoxious, but a good guy and a
decent investigator.

"Stan's out here now?"

"Yeah, but Doyle, seriously, leave it alone. What are you, one day
into your suspension?"

"Two, including yesterday."

"Yesterday doesn't count."

"I'm pretty sure it does."

He laughed. "You better figure that out. It'd be typical Doyle
Carrick, come back on the wrong day because you lost count on
day one."

I laughed, too. "Fuck you."

"All right, the girls are coming out. I gotta go. Are you cool?"

"Yeah, I'm cool."

"Just do good time, and it'll be over before you know it."

"Right."

Just before the phone went dead, I heard him telling Becca how
beautiful she looked. It was six o'clock in the evening. I called Stan
Bowers.

He answered with a booming, "Hey, if it isn't Dirty Harry!"

"Hey, Stan."

"Heard about what happened." He started laughing. "Heard you
sucker-punched Tennison just to make it look good." He laughed
so hard he started coughing.

"Yes, it's hilarious."

"Smooth, Carrick," he said, "very smooth. Anyway, I heard you got twenty days. That sucks. The pricks."

"Yup."

"Oh, shit," he said, turning serious. "And your mom died, right? Or was it your dad?"

"My mom and my step-father. Few weeks apart."

"Damn, Doyle. Sorry to hear it."

"Thanks."

"So what's going on?"

"Well, I'm staying in my folks' house in Dunston. *My* house now, I guess. I heard you were working out here. Figured I'd touch base."

"Right," he said. "What do you need?"

"No, nothing. But I heard there was some meth activity out here, figured I'd talk to the man, get the straight scoop."

"That's what you figured, huh? You're on suspension, right?"

"I'm a property owner, concerned about what's going on in my new community."

"Yeah, all right." He laughed. "We got two meth labs that went up. About a month apart."

"Was one of them on Burberry Lane?"

He sighed. "Yeah, one of them was. Why?"

"Nothing, just that I came across the remains of it, had meth lab written all over it."

"Yeah, not much doubt about that."

"Were they related?"

"Looks like. Some crazy-assed Mexican gangbangers out of L.A."

"Mexicans?"

"That's what it looks like." He laughed. "Actually, one of the locals said it was the Russians—bimbo probably wouldn't know a

Russian from a Mexican if he did a hat dance on her head. But we had four crispy critters in each. One of them had a bullet in the head, so they might not have been playing nice, or a gun could have discharged in the heat, who knows. Coroner says they were Mexican. He had to do a lot of work on them, too. Extra crispy, if you know what I mean. Still, he seemed pretty sure of it."

"And they were from L.A.? That's a long way from home."

"Looks like they were part of a gang called the Monarchs, old L.A. street gang. They found a piece of floorboard at one of the scenes, like the only thing left of the house. Had the word 'Monarchs' scratched into it. Some crazy asshole did it with his fingernails, like some fucked up initiation or something. The DNA from the board matched one of the crispies. It was the one with the bullet, so I guess he didn't do it right."

"There a lot of Mexican gang activity out here?"

He laughed. "If you mean landscapers, yeah. Otherwise I didn't think so, but there you go. Aren't you supposed to be on a vacation, anyway?"

"Yeah, yeah. So where was the other place? The other meth house?"

"What, you want the address?"

"Sure."

He laughed. "Carrick, I've never been suspended, but I'm pretty sure that's not how it's supposed to go."

"I just want to see how it affects my property value."

He laughed again, but he gave me the address.

4

As depressing as it was, seeing the burned-out meth house made me feel like I was back in my element, even in the middle of those amber waves of grain. That sense of familiarity quickly faded, though, when I saw a guy in a hazmat suit in the middle of a cornfield, spraying something from a tank on his back. He looked totally out of place in the middle of all that nature. Maybe he felt me staring at him, because his hooded face turned in my direction and he seemed to be watching me until the road curved away.

I was so focused on the hazmat suit that when I glanced in my rearview I was surprised to see the grille of a black Ford pickup, riding high on a monster truck suspension, filling my back window. Maybe I'd slowed down to watch, but I was still doing fifty in a twenty-five zone. Apparently that wasn't good enough. The Ford hung back a bit, then accelerated right up behind me again, right up on my bumper. He flashed his high beams, as if I had a slow lane to pull onto.

I like to think that deep down I'm not one of the true assholes in the world, but nothing brings it out in me like someone who is. So when he blasted me with his horn and pulled into the oncoming lane to pass me, I accelerated, too. And I smiled as I did it.

He accelerated even more, and so did I, laughing now. We were approaching a blind rise, and this guy started gunning it; so I did, too, probably doing seventy-five now. Sure, there might have been an eighteen-wheeler barreling up the other side of the hill, but probably not on my side of the road.

Twenty yards from the top of the hill, the Ford surged alongside me, but before he could pull ahead, he hit his brakes and swerved off the road to the left. As he bounced over a dirt field, kicking up a cloud of dust, the high suspension suddenly made sense. I took my foot off the accelerator, but still crested the hill with enough speed that my tires left the asphalt.

As it turned out, there was no eighteen-wheeler coming the other way. There was a police cruiser. And as I flew past it six inches off the ground, its lights began to flash. The driver's side door said DUNSTON POLICE DEPARTMENT, and I thought, "At least I'm in the right town."

The truck kept going, lurching back onto the road up ahead and roaring over the next rise.

I considered high-tailing it out of there, too, but I figured a high-speed chase with another police department wouldn't be the smartest way to start my official suspension.

As I pulled over, I savored the moment of peace before the flashing lights on the cruiser reappeared over the hill behind me. The cruiser approached slowly, and even though I was already pulled over, the guy let his siren whoop once. Just to be a dick.

He looked close to sixty and he got out of the car slowly, like he was trying to look cool but was probably stiff from sitting on his butt all day. His mirrored aviators looked like they came from the Bad Cliché factory outlet.

As he approached the car, I took out my badge and lowered my window.

He looked down at me through his badass shades. "License and registration, please." His nametag said POLICE CHIEF PRUITT.

I got the registration out of the glove compartment and pulled the license out of my wallet, making sure he saw my badge as I handed it to him.

"You know why I pulled you over?" he asked.

I figured it was for going airborne at three times the speed limit, but I didn't want to get it wrong by being overly specific. "To give me a ticket?" I held my badge a little higher.

He looked down at it, taking his time and moving his tongue around in his mouth, like maybe part of his lunch was stuck in his teeth.

"Am I under arrest?" he asked dryly, nodding at the badge.

I laughed a little and shrugged. "No, I just—"

"Then put that away, and don't let me see it in this town again."

As he spoke, the black Ford reappeared slowly over the next hill and coasted toward us at a respectful fifteen miles an hour. Chief Pruitt waved for him to pass us and turned back to look at me as the truck crept by behind him with the windows down. The driver had a sweaty forehead, a piggish nose, and a big ugly grin on his big ugly face. He made sure I got a good look at his middle finger.

Chief Pruitt was still busy writing out the ticket. He seemed to be writing a lot. I gave the guy in the pickup a smile and a nod.

"You know," I told Pruitt, "the reason I was driving the way I was, the guy in that pickup was trying to run me off the road. You probably saw him. Surprised you're not giving him a ticket, too."

He was quiet for a second as he finished writing the ticket. "I deal with assholes on a case-by-case basis," he said as he tore off the ticket and handed it to me. "You drive safe now, you hear?"

5

The sun was sinking low by the time I found my parents' street—Bayberry Road, not Burberry Lane. A few minutes later I pulled into the driveway next to their big old wooden farmhouse. The house sat on top of a small hill, and I paused on the wide front porch and looked around at the farmland spreading out around it. Split-rail fences on either side separated the property from a rolling mass of wild grasses on one side and rows of small, conical evergreen trees on the other. I smiled as the name came to me: Meade's Christmas Tree Farm. I couldn't remember anything about it, but I could hear my mom's voice saying, "Something, something, something, Meade's Christmas Tree Farm."

Across the street was a smaller farmhouse. Behind it and to the left were fields with rows of vegetables, to the right a wash line ran across the yard, a pair of butterflies dancing with a bra and a few other scraps of clothing fluttering in the breeze. A wall of tall, dense trees seemed to mark the property line then turned abruptly and followed the road to the west.

Off to the east was a small mountain, hazy and green in the distance.

My face went hot as I put my key into the lock. Frank had given me the key after my mom's funeral, and I remembered thinking that if he was planning on locking himself out, he might want a key buddy who lived a little closer. I had also thought that with my mom gone, it might be a while before I was out there again.

The house probably appeared the way it always did; I had never looked that closely. The feeling, though, was totally different. Even after my mother's funeral, her warm presence had still been strong in the house. With Frank gone, too, the place just felt empty.

I put my bag on the living-room floor and walked through the dining room, the kitchen, Frank's little office in the back. The steps creaked when I went upstairs, a couple of them loudly. On the second floor was a master bedroom, then another bedroom that was nominally my room, although it was full of boxes. In the back was a guest room that seemed somehow more lived-in than my room.

It all seemed tidy and neat and very, very strange. I hadn't been there enough times to feel comfortable getting myself a glass of water. Now I owned the place.

Back in the living room, I sat on the sofa and listened to the quiet. My breath grew softer as the stillness of the house became part of me. I hadn't thought about how I would spend the next twenty days, but it occurred to me then that maybe I'd just sit on that sofa.

I thought about finding a nearby watering hole, but it was Saturday night, and I didn't need that. Instead, I grabbed a glass and a dusty half-full bottle of Irish whiskey from the liquor cabinet in the dining room, and went out onto the small back porch. Sitting on one of the weathered wooden rocking chairs, with my feet on the other one, I poured a couple of inches of whiskey.

The vegetable patch was dense and green, but the lowering sun threw an orange tinge over everything. The shade from the house looked bluish in comparison. A warm breeze slid by, then slid back, the air gently sloshing from side to side.

I closed my eyes and relaxed, enjoying the warmth of the booze on the inside and the air outside. When I opened my eyes, the shadow from the house had crept across the garden and was half-way up the side of the small, barnlike garage. I closed my eyes again, listening as the buzz and whine of the flying insects were replaced by the chirping of crickets. By the time I emptied the last of the bottle into my glass, it was nighttime.

Frank and my mom had said they loved it out here, but they were always complaining about something—Frank going on about the neighbors' hedges, or my mom upset about some crazy Mexicans. She didn't used to be like that, but I guess people change when they get old. I could never understand why they had moved out here in the first place—other than that Frank was crazy and my mom wanted him to be happy. Sitting here on the back porch, though, drinking into the night, for the first time, I could see the appeal.

6

When I woke up, the late afternoon sun was streaming full-strength into my room. It was the kind of sunlight that penetrates blankets and pillows and eyelids and skulls. Between the overindulgence the night before and exhaustion built up over several weeks, I wasn't quite done with sleep, and I didn't feel like I would ever be. But it was late afternoon, my stomach was growling, and apparently sleep was done with me.

I took four Advil from a bottle in the bathroom cabinet. I'd read that taking too much ibuprofen could kill you, but if my head stopped hurting, I was okay with it.

I found an empty can of coffee behind the boxes of herbal tea, but my panic faded into depression when I discovered a jar of instant coffee with a quarter-inch of brown crystals stuck to the bottom. I poured a couple inches of hot water into the jar and took it into the shower with me.

Ten minutes later I was feeling almost human, but as I was pulling on my pants, I sensed something was wrong. The quiet was gone. I grabbed my gun from the nightstand and listened from the top of the stairs to the ambient rustle of movement on the first floor. I crept down the stairs, keeping to the side and stepping over the seventh step and the eleventh; somehow I remembered that they were the loud ones.

The sound was coming from the dining room—a soft *whoosh* I knew but couldn't place. As I crossed the living room, it stopped. After a silent count to three, I yelled, "Freeze," and burst into the dining room with my gun two-handed in front of me.

The kid in the dining room let out a screech, but he froze. He was barely twenty, skinny, with a scraggly beard, wearing a T-shirt and jeans with sandals. He had a broom in one hand and an empty dustpan in the other. A cloud of dust was settling out of the air in a circle around him.

"Who are you?" I barked.

"Moose," he whispered. "I work for your parents."

I vaguely remembered them saying something about a guy named Moose helping out around the place, but this guy looked more like a mouse than a moose. "Bullshit," I said, keeping my gun up and taking a step closer. "Who are you?"

"It's Moose, Doyle," he said, a little annoyed now. "We met at your mom's funeral. I didn't have the beard then." He barely had a beard now, but he did look vaguely familiar.

When he realized I probably wasn't going to shoot him, he seemed to relax. "Wow, Frank said you were wound tight."

He leaned the broom against a wall. "Moose," he said, holding out his hand.

I tucked the gun into the back of my pants and shook his hand.

"Doyle. Nice to meet you."

"We met, remember?"

"Right."

"Sorry about your loss. Your losses. Your folks were really nice people. I can't believe they're gone."

I nodded but didn't say anything.

"I was in Vermont, at a pest management workshop. I didn't want to go, you know? This time of year, and so soon after your mom and all? But I got a scholarship. Frank insisted I go."

"Right."

"Anyway, I'm back now, so I can take care of the crops and everything." He stooped to resweep up the dirt on the floor without making any sudden moves or taking his eyes off me.

"Crops?"

"I farm your folks' garden, give them plenty of fresh produce. Mostly I work across the road, on Miss Watkins's farm."

"Oh."

"You know, Miss Watkins, the lady across the road?"

I tried to remember a Miss Watkins from my mom's funeral. No one stood out, but there'd been plenty of white-haired old ladies. I shook my head.

"You'll like her," he said. "She's great. She's got this organic farm business, growing all sorts of fancy stuff for restaurants and caterers and stuff. Purple this and miniature that. Heirloom stuff, not like the supermarket shelf-stable-for-two-years-but-tastes-like-Styrofoam stuff. It's pretty cool."

"Right."

"She's the one who called to tell me about Frank." He looked at the floor as he said it, his eyes welling up. Then he fished a set of keys out of his pocket. "Um, here's the key to Frank's truck. There's another key hanging in the kitchen. Your folks let me drive it . . . *used to* let me drive it."

I raised my hands. "No, you can hold on to it for now."

He nodded. "Thanks."

We stood there awkwardly as he wiped each eye and snorted. I didn't know if I was supposed to hug him or make a funny face or punch him in the arm. I had just met the guy, despite what he said, and I kind of wanted to be alone.

"So," I said loudly after a couple of moments. "I was about to go into town, maybe get something to eat."

"Sure," he said, pulling up his T-shirt to wipe his eyes. "That would be great."

7

As we drove through the cornfields toward town, Moose shared a torrent of details about the place, but he neglected to mention the massive dip in the middle of an intersection that nearly destroyed the undercarriage of my car.

"Oh, yeah," he said after the fact. "Watch out for that."

I slowed almost to a stop, and was glad I did, because a black Lincoln Escalade blew through the stop sign to our left and pulled out in front of us.

It was a big shiny thing, with lots of chrome, spinning rims, and a heavy bass beat. The passenger window was open and a face looked out at me with dead-looking pale gray eyes and an impressive collection of facial piercings. Our eyes met and he stared. I didn't like him.

In my sternum, I could feel the thrum of the music. I assumed it was hip hop, but it was so distorted, it sounded like something you'd hear downstairs from a Greek wedding.

As the Escalade sped away, I resumed driving at a responsible speed, but I also took out my cell phone and punched in a number. Almost immediately, Danny Tennison answered.

"Hello, Detective Tennison," I said.

"Hello, private citizen," he said. "I'm afraid I can't take personal calls right now, but if you want to call back after six, I'd be happy to talk to you."

"Fuck you."

"I knew you'd say that."

"How's it going?"

"Strangely quiet at work. And I'm already getting along better with my wife."

"I knew you missed me."

"How are you holding up?"

"I'm okay. Listen, I need you to do me a favor."

"Of course you do."

I read him the number of the license plate in front of me. "Can you run that for me?"

"Has it been twenty days already?"

"Fuck you again."

"Seriously, Doyle. You're off the job right now."

"Danny, it's a license plate."

He sighed. "All right. What's the make and model?"

"Big-ass Lincoln Escalade."

"Of course it is. I'm in the middle of something. I'll call you later."

"Thanks."

"Maybe you could work on your golf game or something, try to stay out of trouble for the next twenty days."

"I'll look into that."

Moose was staring at me as I put down the phone.

"So the guy cuts you off and you call in his plates?" he asked.

I shrugged. "Something like that. Guy looks suspicious. Out of place. Call it a hunch. Why?"

He shrugged back at me. "I don't know. It's kind of cool. Kind of creepy." As he said it, he turned away from me and stiffened. He immediately started to close his window. "Speaking of creepy, that's scary as shit. Close your window."

"Why?" I asked, but I already saw it.

I couldn't tell if it was the same guy or even the same spot, but there was a hazmat suit, spraying away in the middle of a field.

I closed my window.

Moose growled. "See? That pisses me off. We're driving along, out in the country, we shouldn't have to close our windows because they're spraying poison all over the place. And the worst part is, in a few minutes, when that guy is gone, we're going to open our windows, but whatever he is spraying will still be in the air. And in the water, and on our food, and in the kids."

"How do you know what they're spraying? It's probably harmless."

"If it was harmless would he be dressed like that? But that's just it: I don't know what it is. No one knows. And even if they think they know, they don't. Twenty years from now, they'll say, 'Well, we didn't know it then, but now we know that shit'll kill you.'"

He went on for a while after that, about pesticides and global warming and biodiversity. After a few miles of uninterrupted corn-fields, we passed a small tract of identical new houses and he started in about how developers were buying up all the land and building on the farms, and about the run-off, and on and on.

I didn't completely disagree with anything he was saying, but I was tired and hungover and I just wanted food.

With its tree-lined streets and planters full of petunias, Main Street in Dunston had a small-town feel that was quaint but claustropho-bic. After Moose's rant, I half-expected to see people in hazmat suits walking down the street, but it was a beautiful sunny day and the few people that were out looked normal enough.

Moose directed me to a dark brick building with BRANSON's painted across the front window. I parked a couple of spots down from it, and as we got out, he said, "You go on in. I gotta run around the corner for a second. If the waitress comes, I'll have the meatloaf and an iced tea."

Before I could say anything, he was jogging down the street. I shook my head, determined not to let it bother me, and pulled open the heavy glass door.

8

Bright sunlight streamed through the big front window, but it was quickly absorbed by all the dark wood and deep-red vinyl. The place was half full, tables in the front and booths along the left-hand side. The bar was in the back. A couple of old guys were sitting next to the beer taps, talking to the bartender, a solid-looking guy in his early sixties with a buzz cut and a bar towel over his shoulder. There was a picture of him on the wall by the front door, twenty years younger, balancing a laughing toddler on his knee.

There were no photos of me and Frank like that. He didn't come into the picture until later, when I had already learned how to be surly.

The bartender laughed at something one of the old boys said, but his eyes scanned the room every few seconds.

I scanned the room, too. At the first table was an elderly couple dressed in the same pale blue. The husband coughed and the wife rolled her eyes and told him to cover his mouth. At the second table two guys in denim and plaid were eating in silence. When I got to the third table, I stopped scanning and stared.

She was sitting alone, reading a book and absentmindedly playing with her tousled, shoulder-length blond hair. In front of her was a tall glass of iced tea, full to the brim, sitting in a pool of condensation. On the plate next to it was an untouched turkey club and a pile of chips. She hadn't started eating, and I liked the idea that she would be there for a while.

She had on jeans and a T-shirt, and even sitting, I could tell she had a trim, athletic body. If she was wearing a bra, it wasn't much of one, because her nipples were poking, just a bit. I might have lingered there a moment too long, because when I looked back up, her cool blue eyes were looking right at mine.

Normally, I would have looked away fast and pretended nothing had happened. This time I smiled, and I was pretty sure she smiled back.

When I finally did look away, I noticed the PLEASE SEAT YOURSELF sign right in front of me. I took a seat a couple of tables away and snuck a few peeks while I was waiting, made eye contact once and got another little smile. I don't always know when something is there, but I usually know when absolutely nothing is, and I was not getting the absolutely nothing vibe.

The waitress was a stocky older woman with a pleasant expression that disappeared behind an appraising look when she got to my table. She gave me a menu, and I asked for another one because I couldn't remember what Moose wanted.

The front door opened as I was trying to decide between the Reuben and the BLT. I looked over, expecting Moose. Instead, I saw my pig-faced drag-racing opponent. He looked bigger up close.

He stopped just inside the front door and looked around, nodding to one of the guys at the bar, who nodded back warily. I was giving him a hard stare, but he didn't see me.

He walked up to the blonde in the T-shirt and said something quiet.

If she had looked up with a smile or given him a kiss, I would have had to end it all right then and there. Fortunately, she made a point of ignoring him, framing her face between her thumb and her forefinger and turning her head away to concentrate on her book.

He spoke again, louder, like he was repeating whatever he had said. She continued to ignore him, until he reached down and grabbed a potato chip from her plate. Then her head snapped around. "Back off, Cooney," she said through gritted teeth.

He popped the chip into his mouth, looking down at her for a moment as he crunched it. When he reached out again, she slapped his hand. It was not a playful slap, and the look on her face wasn't playful, either.

With surprising quickness, he grabbed her wrist, bending it back slightly while the other hand reached for another chip. I can be surprisingly quick myself, and before she could wince, I was out of my seat and over there, grabbing a fistful of his greasy hair and poking my foot into the back of his knee.

He spun as I took him down, his eyes wide, but his mean smile returned when he saw my face. The iced tea went over, and I glanced past him and paused, mesmerized as the beverage splashed across the blonde's T-shirt. I'm familiar with a number of martial arts and fighting styles, and none of them recommends pausing in the middle of a fight to ogle. The next thing I saw was stars, as some kind of cross between a fist and a cinder block slammed into my head.

I stayed on my feet, suddenly back at my own table with my new friend closing fast and grinning like he wanted to play some more. I acted dazed, partly to give him a false sense of security and partly because I was dazed. When he swung another right, I ducked and caught his arm, twisting it around behind him and slamming his head down onto my table.

My ears were still fuzzy from the punch, and it took a second for the noise I was hearing to resolve into the sound of the blonde shrieking, "Stop it, both of you! For God's sake!"

It occurred to me then that maybe I should have started by clearing my throat and saying something like, "Excuse me, sir, but I believe the lady would like you to stop eating her lunch." But thoughts like that only come to me after the damage has been done.

I had the big guy immobilized enough that I could look over as she picked up her book and threw a ten on the table. She stormed out, shaking her head and mumbling something about "animals."

In the moment of quiet after she left, I realized everyone in the place was staring at me. I took a step back and released the big guy, giving him enough of a shove that he'd be out of arm's reach in case he hadn't had enough. Judging from the way he came back at me, he hadn't, but by then the guy from behind the bar had stepped in between us.

"Enough, goddamn it!" he boomed, shoving us in opposite directions. "For Chrissakes, Cooney, how many times I got to tell you?"

Then he turned and gave me a glare.

As I headed for the door, my stomach rumbled loudly, letting me know that while it might not have decided between the Reuben or the BLT, it had definitely been counting on one of them.

9

When I opened the door, I almost laughed at the twin images of my face, red where it had been hit, reflected in the lenses of Chief Pruitt's aviators. Instead, I slipped past him as he reached out to hold the door.

Out on the sidewalk, I looked down the street as the blonde disappeared around one end of the block, then looked up the street as Moose appeared around the other end.

Pruitt's cruiser was parked right in front of my car. I wondered if he was there for lunch or if he had seen my car and was checking up.

"Did you order?" Moose called out. He had a brown shopping bag in his arms.

"Get in the car," I said briskly. There was still time to make a relatively clean getaway.

"What?" Moose called back, slowing a step, confused.

"Hurry up. We're out of here."

He still looked confused, but to his credit, he scurried up to the car and got in fast. His bag clinked when he put it on the floor.

"What's going on?" he asked as I pulled around Chief Pruitt's car and drove away at the posted speed limit.

I told him what had happened.

"Damn, Doyle." He grinned, shaking his head. "Frank said you were a people person."

"Is there anywhere else to eat in this town?"

He put a hand over his stomach, and his face grew sad. "I was going to have the meatloaf."

"So where else can we go?"

He shook his head. "Nearest place that's any good is like ten miles away, and it's closed Sundays. There's probably some soup back at the house."

"Isn't there a McDonald's or something?"

Moose looked stricken. "Dude, tell me you don't."

"What?"

"Eat at McDonald's."

"Well, not all the time, but—"

He actually changed color. "Do you know what they put in that stuff? Have you ever seen what they put in a chicken nugget?"

I laughed. "I don't want to know what they put in a chicken nugget. That's why I ask them to cover it in that delicious breading."

"Doyle, seriously, you need to think about what you're eating."

"I think about it all the time. Hell, right now I'm thinking, 'What am I going to eat?'"

"I'm serious, man. This isn't just about dinner, this is about everything."

"Everything?"

"Damn right. You eat that chicken nugget, it's not just about the factory-farmed chicken and the hormones and antibiotics and the GMOs, it's about the people that work with those chemicals and the folks who have to live next to it."

"GMOs?"

"Genetically Modified Organisms, meaning genetically engineered foods. It's crazy what they're doing with all the Frankenfoods these days."

I laughed. "Frankenfoods?"

"You know, like tomatoes spliced with jellyfish genes, or lettuce with firefly DNA."

I shrugged. "It's still just food. It's not like it's going to kill you."

"Don't be so sure of that."

Moose went on for a while like that, but I wasn't listening, distracted by the image of the blonde from the diner. When I noticed it was quiet, I looked over to see Moose staring at me expectantly. I figured I'd rather ignore his stories than be telling ones of my own.

"So, how'd you end up working for my folks?"

He sighed. "I came out here to work for Miss Watkins, like an apprentice. When your mom got sick, your dad needed help keeping the garden going. Then he needed help around the house." Moose shook his head. "They were great people."

He was an annoying little guy, but I found myself liking him. He went quiet again after that, a sad quiet that dragged on until his cell phone went off, as if it had decided that someone had to say something.

Moose looked at the display. "It's Miss Watkins," he said, whispering even though he hadn't answered it yet.

"You're back," he said brightly into the phone. "How'd it go with the garden club?" He listened again, nodding into the phone. "Yeah, I just got back a little while ago . . . No, the workshop was great, but, you know . . . Yeah, I guess it just broke his heart. . . . I'm here with Doyle right now. . . . When, now? Sounds just great. I'm sure we'd love to." He cupped the phone with his hand and leaned over toward me. "She's inviting us over for dinner."

"Inviting us over?" I repeated, unable to think of anything else to say.

"Yes, and she's a great cook. You're going to love Miss Watkins. She reminds me of my Aunt Sylvia."

I had no desire to eat dinner with Moose's Aunt Sylvia, and could think of at least seventeen different ways that having dinner with one of my mother's friends would be suicidally depressing, but before I could say no, my stomach growled loudly and I paused just long enough for Moose to say into the phone, "He'd love to. See you then."

10

Back at the house, Moose got out of the car first and went inside ahead of me. By the time I got inside, the shower was already running. "Make yourself at home why don't you," I muttered.

I checked the fridge for beer, but found only old food in various stages of bad: limp lettuce, sour milk, and moldy leftovers, bread, and cheese. Frank had died less than two days ago, but by the looks of it, this stuff had spoiled that. I stood there for a while with the door open, thinking about Frank, living here alone with a refrigerator full of rotten food. I started to clear it out, but figured it was best to keep it refrigerated until trash day, whenever that was.

"Are you ready?" Moose yelled from the second floor.

It wasn't until he came downstairs wearing a different T-shirt that I realized he was living here. Guess the guest room wasn't a guest room after all. My brain conjured up a vague memory of my mom maybe mentioning it at some point, and I wondered what else she might have told me.

Moose clomped down the steps and stopped to look at me when he reached the bottom. With his hair wet and his face scrubbed, he looked even younger.

"Are you ready?" he asked again, in the same tone Danny Tennison's wife would use to tell Danny that he wasn't.

"Yup."

"Sure you don't want to change?"

"Yeah, I'm sure," I said, too tired to change, almost too tired to get annoyed at him. "Let's go."

Before we left, Moose pulled an unlabeled brown wine bottle out of the bag he had picked up in town.

"What is that?" I asked as we walked out the door.

"Friend of mine makes organic wine."

"Organic wine?"

"Well . . . kind of," he said over his shoulder as we crossed the street. "He calls it squish. It's excellent."

And probably illegal, I thought, but I didn't say anything.

We crossed the road and walked up onto the porch, and as Moose rang the doorbell, I saw something moving out of the corner of my eye: the laundry fluttering in the breeze. From up close, the bra looked like a flimsy little thing. There were also a couple of small T-shirts, a pair of jeans, and a few lacy scraps that I couldn't quite identify, but which got my imagination going.

I was just thinking they didn't seem appropriate for a little old lady when Miss Watkins opened the door. She had a big smile that froze on her face when she saw me.

"Hi, Nola," Moose said cheerfully. He made a move to step inside, but stopped when she didn't step back. He looked back and forth between us. "I'm sorry," he said. "Nola, this is Doyle Carrick."

"So I gathered," she said.

"Doyle, this is Miss Watkins."

"Nice to meet you," I said, grinning slightly despite myself. I didn't let my eyes go any lower than her nose.

"Again," she said.

"Again."

Moose looked back and forth between us. "You two know each other? That's awesome."

"We've met," she said. "Just today as a matter of fact."

"Really?" he said, his voice squeaky with surprise. Then his face fell. "Wait, you mean at Branson's?"

I laughed nervously. "Afraid so."

11

Nola Watkins's home was a mix of low-end modern and Latin American arts and crafts. Her metal-and-fake-wood shelves were cluttered with colorful bric-a-brac, and her simple black sofa was draped with a green-and-brown woven blanket.

The smells from the kitchen were hypnotic and strangely unfamiliar—an incongruous mixture of onions, peppers, and meat, mixed with cinnamon, cloves, and other spices.

"That smells good," I said.

"*Carne guisado*," she said, with a touch of accent that was either authentic or pretentious. "It's a Colombian recipe, but I learned it in Guatemala. I hope you like spicy."

"Spicy is good."

Moose held up the bottle. "I brought some of Squirrel's squish."

"Oh. Great," she said with a forced smile. "How's Carl doing? Living by himself and all."

"He's doing great," Moose said. Then he turned to me. "Me and

Squirrel used to live together. He's a great guy, but he snores like a spoon in a garbage disposal."

The table was set with wineglasses, but Nola asked if I preferred beer. She looked relieved when I said yes.

She let Moose pour from his own bottle, shaking her head as he did. We followed her into the kitchen, and she took two Yuengling Lagers out of the fridge. With her bare hand, she twisted the cap off one and handed it to me, then twisted the cap off the other.

"Cheers," she said, taking a long pull from the bottle. No glass. I kind of liked that.

"Cheers," I said, and took a long pull myself. The beer was cold and good.

"Cheers," Moose echoed. He took a sip of his drink and shuddered, then took a bigger sip.

Nola watched him with a pained expression as she stirred the saucepan. "How can you drink that stuff?"

Moose licked his lips and grinned. "It's delicious. And it's all natural."

"Well, don't drink too much. We need to pick tomatoes across the street first thing." She turned to me. "Frank and Meredith let me grow on some of their land in exchange for produce. I hope you don't mind."

"Of course not."

She smiled, then turned back to Moose. "And don't forget we've got Greg from the caterers coming on Thursday to check on the corn. I want us up early tomorrow to make sure everything looks just right."

Moose snorted. "Nola, it's just corn."

"It's not just corn, Moose, it's organically grown heirloom Lenape Blue, and these people are paying a lot of money for it to look perfect." She sighed and turned to me. "Sorry. I mostly grow for farm markets and some food co-ops in Philly, a couple of restaurants, but I also do some contract growing for some very pricey caterers."

"Sounds like quite a niche."

"It is, Doyle," Moose chimed in. "It's ridiculous, but these people pay major bucks."

"They can be a pain, but I make more from a couple of crazy wedding jobs than a whole season's worth of farmers markets." She turned down the burners. "Next year I'll be certified organic, and I'll be able to charge a little more for what I grow. Until then, this is helping me make ends meet. Let's go sit down."

"Why not until next year?" I asked as she ushered us into the living room.

"It's a three-year process, and it's not cheap. This is the third year. Meanwhile, I grow obscure heirlooms so rich brides can have vegetables to match their bridesmaids' dresses."

Once Moose was sitting in the armchair and I was on the sofa, Nola perched in a straight-backed wooden side chair, curling her legs up under her and somehow looking quite comfortable.

For a moment, the room was still.

"I'm sorry for your losses," she said quietly.

"Thanks," I said. I was wishing people would stop saying that. I guess it was good to get it out of the way.

"And I'm really sorry I missed your mother's funeral. I had a friend going through a medical crisis. I felt terrible not being there. I was very fond of your mother."

Moose shook his head, his eyes welling up again. "They were both really good people."

The room was quiet for a moment, and when I looked up, Nola was squinting at me, with her brow furrowed and her head tilted, like she was holding the last piece of a puzzle and it didn't fit.

"You're not how I pictured you," she said.

"How did you picture me?"

"I guess . . . I guess how you look in your pictures."

"You mean the official police portrait? Or the high school year-book shot?" Those were probably the only two photos of me taken in the last fifteen years.

"Both, I guess. But also just from hearing Frank and Meredith talk about you."

"What do you mean?"

"I don't know. Just different."

"I know what you mean," Moose chimed in. "Different."

I shifted in my seat, uncomfortable at the scrutiny. I was relieved when the timer dinged in the kitchen.

Nola smiled. "Dinner's ready."

12

The *carne guisado* tasted even better than it smelled. I tend to eat pretty enthusiastically, but I made sure to switch back into conversation mode after half a dozen forkfuls.

"So you learned this recipe in Guatemala? What were you doing there?"

"I went down with a group helping to teach farmers about organic farming techniques." She talked about college, and cooking, and traveling around Central America. Moose joined in, and the conversation moved on to fair-trade co-ops and organic farming and GMOs and the many evils of the modern food system.

I was happy to keep quiet and hunker down with the *carne guisado*, but then Moose said Pop-Tarts should be illegal, and I had to speak up. I haven't had a Pop-Tart in fifteen years, but I like knowing they exist, just in case.

Moose leaned forward. "So, I guess you're more of a meat-and-potatoes kind of guy."

"Actually," I replied, "I'm not that into potatoes, unless they're fried."

I could see Nola was trying to tell whether I was serious or not, so I quickly conceded that I could appreciate the idea of organics, even if I couldn't always afford it. "So how did you get so involved in all this anyway?"

Moose glanced over at Nola like he was wondering what she was going to say. She paused, like she was wondering, too.

She took a sip from her beer and sat back. "When I was sixteen, I got sick. Then I got better. Then I got sick again. I got better, I got worse, for six months, in and out of hospitals: breathing problems, rashes, muscle aches." She laughed and shook her head. "Most of the doctors thought I was making it up. At one point, they thought it was a girl thing. Because of the schedule." She paused to finish her beer. "Turned out it was the next door neighbor's lawn guy. Every month, he'd come and spray God knows what on the grass—pesticides and herbicides and chemical fertilizers. It was a great-looking lawn, if you're into that sort of thing. Damn near killed me."

"So were you allergic to the chemicals?"

"Apparently. Not allergic, but sensitive. They said I have something called MCS, Multiple Chemical Sensitivity." She shrugged. "Anyway, my mom asked the neighbors to stop using the lawn chemicals, and they weren't crazy about it, but they stopped and I got better."

"So that's what it was?"

"The MCS? Who knows? Some people don't think MCS is even real. I'm not entirely sure myself. One doctor said that's what it was; the other doctors said she was a quack. A couple of years later, it happened again, a lot worse. It can get worse each time it happens. It's progressive. That time my apartment building got new carpet in all the hallways, and no, they were not going to get rid of it."

"What did you do?"

"What could I do? I moved out."

"And got better?"

She nodded.

"And now?"

"I'm fine. I just have to be careful. Some people have it so bad they can't come into contact with anything, perfumes or dyes, anything sets them off. And people think they're crazy, or making it up. My friend Cheryl, for example. After her third episode, she just basically didn't get better. Now she lives totally chemical-free, in a house out in the woods. But she has to go out sometimes, and occasionally she'll have a reaction to something. That's who I was with when I missed your mom's funeral. Compared to her, I'm lucky. I live my life, I eat in restaurants, travel on planes. It's generally not a problem, I just avoid places with lots of chemicals. For me it's mostly just pesticides and herbicides." She smiled. "That and cheap carpet. Anyway, when I started looking into it, I was shocked at some of the chemicals that are getting into the food stream. That's what got me into organics. And it's not just the chemicals."

"What do you mean?"

"Well, all of it. The GMOs, the clones, irradiation." She got up and went to the kitchen. "It's like food isn't food anymore."

"Again with the clones?" I repeated. "Really?"

"It's for real, Doyle. They're doing that all over," Moose cut in. "They're cloning cows and sheep. They're genetically modifying crops to produce pharmaceuticals, like vaccines and proteins, and heavy duty stuff like interferon. And the genetically modified stuff is everywhere: corn and soybeans and tomatoes. I swear, they let it out intentionally, mix it in with the regular stuff just so they can say 'Oops, too late now, but see? It didn't kill you.' Or at least not yet."

"Come on, don't you think you're being a little paranoid?"

Nola returned with two fresh beers and gave me one. "Actually, he's right. It does get mixed in, and then they sue the farmers for using the stuff without a license."

"So how does it get mixed in?"

She shrugged. "Pollen drift, carelessness, hybrids . . . mix-ups with seed."

The conversation went on like that for a while. Maybe I had eaten my fill, but the more they talked about food, the less hungry I became.

When Nola announced she was done eating, I did, too.

Moose had eaten like a four-year-old girl, but he pushed himself away from the table and said he was full, rubbing his concave midsection like it was a bowl full of jelly.

We cleared the table, and Nola was making coffee when her phone rang. "Excuse me," she said, clearing her throat before answering the phone. When she spoke, her voice sounded bright and professional. "Hello, Nola Watkins speaking." She had turned partially away from me, but not enough that I couldn't see her expression change as her voice did.

"Nola Watkins speaking," she repeated, tentatively. "Hello? . . . Hello?"

I looked over at Moose, and he looked back at me, shaking his head.

Nola made a soft growling noise in her throat and put her phone away.

"Sorry," she said with an apologetic smile. She was trying to act like nothing was wrong, but her face was flushed and her eyes were strained.

"What was that about?" I asked. "Everything okay?"

She shot a look at Moose and said, "Yes, just a wrong number."

I shot a look at Moose, too.

"She's been getting all these hang-up calls," he said with a slightly drunken snort.

"Moose! Stop it." She turned to me. "It's nothing."

"Doesn't sound like nothing. How long has that been going on?"

"Since she turned down the offer from the developers, about six months ago."

"Moose, seriously," she said with a glare. "Shut up."

"Developers?" I asked.

"Oh, yeah," he said. "They're buying everything up out here."

I laughed before I could stop myself.

Nola gave me a sharp look. "What?"

"Well, nothing. It's just that . . . well, Moose was going on about that earlier, and I've seen a little bit of that, but mostly it's all farmland." I laughed again, this time drawing looks from both of them.

"Just because it isn't being developed now doesn't mean it won't be soon," she snapped. "Pennsylvania is losing open space at a rate of three hundred acres a day. And it happens fast. One day a port-a-potty shows up, two weeks later there's a sign saying 'Coming soon, the Estates at Mountain View Village.' Six weeks after that, there's fifty McMansions where there used to be a meadow."

"If you say so, I believe you," I said, leaning back in my chair. "But I wouldn't have thought there was all that much demand for land out here." I smiled to myself, thinking it more likely they'd be pressuring her to buy than to sell.

Moose rolled his eyes. "Tell that to whoever keeps calling and hanging up."

Nola sighed and draped her hand wearily across her forehead. "It's nothing. Really. Despite Moose's conspiracy theories. Yes, there's a developer trying to buy up a lot of the land out here. Wants to build some tracts. And yes, I told him I wasn't interested. I came here to farm."

"And that's when the calls started," Moose added.

"How many calls?" I asked.

"Not that many."

"A couple of times a week," Moose said.

"Always hang-ups?"

"Yes."

"Who's the developer?"

Nola just sighed, but Moose chimed in. "Company called Red-tail."

"Is that who's calling?" I asked her.

"I have no idea."

"Do they block the number?"

"Of course they do."

"Can't you just block calls from any blocked numbers?"

She shook her head. "I don't know how many customers that would cost me, but I can't afford to lose any right now."

"Have you talked to the police?"

She laughed. "No."

I smiled. "Yeah. I've met your police chief. Didn't exactly fill me with confidence, either."

She shook her head. "No, it's not that. It's just . . . I mean, it's nothing."

"Want me to talk to the developer? I could put a little fear of God in him. Or at least fear of the IRS."

Moose leaned forward. "You have friends at the IRS?"

I shook my head. "Nobody has friends at the IRS. But I know some people."

She looked at me with an odd smile: part patronizing, like she thought it was cute, and part annoyed, like she really didn't. "If you want to talk to the developer about paving over all the farmland around here, that would be great. But this"— she reached over and put her hand on my knee—"this is just a minor nuisance."

Then she got up and headed toward the kitchen. I had never thought of myself as having particularly sensitive knees, but my knee was tingling where her hand had been.

Then I noticed Moose looking at me with that same drunk-but-smug look. "It's probably not the developer, anyway," he whispered loudly, his words bumping up against each other.

"What do you mean?"

"If the developer can't assemble the whole parcel, the whole deal could fall through. The developer can just walk away, find another place to pave over. The people who already agreed to sell, the ones who've already made other plans, picked out other houses and spent all that developer money—I bet that's who's calling."

13

Nola and I switched from beer to coffee after dinner, but Moose stuck with his squish and the effect was visible. He poured another inch into his glass and sloshed some onto the coffee table.

I reached over and grabbed the bottle as he put it down. "What the hell is this stuff, anyway?" I sniffed the mouth of the bottle. It smelled like a cross between dry wine, rotten apples, and vinegar.

"Try it," he said, sliding back in the armchair and closing his eyes for a second. "You'll like it."

I poured an inch into my glass and sipped it.

"Not as bad as I expected," I said, surprised.

"It's not just the taste that's the deal breaker," Nola said, returning with a plate of brownies. "Have a few more and tell me how you feel."

Moose let out a drunken giggle and closed his eyes.

I finished what was in my glass, but didn't pour any more. The events of the past few days suddenly weighed heavily on me, pushing me down against the sofa. I broke a brownie in half and went back to my coffee.

"Hey, sleepyhead," Nola said loudly, nudging Moose's leg with her toe. "You want a brownie?"

He flopped an arm over his belly. "Stuffed," he said without opening his eyes.

"See what I mean about that stuff?" she said, turning to me.

"Point taken." I sipped my coffee. "So who was that guy, anyway?"

"Who?"

"The guy who swiped your chip. Back at Branson's."

She frowned. "Oh, that."

For a moment, I regretted reminding her about it.

"That's Dwight Cooney." The way she said it sounded like she was more annoyed at him than me. "He's harmless. Just a meathead with an underinflated sense of his own repulsiveness."

"You got a lot of them out here?"

She smiled sweetly. "Not just around here."

I put my hand against the slight swelling along my cheekbone. "I don't know if I'd say he's that harmless, by the way."

"No, he is. Annoying, but harmless. Besides, you seemed to be able to handle him without much trouble." She smiled. "Until you got distracted, that is."

I could feel my face warming. "Right."

"I suppose I should say thank you for coming to my rescue and all," she said, reaching over to run her fingertips lightly across my bruised cheek. Apparently, my cheeks are sensitive, too. "But I had the situation under control, so I won't."

She grinned at me as she took her hand away, letting me know she was yanking my chain. I grinned back at her, because I couldn't help myself.

If I had been better at that sort of thing, I might have gone in for a kiss. I was still considering it when Moose snuffled loudly and let out a long sigh.

It was an undeniable cue to call it a night, and a pause hung in the air, waiting for one of us to acknowledge it. Instead, she got up from her chair and sat next to me on the sofa. "So how does someone end up being a cop, anyway?" she asked.

I smiled. She didn't want me to leave. She smiled back conspiratorially, like she knew I knew, but she expected me to go along with it.

I laughed. "By ignoring lots of good career advice."

She laughed, too, putting her hand on my knee again, this time leaving it there. Now, my knee is connected directly to my thigh. And I don't want to get into what my thigh is connected to, but her hand had an effect on me. It might have shown on my face, because she smiled mischievously as she took her hand away.

"Come on," she said, "seriously."

"Seriously?" I shrugged. "A buddy of mine talked me into going into the police academy with him. He washed out; I didn't."

"Hmmm. The thing is . . . you don't seem like a cop."

"Yeah, I get that a lot. My lieutenant tells me that all the time."

"But you're a detective, right? So you must be pretty good at it."

"That's where you and my lieutenant differ. But I am pretty good at parts of it."

"So what do you have, issues with authority?"

"You don't?"

She shrugged.

This time, when Moose snorted, he opened his eyes and looked around, confused.

I looked over at him, and when I looked back at Nola, she was stifling a yawn.

"I guess it's that time," she said, looking at her watch. "And I guess I'll be picking the tomatoes by myself. I have some other crops to check on as well, so don't be alarmed if you see me sneaking through your backyard early in the morning."

Moose let out a sigh and fell back to sleep. Nola shook her head. "You can leave him here, if you like."

"Nah, he'll be all right," I said, for some reason not crazy about the idea of Moose spending the night there. I slipped a shoulder under his arm and hoisted him out of the armchair. His eye opened but remained unfocused. "But he's going to be a mess in the morning."

14

I got up at seven the next morning, not hungover but tired and unprepared for the horrifying revelation that now there was no coffee at all. I managed to assemble a lukewarm cup of tea that not only confused my metabolism, but I think actually pissed it off.

I had an appointment with a lawyer to read Frank's will at nine and an appointment at the funeral home at nine forty-five. I told myself I had gotten up early to get a jump on the day. But I lingered by the kitchen window and pretended to drink tea until seven-thirty, when Nola showed up in the backyard. I took a step back and watched as she walked barefoot up the path between the tomatoes, carrying a large basket. As she bent over to pick some tomatoes, I leaned closer. She stopped and turned, smiling right at me.

I smiled back and waved. Busted again.

* * *

Moose woke up as I was getting ready to leave. He looked worse than I felt, stumbling downstairs in the same clothes he'd been wearing the night before.

"Tell me there's coffee," he mumbled as he entered the kitchen.

"You look like shit."

"Coffee?"

I picked up the empty coffee can and tapped it loudly with a spoon.

He winced and groaned and covered his head with his hands. "Shit, that's my bad. I finished it before I left. I meant to pick some up."

I let him take the rap; instant doesn't count. "I wish you had, because I just started my morning with a lovely cup of *tea*. I'm going into town, and I'm definitely getting a cup of coffee. If you want, you can tag along, but we're leaving now."

He groaned. "Can you wait ten minutes? I just have to go out back and pick some tomatoes."

"I think Nola already picked them."

"She did?"

I nodded.

"Damn. She's going to be annoyed." He seemed perturbed for half a second, then he said, "Let's go."

We drove in silence marred only by an occasional soft groan as Moose massaged his temples. I thought about cranking up the radio, just for laughs, but I wasn't too far away from a headache myself. As it was, Moose winced when my cell phone started playing "Watching the Detectives."

I snatched it up. "Danny-o!"

"Doyle. You sound distressingly chipper. Staying out of trouble?"

"One day at a time."

"Got those plates back on your friend there."

I'd almost forgotten I had called. "The plates, right. So what's the story?"

"Well, it's no epic, but there's a story. George Arnett. Assault, a couple of possessions, possession with intent. Nine months at Graterford. Got out two months ago."

"Any good reason he would be out here?"

"Nothing that jumps out. Born in Kensington, raised in Kensington, went to school in Kensington, arrested in Kensington. I think the trip to Graterford was his first time out of the 'hood."

"Well, it's nice that he got a chance to get out and see the world. Hey, does he have any piercings?"

"Piercings?"

"Yeah, you know, nose rings, that sort of thing."

"No, nothing like that in the mug shot."

"Why don't you send me the mug shot anyway?"

"Doyle . . ."

"Danny, come on, it's just a mug shot."

He sighed. "So what's your interest in Arnett, anyway?"

"Nothing really. A big Escalade driving around Dunston looking suspicious, all out-of-place with its rims and tinted windows."

"Got the old Spidey sense tingling?"

"Something like that. It's a hell of a car for a loser just a few months out of jail."

"You know, technically, you're not supposed to be using your Spidey sense."

"It's okay—I'm only using it for the forces of good." My phone beeped to let me know I had a message. It was the photo from Danny.

Arnett didn't look familiar, but he looked like a lot of other losers I'd known. His eyes were half-closed in the picture, trying to look tough but coming off stupid. He had too much forehead and not enough chin, with reddish brown hair that was very short on the sides and nonexistent on top.

I had only caught a glimpse of the guy in the Escalade, and this wasn't him. But that made sense; Arnett would have been the one driving.

"Seriously, dude," Danny said. "You got a few weeks of this to go yet. Don't be getting in trouble right off the bat."

"I know. I'm cool."

"Yeah, all right, you lying dirtbag. Take care of yourself, okay, buddy?"

"I always do."

We stopped at a mini-mart on the edge of town and got two coffees and a bag for later. I filled a bag with cans of chili and boxes of granola bars, food I could eat without thinking. As we stepped outside, I took a long, scalding sip that immediately improved my outlook.

In the parking lot, we bumped into a skinny white kid with a dirty neck and an awkward attempt at dreadlocks. I thought he was going to ask us for money, until Moose said, "Hey, Squirrel!"

The other kid's eyes widened, but just a little. "Moose. Yo, what's up, man?" He looked at me the way skinny white kids with dreadlocks look at people they think are cops. "Hey," he said warily.

"It's cool," Moose said. "This is Doyle. Mrs. Menlow's son." Then to me, "Doyle, this is my friend Squirrel."

"Right." Squirrel stared at me for a second, his eyes suspicious and strangely pale. His pupils were tiny. "I'm sorry about your folks."

I nodded. "Thanks." Then, turning to Moose, "Anyway, I got to get going. I'll be heading back in an hour and a half or so if you want a ride."

Moose turned to his friend. "Where're you headed?"

"Back home. Want to stop by?"

"Sure." Moose turned back to me. "I'll see you back at the house."

Squirrel immediately took a step back, like he couldn't wait to be away from me. "Good to meet you," he said, wiping his nose with the base of his thumb.

"You, too," I replied.

I watched for a moment as they walked down the street. Squirrel looked back at me over his shoulder.

Sydney Bricker, Esq., had a brick storefront on the last commercial block at the center of town. If it wasn't for the planter full of petunias out front I would have wondered if the place was technically still in the business district. Across the street was a row of stucco singles with big lawns.

Bricker wasn't exactly what I had expected. First off, she was a she. Late forties, tall, blond, and striking, if not exactly attractive. Her legs were long and her skirt was short, and her blouse had enough buttons undone to show a little cleavage. She seemed incongruously polished, like someone had forgotten to tell her she was working in Dunston. I wondered if she was involved in local politics, maybe with an eye on Harrisburg.

"Mr. Carrick," she said, shaking my hand firmly. "I'm Sydney Bricker."

I smiled and shook firmly back. "Nice to meet you."

"You were expecting a man," she said with a knowing smile, leaning back against her desk.

I had pictured Sid Bricker as a short, fat, bald guy, but I wouldn't admit that. "I was expecting a lawyer."

"So, I understand you're a detective," Bricker said, leaning against her desk.

"That's right," I replied. "So, should we get right to it?"

I knew the meeting wouldn't take very long. The will would be simple, and since the lawyer was a lawyer, I figured she'd be unlikely to waste much time with unbillable chitchat. And since I would be paying the bill, I knew I wasn't going to waste much time on billable chitchat.

Frank and my mom had left everything to me. There were some stocks, some life insurance, and some money, and there was the house and the land. Bricker gave me a list of insurance and bank documents I should look for at the house.

After a brief recap of the will, I signed next to the red tab on a dozen pieces of paper. The whole thing took thirteen minutes. I figured Bricker billed in tenths-of-an-hour, six-minute chunks, meaning I had just crossed into the third tenth of an hour.

So when she asked me if I wanted some advice on what to do with the place, I figured if it took less than five minutes, I was all ears. I had time to kill before going to the funeral home anyway.

"By far the biggest asset left to you is the real estate," she said. "You're not in a great market right now, and there's not usually much demand out here, even in the best of times."

"But?"

"I know a developer putting plots together." She shrugged, giving her hair a practiced toss. "Your property might be a little too far, and you might have missed the boat already, but if you were planning on selling, this might be a smart time to do it."

"Thanks for the tip."

"I also have a real-estate license. If you're interested, I might be able to broker that for you."

"I'll think about that." I looked at my watch. "One more thing: Where can I get breakfast around here?"

"Branson's is great. It's over—"

"I know where it is. That's the only place?"

"Unless you feel like driving."

Sixteen minutes. Best not to cut it too close. I stood up. "Thanks."

*   *   *

I got to the funeral home early, but they didn't seem to mind. The place was called McClintock's, and Alfred McClintock himself came to meet me. He was a gaunt man with thinning hair that had turned translucent on its way from red to gray. He gave the impression that he was ready to share whatever sorrow was around without soothing any of it.

He assured me that Frank had arranged everything, but still insisted on walking me through all the different options. He'd wait for me to say, "Okay, that one," then he'd smile sadly and say, "Actually, Mr. Menlow selected this one." Like it was some sort of quiz, a test to see how poorly I knew my deceased stepfather, to show what a terrible stepson I was.

I didn't need that. I already knew it.

Frank had arranged for his remains to be cremated and his ashes placed in an urn matching the one he'd selected for my mother. There would be a memorial service on Wednesday, after which he would be buried beside my mother in the small plot next to the chapel.

He asked if I wanted a reception afterward, invite people back to the house.

I stared at him for a moment, remembering the excruciating awkwardness that had followed my mom's funeral. "No."

He nodded sadly, like he already knew the answer. "Mr. Menlow said you wouldn't."

When we were done, McClintock walked me outside, clapped a hand onto my arm and gave me what I think was a smile. I felt new respect for Frank, who'd had to deal with this guy to arrange my mom's funeral as well as his own.

I said thanks as I approached my car, then I got out of there as fast as I could.

15

When I walked into Branson's, I expected one of those scenes where the music stops and everyone turns to look at me. But there was no music, just the buzz and bustle of breakfast. That didn't stop, either.

The PLEASE SEAT YOURSELF sign was still up, so I sat in the same table as the day before and hid behind a menu.

I knew I was getting the two eggs, wheat toast, and home fries, but as I was trying to decide whether to get bacon or sausage or both, a cup of coffee appeared on the table, and I looked up to see the guy from behind the bar standing there holding a second cup.

"Sorry," he said. "A little short-staffed." I was about to give him my order when he said, "Mind if I join you?"

I moved the menu out of his way, and he sat, sipping his black coffee before putting it on the table. "Sorry about yesterday," he said, taking another sip.

"Me, too."

"You're Frank Menlow's kid. Doyle, right?"

Close enough, I thought, as I nodded.

"Sorry. Frank was good people. Meredith, too. Classy lady."

"Thanks."

He put out his hand. "I'm Bert Squires."

"I thought maybe you were Branson," I said, shaking it.

He laughed. "Branson died thirty years ago. But yeah, this is my place. I didn't want you to think that what went on yesterday was normal behavior around here."

"It isn't? Didn't seem like the first time that guy had pulled something like that."

"Who, Dwight?" Squires laughed and scratched the back of his neck. "Yeah, Dwight Cooney is a piece of work, but he's mostly harmless."

Let him punch you in the head, I thought, then tell me he's harmless. "He didn't seem harmless when he grabbed the lady's arm."

"Yeah, well. He's got it bad for her."

"He's got a strange way of showing it."

He leaned forward, the wooden chair creaking under him. "I'm afraid Dwight never got past the pigtail-pulling phase of male-female relationships."

It seemed like more than that to me, but the guy was making an effort, so I let it go.

"Anyway," he said, pushing himself to his feet. "What'll you have?"

I went with the bacon. The food came out fast, and it was excellent: eggs a little runny, bacon crisp and even. When I was done, Squires came back and told me it was on the house.

"Thanks," I said. "If I'd known ahead of time, I would have gotten the sausage, too."

"That's why I didn't tell you."

* * *

Stepping outside Branson's, I practically bumped off of the heat. Nothing like a big fried breakfast to help you enjoy the summer weather. Still, the way the grease was sitting in my stomach, I figured a quick walk around town might help. The retail district was barely two blocks long, and I'd already walked half of it. I turned in the direction away from Bricker's office and walked past a handful of shops and a bank before I came to a vacant hardware store and a rusty but operational gas station. That was it. I turned the corner and started heading back along the next street up, figuring I'd circle back to my car.

The street was more like an alley, a couple of fenced yards on the left, some Dumpsters and the backs of the stores on the right. Someone was leaning against a utility pole halfway up the block, smoking a cigarette. He was doing something with his hands, but I couldn't figure out what.

He was big, maybe six-four. As I got closer, I saw sunlight reflecting off something shiny on his face and I recognized him as the guy from George Arnett's Escalade. He looked like he recognized me, too, staring at me with that bored expression some people think is intimidating.

I looked back at him with a steely gaze that I thought was intimidating, but he looked away from me, uninterested, and went back to what he was doing with his hands.

As I got a little closer, I realized he was holding a pack of matches, and he was flicking them, lit, toward a row of fences. When I was twenty feet away, he put the cigarette to his lips and took a long pull, like there was more than one drag left in it, but he needed to finish. Then he flicked it onto the ground between us.

I watched it bounce on the cement. Then I looked up at him. "That's littering," I said.

He gave me that same bored stare and as he tore off another match, I heard a raspy mewing sound. Following both the direction of the sound and the trajectory of the matches, I looked down and saw a scruffy gray tabby backed into a corner where two sections of fence met. Its ears were flat against its head and its spine was arched. The ground in front of it was littered with matches, a few of them still lit.

The asshole leaning against the pole was pressing another match to the flint strip on the cover. Before I really thought about it, about how I was suspended and out of jurisdiction, I reached out and slapped the matches away from him.

Before they hit the ground, his hand shot out and smacked my face, enough to sting. I brought up my right, a tight fist with a little too much behind it.

One moment he was there, then suddenly he wasn't.

One moment I felt his arm on my neck, then suddenly—well that was about it, really.

Technically, I wouldn't call it a K.O., but the next thing I knew, I was horizontal on the sidewalk, and I was alone. The spent matches were less than a foot from my face. One of them was still lit, but it went out as I watched, releasing a thin thread of smoke that made little loops in the turbulence from my breath.

The cat was gone.

I sat up slowly and looked around, but the street was empty. My head felt like it was full of overcooked oatmeal. I checked myself for injuries and found no lumps, no bumps, nothing other than a tingle where he'd slapped my face, and a similar sensation on the left side of my neck. I'd heard of martial arts moves that could put a man out with a slap on the carotid artery, cause the blood pressure to go haywire. I'd read that they were frowned upon because while the victim usually woke up unharmed moments later, sometimes the victim didn't wake up at all, having bled out from a torn carotid artery. I guess that was a chance my new friend was willing to take.

The world sloshed unpleasantly as I pushed myself up off the ground. I steadied myself on the utility pole and dusted off my shirt and pants, keeping my anger in check and directed at myself. Walking stiffly back toward my car, I thought about how much I hoped to run into that guy again, and how much that town was starting to seriously piss me off.

Halfway home, I came upon a figure walking along the side of the road, looking as pathetic as I felt—shoulders slumped, feet dragging, and a big wet spot in the middle of his back.

I pulled up next to him and lowered the window. "Moose."

His skin was blotchy, and his face was dripping, like he'd been walking in the heat long enough to remember how much he'd had to drink the night before.

He walked around to the passenger side and got in. Without asking, he reached over and cranked up the air conditioning, moving the vent in his direction. "I feel like crap."

"Mmm," I said with a sarcastic smile. "Squish."

Normally, I might have piled it on a little thicker, but having your ass handed to you is humbling, and I still felt a tiny bit woozy. He sank back in his seat and closed his eyes.

"So that's your friend Carl?" I asked.

"Yeah."

"You didn't mention he was a junkie."

"What?" He opened his eyes and sat up a little. "Squirrel's not a junkie. Are you kidding? He's like, Mr. Healthy Natural. That's why he makes his own hooch. He doesn't want to put chemicals into his body."

"He wouldn't be the first to make an exception for drugs." I shrugged. "Maybe it's organic junk, but he's using."

"Dude, you are so wrong. You're just thinking like a cop."

I gave him a look. "His eyes were half-closed, his pupils were constricted, and his nose was runny."

"That's probably hay fever or something. Squirrel's just high on life."

"You don't think he seemed stoned?"

Moose shrugged and closed his eyes again. "Maybe he was a little more high on life than usual, but that's all."

Moose was practically asleep by the time we got home. His head had left a smudge where it slid down the window.

I was feeling a little worse for wear myself, and after I stopped the car in the driveway and shut off the engine, I let my eyes rest for a moment.

When I opened them, I saw Nola Watkins charging up the driveway toward me with a look of murderous rage. My brain scrambled through everything I had said or done in the last twenty-four hours, but I couldn't think of anything particularly egregious. That scared me even more, because usually it was the infractions you didn't know about that got you in the most trouble.

I put the key in the ignition to start the car, but she walked around to the passenger side. That's when I realized she wasn't coming for me. She was coming for Moose.

16

"Uh, Moose . . ." I said, giving him just enough warning to open his eyes before she opened the door and he tumbled onto the ground.

"You *idiot*!" she shrieked.

Moose put up his hands like he thought she might actually hit him. "What?"

I climbed out of the car and hurried over in case I needed to get between them. Nola held up her left hand, and I saw that she was holding an ear of corn. "Look at this!"

Moose stared up at her, confused but too scared to ask her to clarify.

With an exasperated growl, she grabbed a handful of husk and silk and tore it away, exposing half the ear.

Moose squinted and tilted his head, screwing up his face as he stared at the ear of corn.

"Look at it!" she yelled at him. "It all looks like this!"

"What is that?" he asked.

The corn was mostly blue, but it was speckled with kernels that were a sickly gray color.

"Well, that's a damn good question," she said through gritted teeth.

"I . . . I . . ."

"I know," she said. "You, you . . . You were supposed to take care of that plot. You said you knew heirloom corn, and I trusted you." As quickly as it had erupted, her anger faded and her lip started to quiver. "I needed this client."

She teetered for a second, like she was going to fall over, then she seemed to collapse inward instead. Moose got up and went to her, but she swatted him away, still too annoyed to take comfort from him.

That left me.

I didn't want her to think I was taking advantage, but she was crying now, and she seemed like she needed a shoulder to do it on. I took a step closer and put my arm lightly around her, resting my hand on her upper arm.

She swayed into me. I could feel her warmth, and the slightness of her small frame. Even slack, though, her muscles felt strong and supple.

Her body shook once, a single deep, silent sob. She put her head against my chest and turned me toward the house. I felt like I was driving but she was steering.

Moose looked at me wide-eyed, shaking his head, his hands upraised, protesting his innocence as we walked past him. I shook my head back at him. Now was not the time to argue the point.

Nola's effect on me had been strong since the first time I laid eyes on her, but as I walked her inside and we sat on the sofa, the effect was even stronger. Part of me wanted to make a move. Several parts, actually. But instead, I sat upright so she could lean against me. I smoothed her hair away from her face, and I waited until she was okay.

After ten minutes, she stiffened slightly and the pressure of her leaning against me lessened perceptibly. My back was cramping, but I didn't want her to move any farther away, so I stayed where I was.

"Sorry," she said in a whisper.

"It's okay," I whispered back.

I felt her head move against me, and when I looked down, she was looking up at me, her cheeks and the tip of her nose a soft pink. Even rimmed with red, her eyes were clear and strong.

The desire to kiss her was almost overwhelming, but she smiled self-consciously and gave me a pat on the cheek, then moved a few inches away. The air felt cold where her body was no longer touching mine.

"I put everything I had into this business," she said, watching as I pulled a box of teabags out of the cabinet. The coffee was still out in the car. She had a crumpled tissue in her hand, occasionally dabbing her eyes, but she had regained her composure. "I just need to get to year three, get my organic cert, then I'll be okay. It's taken a while to get the crops growing right, get the business plan ironed out, get some steady customers. The restaurants are a good market, but this specialty catering thing—the high-end weddings and stuff—that's what was going to keep me going until I got the certification. It's all word of mouth, and a couple of jobs can make you or break you."

The kettle started clearing its throat. Before it could start to sing, I turned off the burner and poured water into the two cups.

"It's not just that I like working with the soil, out in the fresh air. There aren't many jobs out there where you don't have to worry about being exposed to some chemical or another. So far I've been lucky, my MCS isn't real bad, and maybe I'm overly cautious, but I don't want to push it and make it worse. I don't want to end up being the crazy lady in the cubicle at the end who's always asking people not to wear scented deodorant. This is a job where I know I can have a good life. A normal life. My last bit of operating capital went into that field of blue corn." She shook her head. "Honest to God, chosen to match the bridesmaids' gowns."

I opened the refrigerator and grabbed the quart of milk, but immediately turned on the taps and emptied it down the drain. "Sorry," I said, handing her one of the cups. "I hope you don't take milk."

She smiled. "It's fine. I like it like this." She held the cup with both hands, absorbing the warmth into her body.

"So what now?" I asked.

She shrugged, closing her eyes as she sipped her tea. "Who knows? I don't even know what it is. It doesn't look like smut or blight or wilt or any of the usual problems."

She took another sip, so I did, too. It wasn't coffee.

"What are you going to do?" I asked.

"I know a horticulturist who works at the college out here."

I smiled. "There's a college out here?"

"Don't be mean. Pine Crest Community has a very fine horticulture department."

"So, when are you going to call her?"

"Him," she said, looking at her watch. "He's actually lecturing right now. It's not far. It would probably be better if I just took the corn out there." She paused again. "Any chance you feel like coming with me?"

"Um . . . sure."

"It's just that, well, I don't want him to think there's anything going on between you and me, but I definitely don't want him to think there's anything between him and me, either."

I laughed ruefully. She wanted me to cock block for her.

"What?" she asked, reading my expression. "You don't have to. It's okay."

"No, that's fine," I said, forcing a smile. "Happy to help."

Moose was sitting on the front steps, looking like a dog that had pooped on the rug. When we stepped out, he sprang to his feet.

"Nola, listen, I'm really sorry," he said. "But I swear, I did everything you said, just the way you said. Everything."

She put up a hand to silence him. "It's okay, Moose. It's all right." She spoke calmly, but she didn't look at him.

"Where are you going?"

She closed her eyes, like she didn't want to answer him but she didn't want to be rude. "We're taking it to Jerry Simpkins," she said, holding up the ear of corn in a big Ziploc bag.

"Nola, I'm really sorry."

She put up her hand again. "Farming is like that."

I got behind the wheel of my car without thinking about it. Nola got in the passenger side without a word. Guess I was driving, then.

"Make a right," she said as I pulled out.

I looked back at Moose, sitting down on the steps. I felt bad for him, whether he had screwed up or not. I could see on his face that he felt terrible.

"Nice car," she said as we drove away, looking at me with an amused expression.

She was right, it was a sporty little thing, a Nissan Z with more bells and whistles than I could really afford. She seemed to be waiting for an explanation. I didn't want to give her one, but I didn't want her thinking I was compensating for anything other than the fact that I spend too much time in my car and have no life.

"It used to belong to a guy named Oscar Quezada," I told her, "a coke dealer who liked to laugh at my Corolla. When Quezada was busted and his car was seized, I made sure I knew when it was coming up at the auction."

I could feel her staring at me, trying to decide what to make of the story. I was still trying to figure that out myself.

"I probably bid more than it was worth," I said, "but I made sure I got it. And I made sure he saw me driving it."

17

Pine Crest College was twenty minutes away, just off the inter-
state. It had that college campus look, all stone walls and brick walk-
ways, but if you looked closely, you could see it was all textured
concrete.

We walked across a small quad, weaving between groups of
students reading or talking, to a three-story stone building with
"Markson Science Annex" etched across the top floor. We entered
through a small glass atrium and went up half a flight of stairs to a
long sunlit hallway with large windows along one side and double
doors every thirty feet on the other side.

As we approached the first set of doors, Nola looked at her watch
and said, "One-fifteen."

The doors swung open, and a steady stream of students started
filing through, the ambient sound in the hallway getting louder and
louder with each additional voice.

Through the doors, I could see the professor, holding court over
a cluster of female students. He had curly blond hair, just over his

collar, but he was about my age, maybe older, and slightly thick around the middle. He had a sly smile, like he thought he was really something. The adoring gazes of his students said they thought so, too.

One by one, he was charming them, moving his gaze from one to the next like a rich kid shopping in his favorite candy store.

When he caught sight of Nola standing out in the hallway, however, his attention was on her and her alone. He swam through the students like a fish against a strong current, never taking his eyes off her.

"Nola Watkins, what a pleasant surprise," he said with a flourish, giving her the same sly smile he'd used on the girls now standing dejectedly inside the lecture hall. "You're looking very well."

I was prepared not to like the guy, and I didn't. But when his eyes went up and down Nola, the dislike intensified.

When he was done looking at her, he stepped closer.

Nola pulled back a bit and said, "This is my friend, Doyle. . . ."

Before she finished the introduction, he had already dismissed me with a glance and resumed staring at her. "Professor Simpkins," he said without extending his hand.

"*Detective* Carrick," I replied, because I can be a prick, too. Some people think I'm pretty good at it.

He stopped and glanced back at me for a moment. I gave him a grin that said, "Yes, I *am* being a prick."

"To what do I owe this pleasure?" he said, turning back to Nola.

She held up the baggie with the ear of corn. "Jerry, I was hoping you could take a look at this."

He looked at the bag, then looked at her, his expression changing from curiosity to suspicion to disappointment at the realization that she was not there because she missed him. When he glanced over at me, he looked resigned, and I'd like to think a little nervous, too.

As we stood there, the cluster of girls gave up and filed past us down the hallway.

Simpkins turned back to Nola, looking hurt and annoyed. He put on his reading glasses and took the bag out of her hand, squinting as he held it up in the light from the windows.

"Yech." He smiled condescendingly. "There's a lot that can go wrong being a farmer, isn't there, Nola? What is this, Mexican Black?"

"Lenape Blue."

"Looks terrible."

"I know. Do you recognize it?"

He opened his mouth, like he expected an answer to come out. But then he just closed it. "I don't know," he said after a moment. "Let's have a closer look, shall we?"

We followed him to a lab in the basement, where he perched on a stool and put the corn on the work surface. He pulled over an illuminated magnifying glass on a spring-balanced arm and switched on the light, examining the corn closely from a number of angles. After grunting a few times, he wheeled his stool to a microscope a few feet away. Popping one of the gray kernels with his thumbnail, he smeared some of what came out onto a glass slide. He placed a glass cover over it and slid it under the microscope.

After several minutes, he sat back and rubbed his eyes, gesturing for Nola to look in the microscope. As she did, he said, "I don't know what you've got here. It doesn't look quite right, that's for sure, but there's no sign of disease. No fungus or anything. The way it's localized, I wonder if it is cross pollinated."

Nola looked up. "I wondered about that, but cross pollinated with what? Those strange kernels don't look like anything I've seen in a seed catalogue. Or would want to."

"No, they don't, do they?" He bit his lip for a moment, thinking. "I do know of a guy. Jason Rupp. A plant geneticist, among other things. I don't know him very well, and he's not here at the college, but he lives nearby. He might be able to shed a little more light. I've only met him a few times. An odd bird, but apparently quite brilliant. He was a finalist for the Gairdner Award. Very prestigious. Anyway, I could give him a call, if you'd like."

We followed Simpkins across the hall, into a small, windowless room with books and papers everywhere. He sat behind the desk and flicked through a Rolodex for a moment, then picked up his phone and punched in the number.

"Jason, hi. This is Jerry Simpkins. . . . Pine Crest, yes, that's right. Oh, thanks, yeah, maybe one day." He rolled his eyes. "Anyway, I'm here with a former student, and she has kind of an interesting problem with some Lenape Blue corn. I was wondering if you might be able to take a look at it. . . . Well, I don't know, that's why I'm calling you."

He put his hand over the mouthpiece. "He says he can call you in a few days, maybe he can look at it then."

Nola bit her lip. "Actually, can you ask if there's any chance he could look at it today? I have a client coming tomorrow, and I need to know what to tell them."

Simpkins raised one eyebrow dubiously, and then took his hand away from the phone. "Actually, Jason, I know this is asking a lot," he said, looking up to make sure we caught that. "She was wondering if she could bring it by today. It seems this is more urgent than I had realized. . . . Yes, I understand . . . I don't know, Jason, that's why we're calling you. . . . It's blue corn. It looks like maybe some kind of smut, but it's only affecting isolated kernels, as if it was a pollination issue. . . . They're kind of discolored, gray and bloated. . . . Okay, I'll tell them. Thank you." He scribbled on a piece of notepaper. "Yes, thanks again, I'll think about that."

He hung up the phone and looked at Nola. "He can see you at his house, but he's leaving in an hour, so you'll need to get a move on." He told us how to get there as he wrote Rupp's address and phone number on a piece of paper and handed it to Nola.

She glanced away, not meeting his eyes as she took it. "Thanks, Jerry."

He stared at her, aware of her averted gaze, and he smiled sadly. "My pleasure."

18

Back in the car, Nola seemed pensive. I wasn't sure if it was because of the encounter with Simpkins or the problem with the corn. She handed me the paper with Rupp's address and I drove as fast as I dared, my previous run-in with the local authorities still fresh in my mind.

Once we got onto the main road, the silence stretched out enough that I had to say something.

"So, I'm perfectly fine going to see this guy right now. It's not like I've got anything else to do. But why is it so important that we see him right now?"

"Because the caterer is coming tomorrow, and I need to be able to tell them what's wrong with the corn. I need to know if this is something I can cut around and use the rest. Is it something that can spread to my other crops? I need to know what I'm up against. Plus there are contractual aspects. Some things I'm not liable for, some things I am."

"And this blue corn, they can't get it anywhere else?"

"Not at this point. I doubt it."

"Maybe something just like it."

She sighed deeply, like she was talking to an idiot, like she was trying not to get annoyed but her efforts would not succeed indefinitely. "You don't understand. The bride was very specific. She chose this particular strain of corn to match the bridesmaids' gowns. The entire meal is going to be blue: The cake is blue, the pork medallions glazed in blueberry, the champagne will have a few drops of blue Curacao. It might be beautiful. It might be tacky as hell. But it will be very blue, and it will be very hard to replace at the last minute."

"Well, maybe they can—"

"No," she cut me off, "they can't. Look, I appreciate your help. I do. And I know you're just trying to help some more, but you really just don't understand."

I've been single a lot more than I haven't been, but one thing I know about women is that when they say you just don't understand, any attempt to convince them otherwise simply proves their point. Instead, I looked straight ahead as I drove, kept my Smurf jokes to myself, and tried not to do or say anything to make matters worse, like telling her what I really thought—that this was a fool's errand and that no matter what the guy said, she was screwed.

As we drove, Nola's silence turned from stressed to exhausted. Before long, she let out a soft sigh and her head pressed against the window, near the smudge Moose's head had left. I leaned forward to see if she was asleep, and looked back just in time to swerve out of the way of a black Saab coming at us way too fast and drifting into our lane. It had tinted windows, gold trim, and fat tires, but what stuck out in my mind was the face in the backseat, looking out the open window as it passed us.

He had curly dark hair and a single eyebrow. Apart from that there wasn't much memorable about it, except for the fact that I remembered it. In my line of work if you remember someone's face, they're probably either a cop or they're something bad. This guy was not a cop.

"What?" Nola asked, sitting up and blinking as I straightened out the car.

"Nothing," I said, finishing my turn. "Guy was going pretty fast."

She mumbled something about young kids driving too fast on country roads, but my mind was somewhere else, flicking through the mug shot book in my head, trying to place that face.

A few minutes later, she was asleep. I called Danny Tennison.

"About five years ago," I started, as soon as he picked up. "You and Ralph Ritchie took down some dumbass in an ice-cream truck in Port Richmond. Real badass, thought he was cool selling crack in the bottom of ice-cream cones."

He laughed. "Mr. Softee we called him. Yeah, I remember. Ugly kid with a unibrow. Why?"

"I think I just saw him up here."

"Mr. Softee? Nah, he got like ten years, remember? Fought a little bit when we picked him up."

"Can you check?"

"Dude."

"Just check."

"Do you have cable up there? 'Cause you can get a satellite dish, if that's the problem. Even just for twenty days, it'd be worth it."

"I'll look into that."

"You could probably even get one of those intro deals, first month free or something. . . ."

He was still talking when I put the phone back into my pocket.

19

Jason Rupp lived in a small, nondescript, wooden ranch house. Apart from a shiny black Mustang looking out of place parked out front, there was nothing decorative at all: no window boxes, no shutters, no sign posts, no garden, no welcome mat, no lamppost. Nothing. Actually, it was probably what the outside of my place would look like if I didn't rent an apartment.

Nola woke with a start when I killed the engine. "Are we there?" she asked, looking out the window.

She took a moment to collect herself, then we got out. She cleared her throat and pressed the doorbell.

A voice from inside yelled, "Come on in."

The inside of the house was as spare as the outside, but it was clean, with modern furniture, a massive TV, and an elaborate computer workstation. Sitting on the computer chair, bending over as he pulled on a pair of socks, was a chubby guy with pale skin, frizzy brown hair, and bushy, uneven sideburns.

He paused between socks and looked up at us. "Hey."

Nola cleared her throat again. "Jason Rupp?"

"Yeah." He looked at her appraisingly, holding his breath as he pulled on the second sock. "Are you the corn lady?" He had a tiny trace of an accent or an affectation, like he was from the same country as Madonna and Tina Turner.

Nola smiled nervously and held up the bag.

Rupp put out his hand and wiggled his fingers. As she crossed the room to bring him the bag, he glanced over at me. "Who's he?"

I thought about throwing out my own cheesy accent, and the phrase "I'm your worst nightmare" came to mind, but Nola was asking for a favor, so I didn't.

Maybe she sensed my temptation, because she quickly said, "He's my friend Doyle. He drove me here."

Rupp looked back at me, lingering suspiciously for a moment before glancing at the bag. When he looked back up at Nola, he paused and smiled as if he was actually seeing her for the first time. "So you're a horticulturist, huh? Are you one of Jerry's kids?"

"At Pine Crest?"

He nodded.

She smiled. "Oh, no."

"No?" He sat back, looking at her again, ignoring the bag. "So how do you know him?"

"He was a grad student when I was a senior at Cornell. He was one of my teaching assistants."

"Cornell, huh? Good program."

"Yes, it was great. How about you?"

He paused, and his expression soured. "Pine Crest, briefly. Then Penn State, and grad school at MIT." He paused again like he was thinking or making a decision. "So now you're a farmer?"

"That's right."

He looked her slowly up and down. "You don't look like a farmer."

I couldn't argue with his conclusion, but I wasn't crazy about his methodology. Still, this was Nola's show. And my previous attempts at chivalry hadn't gone so well.

"Where's your farm?"

"In Dunston. On Bayberry, just up from Valley Road."

His eyes narrowed slightly. "You didn't sell?"

She shook her head and smiled. "No, so far I've been able to resist all the pressure."

"Pressure? What kind of pressure?"

I think she may have blushed. "Oh, nothing. I've gotten some calls, that's all. But I'm staying."

"Calls? Like what?"

"Nothing, just hang-ups, but—"

"You probably could have made a lot of money selling."

"If I was in it for the money, I wouldn't be farming."

He smiled as if he thought that was cute. "Good for you."

I would have wanted to smack him—hell, I did want to smack him—but Nola just smiled nervously and looked down at the bag with the corn.

Rupp's eyes lingered on her for another second. Then he pulled the bag closer and flattened it out so he could see it better. He turned on a desk lamp and grunted.

Nola leaned closer. "What?"

"Nothing," he said abruptly, shaking his head. "This corn is not well."

"I know. I thought at first it might be some sort of weird smut," she explained, nervously rubbing her fingers, "but the way it only affects certain kernels, I thought it had to be some sort of cross-pollination issue, only there's no other corn nearby."

He looked up at her with an unpleasant smile, his condescension now undiluted with any effort to charm. "Cross-pollination?"

"Yes," she replied. "And Jerry agreed that—"

"Cross-pollination with what?"

"Well, I, I . . ." Nola stammered. "What do you mean?"

"Look at these kernels. They are obviously diseased. With what, I don't know, but something. There are so many different types of smut. There are wilts, kernel rots. I can't say for sure."

"But Jerry said—"

"Jerry said what?"

"That it looked like a genetic issue, too. Look at how—"

Rupp waved his hand dismissively. "Everybody thinks everything is genetic these days. Look, the simple fact is that there are thousands of bacteria and viruses and fungi out there, all of them waiting for a chance to infect a host, for a weakness they can exploit—too hot, too cold, too wet, too dry, too windy, whatever."

"Well, yes, but—"

"Why did Simpkins tell you to ask me about this?"

"Why? Well . . . he said you're an expert."

"Exactly. More of an expert than him, that's for sure." He snorted. "If he were an expert, he wouldn't be teaching at Pine Crest, would he?"

Nola's mouth hung open.

Rupp paused for a moment. "Look, I have to get going. If you'd like, I can examine this more closely." He looked up at her again, up and down, a bit of the leer returning to his smile. "Maybe we could meet in a couple of days, discuss it over coffee."

"Well, um, actually, I need it asap. I have a client coming up to check on it tomorrow. Maybe I should just take it to the county agent. If it is some rare disease, the Department of Agriculture is going to—"

Rupp laughed, shaking his head. "Look, I can tell you just by looking at it, this is diseased. But I'll look into it. Give me your number, and if I can find out anything more about it, I'll get back to you as soon as I can."

Nola gave Rupp her card and moments later we were standing out on the front step with Rupp's front door closed firmly behind us.

20

"What a putz," I said as we got into the car.

Nola shook her head. "Academia is filled with that type. I *so* don't miss them."

Rupp was indeed a putz, but he had become noticeably more so halfway through the conversation, and I hadn't said a single word. Maybe I no longer needed to speak to have that effect on people, or maybe it was something else. Usually, when I get that reaction, it's a reaction I am trying to get. If we had been asking about anything other than corn smut, I would have thought Rupp was acting as if his cage had just been rattled.

When we got back to the house, Moose was sitting on the steps, right where we'd left him.

"Did you find anything out?" he asked as we got out of the car.

Nola sighed as she walked up to him. "Probably some sort of smut. We might know more tomorrow. Simpkins sent us to another guy, Jason Rupp. He said he would try to study it tonight or tomorrow."

"Hmm. You want to know what *I* found out?"

"Actually, Moose," she said, "I think I want to go inside and take a bath."

He held up another big plastic Ziploc bag. Inside it were half a dozen stripped ears of corn. Instead of a sprinkling of bloated grey kernels, these ears were composed entirely of them, swollen and baggy and sickly and misshapen. "I found an entire field of this stuff growing next door."

Nola rushed over and took the bag from him, studying it closely. "Where?"

"Next door."

"You went in there? How did you know?"

"Because I'm a genius."

We followed Moose across the street, through Nola's tomato and herb patch, past the blue corn, to the split-rail fence that separated her property from the adjacent land. Just past the fence was a massive wall of dense green foliage, twenty feet high.

"Siberian elm," Nola said, looking up at it. "It's amazing how big those trees have grown in two years."

"They planted *that* two years ago?" I asked.

She smiled sardonically. "Good fences make good neighbors, right?"

Moose hopped over the fence. "Luckily, it's on the north side, otherwise it would really take out some sunlight. You guys coming?"

I wasn't above a little trespassing, but I waited for Nola's response. She looked at me and shrugged, then hiked a leg onto the fence and hopped over it. I followed suit.

Moose plunged into the greenery, and I went next, holding back some of the thicker branches so they didn't whack Nola in the face. I put out a hand for her, and she took it—a purely utilitarian gesture that reminded me of a girl named Cindy Mailer and a walk home from school in the sixth grade.

We emerged twenty feet later in front of a ten-foot chain-link fence. It stretched out to our left for at least a quarter mile. To our right, it turned sharply after a hundred feet, angling away from us to follow the hedges that lined the road. Every forty feet or so was a sign that said POSTED: NO TRESPASSING.

"That's a big fence," I said.

Just beyond the fence was a field of corn, not very tall, looking slightly gray and withered. A pair of butterflies fluttered down one of the rows. They were a muted orange and black, but looked colorful compared to the drab stalks.

"That's where you got it?" Nola asked.

"Yeah," Moose replied. "And it's all like that."

"I thought they were developing this land. I didn't know they were farming it."

I stepped to the side so I could look down the rows; they were straight and they were long. "So whose land is this? The people who want to buy your property?"

"Who, Redtail?" Nola slowly shook her head. "I called them about something a few months ago. They said it wasn't theirs. It used to be Mr. Rudner's, but he died four years ago. It's changed hands a few times since then. The banks that owned it have changed hands, too. I don't know who owns it now."

I turned to Moose. "You went over that fence?"

With a grin, he jumped up and hooked his fingers through the fence. Scrambling up to the top, he swung his legs over it and scrambled halfway down the other side before jumping to the ground.

Nola looked stricken. "Moose! Get back here, right now!"

Instead, he ran over to the nearest row and pulled an ear off one of the stalks.

"Moose!" she scolded. "Now!"

Moose galloped back, still grinning. He tossed the ear to me over the fence, then clambered after it, repeating his earlier maneuver and dropping to the ground right in front of us.

I handed the ear to Nola. She gingerly pulled back the leaves, just enough to see an inch or so of the corn. Then she held it up for us both to see. Instead of firm white or yellow or blue, the kernels were bloated and puffy and a sickly gray.

"So what does this mean?" I asked.

Moose shrugged. Nola's brow furrowed.

"I mean, if whatever is wrong with your corn is that much worse on this corn, does that mean this is where it came from?"

"Yeah," Moose said, turning to Nola. "It could, right? I mean, if it's a fungus or disease, it could have spread from here."

She nodded slowly.

"And if it's a pollen drift issue," he continued, "it could definitely be coming from here."

As he said it, a slight breeze picked up. Nola turned to look the way we had come, in the direction of her own corn. "It might."

Moose held up the ear of corn and looked at it suspiciously. "Probably some fucked-up, tasteless, last-for-six months, shelf-stable, herbicide-resistant, GMO crap."

Nola looked at me, then at Moose. "You think?"

Moose shrugged. I didn't bother. It was obvious I had no idea.

"I'll tell you what," she said. "If it is, they're not allowed to have it within a hundred and fifty feet of the nearest crops."

"So what does that mean?" I asked.

"It means that's a big-time violation."

"So what are we going to do now?" Moose asked.

Nola thought for a second. "About this? I don't know. But I need a drink."

21

By the time we got back to Nola's porch, the sky was a deep blue with a spray of bright pink clouds rapidly turning to gray. Nola went inside for beers, leaving Moose and me on the porch. He looked tired, but satisfied with himself.

"Pretty good call," I said, "checking next door for that funky corn."

He smiled. "I don't know what the connection is, but I've been waiting for something bad from those guys since they took over the place."

"Who?"

"Whoever owns that land."

"What do you mean?"

"Just a vibe, I guess. But when a shadowy corporation moves in next door and plants these huge steroid hedges, it doesn't seem right."

"Shadowy corporation? I thought Nola said it was a bank."

He shrugged. "Maybe it is. And maybe they had nothing to do with any of it. Maybe I just fucked up."

"But you're pretty sure you didn't, aren't you?"

He stretched and yawned. "I was."

Nola came out with a tray of sandwiches and beers. In the time she had been gone, the sky had darkened to a royal blue.

"You were what?" she asked.

"Hoping you were bringing out sandwiches." He picked one up and took a small bite.

"Thanks," I said, as she handed me a sandwich. I was afraid it would be grilled tofu with arugula, but it was thick-sliced ham and thin-sliced Swiss with mustard, and it was delicious. I ate half the sandwich in two bites, washing it down with half my beer.

Nola nibbled at her sandwich, staring at a spot on the floor. I moved my foot into her line of sight and tapped it, prompting her to look up at me.

I gave her a smile. "So what's next?" I asked.

She shook her head. "I don't know. First off, I need to find out who owns that land. Find out what they're doing over there."

"How are you going to do that?" Moose asked, stifling another yawn.

"I don't know," she admitted. "I tried looking online, but I didn't get very far. The county's website is not very good, and it's hard to tell what's what because so many parcels have been consolidated and reconsolidated, and they all seem to be owned by holding companies with no contact information other than a post office box. I wish I could just go over there and ask."

"And you can't?" I asked. It seemed weird to me that you wouldn't know who owned the land next door, but it wasn't like I knew the names of anybody who lived on the same floor as my apartment.

Nola shook her head. "Not really. Sounds crazy, I know, but I don't even know what their address is, or how to get onto the property to ask them. And it's probably changed hands half a dozen times."

"That's what I'm talking about with these developers," Moose said. "It might not look like it, but piece by piece they're buying up the whole town."

"So what's next, then?" I asked again.

As Nola paused to think about it, her phone rang inside the house.

Moose sat up, looking suddenly awake. "Want me to get that?"

"I got it," she replied, getting up to go inside.

Moose and I exchanged a look in the gathering darkness.

"Hello?" we heard her saying. "Hello?"

Moose shook his head, his eyes angry and frustrated.

Nola turned on the porch light as she came back out, but she wouldn't look at either of us.

"Another wrong number?" Moose asked sarcastically.

She gave him a dirty look in reply.

"I know your man Barney Fife is useless," I said, "but you need to report this, get it on record."

"Just drop it, okay?" she said in a weary, pleading tone.

I didn't think I should, but I could see her pale eyes in the darkness, and I knew I would do whatever she asked.

"It's crazy," Moose said.

"Drop it," she snapped in a tone I was glad wasn't directed at me.

Moose put the last of his sandwich into his mouth, and I could see his jaw working hard in the moonlight. As soon as it stopped, he tilted his beer and drained it.

"I'm beat," he said flatly. "Thanks for the sandwich."

We both said good night, watching as he crossed the street in the moonlight and went inside the house, letting the screen door slap behind him.

"He's right, you know," I said.

"Don't you start. Please."

I took a quiet sip of beer, and so did she.

"I appreciate your help today," she said. "It meant a lot to me. Thanks."

"My pleasure. So how are you going to find out who's next door?"

"I don't know really. You're a detective; what would you suggest?"

"If I was in Philly, I'd have my sources. Out here, I don't know. Probably start in the hall of records. Look through the real-estate transfers."

She nodded, thinking about that. "I'm thinking tomorrow afternoon, after I meet with the caterers, I'm going to get in my car and make a left onto Bayberry, and keep making lefts. I figure I'll stop at every house on the left hand side of the road, make every left turn I can, and eventually, I'll either find the entrance to the place, if there is one, or go in a circle and end up back at my house."

"Door to door? Really?"

She shrugged and nodded, but she looked a little apprehensive.

It sounded crazy, but there was a certain old-fashioned police-work angle to it that I liked. "Tell you what; if you want, I can go with you. In case you run into any nut jobs."

She laughed. "That's a nice offer, but I took up a lot of your time today. Don't you have stuff you need to do?"

"Actually, I have some . . . time off from work. Frank's funeral is on Wednesday, but apart from that I'm open." Technically, I was supposed to be finding some of Frank's papers for Bricker, and there was no telling what kind of mature and healthy emotional processing that could provoke.

"Are you sure?"

"Positive." It was the perfect combination of tasks that I would try desperately to put off as a matter of course.

I knew she didn't want to ask me for any more help, but the relief on her face was unmistakable. "You're a heck of a guy."

"I keep telling people. Can I ask you a question?"

"Hmm. I guess so."

"What's the deal with you and Simpkins, anyway?"

She sighed and looked down. "You saw him with his gaggle of adoring fans, right?"

"I did. And I saw them vanish from his consciousness when he saw you. Did you two date?"

"No, no, no. Honestly. When we were at Cornell, he was very, um . . . attentive. I just thought he was being very conscientious." I could practically hear her blushing, and I smiled in the darkness.

"So?"

"Senior year he was one of my teachers. Even for grad students, fraternizing with students you are teaching is a big no-no."

"So what happened?"

"The same time I finished my degree, he got his Ph.D. and the job at Pine Crest. He knew I was looking for a small patch of farmland, so he calls me and tells me this parcel is for sale. . . . It was a really good price. Not too far from the city. College nearby."

"I was wondering how you both ended up in the same town."

"It wasn't until I bought the place that he made his move."

"How'd that go?"

She laughed. "Not the way he'd hoped."

"I see. Any tips on how to avoid the same fate?"

"Hmm. First, try not to be a schmuck."

"Anything else?"

"Yes," she said with a smile, standing and collecting plates and bottles. "You have to be very, very patient."

22

I was exhausted as I got into bed, but an hour later, I was still awake. Partly it was the sound of Moose snoring in the back bedroom. Partly, it was images of Nola drifting through my head—her pale eyes in the darkness, her shy smile as she asked me to come with her to see Simpkins. And yes, her drenched T-shirt at the diner.

But when it got really late, when I finally drove those thoughts from my mind, that's when it hit me that my mother was dead, and so was Frank.

Lying in her house, in the quiet and the dark, I could feel the presence of her absence, a cold, hollow ache that I'd been desperately trying to avoid. Memories of my childhood came back—the days before Frank was on the scene, the days when it was just my mom and me: trips to the beach, meetings with teachers, an awkward talk about condoms, lying on a blanket in the backyard looking for shooting stars. Christmas morning with my dad.

That last one blindsided me, so stunningly vivid I gasped. There was my dad, Christmas morning, bleary-eyed and unshaven, wearing his plaid flannel robe, a coffee cup in one hand, his other arm around my mom. They were both looking down at me as I opened a present, the tree blinking and twinkling to my right.

I hadn't thought about that moment in years, but I remembered it clearly. I had just unwrapped the remote control stunt car I'd been wanting since early the previous January. The smell of coffee and bacon hung in the air, and I looked up at my mom and my dad, and I thought to myself that life couldn't possibly get any better.

As it turned out, I was right.

The hollow ache opened into a chasm, a deep sorrow I hadn't felt since I had started covering it up at my father's funeral.

It occurred to me that just as Frank's death meant one less connection to a time when my mother was alive, losing her meant losing a connection to my dad that I had been holding on to for twenty-five years. I missed her because I missed her, but I missed her even more because I missed him, too.

My throat felt tight and my eyes felt moist, but I didn't cry, because I don't. Maybe I should have.

The last time I looked at the clock, it was just after two o'clock. I don't know when I fell asleep, but when the phone rang at three, I woke up with a start.

The caller I.D. said "N. Watkins," and I glanced out the window before I answered.

For a brief instant I pictured her lying in the dark, unable to sleep because she was thinking of me.

"Hey," I said into the phone.

"There's someone outside!" she whispered tersely.

I swung my feet onto the floor and sat up. "What?"

"There's someone outside my house. I heard them."

"Sit tight, I'll be right over."

I pulled on my jeans and my shoes, and I grabbed my gun from under the mattress. Five seconds later I was crossing the street in the darkness. I circled the house once, then tapped on the glass of the front door. A couple of seconds later, Nola's face appeared in the window, eyes wide. Then the door opened.

"I'm so glad you're here," she said, putting a hand on my chest.

"What did you hear?" I whispered.

"I heard someone outside. I thought it was a raccoon or something, but it sounded like a person. Then I heard someone on the front porch. That's when I called you."

"Wait here," I told her. "Lock the door and don't open it unless it's me."

She nodded and closed the door.

I waited until I heard her lock it, then I went back down the steps and had a more thorough look around. I circled the house once again, then checked the lock on her shed. I checked the two main fields behind her house—crisscrossing them a couple of times and pausing in each one, then in front of the thick green Siberian elm, listening for any sounds of intruders. Some of the plants were bent or broken, like someone had walked across them, but there was no way to tell whether the damage was new or whether the culprit had been a deer or a person.

When I returned to Nola's porch, her face appeared in the window before I had a chance to tap on the glass. I nodded and motioned that she should open the door.

"Did you find anything?" she whispered.

I shook my head. "Not really. Maybe some plants were flattened, but I don't know if that means anything."

"Well, I definitely heard something," she said defensively.

"You're sure it wasn't a deer or a raccoon?"

She gave me a look. "It wasn't a raccoon."

"Okay." She seemed like she didn't want me to leave but she didn't want to invite me in. "Do you want me to stay?"

She gave me a dubious look.

"Downstairs, I mean."

"That's okay," she said. "I'll be all right. I'll see you tomorrow, right?"

"Absolutely."

As I turned to go, she said, "Doyle," and reached out to put her hand on my chest again. "Thanks."

I started to say it was nothing, but then she got up on her tiptoes and put a soft kiss on my cheek. I stayed quiet as she smiled and closed the door.

23

When I got up in the morning, I celebrated the fact that I had coffee by drinking a lot of coffee. By nine-thirty I was fidgety and restless. I wasn't supposed to meet Nola until noon, so I decided to do some sight-seeing. I got into the car and drove for fifteen minutes, until I found a small street called Maple Lane. A few minutes later I pulled over in front of a driveway with crime-scene tape stretched between a lamppost and a small tree.

As I got out of the car, I was hit by that familiar odor of burnt plastic and wet ashtray. The smell made my skin prickle. For an instant I thought about the four people who had died, and how, but I chased that thought out of my head. I ducked under the crime-scene tape and walked up the driveway, fifty yards, to a concrete slab parking area next to a black rectangle surrounded by weeds and cinders. The building had been small but, reduced to two blackened dimensions, it seemed tiny.

There was so little debris I would have thought it had been

cleared away if not for the tangle of pipes. But it was all there, just burned down to ashes.

Surrounding the house was the melted remnants of a vinyl fence. Careful not to touch anything, I walked in a circle, between the melted vinyl fence and the charred black remains of the house.

There was no sign of cars. The parking area was between the house and the fence, so a car would have been destroyed for sure. But there was no sign of burnt or melted tires, no outline where it had scorched the earth.

As I drove back toward home, I called Stan Bowers.

"What's shaking, Carrick?"

"Just checked out that other meth lab, the one on Maple Lane."

"Why you doing that?"

"I'm bored, okay?"

"Yeah, I hear you. Fucking mess, right? I don't know if these assholes don't know what they're doing, or they're onto something new, or what."

"What do you mean?"

"Doesn't look like the standard setup. I mean, both places went up so hot there was hardly anything left to investigate, but we didn't find much in the way of the cough medicine. Each place, it was like they only had a few bottles of Vicks, as far as we could tell. Maybe they're using something else, or maybe the stuff they had just totally incinerated, or that was as much as they could get a hold of. They had all the beakers and shit, and a boatload of acetone. Way more than usual."

"So that's why the places went up like they did."

"I guess. Not much in the way of explosions, either. I mean, usually, these places go up, they go boom. Not these two. There may have been some minor stuff, pop, pop, but nothing that threw out debris, and nothing that blew the fire out. Both places, by the time the fire department got there, they were almost burned completely out, nothing left to burn."

"Were there any cars there?"

"Cars?"

"Yeah. At the Maple Lane place, the fence is all melted, fifteen feet away, but there's no sign of any cars, damaged or otherwise. And I don't remember seeing signs of any cars at the Burberry place, either."

He grunted, thinking. "I don't know. I don't remember seeing any, but that's not what I was looking for. Maybe someone got away."

"Well, that's what I'm thinking. Or maybe the places were torched."

"Hard to tell, as careless as these knuckleheads are."

"Hey, you know a guy named George Arnett?"

"Arnett? Doesn't sound familiar. Who is he?"

"Just some asshole from Kensington. How about the ice-cream man? Ralph Ritchie busted him."

"Mr. Softee. Yeah, I remember him. Why?"

"I've seen both of them this week, right here in Dunston."

"No shit. You're sure?"

"Pretty sure. Ran the plates on Arnett."

Stan sighed. "Well, that's what I'm saying. It ain't Rockwell's America out here anymore. Getting as bad as the city."

"Crazy stuff."

"Doyle, I've seen more crazy shit out here these last six months than the last two years working out of Philly."

Not two minutes later, I saw a little craziness myself: Just outside of town, Mr. Softee coming out of the mini-mart carrying two bulging plastic shopping bags.

He was with two other guys. One looked like Fabio, but skinny.

The other one had creepy gray eyes and a face full of hardware. The guy who took me down in the alley behind Branson's.

Anger flared hot inside me, and even though it was tempered by a cold dose of justifiable trepidation, I felt a strong urge to try my luck with him again, maybe a little more cautiously this time. Instead I turned away and watched in my mirror.

Softee was snickering about something and looking in one of the shopping bags as the three of them walked up to the black Saab. Fabio got in behind the wheel. Softee swaggered up to the front passenger side door. Gray eyes stopped a few steps away and stared until Softee looked back and jumped, scurrying over to the back door and getting in the car in a hurry. Like he was scared.

I had to smile, thinking, *I hear you, dude.*

As I watched in the rearview, the Saab pulled out. I tried to be slick, waiting until the Saab took the first left before I pulled out after it. I had to turn around in a hurry, and my tires sang a little as I took the left, but soon the Saab was back in front of me and I slowed down, keeping a couple of blocks between us. Tailing wasn't my strongest suit, and I was worried they'd spot me on those long stretches of road farther outside of town, but after half a mile, they turned onto a small block of tiny bungalows. I pulled over just on the other side of the next hill, sixty yards away, and watched as Mr. Softee, Fabio, and Prince Charming got out of the Saab and walked up to a tiny, one-story place with vinyl blinds in all the windows and a new-looking white Ford Econoline van in the driveway. The three of them slipped through the front door, and before it closed behind them, a head popped out and looked up and down the street.

Dwight Cooney.

As I was sitting there pondering that relationship, my phone started playing "Watching the Detectives."

"What've you got for me?" I asked.

"You know, I think the magic has gone from our relationship."

"Don't be like that. You know I love you."

"Softee's name is Derek Roberts. He had a bunch of priors, but when Ralph popped him, he got five years for possession with intent and resisting. He seemed to be moving up in the world."

"That was five years ago?"

"Three years. Roberts got out last March."

"Interesting. Any connection to Arnett?"

"They're both assholes. And yes, they're known associates."

"Hmm. Got another one for you."

"Wait, when does this suspension of yours start, anyway?"

"Guy's name is Dwight Cooney."

"Jesus Christ. You're relentless."

"That's part of what makes me so good."

"It's part of what makes you a pain in the ass."

"Dwight Cooney." I spelled it out. "You got it?"

He sighed loudly. "All right, hold on a second. I'm at my computer right now." I could hear him tapping at his keyboard. "Okay, Dwight Cooney . . . 1255 Mill Road?"

"That's the house I'm looking at."

"Yeah, he's an asshole, too. Maybe they met at a chapter meeting. A couple for assault, a couple for possession, drunk and disorderly. Auto theft. Hasn't done much real time, mostly fines and probation."

"Well, he just let Roberts and two other guys into his house. If Roberts is on parole, they're both violating something, right?"

"I guess so." Danny sounded bored, like he was stifling a yawn.

"They're definitely up to something."

"Yeah, maybe, Doyle. But you're not, remember?"

"What do you mean?"

"I mean you're leaving it alone. You're on suspension. If you think something is going on, it's not your job, because you're not on the job. You need to tell local law enforcement, then leave it alone."

"Local law enforcement is a joke around here. Maybe I should go to DEA."

Danny sighed. "Look, if you really think you have something, you can call DEA, but you know you're supposed to go through local first. You know that. Especially if all you really have is a parole violation."

He was right, but I didn't like the way he was telling me. Before I could say something obnoxious, though, Chief Pruitt drove by, giving me a good eyeballing.

"Yeah, okay. Thanks."

I knew it was pointless, but I drove after Pruitt anyway, sinking low in my seat as I drove back past Cooney's house. I caught up with him a couple of blocks away. I don't know if he saw it was me or if he knew something was up, but he coasted over onto the side of the road. As I pulled up behind him, he put his lights on, a little less discreet than I had hoped.

I could see his shades, watching me in the wing mirror as I walked up to the side of the car.

"And how can I help you?" he asked.

"Look, I'm sorry we got off on the wrong foot," I said, exhausting the entirety of my butt-kissing capacity. "But you've got a convicted drug dealer violating his parole by associating with another convicted felon, Dwight Cooney, inside Cooney's house."

"Is that right?"

"Saw it with my own eyes, less than ten minutes ago. They're still there as we speak."

"Well, I think you're supposed to be suspended from duty, and this ain't your jurisdiction anyway, so I don't know what the hell you think you're doing, wandering around spying on the citizens of this fair town. I also think you got some kind of hard-on for Dwight ever since he kicked your ass at Branson's."

He smiled and I knew he was trying to goad me into doing something I'd regret. I wanted to slap those shades off his face, and he seemed to read my mind, jutting his face farther out the car window to give me a cleaner shot. I decided to say something clever instead, but I was too angry to come up with anything.

Pruitt sighed and shook his head. "Look, son, why don't you just go on back to your daddy's house. Or better yet, go on back where you came from."

24

I somehow managed to get back into my car and drive off without saying or doing anything irresponsible. Pruitt was a dick, but I couldn't decide if it was incompetence or if he was corrupt.

If there was some kind of meth racket out there, paying someone off is a pretty standard budget item. And if Nola was being harassed over her refusal to sell, a deal like that would have more than enough money at stake to invest in local law enforcement.

I was still lost in thought, impartially adjudicating The People v. Chief Pruitt, when I noticed a big GMC pickup pulling up close behind me. The windows were tinted, so I couldn't see the driver. He was driving like Cooney, but I wondered if maybe that was just how people drove out here. I pulled ahead a little bit, and the pickup did, too, staying right on me. As I watched in my rearview, another truck pulled out from behind him, into the other lane. It was an older truck, a rust-colored Chevy, and pretty beat up. I smiled as it started to pass the GMC.

I slowed to let the Chevy pass me, but when it pulled up alongside me, it slowed down to match my speed and veered away then came back hard, slamming into the side of my car. I swerved and shimmied, the car listing as the right wheels slid off the road.

That car was by far the sweetest one I'd ever owned, and I winced at the sound of metal trim clattering on the road, crunching under the tires of the truck behind me.

My tires slid farther down the incline, and I gunned the engine, kicking up a spray of gravel and dirt as I tried to get back onto the road. My wheels were just starting to get traction when the Chevy hit me again and I slid off the road completely. The car tipped up for a second, the passenger side almost touching the bottom of the ditch, then it dropped back down onto all four wheels.

The airbags didn't deploy, but a stream of some of my choicest language did. I stood on the accelerator, trying to grind my way out of the ditch, but it was useless. By the time I clambered up the side of the ditch, the two trucks were gone. Instead I saw Pruitt's cruiser coasting up with his lights on.

He let his siren whoop once. I guess he figured he paid for the damn thing, might as well use it. He pulled up alongside me, craning his neck to look down at the car. He let out a snorting laugh. "What'd you do now?"

"Some of your fine, upstanding citizens ran me off the road."

"Really?" Pruitt looked amused. "Another imaginary friend, running you off the road?"

"Two pickups. A new GMC, I think it was green, and an old, beat-up Chevy. Rust-colored."

Pruitt made a big deal about looking up and down the road. "Any witnesses?"

I didn't say anything.

Pruitt got out of his cruiser. "You know, I've seen the way you drive. I think what happened was, you muffed it and ended up in the ditch without any help at all."

"What? I'm telling you—"

"And then I have to wonder if there's a reason you're driving like that."

"Well, I'm telling you the reason, and if you look at the side of my car—"

"There's no need to get belligerent, Mr. Carrick. Can I see your license and registration, please?"

He smiled sweetly, and again I had the distinct impression he was trying to provoke me, trying to piss me off in front of his dash-mounted camera. It seemed a bit of a coincidence, Pruitt arriving on the scene so quickly, and again I wondered, but I took out my wallet and handed him my license. "The registration is in the car. Would you like me to get it?"

He took the license out of my hand, but didn't look at it. "Actually, I'd like you to stand with your feet together and your arms at your sides."

His efforts to piss me off were working, but so were my efforts to contain my anger—proof I didn't need anger management training.

"Now put your arms straight out to your sides, and then touch your index fingers to your nose."

I could feel my eye twitching, and I thought about touching my fingers to his nose instead, but I took a deep breath and complied.

As I did, a black Saab came around the bend and drove slowly past us. I couldn't see everyone inside, but I could see Derek Roberts looking at me through the driver's window. Our eyes met, and his unibrow furrowed. Then he turned and looked straight ahead as he drove away.

By the time Pruitt got to the part where he said he was letting me off with a warning, a tow truck had arrived and my anger had cooled. I still couldn't tell whether Pruitt was an asshole for hire or just an asshole, but either way, he had it in for me. And the feeling was mutual.

25

The car was crumpled all along the driver side, and the right fender was dented, but it was riding fine. *I* was riding a little rougher. There was a lingering soreness on the side of my head from Dwight Cooney, and compounded by the overall pummeling from getting run off the road, I was hurting. Maybe I was a little more attached to that car than I wanted to admit, or maybe it was one thing too many to pretend to ignore, but seeing it all beat to hell made me feel sadder than it should have.

When I got home and saw Nola sitting on my porch, I felt better. She was wearing denim shorts and a gray Cornell hoodie over the same pale blue T-shirt from the first time I saw her, at Branson's. I wondered if the effect that T-shirt had on me would ever wear off.

She got to her feet when I pulled up. "Your car!" she said when I got out. "What happened to it?"

I didn't want to go into it, but I told her anyway. "Someone ran me off the road."

"*What?*"

"Two of them. One flanked me, the other was behind me. Pushed me off the road, into a ditch. How did it go with the caterers?"

"They were upset but understanding. They're going to get back to me next week." She pointed at my car. "Are you sure it wasn't an accident?"

"Positive. Hit me more than once."

"Why?"

"I don't know." Maybe it was a message. I didn't tell her about my tussle behind Branson's.

"Are you okay?"

"A little sore, but I'm fine. The best part was when Pruitt shows up, and I tell him what happened. Asshole gave me a twenty-minute drunk test."

"He thought you were drunk?"

"He knew I wasn't drunk."

"He really doesn't like you, does he?"

I decided it would be best if I kept my suspicions about Pruitt's motives to myself. "No, I guess he doesn't."

She leaned over and cupped my cheek. "That's okay. I like you."

I couldn't tell if she was messing with me, but her hand felt nice on my cheek. "You ready to go?" I asked.

"I guess. You're sure you're okay?"

"Yup."

"You're sure your car is okay?"

"It's fine," I said, opening the door. "Just a little body work, that's all."

She had a picnic basket, and she put it behind her seat. "I brought lunch, for later."

"Great."

I could feel her staring at me as we drove off. The Siberian elm loomed darkly over the landscape, and sensing she was about to ask again what had happened, I tilted my head toward it. "Kind of imposing, isn't it?"

"And totally invasive," she said, launching into a detailed explanation of how the elms spread and why it's a problem, and probably some other things.

After Meade's Christmas Tree Farm, the right-hand side of Bayberry Road was punctuated with a couple of roads, an antique shop, and a church with a tall white spire. The left-hand side was a green wall for a quarter mile before it angled back from the road to make way for a few houses, continuing uninterrupted behind them.

"That's the Gilbert farm," Nola said as we passed the first farm. "They sold the land to a developer two years ago, but kept the house. She's a schoolteacher, and he got a job at the Home Depot up in Saint Clair. The developer sold the land, and it's changed hands at least twice since then."

Over the next half mile, she repeated the same story three times, but with different names and different post-agricultural professions. Across the street from one of the plots was a farmhouse that looked abandoned.

"That's the old Denby farm," she said. "Otis Denby died six years ago, left behind a big stack of taxes. None of his kids wants anything to do with the place."

As we drove on, the road curved, revealing another sagging farmhouse. A U-Haul truck was parked in the driveway, the back doors open. As I slowed to a stop, a sweaty figure came out the front of the house, staggering a bit under two big boxes. He put them in the back of the truck and slid them in as far as his arms would reach. As he straightened up, wiping an arm across his sweaty forehead, he spotted us getting out of the car and his eyes narrowed, his face bitter in a way that made me think there weren't many people he would have been happy to see.

He coughed against the back of his arm and then spat in the dirt. "Can I help you?"

I hung back a step, letting Nola take the lead. "Hi," she said with a big smile. "I'm—"

"I know who you are," he said brusquely. "Is there something I can help you with?"

Nola stopped, her smile stuck on her face like she didn't know what to do with it. As the silence dragged out, I was about to jump in, but she toned down the smile by half and continued. "Moving?"

"Goddamn right I'm moving. This town is going downhill fast, between the Mexicans and the hippies and the yuppies and the city folks. I got a once-in-a-lifetime deal to sell and get out of here, and I'm taking it . . . unless someone fucks it all up."

I stared at the guy's face, wondering if he was the one who had been making the calls.

"Who you selling it to?" she asked.

He snorted. "You know who I'm selling it to. Same folks who wanted to buy your place."

"Redtail?"

He nodded and stiffened, looking at me then back at Nola. "Why do you want to know, anyway?"

"I'm just trying to find out who owns the land next to my farm. I want to talk to them."

His shoulders slumped as he stifled a cough, and his belligerent eyes suddenly looked tired and vulnerable. "I don't know about any of that, but I'm asking you please don't fuck this all up. If you don't want to sell, don't sell, I don't care. But don't start any other trouble that's going to mess this up."

She was quiet as we drove away, maybe wondering if he was her midnight caller, maybe thinking about the quiet desperation of the other property owners, trying to escape the burden of their farms. Maybe she was questioning her decision to keep her farm, thinking about the implications if it caused the deal to fall through. Maybe she was questioning her decision to buy the land in the first place.

As we drove, the terrain grew hillier and the green wall disappeared behind a swell of pale green fields. A couple of times, Nola told me to slow down for an access road or driveway, but each time, it was gone, graded over or filled in. The road twisted and turned, and I was starting to lose my bearings when we came upon a big yellow farmhouse with a leather-faced figure in overalls and a John Deere hat sitting on a rocking chair on the porch.

We pulled up the driveway, and when Nola got out, the old man sat forward.

"How you doing?" she asked.

"Morning," he replied. "Can I help you?"

"Is this your farm?"

"It's my house."

"It's very nice."

"I sold my land. Now I just own the house. Kind of nice, I can still look out my window and see the land, or parts of it. Kind of sad, cause it reminds me it ain't mine no more."

"You mind if I ask who you sold it to?"

"You another developer?"

"No." She smiled and shook her head. "No, I own a small farm over on Bayberry."

"You're that organic girl."

She smiled and looked down. "Yes. Yes, I'm afraid I am."

He sat back. "Makes good sense to me. I never did much like the idea of all those chemicals and whatnot."

"So who did you sell to?"

"Company called Baker/Anderson. Man by the name of Rogers. But that's not who owns it now."

"Who owns it now?"

"I have no idea."

Nola looked at me and raised an eyebrow. I just shrugged, but I got her point; it may have looked like a lot of undisturbed farmland, but someone had bought it all up, and no one seemed to know who.

"How do you know it's not Baker/Anderson?" she asked.

He smiled sadly. "Had a change of heart a few months after I sold it. Wanted to buy it back, or part of it. I found out who they sold it to, but they'd already sold it, too. I got sick of digging, figured maybe sitting on this porch weren't so bad after all."

26

"Well, I don't know about you, but I think it's totally creepy," Nola said, giving the old guy a cheerful wave as we drove off. "These companies are out here buying up huge tracts of land, the whole area, and no one seems to know who they are or what they are doing."

"No, you're right." I didn't want to feed into her paranoia, and those types of land deals probably go on all the time, but it didn't feel quite right. "I'm sure they're not up to anything nefarious but I'm not crazy about the fact that no one seems to know who they are. It makes me wonder what they are hiding."

"Exactly, and don't be too sure it's nothing nefarious. These people will do anything to make a buck, mountain top removal mining, or massive livestock operations, or whatever. The communities always end up devastated."

A half hour later, we came to another cross street. Nola sighed and informed me it was Bayberry. We were almost home. I flicked on my left turn signal.

"Are you hungry?" she asked.

I shrugged, but my stomach growled.

"Make a right," she said. So I did.

We drove in silence for ten minutes, until we approached a sign that said HAWK MOUNTAIN.

Nola said, "Turn in here."

"Mountain climbing?" I asked as we turned into a large parking lot. I was wearing sensible shoes, but I was tired and sore and I wasn't prepared for an expedition.

"Don't worry," she said. "It's a picnic."

We parked next to a small visitors' center, and I followed her up a wide trail that narrowed as we climbed. Small wooden signs pointed at side trails leading to lookouts and other landmarks, but we were headed to the top.

The incline was gentle, but the top was impressive—a rocky outcropping with a sheer drop and an expansive view. It was barely a mountain, but it was the biggest one I'd been on. The land was dense and green beneath us, except for a white scar of exposed rock. To our left was a patchwork of farm fields. A set of train tracks cut across them, looking like a not-very-realistic scale model.

The height was dizzying, but more striking was the sight of dozens of hawks circling below us, soaring on the air currents.

"Wow."

Nola smiled. "Pretty cool, isn't it? This is a major migration point for hawks and all sorts of raptors. I used to come out here all the time, but it's been awhile."

We stood there side-by-side for a few seconds, taking in the view. I had just put my arm around her shoulder when we heard voices and turned to see a woman in a brown Girl Scouts T-shirt followed by a small group of girls climbing up behind us. Nola rolled her shoulder out from under my hand.

"Not only hawks," the guide was saying, "but also monarch butterflies, which are also migratory. Can anybody tell me where they are headed?"

One of the girls shouted out, "Mexico!"

Why don't you join them, I thought as another moment with Nola slipped away.

"That's right," the guide said. "These butterflies are just passing through. Who can tell me what states they will be passing through?"

The girls' hands shot up into the air, and they started shouting out names of states.

"You're all correct," the guide told them. "Monarch butterflies are amazing creatures. Sorry we couldn't get the larva this year to raise some ourselves, but luckily we have thousands of them coming right through our area. These butterflies will cover thousands of miles, passing through twenty states on their journey south to Mexico, where they will meet up with their cousins who are covering just as much territory on the west coast. And after the winter, what happens?"

"They get eaten by birds," I whispered into Nola's ear.

"No, they don't, smart aleck," she whispered back, giving me a swat on the arm. "They're bitter and poisonous."

"They fly back!" the girls shouted.

"Well, their grandchildren do, but I'll give you credit."

"That's like me, bitter and poisonous," I whispered. "It's a self-defense mechanism. My plumage, on the other hand—"

Nola gave me another swat and pushed me away, but her eyes sparkled as she stifled a laugh.

The guide pointed down toward the treetops below us. "If you look closely, you can see monarchs migrating right now."

I couldn't resist looking where she was pointing, and saw a few butterflies fluttering around the treetops, then a few more. It was like looking for fireflies; the more I looked, the more I saw.

"It is pretty cool," Nola said. "You look at them and you think 'delicate little butterflies,' not an army on the move across two thirds of the country."

As the guide led the Girl Scouts away, I moved my arm back toward Nola's shoulder, but she was already clambering over the rocks, off to the side of the peak.

"Come here," she said, grabbing my sleeve. "I want to show you something."

I followed as best I could, very aware of the sheer drop.

She put the picnic basket between two boulders and took out two sandwiches, handing me one. It was tuna salad, but made with egg and celery and slathered on some kind of toasted sourdough bread. It was very good. We ate in silence for a minute, enjoying the view and the steady breeze. Then Nola reached into the basket again and took out a pair of binoculars.

She edged farther out and reached out a hand for me to join her. I picked my way closer and sat next to her on a small rock, our bodies pressed together.

She scanned the horizon with the binoculars, looking for something. Then she handed the binoculars to me.

"There," she said, pointing off to the west. "See if you can find a white church spire, then follow the road behind it to the right."

I found the church, then the road. "Okay, what am I looking at?"

"See that white house, with the porch wrapping around it?"

"Hey, that's my folks' house! And there's yours, right across the street." I could see the thick green hedge behind Nola's blue-corn patch, and from this angle I could even see the rows of corn behind it. Beyond the corn, barely visible in the hazy distance, was a long, low white building. "What's that white building?" I asked, handing back the binoculars.

She put the binoculars back up to her face. "What white building?"

"Behind your house. On the other side of the fence, past those corn fields."

She looked out through the binoculars for a moment. "Looks like some kind of tent . . . It's huge." She let the binoculars slowly fall away from her eyes. "Huh."

"What?"

"If that's a tent, maybe Moose is right. Maybe it is some kind of GMO thing. Sometimes they use tents to prevent drift."

"What drift?"

"Pollen drift, remember? When the pollen from one plant pollinates another plant. You get a mixture. Usually not such a bad thing, unless you're growing something rare, like my heirloom corn, or if it's some kind of GMO stuff."

"So the tent is to prevent pollen drift?"

"Maybe."

"You think it's a GMO?"

She shrugged again. "I don't know."

"So, shouldn't something like that be registered somewhere?"

She looked at me with sudden clarity. "Yes, it should."

"So how would you find out if it is?"

She looked at me for a moment, but before she answered, her phone chirped. She glanced at it, then quickly closed it and slipped it back into her pocket. A crease formed around her mouth.

"What is it?" I asked.

"Nothing."

"Let me see it."

She glared at me for a second. Then her shoulders slumped, and she handed me the phone. It was a text message: "Sell."

I handed her the phone back. "Call the police," I told her. "Right now."

"I will," she said. "Later."

"That was a threat, and they can trace it."

"It wasn't a threat." She started packing up the picnic, stuffing the food back into the basket. Just as she closed the wicker flaps, her phone chimed yet again. She looked at it, more confused than angry.

"It's a photo," she mumbled, squinting at the screen.

I stepped up next to her, looking over her shoulder at the smudge of bright yellow and orange on her screen. I couldn't make out what I was looking at, but Nola seemed suddenly to recognize it.

"Oh, no," she exclaimed, her voice breaking as she pulled the binoculars out of the basket, scattering the remains of lunch across the rocks. "No!" she sobbed, as she scanned the horizon.

That's when I saw it—a little ball of black smoke in the distance, rising into the air over Nola's house.

I took the phone out of her hand and looked again at the picture, a wall of orange flame, her front porch barely visible through it.

She called 911 as we sprinted down the mountain trail, but we got to her house before the fire trucks anyway. The smoke obscured the house as we approached, but as we bounced up into her drive-way, we could see that the house itself wasn't damaged. For a moment, Nola's face showed relief, but as her eyes welled up I followed her gaze. The heirloom patch was gone. The only thing left stand-ing was the little chicken wire fence that surrounded it. Everything else had been reduced to charred, smoking ash, flames still licking up here and there. The air was thick with the smell of burnt corn and gasoline.

She got out of the car, pulling her shirt up over her nose against the strong smell of gasoline. I went after her, but she only managed two steps before collapsing to her knees and sobbing.

I knew it was futile and I was uneasy at the proximity of fire, but I stomped out a few of the hotspots until my shoelaces caught fire and I retreated, swatting at my feet with my hands.

The sirens grew in the distance, but the last of the flames were already flickering out on their own. I knelt down on the gravel next to Nola and put my arm around her. I couldn't think of anything to say that didn't sound trite and hollow.

As the sound of Nola sobbing was drowned out by the deafening sirens, now almost on top of us, I realized how much she already meant to me, and how much it hurt to see someone hurt her. In my chest, I could feel my muscles tightening and hardening in a rage that wanted to lash out. But before I could let it, I had to find out who was responsible.

27

The firefighters doused the field with water, trampling what little had been left unconsumed.

"You're just trouble, aren't you?"

I thought it was an odd thing for a firefighter to say to a grief-stricken victim, but it wasn't one of the firefighters, and he wasn't talking to Nola.

It was Chief Pruitt, looking down at me through his signature aviators.

Nola looked up at him, too.

"You might not want to get too close to this one, ma'am," he told her. "He's nothing but trouble."

I got to my feet and looked down at him. He smiled.

"This is arson," I said flatly.

"Oh, you think so?"

"She's been receiving threatening phone calls. Whoever did this texted her right before it happened, then sent her a picture on her phone."

"Is that right, Ms. Watkins?"

Nola nodded.

"And you don't have caller I.D.?"

Nola looked down and sighed.

"The number was private," I told him. "She uses the phone for business, so she couldn't block it."

"Is that right?" he said.

She nodded again.

"How long has that been going on?"

"About six months," she replied quietly.

"And you never reported it?" He said it with enough doubt and accusation that Nola's head snapped up to look at him. He shrugged. "Kind of strange, isn't it?"

"What's that supposed to mean?" she asked.

"I mean I never heard of any of this trouble." He flicked a finger in my direction. "This was a quiet little town until this one showed up."

"A quiet little town?" I said with a laugh. "You've had two meth houses go up in flames in the last six weeks."

Pruitt's face turned a deep red, and his cheeks started to quiver. "Those houses were not in my jurisdiction."

"Oh, I get it. So if it's just outside your jurisdiction, it doesn't concern you, is that it?"

"It was outside my jurisdiction because those scumbags wouldn't dare try to pull anything like that in my town."

I laughed again. "You've got known drug dealers driving around your quiet little town, as recently as this morning. But I guess you're not concerned about that, either."

"The only drug problem I know of around here is that little pothead over there."

As if on cue, I heard the screen door slam across the street and turned to see Moose stumbling down the steps, blinking in the sunlight.

"And as for these imaginary drug dealers, well, nobody else is seeing any trouble but you."

I took a step closer. "Well, maybe people aren't telling you about it because they don't think it'll do any good."

"Better be careful, Carrick," Pruitt said. "I know all about you and your anger issues. Be a shame to slip up and get kicked off the force for good, now, wouldn't it?"

Nola looked up at him, confused. She had stopped crying.

"Oh, I'm sorry, Ms. Watson, didn't you know? Detective Carrick here is suspended. Apparently he assaulted a fellow officer and interrogated a suspect by putting a gun to the kid's head. Isn't that right, Carrick? He's supposed to be in anger management class, too, but I don't think he's going."

Nola looked over at me, her eyes filling with the same cold anger I had seen when she stormed out of Branson's. "Doyle, is that true?"

I started to deny it, but Pruitt had his facts right, even if he was ignoring the subtleties of the situation.

"Yeah, I've been doing my homework on you, Carrick," he continued, "and you better not try to pull any crap in my town."

Moose walked up, his eyes wide and uncomprehending. "What's going on?"

Chief Pruitt turned to leave with a smug look on his face.

"Don't you want to see the phone? See who's making these threats?" I called after him. "You know, police work?"

"I'll have someone call you for a statement, Ms. Watson," Pruitt called over his shoulder. "I got more important things to do than investigate a bunch of burnt weeds."

We watched him walk away. Then Nola turned to look at me. "Doyle, is that true?"

I didn't answer her, instead turning to Moose. "Where the hell were you?"

"What?" he asked, groggy and bewildered. "I was asleep, I guess . . . I heard the sirens."

Nola turned on her heel and marched inside.

Moose watched her go, then turned back to look at me. "What happened?"

"Someone torched the heirloom patch. Gasoline. She got a call right before it happened. They sent her a picture of the fire."

"No shit!"

"No shit." I looked at my watch. It was just after three. "And you were asleep?"

"Yeah, I guess I was."

"What's up with that?"

He shook his head. "I don't know, must be coming down with something." He scanned the scorched field, shaking his head.

"Do me a favor," I said, "go keep an eye on Nola. I don't want her alone right now."

He looked at me with his head to one side, then shrugged. "Okay."

I waited until he had followed Nola inside, then I walked around the smoking remnants of the heirloom patch as quickly as I could without breaking into a run. I plunged into the thick line of Siberian elm, knowing what I'd find before I got through it.

Emerging on the other side, I saw a rolling expanse of stubble, row after row of corn stalks, all cut off at the ground. I hate to admit it, but as angry as I was about what was happening to Nola, it was the twist in the case that made my pulse quicken.

I called Danny the way I usually did when I found something in a case and I didn't know what to make of it. When I had told him what happened, he was quiet for a moment.

"Corn?" he said with a snort. "Jesus, Doyle, you're desperate, aren't you?"

I was going to say that if he had seen Nola Watkins, he'd want to find out what happened to her corn, too. Instead I told him to fuck off.

"So what're you doing now?" he asked.

"I'm going down to the town hall, see if I can figure out who owns this land where the other corn was growing."

"Why? Doesn't really matter now, does it?"

"I just want to know what's going on."

He laughed. "I'm telling you, Doyle, there's plenty of movies out there you haven't seen. Hell, you could just about catch up on what the rest of the country's been watching. Maybe start picking up on some of those cultural references that are always going over your head." He laughed, but it died out quickly. "You know, your local law enforcement already called to find out what your story is."

"Yeah, I know."

"He spoke to Lieutenant Suarez, so you can imagine how that went." He sighed. "Doyle, you got like seventeen days. Don't fuck it up."

28

Dunston Town Hall was a low brick building that looked like a small post office. Behind the counter was a surprisingly friendly woman in her late fifties with a mischievous twinkle in her eyes. The nameplate on the counter said NOREEN GOOD.

I gave her what I hoped was a charming smile and said, "Hi, Noreen . . ."

To which she countered, "Hi, Doyle."

To which I didn't counter anything, because I was not expecting that. Instead, I laughed nervously.

"I was at Branson's when you tussled with Cooney," she explained with a sly smile. "Your name's come up a few times since then."

"Oh."

"Don't worry, I'm not Cooney's auntie or anything."

She leaned toward me over the counter. "So what can I do for you?"

"I need to look at some real-estate records. I'm trying to find out who owns a parcel of land near my mom's house. Just south of Bay-berry, just east of Valley Road."

She came around from behind the counter. "I can help you with that."

She led me toward a wooden door with a window, PUBLIC REC-ORDS stenciled across it. As she opened it, a voice called out behind us, "Hey Noreen, you seen Mitchell or Tompkins?"

"Both out sick," she replied without turning around.

"Couple of sissies, those two, I swear. If I ever—"

The voice stopped just as I turned around and saw Chief Pruitt standing in the doorway, wearing his mirrored shades in the fluorescent-lit lobby.

"Where the hell are you taking him?" he demanded.

Noreen gave him a look to make it plain she was unimpressed. "I beg your pardon?"

"You can't let him in there," he said.

"Francis, I know it's probably hard for you to see in here with those ridiculous sunglasses on, but can you read what it says on this door here?" She stepped out of the way to make sure he could see it.

Pruitt didn't utter a sound, but I'm pretty sure I saw his lips moving.

"That's right," she said, "*Public* Records. My, you are making such progress."

He stared at her for a second, his face turning red. Then he turned on his heel and left without a word.

"Don't mind him," she said, ushering me into the records room. "He takes protecting this town very seriously."

"Really?" I asked, following her down an aisle of shelves.

She shrugged. "There's been a lot of new faces in town lately, a lot of change. People are suspicious of outsiders. And I'm not talk-ing about the Mexican workers or any of that—that's something different. I'm talking about outsiders who come in and tell folks the way they've been doing things for generations is wrong."

"What do you mean?"

"Well, like your friend Ms. Watkins. She's a delight. But all this organic stuff? I'm sure she didn't mean to offend anybody, but when you come in saying the way you're doing things is better than the way everybody else is doing them, even if you don't say it, it rubs them the wrong way. You're with the police back in Philly, right?"

"Right." I didn't feel the need to explain the nuances of my current employment situation.

"Well, Chief Pruitt is probably a little defensive about that, too. Big-time city police coming in telling him how he's doing things wrong."

"But I never—"

"Doesn't matter what you said or didn't say. He's filling in all those blanks himself." She pulled a long ledger book off the shelf and laid it out on a table, then she folded her arms under her breasts and cocked a hip. "Now, is there anything else I can do for you?"

I smiled. "I think I'm fine for now."

"Well, you let me know if you need anything else."

Some cops will tell you that a stakeout is the most boring part of the job, sitting in a car for hours, staring at a window or a doorway, that the boredom makes each minute feel like an hour. Dwayne Rowan notwithstanding, stakeouts don't bother me like that. I sit there and wait and I go into a different state of awareness, like hibernation or suspended animation. And in the back of my mind, the whole time, I think to myself, *this still beats sitting in a cubicle.*

Searching through public records, on the other hand, is like jabbing forks into my eyes. Except boring. And often about as productive.

But I did find out that Nola was right—almost all the real estate in the block of land we had driven around that morning had changed hands at least once in the past two years. A lot of it had been purchased by the developer Nola mentioned, Redtail Holdings, Inc., owned by a guy named Jordan Rothe. Redtail's properties formed a ring around a cluster of properties owned by a handful of different companies, and many of those parcels had been divided and separated from the homesteads that fronted onto the road, which meant they were essentially landlocked, with no access in or out.

A thin strip of properties along Bayberry were owned by individuals, and then there was Nola's farm, jutting into the patchwork of corporate-owned parcels. Some of the adjacent plots, outside the perimeter we had driven that morning, had changed hands as well, mostly purchased by Redtail Holdings.

The land next to Nola's farm seemed to be owned by a handful of holding companies: BCD Holdings, RST Development, Inc., and Berks Land Group, none of which listed any information other than a post office box. I looked at some of the other listings, and they were all post office boxes, too, and all out of state. Redtail was the only one based locally, and the only one with a real address and a phone number.

I copied them down, thinking if they were nice enough to leave contact info, it would be rude not to get in touch.

29

When Noreen Good leaned through the doorway and said the place was closing in five minutes, I'd already had more than I could bear. In the time I'd been down there, I'd stiffened up nicely, and by the time I stood and stretched and gathered my stuff, Noreen had her key in the door to lock it behind me.

I thanked her on the way out, and she said she hoped to see me again sometime.

It was hot and sunny outside, and it had been dry and dusty inside. Branson's was only a few blocks away, and sucking down a cold beer was the only logical next move.

When I stepped through the door, out of the sunlight and into the dim interior, I felt a moment of unease, wondering if the guys who ran me off the road were sitting in there, watching me. But as my eyes adjusted, I saw that the most likely candidates were the three codgers sitting at the bar, and my paranoia ebbed.

Bert Squires was behind the bar, drying a pint glass with the towel slung over his shoulder. He gave me a smile and a little nod. "Afternoon, there, Mr. Menlow."

In unison, the three old boys looked at me in the mirror behind the bar, then turned on their stools to see me in person.

"It's Carrick," I said, taking a seat a couple of stools down. "But you can call me Doyle."

Squires tilted his head, confused.

"Frank wasn't my biological father," I explained.

"Really?" he said, somewhat taken aback. "Isn't that something? He talked about you plenty, but he never mentioned that."

I nodded wordlessly for a few seconds, making sure that particular thread of conversation had died out. Then I leaned over the bar to get a look at the taps. "How about a pint of lager?"

He slipped the glass he had been drying under the tap with one hand and simultaneously flicked the tap with the other hand, so the beer and the glass reached the same point in space at the same point in time. Nothing showy about it, just smooth efficiency.

When the glass was just shy of full, he flicked the tap, letting the last few drops create a small, sudsy dome. As one hand moved the beer glass in front of me, the other tossed a cork coaster, and again, the two met simultaneously on the bar right in front of me.

"Hot out there?" he asked.

I nodded as I took a sip, savoring the feel as much as the taste. "I was over at the town hall."

"What were you doing over there?"

I shook my head. "Just looking something up."

"You see Noreen over there?"

"I did. She was very helpful."

He leaned forward and lowered his voice, pointing at me for emphasis. "You want anything done in this town, you talk to Noreen. Woman single-handedly makes this town run."

I nodded and took a long drink. "What about Pruitt?"

One of the old guys laughed and looked away.

"Aw, he's okay."

"I don't know. Somebody torched some of Nola Watkins's crops, and he didn't do a damn thing."

The three old heads turned to look at me.

"Torched her crops? How do you mean?"

"I mean torched them. Doused them with gasoline and set them on fire."

"Why?"

I shrugged. "Trying to get her to sell her land, I think. Some new development or something."

He screwed up his face. "That's hogwash. I heard of people talking about stuff like that, trying to scare people off their land like the old west. But that stuff's not for real."

"You don't think so?"

He shook his head. "No way."

I leaned forward and lowered my voice. "I was with her right when it happened. Someone texted her the word 'sell' on her phone and sent her a picture of her crops in flames."

"No fooling?" he said breathlessly. "And Pruitt didn't do nothing?"

"Said he was too busy to investigate a bunch of burnt weeds."

"He said that?"

I nodded and leaned forward even more. "You think he's on the up-and-up?"

Squires's head pulled back, like he'd been swatted on the nose. "Don't even ask that. That ain't right. No. He works hard. It's just him and a couple of knuckleheads he has part-time a few hours a week. I know Pruitt's no Kojak or whatever, but he's not dirty."

He scowled at me like he thought less of me for even saying it, then took a couple of steps down the bar.

"Good," I said. "That's good to hear."

* * *

I drank the rest of my beer, and when I stepped back out onto the sidewalk, I almost bumped into Sydney Bricker. She stopped and turned on her heel.

"Mr. Carrick," she called out with a smile. "Given any thought to my offer?"

I had no idea what she was talking about.

"The property?" she prompted me. "You said you were thinking of selling it."

"No, not really. Actually, I was thinking maybe I'd sell it to one of the local farmers," I told her, although I don't know why.

Her eyes narrowed, and she leaned back to look at me more appraisingly. "Farmers?"

"Yes. Pennsylvania is losing open space at a rate of three hundred acres a day."

She smiled slyly. "Are you messing with me, Mr. Carrick?"

I smiled slyly back.

She laughed. "I see."

I was about to say something wickedly clever, but just then, I saw a brand-new white Ford Econoline van coming down the street, just like the one I'd seen in Cooney's driveway.

As I stepped toward my car, Bricker noticed the rumpled side and winced. "Ouch."

I got in my car, telling her that if I changed my mind she'd be the first to know.

"Well, don't play it too cool, Mr. Carrick, or you could end up being left out in the cold."

30

Bricker's reaction reminded me how angry I was about the damage to my car. I wondered if whoever was in the van had anything to do with running me off the road. My car had never been exactly inconspicuous, and with the side all banged up, I had to hang back even farther for fear of being noticed. I thought the van's driver must have seen me; he was driving like someone who was nervous about getting pulled over. He kept the speed down, waiting at every stop sign for three full, infuriating seconds, making it even more difficult to keep any distance between us. I was sure he had spotted me when he coasted to a stop, but he pulled into a parking lot behind a small office park and continued around to the back, parking next to some Dumpsters.

I drove on to the end of the block and parked on a side street, up on a rise where I could keep an eye on the van.

The driver-side door opened, and out climbed Dwight Cooney. He walked across the lot and got into another car, a Nissan. I slid back in my seat and tried to shift into stakeout mode, but less than a minute later, I sat back up. Derek Roberts got out the passenger side of a black SUV that had already been parked at the far end of the lot. He got into the van and pulled away.

I thought I saw movement through the SUV's tinted windows, like someone was still in there. But I couldn't be sure. I paused for a moment, then pulled out after the van and called Stan Bowers.

"Jesus, Doyle, again? My wife doesn't call this often."

"I'm pretty sure I just watched a drop-off. I was following a local asshole named Dwight Cooney in a white van that I don't think is his. He parked it behind a small office park on Devon Road. A minute later, Mr. Softee himself, a.k.a. Derek Roberts, gets out of an SUV that was already parked there. He gets into the van and drives away."

"No shit. You're sure it's this guy Roberts?"

"Definitely."

"Where are you now?"

"Following the van, going south on Ridge Road. I just passed Schoolhouse Lane."

"Good man. You got a plate number?"

I read it to him.

"Great. Keep this line open, but don't get involved, okay?"

"You got it."

He called back a minute later. "Okay, the van is a rental, probably a bogus credit card number. We have a mobile unit nearby, and I'm on my way, too. Just keep them in sight and don't do anything, okay?"

"All right, all right."

"Good work, Carrick."

Roberts seemed a little more comfortable behind the wheel than Cooney. He drove a couple of miles above the speed limit, like everybody else, rolling stops at stop signs, like everybody else. Just a normal driver transporting a normal vanload of illegal drugs.

After a mile, he made a left onto Shady Lane, another one of those narrow country roads. I hung back again, letting a little more space accumulate between us. Then I made the turn as well.

This is where it would get a little trickier. The van was two hundred yards ahead of me, enough space that Roberts could easily shake me with a quick turn down a side road, but still close enough that he could pick up the tail as well.

Each time the van disappeared around a curve, I held my breath, waiting for the road to straighten out and the van to reappear in front of me. We had been winding down Shady Lane for a quarter of a mile when the van turned down a driveway on the left.

A weathered wooden sign next to the driveway said CROOKED CREEK FARM.

I pulled into a driveway fifty yards down on the other side of the road and parked far enough up that I couldn't be seen from the street, halfway on the grass so there was enough room for another car to get by. I wrote "Back in Five Minutes" on a Dunkin' Donuts napkin and put it where it would be visible through the windshield. No need to piss off the neighbors and have them call the cops on me.

I called Stan, and while I was waiting for him to answer, I flipped open the glove compartment. After a tiny hesitation, I grabbed my gun.

"Doyle," he answered.

"We're on Shady Lane, about a quarter mile east of Ridge Road. I'm parked in the driveway across the street, but I'm going to walk up, see if I can get a closer look."

"Wait, wait, wait, Doyle, don't . . ." He paused, thinking about it. "Okay, go and look, but that's all. Nothing more, okay?"

"Absolutely," I agreed, tucking the gun into my waistband before I trotted back down the driveway and across the road.

31

The other side of the road was so overgrown with tall grasses and wildflowers that at a low crouch I was mostly obscured. Once I was far enough from the road, I turned and ran parallel to it, making my way closer to the driveway. When the driveway was still thirty yards away, I turned and followed it toward a small cluster of buildings surrounding a gravel lot.

Directly in front of me was a low cinder block building, maybe twenty yards wide. It had two doors, twenty feet apart, each facing out onto the lot. Three or four oil drums sat out front.

To the right was a run-down wooden house, and to the left was a rusted grain silo. Between them was a pair of newer-looking aluminum shacks. One was padlocked. The van was parked in front of the other one, with its back doors opened.

As I watched, Roberts and another guy emerged from the shack. I got down low as they each grabbed an armload from the back of the van and carried it back into the shack.

From where I was, I couldn't see what they had, or what was in the back of the van. I waited in the weeds to see if they were going to come back out for another load. A minute later, they did, and when they went back into the shack, I darted toward the cinder block structure, keeping it between me and them. Then I crept around to the front, past the two doors, and up behind the oil drums.

One of the doors was open, meaning my back was exposed, but there was nothing I could do about that now. I touched my gun, reassuring myself, and peeked out over the drums.

I could see directly into the door to the shack, but the interior was dark.

In the back of the van, a tarp was thrown back, revealing stacks of plastic-wrapped bundles, each containing half a dozen smaller plastic-wrapped bundles sealed with red or yellow tape.

There was a lot.

I ducked down as I heard Roberts's voice. Through a gap between the drums, I watched as the men emerged again from the shack. They each grabbed a bundle. This time, the other guy got careless, and his bundle snagged on a hinge on the van's back door.

A wispy column of white powder fell from a hole in the plastic, and Roberts savagely slapped the guy.

"Goddamn it, Paulie." Roberts bared his teeth in a snarl that made the other guy step back, cowering.

When they retreated back into the shack, I took a photo of the back of the van with my phone, and sent it to Stan to let him know this shit was for real. I turned off the ringer before I slipped it back into my pocket.

That was enough for me. I would wait until Roberts and Paulie came and got another load, and when they went back inside, I'd hightail it out of there and watch from a safe distance.

The only problem was, when they came out of the shack, they didn't grab another load. Instead, they started crossing the lot, directly toward me.

I figured I had five seconds to make a move. No way I could get back around to the side of the building without being spotted. One option was to jump out with my gun drawn and tell them they were under arrest. But even if I wasn't suspended, I was still out of my jurisdiction. Making matters worse, as Roberts and Paulie approached, two other guys came out of the shack to continue unloading the van. One of them was Arnett. I recognized him from his mug shot—that same expression, equal parts badass and dumbass.

I decided to retreat as best I could. Staying low, I slipped through the nearest open door and into the cinder block building.

It was dark inside, but I didn't have time to let my eyes adjust. I was in a narrow corridor about twenty feet long. At the end of it, in the light of a single bare bulb, I could see another hallway, going left to right, and in the middle of it, another doorway.

Pausing at the end of the first hallway, I looked up and down the second one. In addition to the doorway in the middle, there was also one toward each end, both facing back toward the front of the building. I took the easiest option and darted in through the open doorway directly in front of me.

One of the other options might have been better.

Slipping through the door, I almost bumped into a chubby guy with pink cheeks and blond hair awkwardly parted in the middle. He was probably coming to investigate the sound of my frantic footsteps.

He had an automatic rifle slung over his shoulder, and when he saw me, he took a step back, swung the rifle down, and took a shot without aiming. It went over my shoulder, and I hoped it hit one of the guys coming up behind me, because I knew at the sound of it they'd all come running.

I took a shot without aiming, too, but I was better at it than he was. He staggered back against the far wall with a small, red-black hole in the middle of his forehead.

32

I felt bad for a second, because I had just killed the guy, but also because I knew shooting him was going to greatly complicate my life.

As I turned, I could see Roberts and his friend Paulie in the hallway behind me. Roberts was back by the entrance, legs braced wide, two-handing his gun. Paulie was running along the wall.

I held up my badge and yelled, "Police!" then jumped out of the way as they both fired. I fired back, but none of us hit anything.

As I got to my feet, huddled against the wall, I could hear footsteps as Paulie turned the corner and ran toward the doorway down the hallway to the left. I tried to tag him as he ran, but I only got off one shot before Roberts and someone else pinned me back. It was Arnett.

There were three of them now, Paulie to my left and Roberts and Arnett straight ahead.

In the quiet between the gunshots, I could hear a single set of muffled footsteps and the sound of doors opening and closing inside the rooms to the right. I figured the fourth guy had come in through that second entrance, and one way or another, it had led him to the doorway down the hall, to my right.

We traded sporadic bullets for a minute or two, like in a bad cowboy movie: I would shoot at them and duck back, then they would shoot at me.

If I stayed flat against the wall, right next to the doorway, I could see out into the hallway to the room where Paulie was hiding. Natural light spilled through it, which meant there was probably a window. As I watched, I saw the barrel of his gun poke out through the doorway, followed a moment later by his face and an explosion when he fired. From his angle, he was shooting at a narrow sliver of doorway, but I guess he figured if he could get a round through the doorway and into the room, maybe it would ricochet around and hit me. Each time, right before he took a shot, the barrel of his gun appeared, followed a moment later by his face as he scoped out the shot.

Counting the beats between shots, I took a wild shot at Roberts and Arnett, right down the middle, then immediately set up my next shot at Paulie. Sure enough, right on cue, his barrel poked around the doorjamb. I adjusted my aim higher, and when his face peered around the corner, I caught him just above his left eye.

His head snapped back, or most of it did. The rest of it spattered the wall and the doorjamb with red. He did a little flip, his feet coming out from under him, and landed heavily on his back. His feet were poking through the doorway, jerking and shaking for a moment before stopping abruptly.

Roberts and Arnett sent a torrent of bullets my way, but I figured I was okay as long as I stayed back from the doorway. At least, until the wall disintegrated. As the bullets continued to slam into the wall behind me, I was troubled by the thought that wall disintegration might actually be a problem. I was also troubled by the fact that I was running low on ammo.

Most troubling of all, however, was that out of the corner of my eye, the guy with the pink cheeks sitting on the floor across from me looked like he was trying to get up. I was pretty sure that wasn't going to happen: His legs were folded under him, and in addition to the hole I had put in him, he must have been hit a dozen more times. There wasn't much left of his midsection. Still, every couple of seconds he would rise up an inch or two before settling back down again. It freaked me out the first few times he did it. Then I realized the impact from the stray bullets slamming into him was lifting him up. The bullets meant for me.

That freaked me out, too.

I was leaning against the wall across from him, next to the doorway that was letting in all the bullets. I made a mental note that if I ever died in a shootout, I'd try not to do it directly across from a doorway. I'd also try not to do it any time soon.

But while the guy slumped across from me had more than his share of problems, he also had an automatic rifle strapped across him, and as far as I knew, he'd only used one bullet.

The gunfire coming down the hallway had settled back into that call and response rhythm. I slid out my clip and saw that I only had two bullets left, plus one in the chamber.

That meant one for my regularly scheduled exchange of gunfire, and then two to cover myself when I went for my roommate's gun.

I fired my shot, waited for them to return it, and then I sprang across the room, firing as I did.

The strap was wound around the dead guy's forearm, and I knew that if I just grabbed the gun and pulled, it would tighten. Then I'd be standing in the open, wrestling with a two-hundred-pound dead guy. As I slipped the strap off his arm I fired my last bullet through the doorway. That brushed them back for a moment, but then I think they saw me standing out in the open and they poured it on. The sound of automatic weapons discharging in the hallway was deafening. I aimed out the doorway and pumped the trigger a few times, pushing them back again while I got the hell out of the way.

I curled around my new gun in the opposite corner of the room, and as the echo of the gunfire dissipated, I heard a new sound—a tightly clenched moaning sound coming from down the main hallway. Another one down. I was pretty sure it was Arnett.

The good news was that they were down to two and a half. The bad news was, I had wasted half the clip getting the gun and tagging Arnett.

For the next few minutes, I exchanged fire down the hallway with Roberts and the new guy, up the hallway to my right. Occasionally, one of the incoming bullets would hit my dead roommate, causing him to jump in his disturbing parody of life.

I was counting down my bullets each time I pulled the trigger, and I found myself once again down to three. Getting another weapon was the next tactical move, but what I really needed to do was get the hell out of here. Roberts and what was left of Arnett were straight ahead. The other guy was down the hallway to the right.

That left the hallway to the left, with dead Paulie and the natural light. Light from a window. Dead Paulie won.

Wrapping the strap around my hand, I silently counted to three. As I sprang through the door, I sent one bullet straight down the hallway toward Roberts. I sent another one down the hallway behind me as I jagged left. The last one I was saving, just in case.

As I went into my roll, I heard voices on the roof. Then, on the wall ahead of me, I saw my own outline in the reflection of a flash from behind me. The entire building shook, and I heard a bang and a whoosh as I went tumbling airborne. The wall at the end of the hallway came at me fast, already bloody from where I'd shot Paulie.

I hit it hard, butt first and upside down, jarring every inch of my body.

Falling to the floor next to Paulie's blood-spattered boots, I could feel myself losing consciousness. I knew about concussions, and I thought I should really be more careful, but as my vision faded, I saw Paulie lying there, the top of his head missing altogether, and I thought, "Things could be worse."

33

When I came to, a pair of agents in DEA windbreakers were running toward me down the hallway, guns out in front, aimed in my direction. They were both shouting at me, but between the ringing in my ears and the way they were shouting over each other, I had no idea what they were saying. I figured they were telling me to stay down, but I had no intentions of getting up just yet anyway.

Then they were both standing over me, holding their DEA badges and their guns in front of my face.

I nodded. "All right, all right," I said. They both seemed too young and too excited.

One kept shouting at me until his jacket suddenly pulled tight around him and his eyes went wide. Then he rose up and away and disappeared altogether and Stan Bowers was standing above me, glaring at the other guy, who suddenly disappeared as well. Stan crouched down, asking loudly and slowly if I was okay.

I nodded, and he reached out a hand to help me up. As he pulled me to my feet, I realized I might have been a little hasty when I said I was okay.

I pitched a little to one side, but Stan didn't seem to notice. He was talking over his shoulder as he walked back down the hall. The strap of the rifle was still tangled around my hand, so I slung it over my shoulder and tried to keep up. I was just starting to make out what he was saying.

". . . asshole out front took a shot at us, so that was that for him. We found one guy still breathing in the room up ahead. They took him to the hospital, but they don't expect he's going to make it, either."

"Did he have any piercings?"

"What?" he asked, like I wasn't making sense.

"His face. Did he have any, like, nose rings, or anything on his face?"

Stan laughed and winced, shaking his head. "Not counting the bullet."

He stopped at the room where I'd been pinned down. "Then there's this guy, all shot to shit," he said pointing at my old room-mate. "Took one in the forehead from not too close." He turned to me. "You do that?"

I nodded. "They started it," I mumbled.

"'Look, but that's all,' I told you." He laughed and shook his head. "Fucking Carrick. Anyway, good shot. We'll need some paperwork on that."

"Yeah, I know it."

"You sure you're okay?"

I nodded again.

"All-righty then." He turned down the hallway that led outside. "Good call on the van. We're talking some serious weight."

We walked out onto the gravel lot, now swarming with agents in DEA windbreakers. Roberts and Arnett were both dead on the ground. It seemed unnaturally bright outside after the gloom inside.

A medic came up and checked my pupils, then started dabbing my forehead with a cotton pad. I swatted him away.

"I'm eyeballing it at something like fifty keys," Stan continued. "Field test is positive for heroin."

That penetrated the fog. "Heroin? Not meth?"

"Heroin, baby. High grade, too."

"Jesus," I said. "Fifty keys of heroin?" Meth houses and heroin busts; what wasn't going on in that town? I took the gun off my shoulder and leaned it against the wall.

Stan stopped and gave me a big smile. "That's right, my friend. Massive."

As he said it, part of the buzzing in my ears resolved into a rhythmic thumping, and I looked up to see two news choppers from Philly stations circling overhead.

Stan followed my gaze. "Yeah, word gets around fast. Big fucking bust."

A pair of ambulances drove slowly up the driveway. Behind the second one, almost on its bumper, was a familiar car with the Dunston Police Chief decal on the door.

I tapped Stan on the elbow. "Locals are here."

Pruitt stopped his car in the driveway and got out, red-faced and sputtering. "Who's in charge here?" he roared.

A couple of people looked up at him, but then they went back to what they were doing. Stan held up a hand and opened his mouth to speak, but Pruitt had already spotted me.

"*You?*" he screeched, his rage now mixed with disbelief.

Stan held up his ID and stepped in front of me. "I'm in charge here," he said. "Special Agent Bowers, DEA."

Pruitt glanced over at him, then back at me. "What the hell is going on here?" he demanded.

Stan stepped to the side and held out his arm. "Can I have a word with you, sir?"

Pruitt's eyes shifted back and forth between Stan and me. Then he took a few steps along with Stan.

Stan put his arm on Pruitt's shoulder. He spoke in a quiet voice that was nonetheless clearly audible. "Chief Pruitt, I apologize for the breach of protocol, but I'm going to ask you for your cooperation, retroactively."

"Retroactively? What the hell are you talking about?"

"Sir, we had live, real-time intelligence that this drug deal was going down, and there simply was not enough time to follow proper procedures. It was either act immediately or lose the opportunity. I'm sure you're just as relieved as we are to have these dangerous drugs, and these dangerous people, off the street."

Pruitt hooked a thumb in my direction. "Why's that asshole here?"

"Detective Carrick was acting as a concerned citizen. He spotted the deal going down, and he called me. We're very grateful for his assistance."

Pruitt snorted and rolled his eyes.

Stan continued. "Chief Pruitt, in about two minutes, the press is going to be here asking for a statement." He smiled. "There is nothing I would like more than to say that this operation was part of a joint effort between DEA and the Dunston Police Department. But I can only say we're cooperating if we are. Are you on board?"

Pruitt's eyes narrowed as he looked back at me, but then he nodded. "Yeah, all right." He turned back to me again. "But I've still got my eye on you."

Stan's boss, Munschak, showed up just ahead of the TV crews. He was short and intense, in his mid-thirties, and looked like the kind of bureaucrat who could really annoy a guy like Bowers. While the state police loaded up the seizure, Munschak went to work on setting up a press conference. Pruitt wandered closer to him, as if taking mental notes on how it should be done.

"Don't you think a press conference is a little premature?" I asked Stan.

He shrugged. "It's a big-ass bust, and Munschak's been catching a lot of grief about how those meth houses caught us totally by surprise."

I smiled and waved him off. "Okay, whatever, but the guy that gave them the van is still out there. We need to wrap him up before he catches wind of this and takes cover."

Stan nodded. "He's a local, right? What was his name?"

"Dwight Cooney."

"Dwight Cooney?" Pruitt said, walking up behind us. He screwed up his face. "Are you shitting me? Dwight Cooney is a dumbass, that's for sure, but he ain't involved in anything like this. You got to be kidding me."

Stan listened to Pruitt. Then he turned back to me and cocked an eyebrow.

"Dwight Cooney," I repeated emphatically. "It was definitely him."

Pruitt shook his head. "Aw, this is horse shit."

"Chief Pruitt," Stan said evenly, "Detective Carrick gave us solid information and put himself in some jeopardy to do it. If he says it was this Dwight Cooney, then I have to take him seriously. And if it wasn't, I'm sure Mr. Cooney will understand."

As it turned out, Mr. Cooney did not understand.

His front door was open when we got there, and Cooney was sitting at his kitchen table, like he was waiting for us.

There was a small bullet hole in his temple, and even from a distance, I could see powder burns around it. There was no exit wound. It was a small caliber gun, fired at close range, so the bullet could bounce around in that thick skull for a good long while, making sure everything was nice and scrambled.

His eyes were glassy and his face slack—actually not much different from every other time I'd seen him.

Pruitt walked up and stooped over to give the bullet hole a close look. I was impressed he'd come with us. I could tell he was dying to hang out for the press conference.

"Aw, shit," Pruitt said, straightening up and giving me a look like it was my fault.

I went outside after that, leaning against my car and staying out of the way and minding my unofficial capacity while the professionals did their work. Eventually, Stan came out with an evidence envelope and pulled out a clear plastic sleeve with a piece of looseleaf paper covered with uneven columns of dates and amounts—big, lopsided characters written in red felt-tip marker. "Pruitt says he's seen Cooney's writing and this looks like it."

He noticed the damage to my car. "How'd that happen?"

"Long story."

He nodded and slid the paper back into the envelope. "Anyway, I know you're in a delicate spot at work, but I want you to know, I'll tell anyone who'll listen that you made this bust happen."

I shook my head. "No, Stan, that's fine." Part of it was modesty, part concern about aggravating things back home, but mostly, it was because all I could think about was going home and getting some rest.

34

When I saw Nola waiting in the darkness on my porch, I thought the cool hands of a beautiful woman would go a long way toward soothing my pain. But then I saw the look on her face, and I wondered if the worst beating of the day was yet to come.

Before she could get started, though, she looked at my face and her expression softened. "Jesus, Doyle," she said, as she reached up to touch the lump on my forehead. "What happened to you?"

"Nothing," I said. "I'm fine." I was quiet for a moment, trying to figure out what to tell her about the bust. I decided on not much. "I just helped out a friend of mine at DEA with a bust."

She took a step back and pursed her lips, torn between sympathy and disapproval. "Are you supposed to be doing that when you're *suspended*?"

The way she enunciated it, I could tell she was still trying to decide what difference that made.

"Not technically, no."

I sat down next to her on the swing and told her the story of what had happened with Dwayne Rowan. The day my mother died. I put a lot into it, made it quite a story, even made her laugh once or twice. By the time I got to the part about my mother dying, I could see the concern on her face. It wasn't until I finished that I realized my eyes were wet, and I turned away to wipe them.

"Oh," she said, after a few quiet moments.

"Yeah. It was a tough situation, but it was a stupid thing to do."

"But they got the bad guy, right?"

I gave her a sideways look. "Who are you, Dirty Harry all of a sudden?"

"No, not at all. It's just . . . No."

I smiled. "It's tricky when you get into it sometimes."

"I'll bet it is."

She had turned to face me, her bare feet up on the swing. She slid one of them under my thigh, a little bit of physical contact as a peace offering. "I didn't know where you'd gone today. I was worried about you."

I smiled. "You don't have to worry about me."

"Never?"

"Never." Talk about worry reminded me that I'd asked Moose to keep an eye on her. I looked around, but there was no sign of him. "So where is Moose, anyway?"

"Moose? I don't know. I think he went to Carl's."

"Hmm."

"What?"

"Carl. Moose swears he's Mr. Healthy Natural."

"He is. He's pretty hardcore about it, too."

"He's a junkie."

"Carl? No, he isn't. . . . Really?"

"He's got all the signs."

"Wow."

"I have my doubts about Moose, too."

"Oh, come on. Now you're being ridiculous. What do you think, everybody out here is doing heroin?"

I had just seen enough heroin to keep every resident of Dunston stoned for the next six months, but I shrugged, letting her know she didn't have to believe it but I still had my doubts. I decided to change the subject. "What did you do with the rest of your day?"

She looked down. "Spent a lot of the day making awkward explanations to disappointed clients, or former clients. I called my insurance company, inventoried what was left. Read up on gasoline spills and organic certification."

"And?"

She shrugged and shook her head. "It's not a death sentence, but it's not good. Soil excavation, testing, bringing in new organic soil." She sighed.

"What about you, with your MCS? Is the gasoline an issue with that?"

She shrugged again. "I've never had a reaction to gasoline before, and I feel okay, considering, so it's probably okay. But something like this happens, you never know."

"Did you check the other corn?"

"There was no other corn. That was all of it."

"No, I mean next door. The corn on the other side of that fence."

She stiffened and sat up. "No, I didn't even think about it. Should we—"

I shook my head and put my hand on her knee. "It's gone."

"All of it?"

"As far as I could see, yeah."

"Wow." She frowned. "Seems like a bit of a coincidence."

"That's what I thought when I went to check it out."

We were quiet for a moment after that.

She looked like she was about to say more when a pair of headlights swept across us. We both turned to see Moose pulling into the driveway in Frank's pickup truck. His tires ground into the gravel on the side of the road as he misjudged the turn.

"Moose is home," she said, standing up and straightening her shirt in a way that made it look like we had been up to more than we had.

"Yay," I said.

She bent over and kissed the top of my head. "You look exhausted, and you've got a big day tomorrow."

"Tomorrow?"

"Yes, the funeral."

The funeral was tomorrow. "Right." I hadn't forgotten about the funeral, but I had let it sneak up on me.

"Get some sleep, Doyle Carrick," she said, skipping down the steps as Moose opened the car door.

With the dome light on, I could see he was having trouble getting it together enough to get out.

"Good night, Moose," she said, as she walked past him.

"What?" he said from inside the truck. "Oh. Hi, Nola. Good night."

I watched as she walked across the road and into her house. One by one, her lights went on then off: living room, hallway, bathroom, bedroom.

Finally, Moose got out of the car. He seemed to be moving in slow motion as he shuffled up the steps. I didn't say a word, sitting in the darkness, listening to him grunting and breathing loudly as he got to the front door and fumbled for his keys.

When he saw me out of the corner of his eye, the keys squirted out of his hands and up into the air. I caught them as they came down.

"Jesus," he said, slumping against the door. "You scared the shit out of me."

"What, did you think I was some goon come to rough you up?"

"Hey, that shit could happen." His voice was thick and slow.

"I know. That's why I asked you to keep an eye on Nola."

"She didn't want me to keep an eye on her."

"I know. That's why I didn't ask her first." I tossed him the keys. "I asked you to do one thing, and you messed it up. Nice job."

"Jesus, you sound like my dad. But even he's not such an asshole." He sighed loudly and tried the keys again, but dropped them.

"Look at you. You're a mess."

"What? I had a couple drinks."

"You're drunk out of your mind. Or is it something other than booze?"

In the dark, I could see the little rat bastard roll his eyes at me as he tried to unlock the door. "What are you talking about?"

I didn't tell him it wasn't locked. "I'm talking about you and your little junkie friend Squirrel. You're a little too stoned for just a few drinks. So what are you on?"

"What are *you* on?"

"Goddamn it, Moose—"

"Look," he said, cutting me off as he finally opened the door. "I'd be happy to have this conversation with you in the morning." At least, I'm pretty sure that's what he said. He was in no shape to be saying "this conversation." "But right now, I'm going to bed."

I sat on the porch and seethed for another five minutes, then went inside to watch coverage of the press conference on the Channel Sixteen eleven o'clock news.

It all looked very impressive. A conference room at the DEA's field office in Allentown, a folding table piled high with stacks of one-kilo bags of white powder, a few secured with red tape, the rest all sealed with yellow tape. Lined up across a tarp on the floor in front of the table was the arsenal of weapons confiscated at the scene: half a dozen automatic rifles and the same number of handguns. It occurred to me as I watched that just a few hours earlier most of those guns had been firing at me.

Munschak was master of ceremonies, praising Police Chief Pruitt's cooperation and saying with a straight face that this was the kind of positive outcome that occurs when local and federal authorities act together. He outlined a version of how the bust had taken place, referencing an anonymous tip. Afterward, he took questions from the press, mostly about weights and street values, which he declined to specify, since the haul had not all been tested yet.

The reporter did a quick "back-to-you," and I was just about to turn off the TV when they cut to aerial footage of the crime scene earlier that day. There I was, right in the thick of it, talking to Stan Bowers with an assault weapon over my shoulder. A medic came over and wiped some blood off my forehead, but I heroically waved him away.

Three minutes later, my cell phone started ringing. Danny Tennison. I almost didn't answer it, but I figured it could be the last friendly voice I heard for a long time.

"So, what are you, moonlighting out there?"

"Look, I was driving along, minding my own business when I saw them switch off on the van, so I called Stan Bowers."

"You just happened to have an assault weapon with you?"

"No, I picked that up at the scene."

"Because . . ."

I sighed. "Because I had already emptied my gun. I know. Jesus, Danny, I'm screwed."

"Probably so."

"Maybe no one else saw it." As soon as I said it, another call came in.

"I saw it on two channels in Philly. I imagine it was on the others, too."

The incoming call was the Philadelphia police. I didn't click over.

Danny laughed. "If you need to take that call, I can hold."

"No, that's okay. I have a feeling they'll call back."

"Probably a good bet. I'll see you at the funeral tomorrow. Try to get a good night's sleep, okay? I don't want to have to listen to Laura the whole way home going on about how you look like shit."

"I love you, too."

35

McClintock, the funeral director, called at nine to remind me the car would arrive at ten. I'd been up since five—not due to any virtue or industry, but because what little sleep I was getting was not of the fun variety.

By the time I'd gotten to bed, I'd stiffened up enough that it hurt just to toss and turn, but I had enough on my mind that I tossed and turned anyway. And my mind was twitching and fidgeting even more than my body, between the ache and sadness over losing my mom and Frank, stress over what was waiting for me back in Philly, and a nagging suspicion that the case that just wrapped up hadn't wrapped up at all.

I hadn't forgotten about Frank's funeral, but maybe I kind of tried to, sinking my teeth into a case I shouldn't have been involved in to take my mind off the things I didn't want to think about. And now that the case was supposed to be over, my brain kept insisting there was something else to it. I had to wonder if I just didn't want to let it go.

But there was still George Arnett's friend with the piercings, the guy who cleaned my clock. He wasn't any of the bodies at Crooked Creek Farm, so unless he was sitting in a trailer behind his mother's house with a bullet in his head, he was probably still running around out there. Hell, he was probably the one who did Dwight Cooney. And even apart from that, I had a sense that something else was going on, that this bust was not the end of it.

When I finally got to sleep, I dreamed about kids eating ice-cream cones with crack in it, and monster stalks of corn that were bloated and sickly. There was also a dream from when I was a kid. It was the one where I come home, and there's no one there, just the faintest scent of smoke. When I was a kid it scared the crap out of me. I hadn't had it in a while. As I've gotten older, a strange nostalgia sometimes accompanied it, memories of my mom coming into my room to make sure I was okay, stroking my forehead and making me smile, lying with me until I went back to sleep. No matter how long it took.

There may have been plenty of terrible things out there in the real world, but the things that scared me the most, the horrible figments of my own imagination, were powerless in the presence of my mom. It was a feeling of absolute safety and security. This time, though, when it woke me up, that nostalgic feeling was followed by the aching awareness that she was gone.

That's when I got up and started drinking coffee.

After McClintock's call, I gave Moose's open bedroom door a loud, coplike bang. He awoke with a start, and immediately grabbed his head with both hands.

"Car's coming at ten o'clock," I said, a little bit louder than necessary.

He groaned.

I put on my suit, went downstairs and called Nola to see if she wanted to ride in the car. She didn't answer and I didn't leave a message.

Moose came downstairs forty minutes later, showered and wearing a suit but looking rough. The suit looked like he had bought it before he finished growing, but I gave him credit for having one. What really looked like crap was his face: pale and drawn with dark rings under his eyes.

He put on a pair of wraparound sunglasses, and sat quietly on the sofa until the car showed up.

McClintock was sitting up front with the driver. Moose and I got in the back and looked out our respective windows.

The service was in the little church with the white steeple, the one we had seen from Hawk Mountain. Having seen the view from the mountaintop, I could picture where the church was in relation to the house and the rest of the town.

Nola was standing outside the church when we got there. Her hair was up and she had on a plain black dress and heels, a string of pearls, and a little bit of makeup. She gave me a tight smile and patted me on the shoulder. "I saw the news," she said, her hand coming up to touch the bruise on the side of my face. "That was a bigger deal than you let on. You okay?"

"Yeah," I said, "I'm okay." The events of the last few days had taken my mind off Frank and my mom. Now I felt like I was back inside that bubble.

McClintock had every detail under control. He led me to the bottom of the steps and stood with me while I accepted condolences from the two dozen people who showed up. Most of them were older, friends of my mom and Frank. A lot of them looked vaguely familiar, either from decades earlier, or from my mom's funeral. There weren't as many as showed up then, and I wondered at first if she was that much more popular than Frank. She had a lot of friends from volunteering at the library. But many of the attendees forwarded regrets from spouses or friends who were under the weather. Maybe they had the same thing as Pruitt's absentees. I wondered if he would call them sissies, too.

Singly and in pairs, they came up and shook my hand and said how they knew Frank or my mom and how they were sorry. Then they headed up the steps into the church. At the end of the line were Danny and Laura Tennison. I was relieved to see them, a breath of normalcy that breached the bubble, even if just for a second.

"Hi, Doyle," said Laura. She gave me a kiss on the cheek, then wiped off the lipstick, looking up at my face with an expression of genuine concern. "How are you holding up?"

"You know me. I'm okay."

Danny leaned forward and spoke quietly. "You look like shit."

"More than usual?"

"About the same. Like the suit, though."

They headed up the steps, and as I started to follow them, I heard a soft whistle, and I turned to see Stan Bowers walking up, wrapping a tie around his neck. In the time it took him to close the six paces between us, he looped the tie into a tight little knot.

"Hey, Carrick. How you holding up?"

"You know."

"Yeah, I do. You don't look too banged up, considering."

"Thanks for coming."

"You know it."

McClintock cleared his throat beside me and glanced down at his watch.

"All right," I said. "I got to get in there."

"I'll see you afterward."

It seemed that McClintock touched my elbow and suddenly I was seated in the front of the church, just like at my mom's funeral. Everything about it reminded me of my mom's funeral, including my efforts not to think about her because I was worried I would lose it if I did. The biggest difference was that Frank wasn't sitting next to me. I was so busy not thinking about my mom, I forgot to not think about Frank, and when I looked at the empty space on the pew beside me, I felt the muscles tighten in my jaw and my throat.

Nola was sitting on the other side of the church, Moose right next to her, still looking like hell. The urn with Frank's ashes was sitting on a pedestal. The service itself was a blur, a lot of stifled coughs while the reverend recited a mixture of prayers and platitudes, with just enough vague personal details sprinkled in to make you wonder if at some point he had actually met Frank. Not that I could have come up with anything better.

Lost in my own thoughts—about Frank, about my mom, my dad, memories from my childhood—I felt like a spectator, of the service as well as the memories. It was like watching Nick at Night: sepia-toned childhood memories interrupted by commercials from the present day—drug dealers, land developers, crop fires, trucks running me off the road.

By the time the service was over, my feet were itching in my three-hour shoes and I was desperate to get out of there. But McClintock steered me back to the steps in front of the church so I could graciously receive everyone's condolences yet again. With all the coughing going on, I made a mental note to track down some hand sanitizer.

Moose was at the front of the line, with Squirrel, whom I hadn't realized was there. They both mumbled something and shook my hand before disappearing.

The rest of the crowd was kind enough not to disperse until everyone had a chance to shake my hand once more. While I was chatting with a blue-haired old woman whose name I had forgotten in the hour since we'd last spoken, I noticed Bowers and Tennison standing off to the side. They were quietly chatting and sharing a furtive laugh. At one point, they both looked over at me, then both looked away. I had the distinct impression that they were trading Doyle Carrick stories. Pricks.

As another old woman stepped up to tell me she was still sorry, I noticed Nola chatting with Laura Tennison. I liked that even less.

I don't think McClintock had approved when I said no, I did not want a reception. Standing there holding hands with the last old lady in line, I knew I had used up all my civility, and I was grateful I had stood my ground.

When it was all over, Nola came up and told me that she had to drive over to Harrisburg, but that she could blow it off if I wanted some company. As much as I didn't want to say no, the fact was I needed to be alone.

I think she understood. I think she was relieved.

McClintock packed me into the limo and drove me home. He opened my door, gave me a small, sad smile, and shook my hand. Then he got back into the car and drove off.

I watched as the car curved along Bayberry Road and disappeared, and suddenly I felt very alone.

A warm breeze swept across me. I closed my eyes and enjoyed the feel of it for a moment before slowly climbing the steps. It felt like the end of the summer. A butterfly floated by, and I thought about Mexico, about finding out where the butterflies were headed and going down there to wait for them. Entering the house, I also thought about going to bed. But I knew that if I did, I might stay there for a week.

Sydney Bricker had given me a list of papers I needed to find— life insurance, bank statements, deeds—and a strong suggestion that I do it sooner rather than later. So instead of going upstairs, I went into Frank's office, confronting two of my greatest phobias: paperwork and awkward personal matters.

It felt like I was violating his inner sanctum, rude just to be in there when he was so powerless to stop me.

Behind the desk was a wooden credenza, and inside it were boxes of all sorts of papers. They were stacked neatly, if not exactly filed, and I was pretty sure I would find what I was looking for inside them.

When I opened the first box, I caught a whiff of something so faint I didn't completely recognize it at first. But part of me did: a combination of leather and aftershave and something else, like tweed. It was Frank. I smiled when my brain caught up with my nose, but my eyes were already wet.

Within five minutes I'd found everything I was looking for. Alongside neatly bundled stacks of bank statements and utility bills was an accordion folder marked "Important Papers," with each of the tabs marked with one of the items on Bricker's list. I wondered if they had been in cahoots, or if this was something normal grown-ups did.

It was cathartic, but almost anticlimactic. I had nothing else to do, so I put the papers I needed on the desk and moved on to the next box. This one was clearly my mom's, and the fragrance totally different, mostly Chanel. My throat caught as I opened it. There was an envelope of old photos, mostly her and me. I was a kid, and she was a beautiful young woman. There were some old tax returns, a few résumés. I lifted out a stack of old manila envelopes, and felt something bulky in one of them. I opened the flap and slid it out: my dad's wristwatch.

I felt a surge of emotions, but before they could assemble into anything coherent, I caught a whiff of smoke and ashes, the faint but acrid smell of something burnt that was not meant to burn. The hairs on my arms rose up as I recognized the smell from my nightmares. I quickly slid the watch back into its envelope. But before I could put the envelope back in the box, I saw something that stopped me.

A restraining order.

"Meredith Carrick," it said across the top. Scanning it, I picked out words like "protection from abuse" and "battery." I felt a jarring sense of disequilibrium. I'd had my problems with Frank, especially in the early days, but strangely, in the days since he died, I felt closer to him than ever before. Now this. I would never in a million years have suspected him of this.

Then I saw the date. Three months before the motel room fire that killed my dad. Then I saw the name. David Carrick.

At first it made no sense to me. Then it came back in snippets: arguments, shouting and cursing, broken furniture, tears. Apologies. I remembered driving with my mother at night, wondering where we were going. It was a school night, and it was an adventure, staying in a hotel, but the gnawing feeling in my stomach came back to me so clearly that I felt it again sitting there on the floor. I remembered coming back home the next day and knowing that my dad no longer lived there.

Suddenly, I felt completely devoid of energy. I left everything right where it was. Feeling sore and stiff and creakier than the steps I was climbing, I went upstairs to bed.

36

It was after dark when I awoke. A gusty breeze was rustling the trees and billowing the curtains. The windows were open, and I lay there in the darkness, feeling the air on my skin and the electricity of an approaching storm. I tried not to think about the restraining order, or anything else.

I tried to go back to sleep, but that wasn't happening, so I moved on to plan B.

Pulling on my jeans and a T-shirt, I went downstairs without turning on the lights. I banged my toe, but took it as fair punishment for not knowing the layout of the place a little better. In the darkness, I grabbed a square bottle from the bar, pretty sure it was Jack Daniel's, and went onto the front porch. In the back of my mind, I wondered about Moose—if he was asleep or out somewhere. At some point I'd have to figure out what to do with him long term. I definitely didn't want to be roomies for life, but I probably wasn't going to keep the house anyway. At the moment, I was just glad to have some time on my own.

The first sip tasted harsh and raw and smooth and warm, sliding down my throat and curling around in my stomach, getting comfortable. I followed it up with a nice long gulp, and that tasted even better. They kept getting better after that.

The storm was approaching from the west, and it looked like a good one. It wasn't raining yet, but the wind was picking up. The lightning itself was too low on the horizon to see, but its reflection lit up the clouds.

The plan was to sit out on the porch, drink too much from the square bottle, and watch the storm. But before long, I remembered all those open windows. When I went upstairs to close them, I was stunned by the view from the hallway. Out over the roof, thunderheads were rolling in, each flash of lightning illuminating the countryside below.

I climbed out the window and onto the lower roof. The sky was dramatic, and maybe the whiskey was already clouding my judgment, but after a few minutes of watching and drinking, I looked up at the upper roof behind me and wondered what the view would be like from there. As I pulled myself up, lightning flashed, casting my silhouette against the roof, just like the stun grenade the day before. My body tensed as I waited for the concussion, and I felt a moment of panic before I realized it was just thunder. Still, I almost dropped the bottle.

Once I got up there, the pitch wasn't bad, but the wind was fierce and there was plenty of lightning.

I was drunk, but not so drunk I didn't know it. I kept low and moved cautiously until I was comfortable, lying back with my hands behind my neck, relaxing and watching the storm.

The wind got up even more, surging and swirling around me. Occasionally, a volley of heavy raindrops would blow over from somewhere it was really raining, splattering loudly on the tarpaper shingles, and on me.

I figured I would stay up there until it started raining hard. I don't know how long I'd been out there, but the bottle was empty and the storm was still approaching when I heard a crack of thunder that didn't sound like a crack of thunder. There was no rumble or roll, just a single sharp crack so brief and so familiar it could have been my imagination.

Propping myself up on an elbow, I looked out over the countryside and tilted my head, listening. All I could hear was the wind and the rain and the slow, distinctly different rumble of thunder in the distance.

As I was lying back down, I saw a string of lights in the distance, four of them, like little dots, snaking through the fields behind Nola's farm. The lightning was picking up again, and between that and the darkness and the swell of the undulating fields, it was impossible to tell how big the lights were or how far away. It was only when one of them stabbed into the sky that I recognized them as flashlights. My brain seized that bit of information, filling in the blanks to give them scale and distance and meaning.

A blinding flash of lightning made them disappear for a moment, but then they were back, four flashlights in the distance, moving at a decent clip. As I watched, they spread out, from a single column to a single row, now sweeping across the field. The lights were flickering now, maybe sweeping back and forth.

I stood up to get a better look, and the roof seemed suddenly steeper than before. Maybe it was the whiskey, or maybe it was the storm, but I had a hard time keeping my feet under me.

The wind was howling now, and it finally started to rain in earnest, but I stayed up there on the roof, watching the light show playing out across the fields. The lightning was getting closer and brighter. Each flash erased my night vision, causing the lights to disappear again, and as the rain intensified, it became harder and harder each time to find the flashlights again.

An impossibly bright flash of lightning was accompanied almost simultaneously by an explosion of thunder that sounded like it was right on top of me. I dropped to the roof, clinging to it, cowering and fighting the urge to clench my eyes shut. The bottle slid down the roof and wedged in the gutter. The flashlights changed formation yet again, the two in the middle holding steady while the two on the edges moved forward and closed in, forming a box.

They held steady like that, and I realized I was holding my breath. When I breathed again, I caught a strong whiff of ozone and my skin started to tingle. I dropped down, trying not to take my eyes away from those four points of light. But then the world exploded in brilliant white light and a clap of thunder that drove the air out of my lungs. My eyes clamped shut, and I pressed myself against the roof.

When I opened my eyes, the four lights were gone. I stared without blinking, my eyes sweeping the darkened landscape, probing the spot where I thought I had seen the lights. I lay there soaking wet as the storm moved away and the night turned dark and quiet, my eyes straining into the darkness until eventually, they closed.

37

When I opened my eyes again, the sky was beginning to pale and the birds were making a racket. It felt like they were talking about me.

I was cold and wet and stiff and sore. And on the roof.

The buzz from the whiskey had long since worn off, replaced with an ominously throbbing headache. Lying there for a moment, I thought about the strange procession of lights and wondered if I had dreamed the whole thing.

As I rolled over, the headache flared with an intensity that made me feel nauseous. The rest of me hurt, too. I crawled toward the edge of the roof, gulping air and clenching my jaw against the urge to be sick. I paused at the edge and got to my feet, trying to keep my balance as the roof swayed under my feet. I looked out at the land rolling gently in the morning haze. Once I had fixed in my mind the general area where those lights had been the night before, I slowly slid over the edge of the roof.

Stiff and sober, climbing down off the roof was much scarier than climbing up had been.

I lowered myself over the edge, to the slightly pitched lower roof. For an instant, my arms went wide, making goofy little circles until I regained my balance.

The window was still open, and I shook my head; the reason I had come upstairs the night before was to close it. I pulled the window open a little more and half-crawled, half-tumbled inside to the second-floor hall. I had just closed the window when I turned and found myself face-to-face with Moose, coming out of his room.

He stopped and looked at me, down and then back up. "You look like shit."

"Fuck you, too."

"No, seriously. You look awful. What, did you sleep in your clothes?"

"Something like that."

"Are you okay?"

"Rough night. I'm fine."

"Okay." He said it like he didn't believe me. The corner of his mouth tugged up into a slight smile. I gave him a look that made the smile go away.

"Okay, then," he said. "I have to run some errands for Nola. She's still in Harrisburg. Then I'm supposed to help Squirrel with something. You should maybe try to get some rest."

I answered him with a grunt. As soon as he was out of my way, I headed straight for my room, where I peeled off my wet clothes and climbed into bed.

It felt like only a few minutes had passed, but the sun was brighter when Moose woke me up again.

He seemed agitated, and sounded like two people talking at once.

I held up a hand. "Slow down a minute. What are you talking about?" My voice sounded croaky, and my throat was sore.

He plopped down on the side of the bed. I sat up and gave him a look to let him know he was crossing a line.

"It's Squirrel," he said. "He's missing."

"Missing?"

"Yeah, I was supposed to meet him at his place this morning, and he wasn't there. I can't find him anywhere, and he's not answering his cell phone."

I sank back and laughed. "Moose, your friend is a junkie. They're not really known for being reliable."

"Doyle, that's bullshit. This is serious."

"I am serious. Your friend's a goddamn junkie. And I don't know if you've been watching the news, but six drug dealers were killed right here in Dunston. Now, maybe Squirrel didn't have anything to do with those guys, but he probably wasn't too many steps removed from them, either."

"Jesus, for the last time—Squirrel's not using drugs. What is it with you?"

I glared at Moose in reply, but he took a deep breath and continued. "His car was missing, too—"

"So? He probably went out—"

"I found it."

That stopped me. "You found it?"

He nodded.

"Where?"

"Not far. On the side of the road."

"Did you check the gas gauge?"

"What?"

"The gas gauge. Did you check it?"

He looked at me like I was crazy. "No."

"Well, maybe he ran out of gas."

"Oh." He sat there for a moment, thinking about that. "All right, that's true. Well, we can check it."

"We?"

"Yeah, come on. I need you to come with me to check it out. Give me your cop-ly take on the situation."

"I can tell you that much right now. Your friend's a junkie, which means he's a fuck-up, which means he blew you off and he's probably out dozing off his latest fix."

"Doyle."

I'd met retired cops who spent their lives looking for mysteries to solve: wondering whose dog was crapping on their lawn or which neighbor was stealing cable. Sure, some of my suspicions had turned out to be right, but I had also spent the better part of three days doing background checks on a vegetable patch. I didn't want to become that guy. But the look on Moose's face told me he wasn't going to drop it, and I was curious about whether Squirrel's whereabouts maybe had something to do with Roberts and Arnett. My cop-ly instincts were intrigued.

"All right. Go make some coffee."

38

Moose brought me two granola bars and a cup of coffee that I suspected was reheated, but that was fine. At this point I was just looking for the active ingredient.

When I got outside, he was sitting in the driver's seat of Frank's truck with the engine running. I gave him a look as I walked to my car and got in. Somehow I could tell Moose wasn't the kind of driver I'd have the patience to ride shotgun with. And even though my car was beat up, it was running fine. I started the engine and Moose got in next to me, giving me some kind of look, but I didn't look over at him.

Squirrel's truck was barely half a mile away, so we went there first, to make sure it was still there and that Squirrel wasn't asleep in the back.

Moose directed me down Pear Tree Lane, just off Valley Road. "It's right up here," he said as we came around a bend in the road.

I slowed down to look, and still had to jerk the wheel to miss it.

Some kind of old panel truck, like a station wagon on steroids, rust–colored and beat to hell. It was parked between two trees, per-pendicular to the road with its rear wheels resting on the edge of the embankment. The tailgate was down, jutting out into the road right at windshield level, like a blade.

"What?" Moose asked, apparently oblivious to how close he had just come to decapitation.

"Thanks for the warning."

I pulled over just past it, and we got out.

"The Bronze Bomber," Moose said with affection as we walked up, patting the side of the truck. "A 1983 Jeep Wagoneer. Thing's just about indestructible."

Not only did it look destructible, it looked halfway destructed.

The driver's side window was partially open, and the seat was damp from rain. The gas tank was half full. In the back was some lumber and a couple of milk crates, one filled with empty canvas bags, the other with plastic tubing and a couple of beakers. I picked up a beaker and looked at Moose.

"That's just supplies for making his squish," he told me.

Nothing else looked suspicious. I put the beaker back and closed the tailgate, but a second later it fell open again.

Moose nodded sheepishly. "Yeah, the latch is tricky."

I closed it again, this time with a little more force, but it fell open again. This time I ignored it. "So where else did you look?" I asked him. "And where else didn't you look?"

We started at Squirrel's house, a tiny square bungalow surrounded by a lawn that Moose informed me was not weedy but "native." The tiny, unpainted wooden porch had no steps.

Moose had keys, but I knocked on the door twice and waited a couple of minutes in between. When there was no answer, I stepped back and motioned for Moose to have at it.

He stepped forward and raised the keys, but stopped. "You're here as a friend, right?"

"What are you talking about?"

"I mean, you're not here on official business, right?"

"I'm not anywhere on official business. I'm suspended, remember? Why?"

"Well, this is where Squirrel makes his squish, and I don't want him to get arrested or in trouble or anything."

"Don't worry. It's not even illegal unless he's selling it."

Moose gave me an awkward smile.

"Beautiful. Well, I don't give a crap about any of that." I wasn't going in there hoping to find evidence of an illegal still. I was hoping to find evidence of his drug involvement. "But if we're going in, let's go in."

With a shrug and a sigh, he opened the door and we stepped inside.

I was expecting a drug den, but the place was clean and about as tidy as my apartment back in Philly on a good day.

The furniture was old but solid, a mish-mash of styles, like a used-furniture showroom. In the middle of the coffee table was a note Moose had left, asking Squirrel to call him. We walked through to the kitchen, which was yellow and white, with a lumpy linoleum floor. The yellow Formica countertop was worn white in places.

In the bedroom, the bed was tightly made, the corners of the covers folded crisply under the mattress. Moose held up his arms. "See? He hasn't been home all night. The bed's still made."

"He always makes his bed like that?"

"Yeah, ever since he got out of the army."

"The army? That little flea?"

Moose nodded solemnly.

"Well, he probably made it again, right after he got up. That's how they do it in the army."

Moose shook his head. "He doesn't make it until after lunch, because that's when he knows whether he's going back to bed or not."

Any respect I had for Squirrel because of his stint in the army evaporated. "Are you serious?"

"It's like a routine with him. A ritual. I actually teased him about it."

"I bet you did," I said lightly, but I could see in Moose's eyes that he was seriously worried. "Is there a basement?"

Moose nodded, then paused before leading the way through a door in the kitchen. The basement was dirty and unfinished, smelling of dust and vinegar. An old washer and dryer sat in one corner. There was a concrete laundry sink and a floor-to-ceiling cabinet against one wall. On a table across from it was a disassembled electric juicer. The rest was taken up with a dozen empty five-gallon buckets. I opened each of the cabinets, poked around inside. Mostly it was empty wine bottles and plastic jugs, but I moved stuff around and looked under it and behind it. I saw no signs of drug paraphernalia, although that could have been hidden anywhere, but I also saw no reaction from Moose, although that didn't prove anything, either.

When I was finished looking around, I turned to Moose and shrugged, then followed him back up the steps and out onto the porch.

"Look," I said. "If you really think he's missing, you should probably just go to Chief Pruitt."

Moose shook his head vigorously. "No. I'm with you on that guy. He's a dick. Plus, I don't want him to see Squirrel's setup here."

"Okay, well, if you really want my help, you have to tell me everything you know, and I mean including anything about drugs."

Moose rolled his eyes, but he looked like he was going to cry. "Doyle, I swear to you. Squirrel is not into drugs. At all."

I sighed, wondering if he really didn't realize his friend was a junkie. "Okay," I said, against my better judgment. "So, where else do you think he might be?"

He took out a piece of paper and started to unfold it. "I made a list."

For such a small town, it turned out there were a lot of places to look. Over the next four hours, I learned more about Squirrel's day-to-day habits than I ever wanted to know. We went to the mini-mart first, where we also got lunch, burritos that we ate as we drove to the library. Then we went to a comic book store, two picnic spots, and three friends' houses.

The friends eyed me warily, even after Moose assured them I was cool. Two of them looked like they'd been using. None of them knew where Squirrel was.

By the time we got home, the lines on Moose's face were deeper than when we'd left. He'd been worried before, but now he was seriously considering the possibility that something bad had happened to his friend. I was considering it, too.

"Look," I said as we parked. "If you're that worried, the police are the only ones with access to the resources you need."

"Yeah, maybe."

"Or just wait a bit. He's probably fine, and he'll be wondering what you were so worked up about."

"Right. I'm going back to his place. See if he turns up."

"All right. Don't sweat it. He'll turn up."

39

I sat on the porch steps, watching as Moose got into the truck and drove off. He was obviously worried about Squirrel, and I wondered again if he honestly believed Squirrel wasn't using. Then I reminded myself that Moose was probably using, too. Maybe he was worried because he knew more than he was letting on.

Once he had disappeared around the curve, I abruptly got to my feet. I immediately felt a slight wave of nausea, bringing back a taste of the misery I'd felt when I woke up on the roof.

I closed my eyes again and put a hand on the railing. But as I waited for the moment to pass, I also remembered the strange lights I'd seen in the fields behind Nola's farm. When I opened my eyes, instead of going up the steps and into the house, I crossed the street to Nola's house, went around back and plunged into the bushes.

When I emerged from the dark thicket of green, the sky had streaks of happy orange clouds that somehow made that tall fence look more sinister in contrast. I walked along the fence for fifty yards, looking down the rows of corn stubble and slowing when I reached a spot that was roughly even with where I had seen the lights. I didn't know what I was looking for, but I squinted into the twilight, staring down one row after another until a spot of color in the growing darkness caught my eye.

I strained but couldn't make out any details, just a little smudge of red against the faded corn stubble and the dark earth. The fence seemed even taller up close, but it was still just a simple chain-link fence.

And if Moose could do it, I damn sure could.

Hooking my fingers into the links above my head, I kicked off the ground, pushed with my toes, and started pulling myself up.

The musical ring of the chain-link against the pole brought me back to younger days—as a uniform chasing lowlifes, or even younger, scrambling over fences just ahead of one angry pursuer or another. But it was always either chasing or being chased. I couldn't remember ever just climbing a fence like this from a standing start. Without the adrenaline rush, I bogged down just shy of the top. With no forward momentum, my toes had a hard time gripping the chain link, and I had to rely on arm strength alone to pull me up to the top. The no-tresspassing sign seemed even louder as I ignored it.

I paused at the top, just for a second. It was brighter up there, closer to the sky, but the shadows on the ground looked even darker. The red smudge I had spotted earlier was barely visible now. I felt exposed, perched up there in the open.

I swung my leg over and lowered myself down to the other side. It occurred to me, as my feet hit the ground, that a trespassing arrest could turn into a major problem with my recent history. Pushing that thought out of my mind, I trotted down the rows of stubble, toward the red spot. Even crouching right over the thing, I needed a few moments to see that it was an apple, halfway embedded in the mud.

Kind of strange, an apple in the middle of a cornfield. I stared at it for a few seconds, wondering if it meant anything at all. Probably not, I decided, but as I stood up and looked around to see if there were any other apples, something else caught my eye.

Looking one way, I saw rows of corn stubble extending evenly back to the fence. Looking the opposite direction, I saw the same rows extending just as evenly into the distance, disappearing over a slight rise forty yards away. But looking out across the rows, I could see a jerky, wavering line cutting a crude diagonal across the rows. The line was made of mud and crushed corn stubble, as if something had churned the soil. I thought I could make out footprints, but in the gloom it was hard to tell.

I turned and looked behind me, but the line ended under my feet. At the apple.

Images from the night before came back to me, a line of lights snaking across this field in the darkness. Closing my eyes, I tried to picture it, tried to superimpose those lights over the path that cut across the field. But between the lightning and rain and the alcohol last night, and now the darkness and the different perspectives, it was useless.

I looked back at the fence for a moment, at the blank back of the NO TRESPASSING sign. Then I looked at the diagonal line, and took off at a jog along it.

The field was bigger than I expected. The landscape rolled gently, and I dipped and rose with it. The fence and the trees quickly disappeared behind me. Eventually, I came over a rise and paused. Down the slope in front of me, the path that I had been following ended at a small grove of trees enclosed in a fence. Beyond the grove, angled off to the right, was a large trailer, like you would see on a construction site. A couple of pickup trucks were parked on a graveled area next to it. One was green, but I didn't see any marks on it, and I couldn't tell if it was the one that had run me off the road.

I approached the trees cautiously. My gun was back at the house, tucked safely under my mattress. I was acutely aware of its absence. The stand of trees was thirty yards across, and it was surrounded by another chain-link fence, similar to the one I'd scaled to get onto the property, but only six feet high. Still, I wasn't crazy about the thought of scaling another fence. I crept along the fence and came to a gate, but it was padlocked.

Just past the gate, a branch extended out over the fence. The sky was almost dark by now, but even in the dim light, I could see an apple hanging from the branch. I reached up to touch it, maybe to pick it, but as my hand approached, I heard a loud crack and the apple exploded.

40

Three men were coming at me, running. One of them stopped to aim a rifle, and as I dropped to the ground, I heard another shot and a bullet passing right over me. Staying low, I sprinted off in the opposite direction. When I reached the next bend in the fence, I grabbed the pole and swung myself around the corner.

Ahead of me, seemingly adjacent to the fenced-in orchard, was a long white tent, looking almost blue in the last of the twilight.

I ran straight at it, locked into my route by indecision. Whoever was chasing me would be rounding the corner behind me any second. If I angled out to the left, toward the far end of the tent, I'd be outlined against it, an easy shot for even a mediocre marksman. If I stopped and tried to scale the fence surrounding the orchard, I'd be an even easier target. And if I somehow made it over, I'd probably be trapped inside the enclosure. My only hope was if there was a space between the tent and the fence surrounding the orchard, I could slip in between them.

When I heard the men shouting at me to stop, I found a little more speed. I had almost reached the tent when I heard the crack of a gun, and I almost went sprawling, trying to duck and still keep my feet underneath me and pumping. When I looked up, I cursed; the tent and the fence were tightly tethered to each other. But with the next crack of a handgun, another option presented itself.

The wall of the tent snapped and billowed as the bullet punctured it, and I saw two bullet holes, maybe a foot apart, right at waist level.

The tent looked like plastic sheeting, or at least I hoped it was, and not some coated canvas. I had no idea what was inside it—a brick wall or a Bengal tiger or a dozen armed men like the ones behind me—but at that point, I was committed.

I pumped my legs a little harder those last few steps, then launched, feet first, aiming for the two bullet holes in the tent.

My feet hit one of the holes and penetrated it, followed by my legs and my hips and my waist. And then I stopped. My shoulders, arms, and head were protruding from the plastic, which was now pulled tight around my ribs. I couldn't see my pursuers, and hanging there, half inside the plastic and half out, I expected a hand to grab me at any moment, or a bullet to end it all.

Reaching up, I hooked both index fingers into the second bullet hole and pulled, tearing the plastic, trying to join the two holes. But the plastic stretched as much as it tore, like a bad dream, the holes weren't getting any closer. The plastic constricting my ribs made it hard to breathe. I started to feel lightheaded, and my arms were growing weaker. I could feel the edges of panic and it occurred to me that, if I didn't get out of there, I could pass out and die of asphyxiation without anyone laying a hand on me. But at the sound of footsteps thudding on the dirt, I gave a last frantic tug. The two holes finally merged and I slid to the ground, my lungs filling with air. Inside the tent, I pushed myself up onto my feet and scanned my surroundings.

The tent was unlit, but the roof was clear and in the light coming through it I could see the space was huge—maybe fifty feet wide and eighty feet long. Five rows of tables ran the entire length of the tent. The tables were covered with plants, with racks running down the center of each table. On the table in front of me, I could see stacks of clay pots and saucers and various tools hanging from hooks.

Overhead was a lattice of thin pipes, like a sprinkler system, and unlit fluorescent lights above them. The place smelled like a greenhouse—fertilizer and chemicals and dirt and humidity—but with something else, too; flowery but with a hint of decay. The air was damp and warm, and I could feel sweat trickling down my skin in half a dozen places.

I could make out what looked like potted flowers, but in the darkness, the colors seemed drab and dull. Other plants grew taller, with some sort of fruit or pods hanging from them. As I was reaching out to touch one, I heard voices through the hole in the tent.

I grabbed a trowel and turned to face them. For a moment, it sounded like the men were arguing among themselves, voices lowered but harsh and angry. Then a leg and an arm appeared in the hole I had made, and I looked down at the trowel in my hand.

The far side of the tent was forty feet away, with half a dozen rows of plants and racks and tables between me and it.

As I looked back, the arm and the leg were joined by a head. I grabbed a clay saucer and flung it hard, like a Frisbee. My knack for Frisbee had never before proved useful, but the saucer caught the guy in the side of the head and exploded into shards as he slumped to the floor. Climbing up onto the potting table, I jumped over the rack and onto the next table, ducking under the sprinklers. I repeated the maneuver three more times, making my way to the far side of the tent.

The last table wasn't as wide as the others, making room for a standpipe that was connected by a hose to the overhead sprinklers. My foot slid out from under me as it caught the edge of the table, but I grabbed at one of the overhead pipes and caught it, regaining enough balance to drop down into a crouch.

Another trowel was hanging from a hook, and I grabbed it and slipped between the table and the wall of the tent, stabbing at the plastic, puncturing it, then again, three more times. This time, when I pulled, the holes readily tore along the perforated line. I plunged through the hole—and immediately banged against a wide metal surface. It seemed like I had emerged into some sort of cell, and for an instant, panic gripped me, squeezing my chest tighter than the plastic of the tent. Then I felt the cool air against my damp skin, and I realized I was outside.

The air smelled fresh and clean compared to the inside of the tent, but I could also smell gasoline. I had emerged in the small space between the tent and a large tank—maybe five hundred gallons—with a hose coming off of it like an old-fashioned gas pump. Looking out from behind the tank, I could see the trailer extending off to my right. In front of me and to my left was corn stubble as far as I could see.

I couldn't see the tiny orchard, but I turned and sprinted off at what I hoped was a perpendicular angle to the way I had come: back to the road and away from whoever was chasing me, but without leading them back toward Nola's house.

The sweat cooled on my skin and I could feel the air as I pulled it into my lungs and let it out, each breath aching just a little bit more. I ran as fast as I ever had over the rows of corn stubble, one step between each row, repeated again and again, feeling momentarily safer each time the land dipped down low, then vulnerable again as it rose up once more.

After the second rise, I started looking for the fence. Each time I topped a hill after that, I was disappointed that it wasn't there.

The property records had said the parcels of land were owned by a bunch of different companies, but I had covered a lot of territory—too much territory for it to be any single parcel.

My lungs were burning and I was afraid that I was lost, that I was running deeper into some massive armed compound, when I chugged up a hill and saw the fence fifty yards away. As I ran closer, it seemed to grow bigger than the ten feet I had scaled on my way in.

My legs felt like rubber and my lungs were about to burst, but men with guns was more than enough incentive for me. Without slowing down, I ran up the fence on my toes and fingers and slipped over the top. Lowering myself until my arms were fully extended, I let go. As soon as I hit the ground, I scrambled into the dense growth on the other side of the fence, crouching in the darkness and trying to catch my breath.

I waited ten seconds, then peeked out, relieved to find myself on Bayberry Road, just past the curve, about a hundred yards from my house. As I was stepping out of the thicket, I heard a vehicle approaching fast and I pulled back.

It was a truck, maybe one of those that had been parked next to the trailer, sweeping both sides of the road with high-powered flashlights as it drove slowly up Bayberry, toward Nola's farm and my house. There were two in the back and two in the cab, at least three of them armed with assault rifles.

If they were searching the perimeter, they would probably turn around and come back when they reached the line between their land and Nola's. As soon as they disappeared around the bend, I darted across the road and up the embankment, vaulting over the fence into Meade's Christmas Tree Farm.

The rows of man-sized trees seemed ideally suited to concealing pursuers in the dark and to framing me for an easy shot in the back. I had long since used up my emergency energy supplies, but I found enough fumes to keep me going, jogging down the row of trees in a low crouch. By the time I reached the fence that separated Meade's land from mine, I barely had enough energy to slip through it and onto the ground.

I landed on one of Moose's plants. A tomato squished underneath me, soaking into the back of my shirt, but I didn't care. I lay there on my back, trying not to make too much noise as I caught my breath.

41

When my heart had slowed down and my breathing was almost back to normal, I made my way to the house, careful to stay down low.

The lights were on inside, and I couldn't remember if I had left them that way. It had been daylight the last time I was home. There was no sign of Frank's truck.

The front door was open.

As I slipped inside, I heard a noise coming from the kitchen. My gun was upstairs, and I had run about as much as I could, so I gingerly lifted the fireplace poker out of its holder and crept through the dining room. With the poker held high over my shoulder, I rocked twice on the balls of my feet and sprang.

Nola was just turning from the refrigerator to the sink with a foil-covered casserole dish. When she saw me, she screamed and dropped it.

I pulled up short, backpedaling and skidding, my feet threatening to slide out from under me. The dish hit the floor and smashed, sending shards of white ceramic and scraps of moldy noodles scattering across the kitchen floor.

"Nola!" I said.

She stared back at me, breathing deeply and shaking.

I put down the poker and went to her. "Jesus, are you okay?" I put an arm around her shoulder, guiding her past the wreckage of the casserole and into the dining room. "Sorry about that," I said softly.

She looked over at me, still dazed, but she smiled and let out a little laugh.

"I didn't expect to see you," I said. "What are you doing here?"

"I hadn't seen you since the funeral. I came to see how you were doing. You weren't here, so I came in to wait. I was looking for a beer, but when I opened the fridge . . . All the mold . . . it's disgusting."

"Yeah, I know. I—"

She patted my cheek. "It's okay, I'm just saying. So I started cleaning it out."

I looked over her shoulder. The kitchen trash can was pulled over in front of the fridge. On the counter was a lineup of moldy, expired, and dried-out foods.

"Thanks."

She smiled.

"It's nice to see you," I told her.

"It's nice to see you, too." Her eyes stayed on me a second longer, then she looked me up and down. "You look terrible."

I smiled, about to tell her why, but when I remembered why, I stopped smiling. "You have to leave."

"I . . . What?"

"You have to go."

She laughed and stepped up very close, hooking her fingers into the pockets of my jeans. "Actually," she whispered, coming up close to my ear. "I was thinking I might just stay right here."

"Oh." My resolve softened in inverse proportion to something else.

She lingered next to my ear, breathing on it, putting her teeth on my earlobe. I started to wrap my arms around her, but then I took a step back, shaking my head.

"No," I said, more emphatically than I felt. "I would definitely like you to stay, but you can't. You need to get out of town."

"What? What are you talking about? Why?"

Before she could imagine any other reasons why I wouldn't want her there, I told her a heavily edited version of my excursion onto her neighbor's land. I mentioned the guns but left out the shooting. I wanted her to take things seriously, but I didn't want her scared witless.

"So, you were inside that tent?"

"Yeah, but that's not the—"

"What was in there?"

"Some plants, I guess. I don't know. It was dark, and there were guys with guns chasing me. But the point is, you need to leave town."

"Why do *I* need to leave town?"

"Nola, something very fishy is going on at that place, and there's a lot of men and a lot of guns. Someone just burnt down your crops."

"Yeah, I know, and it sucks. But what makes you think that has anything to do with what happened tonight?"

"I don't know, but if the people who torched your farm are armed like the guys I saw, and they're right next door, this place is too dangerous for you to be around."

"Well, wait a second. Guns are pretty common out here—"

"Not the type of guns I saw—"

"And you were trespassing, right? They've got signs all over that fence."

"Nola, they're driving up and down our street with automatic weapons."

"Then we need to tell Chief Pruitt."

I snorted. "Nola, you heard him—he's got more important things to do than investigate burnt weeds." I could feel my annoyance rising, and I swallowed against it, trying to keep it off my face. "Look, you're in danger, and Pruitt doesn't care. Just go somewhere safe tonight, and tomorrow I'll know what's going on."

She gave me that dubious look again, but then she looked down, like something had caught her eye. Her eyebrows furrowed. She reached over and pulled the tail of my shirt out to the side.

Looking down, I saw what had gotten her attention: a pair of holes, a few inches apart, one on either side of the seam.

"Are those bullet holes?" she asked in a breathy whisper.

I lifted the fabric to get a better look. "Yeah, I guess they are." I hadn't realized it had been that close.

"You didn't tell me they shot at you." Her eyes were changing as I looked in them, the toughness undermined by the slightest quiver of fear.

"They shot at me."

She looked back up at me, now very serious. "It was close."

"That's why we have to get you out of here. Someplace safe. There's plenty of hotels not too far from here."

"Hotels aren't so safe for me," she said quietly.

"What? What do you mean?"

"They're not safe. They're full of chemicals." Her voice was getting louder, her tone almost shrill. "The cleaners and disinfectants and air fresheners. They need carts to move it all from room to room, for God's sake. Not to mention the exterminators, since bed bugs made a comeback. Doyle, I can't just go to a hotel like most people. I'm not like most people." Her eyes were shiny with tears, but she took a deep breath and let it out slowly. "Look, I wish I didn't have to deal with this, but I do. I don't want to see what a third episode does to me, does to my life."

She paused again, but I could tell she wasn't done. "Cheryl had a third episode," she said, almost whispering. "Now she has to live off on her own, in the woods. She can't go to movies or restaurants. Right now, she's driving to Michigan because she can't get on a plane. I don't want to be like that."

Her frustration was so raw I could feel it. But I had to push her to go. "Isn't there anywhere safe you could stay?" I asked softly. I thought about Simpkins, but I wasn't about to share that thought.

She started to shake her head, but I could see a thought strike her, a thought she didn't want to share.

"What?"

She looked into my eyes for a moment, considering it all. "Well . . . maybe Cheryl's house. She's away, and it's clean, and I have a key. I guess I could stay there."

"Where is it?"

"Not too far. Shachterville. A few miles."

"Good. When can you be ready to go?"

"I don't know. First thing in the morning, I guess."

I shook my head. "Tonight."

She nodded reluctantly. Then she slipped her finger through one of the holes in my shirt, touching the skin that would have been punctured if the bullet had been a few inches over. "What about you? Dangerous doesn't affect you?"

"Not the same way, no."

She cocked the eyebrow again.

I took a deep breath. "Look, I've got a gun and about fifteen years handling it. I'll be keeping it very close."

"And what about tomorrow night? What are you going to do then?"

I laughed awkwardly. "I'll have to get back to you on that."

*   *   *

I waited in Nola's living room while she went upstairs and packed a bag. She was trying to keep her tone light and so was I, but her eyes were jittery and nervous.

Thirty minutes after I had surprised her in my kitchen, Nola was in her car, headed out of town. As I drove behind her to make sure she wasn't being followed, I called Moose. He hadn't heard from Squirrel, and he sounded distraught. When he asked me what I was up to, I told him it was a long story. But I told him to stay at Squirrel's for the night, even if Squirrel came home.

He asked why, but when I blew off the question, he seemed relieved. I don't think he wanted anything else on his mind.

I followed Nola onto Route 78, and as we had agreed, she pulled onto the shoulder a hundred yards down the road. I pulled in behind her, watching the on-ramp in my rearview to see if anyone came up behind us. After five minutes, no one did. I flashed my headlights, and we both continued on.

Ten minutes later, we turned off and I followed her for a couple of lefts and a right, making mental notes so I could find my way back. We ended up in a wooded area, in front of a small bungalow with lots of big windows and a narrow uncovered porch. I had been expecting some sort of futuristic bubble house, but then I remembered it wasn't germs that were the problem, it was chemicals.

Nola got out of her car with a large clump of keys in her hand and opened the door. I started to go in first, but she put out a hand to stop me.

"Shoes," she whispered, pointing at my feet.

With a sigh, I took off my shoes, then went in first and had a quick look around. The place was tiny, and the furniture was simple and a bit old-fashioned, but it seemed comfortable enough and there were no hidden goons.

I got the number for the house phone, then warned Nola not to use it, in case it was traced. I also told her to keep her cell phone on and charged. She replied with a tense nod. I also told her not to answer the door for anyone but me. "I'll knock four times," I told her. "Two, and then two more."

I was now deep into cop mode, but as I was leaving, she gave me a kiss, and that stopped me. I went in for another one, a longer one. She put her hand on the back of my neck, and I put mine on the small of her back, then a little lower. For a moment, I thought about staying. To protect her.

When she pulled back, she looked me in the eye. "I worry about you playing cops and robbers—"

"Hold on, I *am* a cop."

"Oh, excuse me," she said sarcastically. "I worry about you playing 'not-suspended cop in his own jurisdiction.'"

Before I could respond with a childish retort, Nola touched my cheek and looked into my eyes. "I mean it. You be careful, Doyle." Then she stepped way from me and smiled sadly. "Now you'd better get going."

As I drove home, I tried to think, tried to make sense of everything that was going on, but all I could think about was turning the car around and going back to be with Nola.

When I got home, I locked the doors and turned off the lights, moving a chair so I could face the front door but still feel the breeze from the kitchen window. Then I sat and I thought some more. With a gun on my lap.

42

I woke up in darkness to the sound of windows rattling and the roar of an engine. I'm not ashamed to admit my first reaction was to jump out of my chair and hide behind it. After a few seconds, the windows stopped rattling and the roar receded, but it didn't go away.

As I got up from behind the chair, the noise began to grow again. I tucked my gun into my holster and headed for the door. I could feel the adrenaline coursing through my system, the sweat seeping out of me, my pulse racing, tingling in my eyes.

At first, I couldn't see the source of the sound, just a thick fog rolling in. With the outdoor lights on, Nola's house was a smudge of light across the street. The scene was surreal, and for a moment, I wondered if I was dreaming. But before my pulse could slow, the noise started growing again, throatier now, seemingly coming from everywhere at once.

I ran to the driveway, then down to the street. My eyes watered in the fog, and my mouth tasted chalky. The roar grew louder, the sound of windows rattling underneath it.

Then I saw a pair of lights, like headlights, but low in the sky. They swooped down lower, and the space between them widened. As they passed directly over me, the roar resolved itself into the sound of an engine up close. I caught a glimpse of a small plane, red with a black-and-white stripe. Then all that was left of it was a blinking red light and a thicker blanket of fog settling down over me, over the street.

In the scant light from Nola's house, I saw a curtain of slightly darker gray dropping down through the gloom, onto Nola's vegetable patch, and I wondered what terrible chemical they were dropping onto it, onto me.

I fired once into the sky, a warning shot, but I could barely hear it with all the noise. I ran down the street, futilely chasing the lights as they pulled up into the sky and the sound faded once again.

Now that I had identified the sound, I could place it as well. Even though I had lost sight of the plane's lights, I could hear it banking around for another pass. I turned and ran back up the road, then stopped, legs braced wide, gun pointed into the sky.

As the engine sound grew louder once more, the lights reappeared, this time right in front of me. I fired another warning shot. Then, as the headlights came at me, I fired again, right between them. The lights tilted crazily, then wobbled back and forth before they pulled away, engine screaming, and disappeared into the night.

The sound seemed to be still fading away when the lights came back behind me, approaching even lower. I whirled and pointed my gun, ready to shoot. But this time it wasn't the plane, it was a station wagon, and it swerved wildly to avoid me. Two of its wheels left the ground. Then it dropped heavily back onto the road, shimmying as it sped off into the dissipating mist, the taillights receding into the darkness.

And then it was quiet. Already, the lights from Nola's house appeared brighter. A light breeze picked up, and swirls of clear air cut through the fog.

By the time I had walked back to the foot of my driveway, the breeze had swept away whatever it was and the air was clear. If not for the chalky taste in my mouth and the gritty feeling in my eyes, I might have thought it had never happened.

But it had. The sweat was drying on my skin, and maybe that's what was making me itch, but I'd been sprayed with something, and I needed to get it off of me. I ran into the kitchen to rinse my face in the sink. The counter was covered with moldy bread and leftovers and wilted vegetables and the floor was littered with shards of the casserole dish and bits of the moldy noodles it had contained. I shoved them out of the way and turned the faucet on full, rinsing my hands and splashing my face.

I went upstairs and took off my boots and socks, resisting the urge to scratch my burning toes. When the shower was scalding and the bathroom was filled with steam, I got in and started scrubbing.

43

By the time the hot water faltered, my skin was pink and raw, and I was pretty sure whatever might have been on me was gone. The scalding water had felt pretty good, and I was thinking that my bed was going to feel even better. But as I turned the water off, I heard banging on my front door and felt a jolt of alarm. Maybe it was one of the gunmen from across the street, or some friend of the Red Baron come to follow up the air assault with infantry. But the knock had a tone and a rhythm that I knew well, because I'd used it often.

I pulled on clean underwear and a fresh pair of jeans and grabbed a T-shirt on my way downstairs.

The pounding at the door started up again as I reached it. I paused at the peephole, taking a moment to savor the sight of Chief Pruitt standing out there with his face red and his jaw clenched. Then I opened the door.

"Jesus Christ!" Pruitt sputtered. "What are you, going to leave me out here all goddamned morning?"

"I was in the shower, actually. Can I help you?"

"You help me? Frankly, I doubt it. Can I come in?"

I stepped out onto the porch and pulled the door closed behind me. The wood floor felt nice and cool under my bare feet. "What do you want?"

"Got a complaint about some crazy bastard standing in the middle of the road shooting a gun in the air. Right outside your house. Know anything about that?"

I thought about saying, "Yeah? Well I'd like to file a complaint about my crazy neighbors trying to kill me." But I didn't know how much I trusted Pruitt, and I didn't want to cop to trespass just then, either. I stayed quiet for a moment, thinking about how to play it. The sky was just starting to lighten in the east, and it seemed like a long time since I'd had a normal night's sleep.

Pruitt laughed. "Yeah, I thought it sounded like you. It was the McCutcheons that saw you. Good people, live in town. They said they could come by for a visual identification, but I told them I was pretty sure I knew who it was. Didn't want to trouble them any more than necessary." One of his hands was idly playing with a pair of handcuffs. "Mind telling me what that all was about?"

If he was in on it, he'd already know about the crop duster. But even if I wasn't getting that dirty-cop vibe off of him, I wasn't about to trust him with much.

"I was attacked by an airplane."

"By an airplane?"

"Yes, an airplane. One of the ones that sprays stuff. A sprayer."

"A crop duster?"

"Yes, that's right."

"They don't usually fly at night, I don't imagine."

"I don't imagine they usually dive-bomb people either, but there you have it."

"So what," he said with a snicker, "you think the terrorists are attacking the Borough of Dunston?"

He stared at me for a moment. Then he let go of the handcuffs and took out a pad. "Okay, what did it look like?"

"What's that?"

"The airplane, dumbass!"

"Red, I think."

"You think?"

"Sorry, it was dark out. It was red, and it had a black-and-white stripe on the side."

He dutifully wrote that down then looked up at me dubiously. "And the plane attacked you?"

"Yes, that's right."

"And what was that, like with machine guns or with Martian brain waves or something?" He wiggled his fingers as he said the last part, then bit his lip like it was a struggle not to laugh.

"No, actually, it was spraying, probably some kind of chemical. I woke up because the windows were rattling. I ran outside and the damn thing was practically flying down the middle of the road."

"So what did you do?"

I thought for a second about what I was going to tell him. From my own experience, when you catch someone in a little lie, it's usually because they're covering up something bigger.

"I fired a warning shot."

"You shot at the plane?"

"No, I fired a warning shot."

"So all you know, this could have been some mosquito prevention program, and you just start discharging your weapon all over the place?"

The way he said it, it did sound pretty bad. I could see the ominous clouds of a shit storm on the horizon if this ever got back to my lieutenant. "It was a warning shot. I fired into the air away from the plane."

"Well, I think you're full of shit."

I didn't say anything to that.

He stared at me for a second, like he was trying to decide what to do next.

"All right," he said finally. "Go put some shoes on and get in the car."

"That's bullshit. You can't arrest me just because some townie says they saw someone with a gun."

"You're not under arrest, asshole. At least not yet. Charlie Brand's the only pilot in the county who's got a crop duster. You and me are going to pay him a visit."

44

By the time I came back outside with my shoes on, the sun was coming up. It looked like a nice day, and the incident with the crop duster seemed even more unreal, like something from a dream. I felt giddy from lack of sleep, and I knew at some point I was going to crash.

I got in the front passenger seat, and Pruitt grunted, like maybe that wasn't the seating arrangement he had in mind, but he didn't make me get in back.

As we drove off, he made a couple of very official-sounding radio calls, and it occurred to me that he was trying to impress me.

"How far's this place?" I asked, biting back a yawn.

"Not too far," he replied without looking at me.

I closed my eyes and leaned my head against the window.

He turned on the radio, and we caught a few bars of Steely Dan. Not my favorite, but pretty good. He must have sensed my approval, because he switched it over to a country western station. When I looked over at him, he seemed pretty happy with himself.

I closed my eyes again, serenaded by some cowboy. When I opened them, we were turning into a driveway next to a sign that said "Brand Agricultural Aviation Services." It sounded like the same guy was singing, but a half hour had gone by.

Fifty feet up the driveway was a nice looking Cape Cod with a wide porch in front that wrapped around the right-hand side, a small strip of garden wrapping along with it. The driveway wound around to the left, leading past a wooden two-car garage and onto a wide, corrugated metal shed in the middle of a large field.

A sign next to the driveway said OFFICE, and pointed to the shed in the back.

Pruitt drove straight back and parked in front of the shed.

"Come on," he said as he killed the engine and got out.

I got out, too, rubbing my face and blinking. I wasn't sure what to expect, but I suspected Pruitt probably was—otherwise he wouldn't have brought me with him.

By the time I caught up with him, he was already tapping on the unpainted aluminum screen door set in the side of the shed. He stepped back, hands on his hips, rocking back and forth on the balls of his feet, as if he was hoping someone would answer the door before I caught up with him.

It was a tie.

The woman who answered the door wore pink lipstick and had curly blond hair, bleached and going gray. She opened the door with a big, customer-service smile, but when she saw Pruitt's uniform and the cruiser parked in the driveway behind us, her expression reflected the fact that it wasn't quite seven o'clock. Her eyes lingered on me, probably wondering if I was responsible, then she looked back at Pruitt.

"Kinda early. Can I help you?"

Pruitt widened his stance. "Is Charlie here?"

She shook her head. "Nope. You need some spraying?"

"No, ma'am," he replied. "I just need to ask Charlie some questions."

She took a drag of a previously hidden cigarette and shook her head. "He's down in Carolina."

"He been down there long?"

"About a week, I guess."

"You expect him back anytime soon?"

She shook her head again. "Maybe not till next week, but I'm not sure. Why? What's this about?"

"Nothing you need to worry about. You do all the spraying around here?"

"We better. Hardly enough of it to go around. I'd hate to think folks was bringing someone in from outside."

"Who's your closest competition?"

"Oh, I don't know. Probably Fred Tate up in Luzerne or Joey Colino in Mifflin. But they're both a hundred miles away. That's a lot of fuel. Even if they was cheaper, I can't imagine they're that much cheaper."

Pruitt glanced at me out of the corner of his eye. "Well, thanks for your time, ma'am."

She seemed relieved it was over. "Always glad to help, officer."

"Actually, I have a question," I said. "How long would it take Mr. Brand to fly back here from where he is?"

She looked at Pruitt before answering, and I got the distinct impression she was checking with him for permission to ignore me. When he didn't give it, she shrugged. "I reckon three hours. But he'd be driving, and that would take longer."

"Why would he be driving?" I asked.

"Because he don't got the plane. It's parked in the shed."

I sighed, but Pruitt silenced me with his hand.

"You mind if we take a look at that plane?" Pruitt asked with a smile.

"You got a warrant?"

Pruitt's smile got smarmy and big. "You telling me I need one?"

"No need to be like that. Go on back, if you want," she said, hooking a thumb toward the garage door around the corner of the building. "Look all you like, but don't touch anything. Charlie'll know it if you do."

Pruitt cocked an eyebrow, giving her a look like he appreciated the permission but not necessarily the attitude. He turned and started walking around to the garage door. I followed him.

There was a pair of large, swinging hangar doors, a window in each of them. Pruitt checked the door, but it was locked, so we both converged on the same window.

Inside was a single-wing, single-engine plane, bright yellow, with no stripe.

Pruitt looked over at me, but I kept my eyes front, because I didn't want to deal with him. I was still staring at the plane when the radio crackled and the dispatcher paged him.

Pruitt walked away without a word. I turned to watch him and saw that the woman had followed us up the driveway, keeping an eye on us. I walked over and gave her my card, asked her to have Brand give me a call. She looked at the card, then studied me for a second before turning away without a word and walking back down the driveway.

When Pruitt came back, his shades were in his hand, his eyes were red and wet, and his face was ashy and gray. He seemed ten years older. "Come on. We're going back."

"Everything okay?" I asked.

"Friend of mine's kid died."

"Jesus. I'm sorry to hear it."

"Just get in the goddamn car."

45

We drove back in a stony silence until we pulled up next to my driveway and Pruitt turned to look at me, chewing the inside of his bottom lip. "Look here, Carrick, I brought you out there out of professional courtesy, understand? 'Cause you did okay on that bust. But I've had enough of you for a while. I'm going to leave this alone because I have other things to do, but I want you to lock up your weapon somewhere safe and keep it there. And then I want you to stay off my radar, you hear? I know you're in the shit back in Philly. You cause me any more work, I'll make sure they hear about it, okay?"

I nodded.

"Okay, now get out, and let's you and me not run into each other for a while."

As I got out of the car, I said, "Sorry about your friend," but he sped off without looking at me.

Little more than an hour had passed since Pruitt came knocking on my door, but it seemed like a lot longer. The thought of sleep entered my mind as I walked through the front door, but then I saw the mess in the kitchen, the rotting food Nola had left on the counter, the bits of casserole dish scattered across the floor. As sleep seemed less and less likely, I felt more and more tired.

I took a broom from the closet and swept the shards of Corningware into a pile in the corner then grabbed a trash bag from under the sink and started with what was on the counter. It didn't seem as bad as it had the night before. I could picture the bread and the strawberries covered with mold, but now they both just looked kind of wilted. The mushrooms were a mess, reduced to a brown slime, but the rest of it didn't look so bad at all. I puzzled over it for half a second, then dumped it all into the trash.

Grabbing a yogurt from the fridge, I checked the date, then gave it a brisk shake and opened it up. For a brief moment, I stood there drinking my yogurt and wondering which domestic chore should come next, or if I should take another stab at sleeping.

Then I noticed a thin film of white powder on either side of the kitchen windowsill, and I remembered there were more pressing things to consider. Like what the hell was going on in this crazy-assed town, what kind of death from above was being sprayed in the middle of the night. Like why Nola's neighbors tried to kill me instead of saying, "Hey, you going to pay for that apple?" Or where Squirrel was. Or whether any of it had anything to do with Roberts and Arnett, or if it was some bored paranoid fantasy and that was just how things worked out here.

A light breeze came in through the opened window, and I closed it so as not to disturb whatever was on the windowsill. Using a spatula, I scraped the powder into a Ziploc bag and taped it closed. As I was washing my hands and the spatula, the phone rang, a blocked number, and I kept right on washing, making sure I did a thorough job before I answered the phone.

"Doyle?" said a voice that sounded like the woman at the crop-dusting place but with twice the nicotine habit.

"Nola? Is that you?"

She coughed into the phone. "Yeah, more or less," she croaked. "I want to come home."

"You sound terrible."

"Thanks. I feel pretty lousy."

"But you're okay, right?"

"If you mean are any bad guys messing with me, I'm okay. Other than that, I feel like poop." She coughed again. I thought about all the coughing during the funeral, Pruitt's sick cops. "How are you doing?"

"Me? Um . . . I don't know. Okay, I guess. We had a bit of an incident last night."

"What kind of incident?"

It wasn't until that moment that it really sank in, the implications for Nola's farm of what had happened the night before.

"I'm not sure, really. Last night, late, a crop duster dive-bombed our houses."

"A plane?"

"Yes. A crop duster. One of the ones that sprays crops and stuff." If someone knew how devastating this could be for her, for her farm and her organic certification, it could be an easy way to get her to sell.

"A crop duster." She paused to cough. "Did it . . . spray anything?"

"Yeah, it did."

There was a long silence on the other end. "On my crops? On my house?"

If someone knew she had chemical sensitivity, it could be attempted murder. "Yeah, both."

Through the silence I could hear her breath becoming wet and thick.

"So, what does that mean?" I asked.

"I don't know," she said, practically a sob. Then she inhaled deeply. "It means I want to come home and I can't."

When I got off the phone with Nola, I called Stan Bowers.

"What's up, Doyle?" he answered.

"I need a favor."

"A favor, huh?"

"I need you to get me some lab work."

He laughed. "Don't you have friends who can do that for you?"

"Just Danny, and if our lieutenant finds out Danny's doing that for me, he's toast. C'mon, who just got you your biggest bust of the year? Fifty keys of H has got to be worth a little lab work."

He sighed. "What've you got?"

I told him about the incident with the crop duster.

"Jesus," he laughed. "You can't even take a couple of weeks in the country without some kind of shit storm finding you."

"Yeah, it's hilarious. Anyway, whatever the guy was spraying, it settled onto my windowsill, some kind of white powder. I figured, if anybody can get away with sending an unidentified white powder in for analysis, it's my best buddy at DEA, right?"

"White powder, huh?" He suddenly sounded serious. "You think it might be anthrax or something? I'm at a breakfast meeting with Homeland Security, should we get them involved?"

"I don't know, Stan. They spray shit all the time out here. Could be pixie dust for all I know, but I'd really like to find out."

"Yeah, all right. They're a bunch of assholes anyway. You got no idea what it is?"

I didn't want to give him any excuse to back out, so I left out the part about the neighbors trying to shoot me. "I don't know. There's a woman next door, has a small organic farm. There's been some pressure on her to sell her land. Could be an herbicide or pesticide, something to kill her crops or contaminate them so she can't sell them as organic."

"That's pretty obscure."

"Maybe, but someone already torched some of her crops with gasoline. I don't know, I'm just guessing. She's also sensitive to chemicals, like allergic. They could be trying to hurt her that way, or make the place uninhabitable."

"All right, I got you. I can put it in, but my guys are pretty busy. Could take a little while."

"Even if they know it's for you?"

"Jesus, Doyle. You're pushing it, you know that?"

"But you love me anyway, right?"

"Yeah, but only as a friend."

46

I had arranged to meet Stan at a Dunkin' Donuts in a town called Hamburg, about ten miles away. I'm not a huge fan of Dunkin' Donuts coffee, but with a shot of espresso and a doughnut on the side, it ain't bad. I was finishing my second coffee when Stan came in. He had a suit and a briefcase and an adhesive "Hello, My Name Is" tag, with "Stan" written across it in big, blocky letters.

He ordered a large coffee and brought it over to the table.

"Hope you're not working undercover, *Stan*," I said, making it obvious that I was reading his tag.

He looked down and peeled it off, then folded it up and threw it at me. "Asshole. You've worked cases with Homeland Security, right?"

"Couple times."

"You know a guy there named Craig Sorenson?"

"No."

"You're lucky. Guy's a complete tool." He paused, studying my face for a moment. "Jesus, look at you. You look like *you're* under-cover. I've seen meth addicts with more color in their cheeks."

"Thanks. I've been working on it."

"Apparently. Being attacked by airplanes, huh? That's impressive, even for you. Who'd you piss off this time, the Air Force?"

"That would explain it."

"So why don't you take it up with local law enforcement? I mean, apart from the obvious."

I shrugged.

"You think they'll fuck it up?"

I shrugged again.

"By accident or on purpose?"

One more shrug.

He shook his head. "Right. I don't want to hear about any of that. Munschak's dad is chief in some bumblefuck town near Scranton. Thinks these salt-of-the-earth types can do no wrong." He took the lid off his coffee and slurped it, then put the lid back on. "So what've you got?"

I slid the envelope across the table.

"It's sealed?" he asked before touching it.

I gave him a look to remind him I wasn't an idiot, but I nodded.

He shrugged a mild apology as he palmed it and put it in his briefcase. "Like you haven't done some dumb shit lately."

"Point taken."

"I'll get it back to you as soon as I can."

"Thanks, Stan."

He picked up his briefcase and stood, looking down at me. "Try to stay out of trouble, okay, Carrick? Doesn't look like suspension is agreeing with you."

* * *

When Stan left, I ordered another coffee, to go. I didn't know how long it was going to take to get the results back on the white powder, and I didn't know what my next step should be. At some point, I needed to get some sleep, but I had too many unanswered questions to sleep well. For the moment, caffeine would have to do.

When I took out my wallet to pay for the coffee, though, I found the slip of paper with the information I had written from public records: Redtail Holding Company, Reading, PA, Jordan Rothe, CEO. I called the number and asked if Mr. Rothe was there. The receptionist said yes, but that he was in a lunch meeting.

"When do you expect him to be finished?"

"At least an hour, maybe a little longer. Can I ask who's calling?"

"Thanks. I'll try again later."

Redtail Holding Company occupied the tenth floor of an eleven-story brick building in the center of Reading. There was a historical plaque out front, but I didn't read it. The lobby was funky, like it had been restored on the cheap. Or maybe it had never been all that nice to begin with.

I got off the elevator on the tenth floor and was greeted by a small woman in her late sixties sitting at a reception desk. She had a sweet face and smart-looking eyes. She reminded me a bit of my mother. Behind her was a wall of pale blue glass, and behind the glass was a seating area with four low angular armchairs and a massive glass coffee table.

"Can I help you?" she asked, friendly but efficient.

"Yes, I'm here to see Mr. Rothe."

"But you don't have an appointment."

"No, I don't."

She smiled. "You're the gentleman who called earlier."

"Yes, I am."

"Well, your luck is good, but I don't know about your judgment. Mr. Rothe just had several meetings cancelled, but I doubt he'll see you without an appointment. What is your name?"

"Doyle Carrick."

"Can I ask the purpose of your visit?"

"Some real estate over in Dunston recently came into my possession, and I understand he has an interest in that area."

She eyed me for a second, then picked up the phone on her desk and spoke quietly into it. When she put the phone down, her face conveyed nothing.

"You can have a seat, Mr. Carrick."

The chairs were more comfortable than they looked. After fifteen minutes I was starting to wonder if she had parked me there so Rothe could leave through the back door, but at that moment he appeared down a hallway and strode across the waiting room with his hand extended. He had a friendly face, with the more-than-skin-deep polish of someone who has been in sales from an early age.

"How do you do, Mr. Carrick?" he said.

He gave my hand a hearty shake, and I returned it. "Thanks for seeing me," I said.

"Come on back to my office," he said, turning. "I only have a minute. But tell me what I can do for you."

"I understand you're planning a development in Dunston?"

"Yes, that's right. The Village at Mountainside Meadows. But it's more than a plan at this point. We're breaking ground in a few weeks."

"Really?"

He stopped for a moment and looked back at me. "You sound surprised."

Then he was walking again, cutting a sharp left into a spacious office with a large desk. In the middle of the room were four tables with white, three-dimensional models of houses. The walls of the office were covered with aerial photographs of existing residential developments. Rothe didn't break stride as he went behind his desk.

I stopped in the middle of the room. "I didn't realize you had already acquired all the property you needed for that project."

"Not officially. A lot of it is still under agreement. But we'll be closed on it all by the end of the day."

"Today?"

He nodded, a little smug.

"All of it?"

"All of it we need."

"What does that mean?"

"Why are you here again, Mr. Carrick?"

"Actually, it's Detective Carrick." I paused to let that sink in, but not long enough for him to ask to see my badge, or where I worked, or if I was suspended or anything. "A friend of mine has been pressured to sell her property. She's being harassed and her property vandalized. I'm going to make sure it stops."

A few cracks formed in the salesman's smile. "Ms. Watkins."

"How did you know?"

"Everyone else sold. So, you're not really interested in selling a property in Dunston."

"I might be."

"Where is it?"

"North of Bayberry. Just east of the Watkins property."

He shook his head. "Not interested. Sorry, but it's not contiguous. Although I think you already knew that."

"That's too bad. Now, I want you to make sure these bad things stop happening to Ms. Watkins. Now. Before bad things start happening to other people."

He smiled patronizingly. "*Detective* Carrick," he said with emphasis, "we are a respectable development company. We do not engage in those types of activities. We made an offer, Ms. Watkins refused, that's that. I mean, we never made it a secret to the other townsfolk that holdouts could jeopardize the deal," he said with a shrug. "But we've long since moved past that."

"What do you mean?"

He smiled. "We game-planned around it, used it as a selling point. We figured it actually made sense to keep more of the farms. It adds to the scenic charm. Frankly, if she changed her mind at this point, I'd probably say no, because it would cost too much to change the plans."

"And you already control all the land?"

He nodded. "We either own it or we have it under agreement. We'll own it all by the end of the day. Next month, we'll start digging, have people moving in before you know it. Shame you didn't come to me earlier. Don't worry, though." He actually winked. "Once the development is finished, your property value will probably double." He looked at his watch. "Now, if you'll excuse me, Mr. Carrick, I have to get to a closing over in Fleetwood."

"Thanks," I said, a little stunned that no one wanted Nola's property after all.

Rothe grabbed his jacket from the back of his chair and pulled it on. When his right hand emerged from the sleeve, it was holding a business card, which he extended in my direction.

"If you're thinking of trading up into some new construction, though, call me and I'll make sure you get a great deal at Mountainside Meadows."

I took the card and by the time it was in my pocket, Rothe was standing next to the door, waiting for me to precede him out.

He closed the door behind me and then passed me down the hall. "Okay, Sara, I'm off to Fleetwood," he said, striding past the receptionist.

She gave me a nice smile as I walked out after him.

"Okay, Sara," I said, smiling back. "I'm off to Dunston."

Between the shock that Redtail wasn't interested in Nola's property and the abruptness of Rothe's departure, I was halfway home before it occurred to me how strange it was that Rothe expected to get all those real-estate deals done in one day. Even with the parcels consolidated, it was still a dozen sellers. I called to ask him about that, but was sent straight to voice mail. I left a message asking him to call me, and before I could put my phone away, another call came in. It was Moose.

"Doyle?" His voice sounded small and afraid, breaking a bit like he was about to cry. I could hear a lot of noise and commotion in the background.

"Moose? What's going on? Are you okay?"

"I don't know. I'm at Squirrel's place. In the bathroom. The police just showed up."

"What's going on?"

"It's Squirrel." He let out a sob. "They're saying he's dead, and now they're asking me all these questions."

"He's dead? What happened?"

"I don't know. But I'm scared."

"Okay, sit tight. I'll be right there."

47

When I got to Squirrel's house, Moose was sitting on the curb out front. His face was pale and wet. Two patrol cars were parked outside, and two uniforms stood by the front steps, looking worse than Moose. I wondered if these were the two "sissies" who had called in sick, Mitchell and Tomkpins, if Pruitt had dragged them in anyway.

Moose stood up unsteadily when he saw me, wiping his nose and making a visible effort to get himself together.

"So what's going on?" I asked.

"I don't know. I drove around the usual places a few times, then came back here to see if Squirrel was going to show up." He was obviously distraught, but I couldn't tell if that was all. "Then that asshole Pruitt shows up, getting in my face and asking me all these questions. I didn't know what was going on. Then . . . then he says Squirrel is dead. And he starts asking me what I had to do with it."

"How did Squirrel die?"

"I don't even know. They won't tell me."

"Okay, where's Pruitt? Is he inside?"

He nodded.

"Wait here."

The two uniforms by the front door were barely old enough to drive. They both looked pale and sweaty. Their badges said Deeley and Ford, and I couldn't help wondering, if these guys were dragging their butts to work like that, what kind of shape were those sissies Mitchell and Tompkins in. I nodded and walked past them before they could say anything, keeping my distance so as not to breathe in any of whatever they had.

Pruitt was sitting at the kitchen table, his face drawn and his jowls hanging low. His shades were in his shirt pocket. He looked up when I walked in.

"Aw, Jesus Christ, Carrick. What the hell are you doing here?"

"Moose called me."

"Well, get out of here and take that little scumbag with you."

"What happened?"

He stood up and came toward me. "I don't know. Maybe you should ask that little maggot out on the curb." His voice was loud and sounded like it was getting away from him. "I don't know what those two have been getting up to, but we found Squirrel under the Stony Creek railroad bridge. Looks like he was walking across and he slipped, but he's got a fresh needle mark in his arm and puke on his shirt, and I don't think that helped his footing any. So you tell that blubbering piece of shit out there he can either tell us what he knows, like where Squirrel got the stuff, or just get the hell out of here. And he better watch his goddamn step or I'll lock his ass up, I mean it. Squirrel was a good kid before he started hanging around with that guy, messing around with all this shit. And if Moose had anything to do with it, I'm going to nail him for it."

From the look in Pruitt's eye and the way his lips were quivering, I could tell he was in a dangerous place. It didn't seem like it would take much for him to snap, screw up both our lives for a long time.

I didn't say a word, just turned and left. Outside, I paused a moment to collect myself, then trotted down the steps as if everything was cool.

The two uniforms waiting outside looked up at me, and I gave them the same nod as when I went in. "Where'd they take the body?"

The guy on the left looked at me suspiciously.

The guy on the right said, "St. Mark's."

I said, "Thanks," and kept walking.

Moose was sitting on the curb again. He stood up when he saw me.

I walked right up to his face and whispered, "Are you stoned?"

"No!" he replied indignantly, shaking his head.

Up close, I could smell the apple hooch on his breath.

"Are you drunk?"

"No," he said, not quite as indignant. "I had a couple of drinks while I was waiting for Squirrel, but—"

"Are you okay to drive?"

He nodded.

"Then go home. I'll follow you."

48

I regretted it as soon as I said it. Maybe it was the drinks, maybe it was the grief, maybe it was just Moose being Moose, but I had suspected he would drive like an old lady, and I was right. It seemed like there was an invisible school bus in front of him; he never got above twenty miles an hour, and still he kept tapping his brakes. If I hadn't known better, I would have thought he was deliberately messing with me.

I used the down time to check in with Nola.

"Hi," she said. Her voice sounded feeble and weak.

"You sound even worse."

"I feel even worse. Is there any word on what they sprayed on my land?"

"Not yet. Did you ever hear back from Rupp about the corn?"

"No. I don't think he's taking it seriously, not that it really matters now."

"I'm afraid I have some bad news . . . Squirrel is dead."

"*What?*" her voice disappeared briefly into a higher pitch than her throat could handle. "What happened?"

"I don't know all the details yet, but it looks like an accident. They think he was stoned at the time."

"Poor Squirrel."

"Yeah. Moose is pretty broken up about it."

"I'll bet . . . Jesus." As she said it, she started coughing, a dry, raspy cough that sounded like it hurt.

"That really doesn't sound good," I said. "Maybe you should see a doctor."

"I called my doctor."

"You did?"

"He said there was something going around."

"I heard," I said. "Some kind of flu."

She let out a small raspy laugh. "This isn't the flu."

"Well, there's definitely something going around. Half the people at the funeral were coughing and Pruitt's down to conscripting twelve year olds. . . ."

"*It's not the flu*," she snapped.

She said it with such authority, such finality, that it made me pause. And it made me realize that I kind of knew she was right. I kept wanting to blame the crop duster, only she hadn't been around for that; I had, and I wasn't the sick one.

"What do you think it is?"

She paused. "I don't know."

"Could it be the chemical thing? The MCS?"

"I hope not," she said, quiet and scared, like she thought it was.

"Is this how it starts?"

She let out a sigh that trailed off into a crackly wheeze. "I don't know, Doyle. It can be different every time. I tried to call Cheryl, to see how it started for her the third time. But I couldn't get through."

We were quiet for a moment. I didn't know what to say. "Can I get you anything?"

"You can find out what they were spraying."

Nola didn't seem the type to scare easily, and the fact that she was scared filled me with dread. Made me think maybe I should be scared, too. I followed Moose up the driveway and parked next to him, waiting while he slowly got out of the truck.

As soon as we got inside, he slumped into an armchair.

I sat in the chair across from him. "So what the hell is going on?"

"Squirrel is dead." His lip started quivering, and his eyes welled up.

"Yeah, I know that, but before I lose you, you need to tell me what you know about it. What was he mixed up in?"

"What do you mean?"

"You know what I mean. What were you two up to?"

He bit his lip. "Before I tell you this, I want you to know, Squirrel was a good guy."

"But he was a junkie."

"No, he wasn't a junkie. Never." Moose seemed to be sinking into the chair. "But he was a scrumper."

"A what?"

"A scrumper. You know he made his squish, right?"

I nodded.

"Well, he didn't exactly buy the apples. He scrumped them."

"You mean he stole them?"

He rolled his eyes like he didn't want to say it. When they stopped rolling, they half-closed. "Yeah, I guess."

"From where?"

"All different places. He'd find a place; then he'd move on. He was good about that. He didn't take too much from any one place, even if he found a really good place, because that wouldn't be fair."

"Great." His eyes were slowly closing. "Something I need to tell you," I said, and they opened back up a little. "Last night a crop duster came and dusted us with something."

They opened wider still and looked around. "What are you talking about? With what?"

"Don't know yet."

He stared at me like he was trying to make sense of it. "Nola's, too?"

I nodded.

"Fuck. Does she know?"

I nodded again.

He thought for a moment, then his eyes closed completely. "I don't even know what to think of that."

In seconds, his breathing became more regular, and just like that, he was asleep. I couldn't tell if he was exhausted from the emotional trauma of the past couple days, or if he was crashing after a high. Maybe both. He shook himself awake, and sat up, momentarily confused. "I'm going to go crash for a while," he said, getting unsteadily to his feet.

I watched him slowly climbing the steps, and after a few moments thought maybe I would do the same. The quiet of the house seemed to be urging me on, coaxing me to sleep.

I sat back on the sofa and closed my eyes, but no more than a few minutes had passed before I heard the doorbell. When I stood up, my entire body ached. The bells started playing again as I was reaching for the door.

It was Sydney Bricker, with a tight little smile on her face.

"Hello, Mr. Carrick."

As I smiled back, I realized even the muscles in my face ached. "What can I do for you, Ms. Bricker?"

She pulled out a leather folio and a pen. "One last paper you need to sign before we can transfer the assets."

She opened the folder to a page with a red plastic tab at the bottom, next to a space for my signature. I started to read it, some innocuous thing about having been informed of some estate tax that did not even apply to me. I could have sworn the page was identical to one I had already signed, and I wondered if she had somehow screwed the other one up. She seemed nervous, and I decided not to call her on it. She handed me a pen with her name on it. When I twisted it open it felt solid and expensive.

"Not many lawyers make house calls, you know," I said, as I signed it.

I expected her to bring up the property again, but she never mentioned it. As I handed her back the pen, she took it between her thumb and forefinger and dropped it into her breast pocket, like she didn't want to touch it, like she was worried about catching whatever was going around.

"Thank you, Mr. Carrick," she said with that same tight little smile. Then she turned and left, as if she was in a hurry to get away from me.

I watched her drive away, but as I turned to go back inside the house, my phone rang. When I looked at the ID, my heart sank. Dunston Police Department.

"Doyle Carrick," I answered, and my phone immediately beeped that it was almost out of juice.

"Chief Pruitt here. I'm over at Dwight Cooney's mom's place, 819 Mill Road, about a quarter mile up the road from Dwight's house. Got something you might want to take a look at."

Cooney's mom lived in a double wide. It was kind of run down, but with window boxes and shutters and a row of marigolds, it didn't look half bad. She was watching from the front door, holding a towel over her mouth. When she saw me look over at her, she disappeared inside.

A pair of ruts in the grass led to the back, where Pruitt was leaning against the back of his cruiser, arms folded across his belly.

Behind the car was a small, weathered travel trailer, its wheels sunk halfway into the dirt.

"Took you long enough," he said when I walked up.

"Sorry. They take traffic enforcement pretty seriously in these parts."

He smiled at that, but not for long. "You know I don't have to show you this, right?"

Going along seemed like the quickest route, and by now I was curious. "Yes, I know."

"Now, I'm short-handed as hell, got a bunch of wusses calling out sick every time they get a sniffle, so I don't want you making anything out of this. And there's no need to, anyway. I'm doing this out of professional courtesy, and as a goodwill gesture. But have no doubt, you fuck with me or piss me off, I will come down on you like hellfire, do you hear me?"

"Yes, sir."

"All right, then, follow me. But don't touch anything."

He turned around and walked toward the trailer. "We found a key on Cooney's keychain, found out he had this trailer parked in his momma's backyard." He shook his head. "Boy's been a thorn in that woman's side since the day he was born."

He fiddled with the lock, then swung the door open and stepped aside, waving me in.

The interior was cramped, dingy, and dark. It stunk of lowlife male: stale beer, old pot smoke, sweaty socks, and garbage, with more than a hint of poorly aimed urine, which was odd since there didn't seem to be a bathroom.

Cooney's fridge was covered with photos, held in place by magnets and tape, and all featuring grainy candid images of the same woman. They looked like they had been taken with a camera phone.

Some of them had been taken from outside a window. There were a lot of them.

Pruitt gave me a moment to look at them. "That's Miss Watkins, isn't it?"

"Yeah, that's her all right."

"I assume she doesn't have photos of Dwight all over her fridge?"

"No, she does not."

"Makes it pretty creepy, then. You said she was getting a lot of hang-up calls, right?"

I nodded.

He held up a Ziploc evidence bag with a cheap cell phone in it. "Prepaid, courtesy of the mini-mart. We'll send it in for testing, but the phone is set so the number is blocked. Almost all the outgoing calls were to Miss Watkins's phone."

I nodded.

"I don't think she'll be getting any more hang-ups, but she should have reported it. If he was stalking her the way it looks like, it could have turned out bad. And if we'd known about it, there's things they could have done to trace it."

"Right."

"Anyway," Pruitt said, motioning me out the door and fingering the key. "I don't know if she needs to be told about all this, since Dwight isn't going to be bothering her anymore. And I don't know if she was really all that upset about those phone calls to begin with, since she never called them in or anything. But I thought I should let you know, so you could tell her she didn't have to worry about it anymore."

I kept quiet about all the reasons why Nola wouldn't have wanted to tell him about the calls, how useless, unhelpful, and indifferent he could be. "When was the last call to Nola's phone?"

Pruitt looked at his notes, squinting. "Tuesday night."

"Did he send any texts?"

"What?"

"The phone. Did he send her any texts. The next day, right before the fire, there was a text, and then the photo."

Pruitt frowned at me for a moment, looking vaguely annoyed, then he shrugged. "Well, I don't know about that. Maybe he had another phone somewhere. I'll keep an eye out for it."

Maybe those crank calls had nothing to do with developers or land deals or anything else. Maybe it was just a lovesick, lowlife dead guy. But I couldn't shake the feeling that something else was going on.

49

The day's events and the lack of sleep had left my nerves jangly and raw. When I got home again, it hit me hard: I needed sleep. Climbing the steps to go to bed, my joints creaked almost as loudly as the stairs. I felt like an old man, and smiled grimly at the thought that the way things were going, this could be as close as I got to being one.

When I got to the top of the stairs, I saw Moose's light on and his door slightly open. I knocked, but got no answer.

I wanted to respect his privacy, but he'd had a hell of a day, too, and I wanted to make sure he was okay. Pushing the door open, I called gently, "Moose."

He wasn't in his bed, but I could hear wheezy, labored breathing. The bathroom light was on, and the door was open.

I called again, louder. "Moose!"

As I stepped into the room, I kicked two empty bottles. They clinked loudly, and one rolled under the bed. From the bedroom, I could see him passed out on the toilet. At least he was clothed.

I'd lost friends before, and I'd gotten pretty drunk when I did. I didn't fault him for that. I figured I'd put him in bed and let him deal with the hangover in the morning.

Then I saw that he'd thrown up on himself, and I thought he could deal with that in the morning, too. But when I bent down to pick him up, I noticed the bluish tinge to his lips. His breathing was shallow and slow. I gave him a little shake.

"Moose!" I shouted, right in his ear. When that didn't get a response, I pulled up one of his eyelids. The pupil was almost gone, a tiny black dot in the middle of his brown iris.

The little prick had ODed.

I slapped his face, but there was no reaction. It pissed me off that he had done this in my mom and Frank's house. I slapped him again, harder. I turned on the water and splashed some in his face.

"You gotta be kidding me," I said out loud, slapping and shaking him. "You do this *now?* Do you know how fucking tired I am?"

The last slap had a little more mustard than might have been necessary, but it woke him up, goddamn it, for what that was worth.

He moaned and stirred, his eyes open but unfocused, looking past me before closing again. He needed attention fast.

I grabbed one of his other shirts off the bedroom floor and draped it over him so I wouldn't get any puke on me. Then I picked him up and carried him downstairs.

Getting out the front door wasn't much of a problem, but the car doors were locked. I put Moose across the hood while I fished out my keys, bracing one hand against his chest in case he started to slide off. Once the doors were unlocked, I put him in the passenger seat.

I started the car, but before I drove off, I reclined his seat, making sure his head was back and his airway was clear. As angry as I was, I realized I was scared, too. As my hands tightened on the wheel and my foot pressed the pedal, I said, "You better not fucking die."

50

St. Mark's emergency room was already bustling when we got there, but when I brought Moose in and announced he was ODing, a cluster of attendants swarmed over him in a frenzy of attention. He was a mess, but he seemed stable, his breathing shallow and slow, but regular.

In a matter of seconds, he was disappearing through the swinging doors, and in the relative quiet that followed, I noticed that the place was packed with sick farmer types, all pale and sweaty. It seemed like half the town was there, and again I wondered if somehow the crop duster was involved. Part of me hoped it was, and that these people were suffering from some kind of chemical exposure instead of a virus or bacteria, something I could catch.

A wave of coughing spread across the room, and I wanted to get out of there as soon as I could, before I got whatever it was they had, what Nola had, but before I could, the intake nurse called me over and started asking questions. I didn't know Moose's real name, or his age, or if he had any allergies. I didn't even know for sure what was wrong with him.

"But I suspect a heroin overdose," I told her.

She stopped writing and looked up at me.

"I'm a cop," I explained. "I've seen it before."

She stared at my face for a moment. "And are *you* okay, sir?"

Judging from the concern in her face, I must have looked pretty rough. "Nothing a week in bed wouldn't fix."

When she was done with her questions, she directed me toward the seating area and told me the doctor would be out to speak to me. I put a handful of singles into a vending machine, and sat in the only empty chair, mechanically chewing cheese crackers.

I'd only been to St. Mark's a couple of times, and never the E.R., but it brought back memories of my mom, sick and frail. This was probably where they brought Frank, too. Alone, without my mom or anyone else with him at the end.

After twenty minutes stuck in there with all those sad thoughts and sick people, I was starting to feel claustrophobic. I was thinking once again of leaving when the doctor came out. She looked familiar, tall with dark hair and big brown eyes creased with stress. The woman at intake pointed me out in the crowd. The doctor came toward me and held out her hand with a harried smile. "I'm Dr. Walters."

"Hi. I'm Detective Carrick. You helped care for my mother, Meredith Menlow."

"Of course." The creases around her eyes softened and fell. "I heard about your father," she said. "I'm so sorry."

"Thanks."

"He was a sweet guy. They both were."

"Thanks. So, um, how is Moose?"

"Moose? You mean Bruce?"

I smiled. "Yeah."

She told me he was stabilized and gave me the basics. "We're pretty busy tonight, but I'll make sure I keep an eye on him. He should be fine. We treated him with Narcan, which counteracts the effects of the opioids, blocks the system from absorbing them. He might not feel too good for a few days, but he'll be okay."

"Thanks, Dr. Walters."

"Call me Janie."

"Call me Doyle."

She smiled, then she looked around the crowded waiting room and her face sagged a bit. "Look, you're not going to be able to see Bruce until tomorrow. You should go home and get some rest."

Now that he was out of danger, my annoyance at Moose was undiluted by concern; I had no desire to see him before tomorrow.

"So was it heroin?" I asked.

"Probably. It was some kind of opioid. A lot of alcohol, too. Bad mix."

I shook my head. "Idiot."

"The heroin is like an epidemic around here."

I glanced around at the packed waiting room.

She followed my gaze. "Yes, it's not the only epidemic. Looks like we're getting an early start on flu season."

I turned back to look at her. "I thought there was more of a problem with meth out here than heroin."

She shook her head. "Not so much. I've heard a lot about meth on the news, but I haven't seen much of it here."

"A lot of heroin, though?"

"A lot of overdoses. We had an eleven-year-old girl come in. She swore she didn't do it, so maybe someone slipped it to her. I've heard of people doing sick stuff like that. There was a big bust just the other day, apparently, so maybe that will help."

I thought about the piles of it being unloaded from the van. "I hope so."

51

I woke up the next day, stiff, exhausted, and fully clothed. My shirt was stuck to the abrasions from where I had hit the wall, and I had to peel it away. As I got into the shower, I noticed that my feet looked strangely pale, and I realized that for the first time in weeks my athlete's foot didn't itch. Maybe things were looking up.

When I got out, I saw that my phone was dead, and while I had been recharging, it had not. I plugged it in and turned it on. My stomach knotted when I saw I had nine messages.

Stan had called twice, sounding strange and asking me to call him. Dr. Walters called to let me know that "Bruce" was doing fine, and that he might be released later that morning.

Suarez called, saying I should give him a call when I get a chance. He sounded like he was holding back laughter.

The next message was from Stan again. He sounded gruff, mumbling something about "flowers or some shit. Just give me a call." Then Stan again after that, saying, "Doyle, where the fuck are you? Give me a fucking call."

There was a call from Nola, sounding sick and concerned that she couldn't get in touch with Moose.

Then Pruitt, of all people, demanding to know what kind of horseshit I was trying to pull.

The last message was another one from Suarez. I called Stan.

"Jesus, Doyle, where the fuck've you been?"

"I had a late night. Something came up."

"Yeah, well, while you've been sleeping off whatever you were up to last night, I've been taking it up the ass from Munschak."

"What's going on?"

"What's going on? That fucking bust, Doyle. Fifty keys of heroin, my ass. Fifty kilos of paperwork, probably, but there was maybe three keys of heroin. High grade, yes, but not enough to justify twenty agents and a jurisdictional dispute. Not enough to justify five bodies. And definitely not enough to justify a big goddamned press conference."

"What are you talking about? I saw it myself. Christ, you put it on TV. There was plenty."

"Yeah, there was a lot of something, but it wasn't heroin. The bag we field-tested was, but the rest of it was bullshit, flour or something. It was nothing."

"So what does that mean?"

"It means I'm fucked," he snapped. "It means I'm in a rowboat in the middle of a category five shit storm. It means that my dickhead publicity-hound super jumped the gun and has turned a minor glitch into a major embarrassment." He sighed, a deep, sad, tired sigh. "And since I covered your involvement, it also means that a slightly tweaked story to cover a comrade's administrative woes could now be viewed like conspiracy to obstruct justice in a capital case."

"Capital case?"

"Yeah, I've got five of these assholes on ice. Six if you count Cooney."

"Hey, come on, Stan, it's not like—"

"No, Doyle, don't 'Come on, Stan,' me. I called Philly and talked you up, now this is biting my ass all over the fucking place. You might be determined to get yourself bounced out, but I'm not going with you. I got to work with these people too, and you just made that a lot more difficult."

"Right. You didn't by any chance get those other test results back, did you?"

"Test results? You're un-fucking-believable. Yeah, as a matter of fact I did get the results back. Where did you say that shit came from?"

"The crop-duster plane. It was all over the place."

"Yeah, but where did you get your sample?"

"I told you, it was from the windowsill in my kitchen."

"Your kitchen, huh? Well, that's hilarious, Betty Crocker, because that was flour, too."

"Flour? Wait a second, Stan—"

"Doyle, I hope we get to work again together in an official capacity, but in the meantime, I want you to write my name and my number on a piece of paper and throw it the fuck away."

And then he was gone.

Before I could get back to that last message, the phone started ringing in my hand. I felt a strong urge to stash the thing under the sofa cushions and run away, but I looked at the display and saw it was the hospital. For a moment it took me back to the call about Frank.

"Hello?"

"Hello, is this Mr. Carrick?"

"Yes."

"Hi, this is Janie Walters from St. Mark's. Bruce is ready to be discharged, but someone needs to come and pick him up."

"Is he okay?"

"He did fine. Sometimes it can be pretty tough when we give

them the Narcan. You know, if they're . . . You know, if they've got a big habit. But he did good."

"So, what was it, anyway?" I asked.

"We don't know, exactly. Probably heroin, maybe morphine. Could have been fentanyl or oxycontin, something like that."

"He wouldn't tell you?"

She paused. I think she could sense my annoyance, and she was choosing her words carefully. "He denies taking anything, but that's pretty common. He's probably scared. The fact that he's not shooting up and didn't have too much trouble with the Narcan suggests he's probably not too far into it, although people can get pretty deep before they start injecting."

"Right. Okay, should I come over now?"

"Sure. I'll have them get him ready."

"I'll be there in ten minutes."

The hospital was even busier than before. There weren't enough seats in the waiting area, and people were milling around while the staff rushed back and forth. Moose was sitting in a wheelchair by the front desk, tapping his fingers on the armrest and fidgeting his feet. I smiled when I saw him. Not because I was happy to see him, but because he looked like he'd been through hell, and I was glad. He deserved to have been through hell. Maybe he'd learn a lesson.

Janie Walters was standing next to him. She looked like she'd been through hell, too.

"Hi, Doyle," she said with a tired smile. Then she looked down at Moose, like she expected me to say something to him.

I didn't. I ignored him completely. It was reciprocated, which annoyed me even more: Who did he think he was, ignoring me when I was there to pick him up? Janie nodded, as if she suddenly grasped my anger at the idiot who had almost killed himself in my

mother's house messing around with substances I was profession-
ally committed to fighting.

"Well," she said, awkwardly clapping her hands together. "You
be careful, Bruce. And remember what we talked about."

To his credit, Moose closed his eyes before he rolled them.
Otherwise I might have backhanded him across the room.

He started to get up, but Janie put a hand on his shoulder and
pushed him back into the chair. "Not until we get outside," she
said. "Those are the rules."

He huffed, like it was a hardship for him to stay in the wheelchair. Janie started to wheel him out.

"Don't be too hard on him," she said, looking up at my face.
"He's had a rough night."

I wanted to tell her a thing or two about my rough night, but
when I looked into her eyes, I caught myself. She'd had a rough
night, too. "Okay. Any special instructions?"

She shrugged. "Just keep an eye on him."

As soon as we were outside, Moose looked up at Janie. "Can I
get up now?"

She stopped and put the brake on. "Yes, you can get up now."

He scrambled out of the wheelchair, almost tripping when his
feet got caught in the footrest.

"If you're going to break something, go ahead and do it here," I
said. "Save me the trip."

He gave me a dirty look and stalked off toward my car.

I gave Janie a smile. "Don't work too hard," I told her.

"Take it easy on him," she said.

Moose slumped down in the passenger seat, one hand covering his eyes.
"Thanks for coming to get me," he said when we were halfway home.

He was making an effort, but I wasn't quite there yet.

"Well . . . thanks for not puking in my car, or dying. Yeah, thanks for not dying in my car when I was driving you to the hospital, or in my parents' house. You know, while you were overdosing."

Moose sighed.

I gripped the wheel tighter, clenching my teeth as well. Janie had said to be easy on him, but having started, I could feel my anger building.

"ODing on heroin?" I yelled despite myself. "Jesus Christ! Are you fucking kidding me?"

"I didn't take any heroin!"

"Oh, you didn't? Oh, that's a relief. You should have told me that last night while you were choking on your own vomit and slipping into a coma. It would have saved me a trip to the fucking hospital."

"I'm not using, I swear to God."

"Oh, well, you must be telling the truth, because a junkie would never lie about using drugs. That's never happened."

"You're a real asshole, you know that?"

We drove in silence after that.

I wasn't totally unsympathetic. I knew he felt like shit. And I know he was upset about Squirrel. I had done some pretty boneheaded things when I was young, too. And boneheaded was still very much in my repertoire. But I hadn't ODed on heroin, for God's sake. And I definitely hadn't done it while staying in the home of a narcotics detective in a precarious professional state.

When we pulled into the driveway, I got out of the car first, but I dutifully hung back and waited for him, making sure he didn't fall. When we got inside, he went straight upstairs, the steps creaking loudly.

I stayed downstairs, but I couldn't relax knowing he was up there. I didn't want to leave him alone in the house, but I couldn't stand the thought of being there with him. Once he was settled in, I got back in the car.

52

Twenty minutes later, I was parked down the street from Crooked Creek Farm, where the bust had gone down. Even at three kilos it was probably still the biggest police story out here in the last ten years, but I was still surprised to see a patrol car parked on the street out front. Between the busted bust and the flu from hell, I didn't think the Dunston Police Department would spare the manpower to guard the scene. I was about to turn around and go when the uniform took a call on his radio. A minute later, he started up his car and drove off—no lights, no rush, like he had just gotten word that he had more important things to do.

I waited a few minutes, then approached the same way I had before, diagonally across the field next to the driveway, so I could say I hadn't seen the police tape. It rankled that the police tape was meant to exclude me along with the other civilians. It made my suspicion seem very real.

As I walked up to the cinder block building, I noticed a distinct quietness, like the place was still in a state of shock after the violence of the bust.

The house was taped up tight, and I left it that way. Walking across the lawn was one thing. Breaking into a sealed house was something else entirely. Through the windows, the place seemed empty of both people and things, and I was relieved. I'd been dreading the sight of pizza boxes and beer cans, the spore of young men who didn't give a shit. Because it would bring home the fact that I had killed three of them. Three lowlife criminals, to be sure. Probably three animals with long histories of violent crime. But three people that I had killed.

I went over to the cinder block building where all the shooting had taken place. Both doors were closed and taped. The oil drums were gone. I walked around the whole building, past the windowless back. When I got to the far side, I saw a single window set in the wall. Cupping my hands around my eyes, I peered through the window and saw a plain room with another doorway at the far end, the frame spattered with blood. Beyond that was the spot where I'd landed in the hallway, where Stan had found me. Next to it was the spot where the guy called Paulie had died, after I shot him.

I stifled a shudder and kept walking. The two metal shacks looked exactly the same as before, except the padlock had been snipped off the second one.

The first one—the one where Roberts and his crew had been loading the bundles of whatever the hell it was that wasn't heroin—was empty. The second shed was not empty. It was half-filled with stacks of wooden crates filled with apples—five high, six wide, and three deep. Ninety cases.

Not what I expected. I hadn't had breakfast, so I took an apple from the case on top of the nearest stack and bit into it. It wasn't very good—mealy and not very sweet, maybe even a little bitter.

When I let the door close, the entire structure sang with the quavery warble of thin metal flexing.

My stomach grumbled when the apple reached it, reminding me how hungry I was.

As I followed the gravel path up toward the silo, I took a few more bites, but the apple didn't get any better. The silo was old and rusty, looming ominously over everything else. It was empty except for a layer of pigeon crap on the bottom and a bunch of pigeons at the top.

I turned and walked back to my car. Apart from a deep melancholy to go with the sick feeling that had occupied my stomach since talking to Bowers, I hadn't found a thing. I took a last bite out of my apple and flung the rest of it at the side of the silo. It banged loudly, splattering in all directions and sending a whoosh of pigeons out the opening at the top of the silo.

I don't know what I had hoped to find there, some kind of clue as to what had really been going on, maybe how the flour fit into this all. But there was no evidence of a sinister bread-making operation, no gangster elves making cookies in a tree. There was nothing.

Even right after the bust, I had known something else was going on, but at least there had been an illusion of closure. Now there wasn't even that. There was just an ominous feeling settling over everything, like that damned mist from the crop duster. In Philly, there was a shitstorm with my name on it, and it was getting worse. In Dunston, the big case was fucked; something was going down and the bad guys were getting away with it. People I loved were dead, and now people I cared about were sick. Maybe the whole town was. Maybe the whole world was.

53

It was noon, and apart from a few bites of apple, I still hadn't had breakfast. An image of it flashed in my mind—eggs, bacon, toast—and the grumbling from my stomach grew louder. As soon as I remembered that Branson's served breakfast all day, I knew where I was headed.

I called Nola as I drove.

"Hello?" she said, sounding worse than she had the night before.

"How are you feeling?"

"Rough night. I feel like crap, and I look like crap. How's Moose?"

It took me a moment to realize she was referring to his mental state after Squirrel's death, not the OD. "He's okay," I told her. "He's upset." She didn't seem ready to handle more than that. "I got the results back from my friend at DEA. That powder they were spraying, apparently it was flour."

"Flour? Like bread flour?"

"Apparently."

"Why would they be spraying flour?"

"I don't know, maybe to send a message. But that's what the tests said. Maybe your doctor was right, maybe it's just the flu. There's some bad stuff going around."

"It's not the flu," she said brusquely. Then she took a deep breath. "Doyle, it's . . . it's not the flu."

She started coughing, and I wondered for a moment if she was doing it for effect. But I immediately felt guilty as the cough got away from her, getting deeper and harsher.

"That sounds pretty bad," I said when she stopped. "Maybe you need to go to the hospital."

"I can't go to the hospital."

"Why not?"

"The chemicals, Doyle." Like it was obvious. "Hospitals are worse than hotels. They're full of sick people and medicines and disinfectants and other stuff. They're so concerned about the germs they don't even think about the chemicals. Last time I got sick, I went into the hospital. It might have saved my life, but it could have killed me. No hospitals."

I could tell she was getting irritated at me. "Okay," I said. "I'll check on you later."

When I walked into Branson's, the glorious smells of breakfast still hung in the air, but the place felt different. The tables were almost empty. Squires was behind the bar as usual, but he wasn't wiping down surfaces or washing glasses or inventorying. He was just standing there.

I thought he saw me and I waved, but he looked right through me.

The waitress came over immediately. She looked tired. I ordered two eggs over, hash browns, bacon, scrapple, rye toast, and coffee.

The coffee came, and as I sat there and sipped it, the exhaustion seemed to sink back in, but it wasn't the aching exhaustion of the night before; it was a mellow, comfortable, almost snuggly exhaustion.

I closed my eyes for a moment and just enjoyed the fact that I was sitting. I heard a noise across the table, and when I opened my eyes, I saw I had been joined by my friend Chief Pruitt.

"Well, you sure screwed the pooch on that one, didn't you?" He shook his head. "Five dead over a vanload of baking supplies."

"And some heroin," I reminded him.

"Yeah, you're right," he conceded, taking off his shades and waving for the waitress to bring him a cup of coffee. He gave her a wink when she did, and I wondered if he was going to pay for it. "Tox results came back on the Squires boy. They said if he hadn't fallen, he probably would have died of an overdose anyway."

"The Squires boy? Wait, you mean Squirrel?"

"Carl Squires, yes." He tilted his head back toward the bar. "Bert's boy, the poor son of a bitch."

Looking over Pruitt's shoulder, I now recognized the pain etched deeply on Bert's face. He'd aged since the last time I'd seen him. A lot. He looked like an old man, like there wasn't enough time left in him to heal those wounds.

"Heard about your friend Moose, too," Pruitt went on. "Seems like that crap's all over the place these days."

I nodded, wondering where he was going with this.

He reached back with one hand to rub the back of his neck. "Stuff like this didn't use to happen in this town," he said. "Anyway, I just wanted to say, yes, you sure fucked up that bust over at the farm. And you should have just come to me. But a couple of keys is a couple of keys. That stuff's out there killing kids. I'm glad you got it off the street." He leaned forward and lowered his voice. "And between you and me, five assholes is five assholes. I'm glad they're off the street, too."

It was a pretty magnanimous gesture on his part.

"Thanks," I said.

It felt good just to sit there, sipping my coffee and listening to

Pruitt be gracious for the first time since I'd met him. My career was probably fucked, but for the moment, just sitting there, I felt happy.

Pruitt leaned forward and looked me in the eye. "You all right?" He sounded kind of concerned, kind of suspicious. "You don't look like you're feeling too good." He leaned closer. "Or more like, maybe you are feeling too good. What's going on with you?"

"I'm all right," I told him with a smile. "I'm just very tired, and I'm enjoying my coffee and looking forward to my breakfast."

My voice sounded muffled in my ears, and I realized as I said it that I no longer wanted my big breakfast. That was a shame, because I'd been looking forward to it.

Pruitt's eyes narrowed. "You look sort of weird."

I was starting to feel sleepy, and I felt my stomach gurgle. "Actually, I am feeling a little . . . something." I got up, feeling slightly unsteady on my feet. "I'll be back in a second."

Pruitt nodded, his head turning to follow me as I walked.

The bathroom seemed far away. When I finally got there, I splashed water on my face and rubbed my face with paper towels.

When I looked in the mirror, I noticed my eyes.

My pupils were two tiny little black dots.

Someone had slipped me something.

My first thought was Pruitt. I'd been sitting there with my eyes closed when he sat down with me. But I couldn't see him slipping something into my coffee in a room full of people.

Whoever it was, I needed to get home.

My limbs felt heavy and clumsy as I made my way back to the table. My food was on the table. It looked heavy and greasy, and the sight of it made me feel sick. Pruitt looked up at me as I came nearer, sizing me up.

I put a twenty on the table. "I'm not feeling so good. I got to get going."

"Sure," he said, standing up.

I walked unsteadily out to my car. As I fumbled with my keys and started the engine, Pruitt came out onto the street, his eyebrow cocked like he was getting a better look.

I drove away with one eye on the rearview, making sure Pruitt didn't come roaring up behind me with his lights flashing, pull me over for driving under the influence.

That would be a mess, I thought; get a DUI while on suspension. I had a little laugh, then realized the car was drifting. I jerked the wheel back a little too hard but got it under control.

My phone started to vibrate. Sydney Bricker calling again. No way was I in any state to talk to her.

The situation seemed funny, but I knew it wasn't. Even less funny was the siren suddenly screaming behind me. At first I thought it was Pruitt, but I recognized the sound even before I saw it in my rearview—an ambulance, driving fast, the way they used to before they realized they were killing more people than they were saving on the way to the hospital. Whatever I was on was still hitting me, and my slow-motion reflexes barely had a chance to pull over before the ambulance had screamed past me. When I saw it turn into St. Mark's Hospital, a quarter mile ahead, I knew that was where I was heading as well.

I pulled into the entrance for the ER and let the car coast to a halt. I couldn't keep driving, but I couldn't check in. That would get back. Even on the remote chance that I could convince anybody that someone had slipped me something, it would still be entirely too embarrassing.

In the seconds that passed while I tried to decide what to do, my lids grew even heavier, and I realized it would be even more embarrassing to be found dead in my car.

54

Wearing shades to hide my pupils, I did my best to walk straight and look straight while I strode through the door to the ER, but once inside, I stopped. It was packed. The seats were full, and people were leaning against the walls, shuffling up and down the aisles between the chairs, all of them coughing and wheezing.

"Jesus," I whispered, momentarily sobered, my addled brain trying to make sense of it.

I squeezed my way through to the admissions desk, where a different woman was working. She looked up at me without batting an eye. I imagine it would take a lot to make someone bat an eye on a day like this in the ER.

"How may I help you?" she asked, in a tone that almost dared me to make her bat an eye. Her nametag said, "Wanda."

"Hi," I said, with what was probably a horribly twisted version of my already dubious charming smile. I thought about calling her by name, but decided against it. "I need to talk to Dr. Walters, please."

"About what?"

"It's urgent."

She still didn't bat an eye, but the left one did twitch a bit.

"Wait here," she said, not hiding the effort it took to heave herself out of her chair and shuffle through the double swinging doors into the patient area.

A couple of minutes later, Janie emerged, annoyance followed by a brief smile, then confusion as she looked closer at me. "Doyle? Is Bruce okay?"

"Hi," I said. I had enough sense to leave out the charming smile. "Yeah, he's fine. I just need to talk to you for a second."

"Doyle, that's great, but we're crazy busy today."

Leaning close to her, I said quietly, "I need to see you alone. It's urgent."

She pulled back and looked at me, her large eyes a little larger.

I gave her a little nod. "Please."

She scanned the room, then grabbed me by the elbow and backed through the swinging doors. She kept going, leading me to a little nook filled with equipment between two patient bays. She pulled a curtain panel around to hide us. "Best I can do," she said. "So what's this all about?"

"Someone slipped me something. I'm stoned out of my mind."

"What are you talking about?"

I took off my shades. "Somebody slipped me something. Some kind of narcotic, I think. Look at my pupils. They're practically gone."

"When?"

"I don't know when. I started feeling it about ten minutes ago."

She frowned. "Is it still coming on?"

I nodded and blinked my eyes, trying to focus. "Definitely."

She paused to look at my eyes. "Yeah, okay, come on. If you ate it or drank it, it can take thirty or forty minutes to take full effect. We need to get you admitted."

"No." I put my hand on her arm.

She looked at me questioningly.

"Not everyone is going to believe me that someone slipped me something. If I check in, that goes on my record, and I can't let that happen right now. I just need some Narcan. If you can't do that, I understand, but I'm just going to have to take my chances and sleep it off."

She stared at me for a second. "Wait here."

She slipped through the curtain, and I closed my eyes. Now that I was about to counteract the high, part of me was sad I hadn't taken the time to enjoy it. But mostly I didn't care, because I was really high.

A minute later, she was back with a sealed plastic bag that she tore open. "This is an overdose kit that we are allowed to give out. It has a Narcan nasal spray, but it takes a few minutes to work, and since we don't know how much you got, I'm going to go ahead and give you an injection." She told me to roll up my sleeve as she stripped the plastic off a syringe and filled it from a vial. "Technically, I am not supposed to treat you without checking you in, but I'm going to cut you a break since I liked your folks. It sounds like you've got enough on your plate, and I know there's enough on mine." She looked me in the eye. "You're not telling me stories, right?"

I held up two fingers, like a boy scout. "Cop's honor."

"Good. We're too busy to check anybody in we don't have to anyway." She smiled as she jabbed the needle into my arm. "You should feel it almost immediately."

As she said the word "immediately," I felt a sudden, lurching, plummeting sensation. Like falling back to Earth. I realized how much better the drug had been making me feel.

She stepped back and observed me for a moment.

The aches and pains I'd forgotten about washed across me.

"Yeah," she said with a wry smile. "I'd say that probably did the trick, huh?"

"Yes," I said sarcastically. "I feel much 'better.'"

She put her hand on my shoulder and gave it a little squeeze, then handed me a tiny pill envelope. "The Narcan only lasts a few hours. Depending on what you were given and how much, the opioids might last longer. If you start to feel a buzz coming on, you need to take two of these. That should tide you over until whatever it is wears off."

"Thanks."

"Just wait a few minutes, let the Narcan really take effect. Then you can get going."

I nodded.

"Okay," she said. "I need to get back out there."

"Thanks."

"Glad to help. But Doyle?"

"Yeah?"

"Try to stay out of trouble, okay?"

We stepped out of the exam bay, and Janie made a left, disappearing into the bustling activity of the ER department. I made a right and pushed open the swinging door back out into the admissions area. When I did, I saw Chief Pruitt leaning on the admission desk, talking to Wanda.

They seemed to have established a rhythm: He'd speak for a few seconds and she'd listen, then shake her head. Then he would speak again, and she would listen and shake her head again.

Eventually, he hooked a thumb over his shoulder, in the direction of where I was standing, by the swinging doors. This time, she sighed and shrugged and nodded.

I ducked back into the equipment nook and told myself that there was no way he would just start searching the exam bays. But sure enough, a couple of seconds later he pushed through the doors and started pulling back curtains, one by one. I ducked behind a big crash cart and a moment later a pair of big, ugly black Oxfords appeared on the other side of it. They stayed there for a moment; then I heard Wanda's voice and they disappeared.

I waited a couple of seconds, then poked my head out. Pruitt was halfway down the ward, talking to Wanda and one of the doctors. He looked like he was trying hard to explain his presence there.

Slipping out from behind the crash cart and through the swinging doors, I pushed through the crowded waiting room and out into the parking lot. Pruitt's car was next to mine. I grinned to myself as I pulled out of the parking lot and disappeared around the corner, but the grin faded as my thoughts turned back to figuring out what the hell was going on.

Anybody in the kitchen could have spiked my coffee, or the waitress, or Pruitt. And that would explain why he had been pretending to be a decent human being, and why he had followed me to the hospital to try to bust me while I was still intoxicated.

I had a box of narcotics field test kits in the trunk, but by now my coffee was long gone. Of course, it might not have been the coffee at all. But if not, then what? The only other thing I'd had to eat was an apple.

I tapped the brakes, slowing down as I considered that possibility. Thinking back, maybe I'd started feeling a buzz before I even got my coffee. I couldn't remember.

But apples? And how would someone know I would even take one, much less which one?

Unless they didn't. Maybe it had nothing to do with me. Maybe it was a coincidence. Maybe it was just dumb luck.

The theory seemed extremely unlikely, but then again, the apples would be easier to test than the coffee. I turned the car around and headed back to Crooked Creek Farm.

55

I parked in the driveway across the street and brought the narco-tests with me. This time, as I approached the cinder block building and the farmhouse, I felt no sense of melancholy. I was focused solely on the apple shed. But when I pulled open the aluminum door, the shed was empty.

I stepped back and looked around me, getting my bearings and making sure I was at the right place. Then I checked to see if I had company.

Barely an hour had passed since I had left there. That wasn't much time to get in, load ninety cases of apples, and get out. Even if more than one person was working, they would have had to arrive right after I left, and leave right before I came back. They had probably been watching, waiting for the patrol car to leave.

With the apples gone, I was in the same boat as with the coffee from the diner—plenty of unlikely suspicions and nothing to test. I walked around the silo, looking for some apple fragments from the core I had hurled at it, but all I could find was a sticky spot with a few tiny bits of apple. There wasn't much, but the tests were pretty sensitive.

I opened the plastic pouch and scraped some of the apple residue into it. Once the sample was in the pouch, the test was self-contained. There were three ampoules inside the pouch, each containing a different reagent. You break them in the right order to find out what you have.

I broke the first ampoule, and as the reagent came into contact with the apple residue, it immediately turned a distinct purple color. Bingo: narcotics were present. When I broke the next ampoule, the reagents mixed and immediately turned lavender. Opioids. The third reagent was inconclusive. I couldn't tell specifically which opioid was present, but it was definitely something.

With my back against the side of the silo, I slid to the ground, staring at the reagent. Son of a bitch. Apples. What was that about?

I sat there for a few minutes, watching the reagent, waiting for it to say, "Sorry, just kidding," and change back.

Looking around at the scene of so much carnage, I knew I shouldn't be hanging out here. If the bad guys came back, it would be bad. If the good guys came back, that would arguably be worse. But I couldn't figure out where to go or what to do.

Why would someone spike apples with heroin? Maybe someone was smuggling heroin into the county in apples that were spiked, like watermelons with vodka. But although apples were pretty hardy, they were still perishable. It was a crazy idea.

Was it a sinister plot to poison school kids? Janie had said the hospital had admitted school kids ODing. The thought gave me chills.

When I was trespassing in the fields behind Nola's property, the apple trees were corralled behind a security fence. That suddenly made sense if the apples were full of heroin.

But the fence wasn't around boxes of apples, it was around apple *trees*. Maybe the heroin was in the apples already.

Moose and Nola had talked about crops that were genetically engineered to create pharmaceuticals. Maybe these were, too. That would explain the fences *and* the guns.

But I didn't know if that was even possible. There was only one person I could think of who knew enough about it to tell me. Jason Rupp.

The fancy black Mustang was parked in front of Rupp's house, just as before. I parked behind it and knocked on his door.

He answered almost immediately, and when he saw it was me, a half smile formed on his face. He looked left and right, maybe for Nola, then said, "You? Look, I'm sorry, but I don't have any info on your friends', corn."

"That's okay, I have a couple of other questions. Mind if I bounce them off you real quick?"

"I'm kind of in the middle of something."

I think he was waiting for me to apologize and go away. I didn't.

He let the silence hang there a good long while before he sighed and stepped back into the house. "Okay. Real quick."

"Thanks."

The place looked barren on the inside, even compared to before. The bookcases were empty, and boxes were stacked in the corner.

"You moving?" I asked.

"What?" He seemed annoyed at the question.

"I saw the boxes. You moving?"

"No. Well, kind of."

"Kind of?"

"I'm teaching abroad for a little while."

"Oh, yeah? Where's that?"

"France," he said, his vague accent suddenly stronger. "University of Paris."

"You speak French?"

"Doyle, that's your name, right?"

I nodded.

"Well, I'm busy here, Doyle. If I had time for chitchat, I'd call my mom or something."

"Okay, sure. So, you're a geneticist, right?"

"That's right."

"So, I've heard that it's possible to genetically engineer plants to produce medicines."

"Yes, that's right."

"Okay, would it be possible to make apples that could create heroin?"

He laughed. "Apples that create heroin . . ." He laughed again. "That's pretty crazy. What are you, writing a science fiction movie?"

"So is that a no?"

"You must admit, it does sound like something a room full of stoners would come up with."

"So that's a no?"

He sighed and scratched at one of his sideburns, like he was trying to think of a way to dumb it down for me. "Production of a compound isn't attached to a single group of cells or a single gene, it's systemic. People think plant metabolism is this simple thing— 'this' produces 'that'—but it's unimaginably complex, with different pathways and molecules interacting in different ways. It is flexible and dynamic and can be as dependent on environmental or developmental factors as genetics."

I was quiet for a moment, and had almost caught up with what he had just said when he continued. "So, the short answer would be no. The longer answer, well, I'm not saying it could never be done.

I'm just saying it hasn't, and it would take an astonishing intellect to pull off something like that."

I was pretty sure I had more questions, but standing there with him looking at me impatiently, I couldn't think of any. When my phone chimed, he clapped his hands and rubbed them together, like we both knew that was my cue to leave.

It was Rothe, the developer.

Rupp nodded indulgently as I thanked him and moved for the door. He closed it firmly behind me, and I heard him lock it. It's an effect I tend to have on people.

Out on the front step, I answered the phone.

"Doyle, here."

"Hi, detective, it's Jordan Rothe. I got your message. Sorry I didn't call you back earlier. We're a little shorthanded, and it's been a hectic few days. What can I do for you?"

"Shorthanded? You mean people out sick?"

"That's right."

"What do they have?"

"What do . . . ? I don't know. The sniffles. There's something going around."

I paused for a moment, wondering again how the whole flu thing fit in. Maybe I paused longer than I thought, because Rothe prompted me with an elaborate clearing of his throat. Unless he was coming down with something, too.

"Sorry," I said. "Thanks for getting back to me. I was just wondering, with all those different sellers, how are you managing to complete all those deals in such a short time?"

"Right. Well, normally yes, something like that would take a long time, especially since there's a one-month lease-back."

"A what?"

"A lease-back, so the purchase is completed, but then the land is leased back to the seller for one month, to give them time to vacate

or find another location. It's not unusual, although it's more common with smaller deals."

"Isn't that risky, leasing it back? What if there's a problem with
the property?"

"Real estate is always risky, especially in a market like this,"
he said with a nervous laugh. "But I doubt there will be any problems a dozen bulldozers can't rectify. We're re-grading the entire
site anyway."

"I was wondering about that, actually. Just out of curiosity: Why
are you investing in a big development way out here, right now?"

"Between you and me, I think it's kind of crazy, too. But I'm
getting an amazing deal on the real estate. That's what's driving
the whole thing. I think some of these other developers overpaid
on their land, couldn't make it work. Now they have to get rid of it.
So I get a great price. I keep my inputs low, keep my costs down, I
can offer a killer price on new construction. I know for sure I can
sell enough units to pay for the land and the infrastructure. If some
of the parcels sit until the market turns around, that's fine. It's still
a good investment."

"You said you were breaking ground next month. Isn't it unusual
to start construction so quickly?"

He took a deep breath. "Look, Detective Carrick, I don't have
time to go into all of the nuances of this deal—it actually get's kind
of complicated when you get down to it—but the sale of the main
parcel includes a clause that construction on the infrastructure
must begin by a certain date. That's probably part of why it was
such a good deal."

"Is that unusual?"

"Not terribly."

"Okay, and the lease-back, doesn't that make the deal even more
complicated? And that brings me back to my first question, how
are you getting all those deals closed so quickly?"

"The lease-back was no big problem, and the deals were all structured the same. Plus, we're dealing with the same local listing agent on all of them. We've structured the deals to make everything as smooth as possible."

"The same agent for every one of those deals?"

"That's right. She made a lot of money from it, but she's been pretty helpful in putting the whole thing together."

"And who is that?" I asked.

"Her name is Sydney Bricker."

56

Sydney Bricker didn't pick up, so I left her a message saying I wanted to talk to her. I didn't say why. I drove in the direction of her office, but I wasn't sure yet if that's where I wanted to go. I wasn't entirely satisfied with Rupp's answers, and I hadn't gotten a chance to ask all my questions, but he had made it pretty clear he didn't want to talk to me anymore.

When I saw signs pointing toward Pine Crest College, I turned to follow them.

I was looking for Simpkins's office, but instead I found Simpkins himself, walking across the quad in the middle of a small cluster of young women.

He must have seen me out of the corner of his eye because his head whipped around and our eyes met. He looked back at one of the girls who had been talking. When he glanced back a moment later, there was resignation in his eyes; I was still there, and getting closer. He took a few more steps, then turned in my direction.

A couple of the girls almost stumbled as they tried to adjust their stride. One of them stifled a cough.

"You're Nola's friend. Carrick, right?"

"Detective Carrick, that's right."

"What brings you to Pine Crest?" Simpkins asked. "Thinking of taking some classes? We have a great continuing ed program."

"I spoke to your friend Rupp, and I wanted to ask you a couple of the questions I asked him, or tried to ask him. Do you have a moment?"

He sighed heavily, then turned back to his retinue. "Okay, everyone, I will see you tomorrow. Remember, if your lab partners were out sick, you need to get them your notes. And Maria, don't forget you owe me a lab report."

As they drifted away, Simpkins indicated which way he was walking and I fell in step beside him.

"So, what can I answer for you?"

"I have a question about genetically engineered pharmaceutical crops."

"I doubt I can help you any more than Rupp can," he said. "He's much more up on that sort of thing than I am."

"Maybe so. Would it be possible to genetically engineer apples to produce opioids?"

"Would it be possible? Yes."

"Yes?"

"Sure, I would think so. Why not? I mean, I don't think anyone has done it, but they've done things like it, so why not? I'm sure there would be hurdles to get past, but there are all sorts of drugs being genetically engineered into plants. The bigger question is why?"

"What do you mean?"

"Why would you do it? Why would you engineer a plant to create a substance that is already created by another plant? Heroin comes from opium poppies. Why go to all that trouble when you can already get it from them? It would be like engineering apples to produce orange juice. Why bother, when there are already oranges, right?"

"Maybe because heroin is illegal and orange juice isn't."

"Point taken." He shrugged.

"And poppies only grow in certain places, forcing people to go to great lengths to transport heroin to other places."

He shrugged again. "I guess it makes some sense, but it seems like a lot of trouble. Then again, people have done much stranger things in transgenics."

"Like what?"

"You mean apart from the glow-in-the-dark puppies and the mice with human ears on their backs?" He laughed. "It's a strange new world out there, Carrick. Why do you ask about the apples and the opioids?"

"When I asked Rupp if it could be done, he said no."

"Really? He probably thought you meant had it already been done."

"He said it was very unlikely, and that only someone with an astonishing intellect could pull off something like that."

Simpkins laughed. "I don't know Rupp all that well, but I think the only intellect he would be astonished by is his own." Simpkins stopped and turned toward me. "Look, I have another class in ten minutes, and I have to prepare. I don't know what you're getting at, but Rupp is much more of an expert in these matters than I am." He shrugged. "Maybe there is something about that plant and that compound that makes them ill-suited for each other. Maybe there is some other reason I'm unfamiliar with as to why it wouldn't work, okay?" He looked at his watch.

"Right. Well, thanks for your time."

*　*　*

As I was getting back into my car, another call came in. I thought it might be Bricker, but I didn't recognize the number. I considered not answering it, but that hadn't worked out so well for me lately. "Hello?"

"This Doyle Carrick?"

"Yes. Who's this?"

"Charlie Brand, at Brand Agricultural Aviation. You were out here looking for me?"

"I was out there looking for a red biplane crop duster with a black-and-white stripe. You got one?"

"Nope. Why you looking for it?"

"I just want to talk to whoever owns it."

"Why's that?"

"Someone sprayed my property in the middle of the night. I wanted to find out what it was and why he did it."

"Right. You're a cop?"

"Philly PD. But in this matter, I'm just a landowner."

"Guy's name is Ricky Spetzer. I got a few questions for him myself. You get here in the next ten minutes, I'll take you along with me."

"I can be there in twenty."

He grunted. "Hurry up."

Charlie Brand came out of the office to meet me. He was a big guy, a couple of inches taller than me and maybe twenty pounds heavier. He had the posture and the demeanor of someone who had left the military with a full pension.

He eyed me appraisingly then smirked as I approached him with my hand outstretched. I gave his hand a firm shake, but that didn't seem to count for much.

"Come on," he said, turning on his heel. "We're out back."

The hangar door was open, and the yellow single wing was out on the grass, waiting to go.

"You're lucky I got a two-seater," he said over his shoulder.

"We're flying?"

My lack of enthusiasm must have been apparent, because Brand's face opened up in a cruel smile. "Yup."

He gave me a helmet to wear and climbed into the front compartment. I put the helmet on, and as he went about checking readouts and flicking switches, the helmet speakers crackled.

"Buckle up," he said. The engine growled to life, then settled into a loud purr. A moment later, we were bouncing down the runway and skipping up into the air.

The scenery was beautiful, but the sensation in my stomach was not. Above the noise from the engine, I could hear a hiss coming from the helmet speakers, so I knew they were on. But apart from an occasional grunt or sigh, Brand didn't say another word during the rest of the half-hour flight.

When the sound of the engine changed and I felt like we were getting lower, I looked down and saw a small clearing below. Off to the side was a double-wide trailer and a large, rusted metal hangar. The clearing grew larger as we made our descent, but it didn't seem to grow larger enough.

I could see that the big doors on the side of the hangar were open, and inside I could see a bright red wing. As we bounced onto the grass field, a door opened in the metal shack and a skinny guy in overalls stepped out. He had a wispy beard, and he looked up at us, squinting into the late afternoon sun. He seemed to tense up, and he took a step back. His head snapped from left to right as if he was trying to decide which way to go, then he took off at an unsteady sprint toward a pickup truck parked on a driveway.

We came down gently and Brand kept the engine going, pulling the plane across the field and angling it toward the truck. As we overtook the guy in the overalls, he looked over at us, did a double take, then slowed.

Brand killed the engine, and when we came to a stop he jumped out of the plane, striding menacingly toward the guy with the beard. The guy took a couple of steps backward and smiled nervously. I hurried out after them, wondering what I had stepped into.

"Where you going, Ricky?" Brand asked, in a gravelly voice that sounded a bit too much like Clint Eastwood to be wholly unintentional.

"Hey, Charlie," Spetzer said. Then he looked at me. "Who's this?"

"Guy's got a couple questions for you." Brand walked right up to Ricky, standing close and looking down at him. "I got a couple myself."

"Sure, Charlie. Whatever you say," Ricky said, taking another step back.

Brand stepped to the side so he was no longer between Spetzer and me.

"That your plane?" I asked, hooking a thumb at the red plane in the hangar.

Spetzer smiled, like maybe he was hoping to make me an ally. "Sure is."

"That plane sprayed my house in Dunston the night before last."

The smile disappeared. "Did it?"

"Yes, it did. And I'd like to find out what it was spraying, and why."

Spetzer looked down and laughed nervously.

"I'd also like to know why you were doing it in the middle of the night."

Brand looked at me, then cocked an eye at Spetzer, waiting for an explanation.

Spetzer laughed again. A jittery smile played across his lips, then trembled for a second and fell. His eyes welled up. "You're the guy who shot at me."

Brand turned to look at me, but I don't think he entirely disapproved. He turned back to Spetzer and waited.

"They had guns," Spetzer whined. "They meant business."

Brand snorted. "You mean they *were* business. How much did they pay you?"

I held up a hand to stop him. "So what was it you sprayed?"

Brand gave me a look to let me know he didn't like my hand. I ignored him, and he got over it.

Spetzer shrugged. "Nothing, they said."

"What do you mean, 'nothing'?"

"They said it was harmless. It was like . . . flour or something. They said it wasn't going to hurt nobody. One of the guys ate some of it in front of me."

It *was* flour. In my mind, an image flashed: sacks of white powder in the back of that van. "Why were you spraying it?"

He shook his head. "They wouldn't say. All they said was, if I did it, no one would get hurt, but if I didn't, somebody would get hurt plenty and it would be me. I figured maybe they was sending someone a message."

"Why was it at night?"

"I don't know. 'Cause they had guns and they said so, man."

"Why were you flying so low?"

Brand turned to look at me again. "It's always low. That's part of the job."

"No, Charlie, he's right," Spetzer said. "It was low. They said it had to be. I figured it was part of the message, or 'cause I was just doing a small area. I wasn't crazy about that part neither, flying so low and at night. But it wasn't like I could say no."

"Right," Brand said, mimicking him. "'They had guns and they said so.'"

"Fuck you, Brand, you weren't there!"

"All right, all right," I said. "So who was it, anyway?"

Spetzer shook his head. "I don't know. There was a couple of them. They was foreigners. They just showed up."

"What'd they look like?"

"One guy was young, a little taller than me, had this long blond hair, like a fucking shampoo commercial. The other guy was bigger, meaner. Had all this junk stuck in his face."

"Junk like what?"

"You know, earrings and stuff."

"In his eyebrows?"

"In his eyebrows, his nose, all that. I think he was the one in charge. He was a scary motherfucker."

Scary, indeed, I thought, picturing the badass who had leveled me behind Branson's. "Get any names?"

"The big guy was called Levkov, I think. The guy in charge. That's all I heard."

"Levkov," I repeated. Now he had a name.

"You done this before?" Brand asked.

He looked down. "Twice before this."

Brand looked over at me, shaking his head, like this proved what kind of lowlife Spetzer was.

"They pay you?" I asked.

Spetzer nodded.

"Cash?"

He nodded again.

"How much?" Brand asked, stepping closer to him.

"Five grand a shot."

Brand stepped even closer. "So here I am, trying to let you keep your fucked-up little territory that you can barely manage to service, and you're doing midnight runs spraying some mystery bullshit in my backyard?"

Spetzer shrank away from him, looking away to the side. "I know Charlie, and I'm sorry. Maybe they knew you wouldn't go along. But I mean it, man, these guys were scary."

"You don't think I'm scary?"

Spetzer laughed at that, then winced, like he was expecting a smack. "Charlie, you can kick my ass or ruin my business, whatever, but no, you ain't scary like these guys was."

57

When we got out of the plane back at Brand's little airfield, he gave me a nod, then turned and walked back to the house.

I yelled thanks, and he gave me a half wave without turning around. My entire body felt rubbery and weird. I wondered if it was the plane ride or the Narcan wearing off.

When I got in my car, I checked my phone and saw I'd missed another call from Sydney Bricker. This time, I listened to her message right away.

"Mr. Carrick, I need to see you, as soon as possible." She didn't sound like a shark in a power skirt. She sounded small and frightened. "I'm at my office. Please call me. It's important."

I called her back and got her voice mail.

"This is Doyle Carrick. I got your message, so call me back at this number. I'm on my way over to your office right now. I'll be there in about ten minutes."

My mouth felt dry, and I wondered if my limbs were starting to feel heavy again or if I was imagining it. I started to put my phone away, but instead I made one more call.

Danny Tennison answered the phone with a sigh. "I'm going to start blocking your calls."

"No, you're not."

"Seriously, Doyle, I know that bust went sour, most of it was bullshit. You're in the shit, and you need to lay low. Way low. Tell me how the weather is out there, and then leave me the fuck alone."

"Guy named Levkov, just one name. But I think he's at the center of whatever's going on up here."

"Doyle! Knock it off! There is no center of whatever's going on up there. If you got something, give it to the locals and walk away from it. If they drop the ball, fine. Leave it dropped."

"Danny, it's just one name—"

"No! I'm hanging up now, Doyle, and if you don't have stories about fish that you caught or movies that you saw or even a goddamn dump that you took, anything other than police work, then I don't want to hear from you until you're reinstated. But I got to tell you, at the rate you're going, I don't see that happening."

"Jesus, Danny—"

"Don't 'Jesus, Danny,' me. You need to grow up, Doyle. You're not a kid anymore, and that whole cliché, rebel-against-authority thing is just you being a fuck-up."

"Yeah? Well, maybe I do have issues with authority, and maybe it is cliché, but I don't think it's normal to have some asshole like Suarez barking at you all day."

"It's called having a boss, Doyle. No one loves it, but most grown-ups learn how to deal with it."

"You know what? I think maybe you're the one who's got issues with authority, like maybe you like it too goddamned much." I laughed bitterly. "Maybe that's why you're so happily married."

Danny said, "Fuck you." Then he hung up.

I immediately regretted having brought his marriage into it, but I knew I would have kept going if he hadn't hung up.

I still couldn't tell if I was getting reintoxicated from the Narcan wearing off, but I figured if there was any doubt after a buzzkill conversation like that, I'd better play it safe. I took out the little envelope Janie had given me and swallowed two of the pills.

A couple of minutes later, I pulled up in front of Bricker's office. I immediately picked up a bad vibe. The exchange with Danny had brought me down, but it was more than that. The streets were strangely deserted, and so quiet I could have been the last man alive. I felt a slight chill. A dark layer of low clouds had developed out of nothing, pushing down on the world.

I knocked on the outer office door and waited, then knocked again and walked in.

The small reception area was empty, and the door to the office was open.

Sydney Bricker was at her desk, or rather across it. Her legs dangled in front of it, her short skirt riding up her thighs as her back arched over the blotter, her arms by her sides. Her head hung over the far side with her mouth wide open.

I took out my gun before moving around to the back of the desk, as if I could protect myself from what I was going to find.

Her left eye was open, staring blindly at the back of her deep leather chair. Her right eye was a bloody ruin, two inches of one of her personalized pens protruding from it, just enough so I could see the gold script *S* in Sydney. A thin red line led from her eye into her hairline, the blood wicking down her hair, which hung down onto the padded seat, curling into the blood that had pooled there.

I'd had a nagging feeling that something else was going on even before Stan Bowers told me most of the heroin from the bust wasn't heroin. But while Sydney Bricker's murder confirmed my vague suspicions, it didn't clarify them. I still didn't know what the hell was going on.

One thing I did know was that I had to get out of there. Pruitt could show up at any moment. Bricker had called me less than a half hour earlier. Careful not to touch anything, I pushed open the door and looked up and down the street. It was empty.

The sky looked even more ominous, but there was something else as well, an atmosphere of dread so thick I could feel it on my skin. Just like Crooked Creek Farm, where the bust went down, this place was haunted now.

58

I walked quickly to my car, keeping my head down in case the streets weren't as deserted as they seemed.

As I opened my car door, I sensed movement behind me and simultaneously felt a sharp pain in the center of my back. For an instant I thought I'd been stabbed, but then I recognized the pain as the barrel of a gun applied with gusto.

"Don't fucking breathe," said a thick Russian accent, right next to my ear. "Or I'll shoot through your spine."

His gun stayed where it was, solid as a rock as his other hand swept over me in a quick but thorough frisk that included my ankles. When he was done, he was holding my gun as well as his.

"Move a muscle and I will kill you," he whispered in my ear. Then the pressure disappeared from my back. He stepped away from me, backing around the car and coming into sight on the other side of it.

It was Fabio, the guy with the long blond hair. A shampoo commercial, Spetzer had said, and he nailed it. I smiled at the thought.

"It's good you can smile," he said with a smirk. He had both guns leveled at me, keeping them close to his body. "Unlock the doors."

I flicked the power lock.

He opened the passenger door, keeping one gun pointed at me over the roof of the car and the other one pointed at me through the interior. "Nice car. You should take better care of it. Now get in."

We both got in, and I fastened my seat belt. He thought for a moment; then he did, too.

"Drive," he said.

I started up the car and pulled out. "Where?"

"Home."

It tripped me up that I didn't know where he meant. "You mean the place on Bayberry?"

He smiled and nodded. "Da," he said, easing himself around so his back was against the door. He seemed relaxed, except for his hands, which both pointed at me—my gun at my head, his gun at my belly. I couldn't decide if I would rather be killed by my own gun or his. Kind of embarrassing to be killed with your own gun. But then again, better it come from someone you know, right?

"So, who are you?" I asked.

He laughed a little to himself, like that didn't deserve even a badass answer. "You can call me Mikhail."

"So what is it you want, Mikhail?"

"I want you to shut up and drive."

I drove slowly, partly because I needed time to think. Also, with two guns pointed at me, I didn't want to hit a pothole and get the festivities started ahead of schedule.

"So were you in business with Cooney, is that it? Some kind of cartel?"

He laughed again. "Cooney? You fuck with me? Cooney is a joke."

"Well, if this is about the drugs, I'd say just leave it alone. The case is closed. No one knows who killed Cooney, but they're thinking it was one of the guys at Crooked Creek Farm."

He snorted. "Drugs are a joke, too. Chump change. Now shut the fuck up and drive."

It was a ten-minute drive, and we were five minutes into it when Mikhail let out a laugh. "It's a shame about your lady friend," he said. "But you shouldn't be so hard on yourself."

I gave him a look, letting him know I knew more was coming but I didn't really care.

"Is understandable, I guess," he went on. "Suspended from your job, about to lose it completely. Now you are using drugs. Especially after the death of your parents, the ugliness with Miss Bricker. It is not surprising is all too much for you."

When I looked at him again, I wasn't trying to convey anything. I was just trying to figure out what the hell he was talking about.

"Is not uncommon among cops like you." He smiled. "Tragic, yes, but not rare."

He wiggled my gun at me, and that's when I understood. My gun, my car, my house. He was going to make it look like suicide, probably set it up to look like I killed Bricker.

It annoyed me that my life needed so little embellishment to justify suicide. I'd have to give that some thought later. Meanwhile, I had about a minute to come up with a plan. Mikhail was armed and I wasn't, and even in a fair fight he probably could have taken me. I was looking for an advantage, and I couldn't seem to find one. Maybe I could insult his hair, get him angry enough to slip up.

I was so intent on finding a way out, I almost missed the turn onto Valley Road.

"Ah-ah!" Mikhail barked, reminding me to turn.

I took the turn a little wide and a little fast, but I made it onto

Valley, bracing myself as we scraped bottom on that damned dip in the road.

Mikhail lurched in his seat, his head almost hitting the roof of the car. "Careful, asshole," he said.

Given the state of the rest of the car, I wasn't too concerned about damaging the undercarriage but I was a little worried about an accidental discharge. Still, Mikhail suddenly seemed a little off balance, and it occurred to me that while this place was new to me, it was still somehow my home turf. There had to be some advantage in that.

Mikhail's eyes narrowed, like he had somehow read my mind. He inched farther away from me, angling his back against the door and widening the space between us. He was taking no chances, his eyes glued on me and both guns held up with great deliberation. He was expecting a move to come from me soon, and I knew it. That was my second advantage.

It didn't amount to much.

Up ahead, I saw Pear Tree Lane, the little road where Squirrel had left his truck. On an impulse, I turned onto it. Mikhail looked out the window, then back at me.

"What the fuck you doing?"

"I'm driving home, like you said." I let my foot sink down, just a bit, picking up a little speed.

"This is not the way to your house."

"What are you talking about? This is the way I always go."

Mikhail said, "Turn the car around."

"What are you talking about? This is the way to the house." We were approaching the bend in the road.

"Turn the fucking car around."

"Look," I said. "I'm not in any hurry to get home, but this is the fastest way, I just go up here and make a left." I was making stuff up now, just trying to sound like I was making sense.

"Turn around now!" he shouted, flecking my face with spit. "Right fucking now!"

"Okay! Okay! I'll turn around the car." I cowered away from him and put up one hand defensively, partly to appear afraid, partly to give him something to look at, keep his eyes pinned on me.

We were doing about forty miles an hour. He seemed to relax just a bit, and God love him, he leaned further back against the window.

I almost wanted to thank him, but I never got the chance.

The next moment passed as a series of distinct images, a slow-motion slideshow flickering in silence: Mikhail turning to look out the windshield, like he'd seen something from the corner of his eye. The windshield exploding as Squirrel's tailgate punched through it. The air filled with fragments of glass, catching the light, sparkling all around Mikhail, like he was in a snow globe. More glass as the tailgate chopped through the windshield's metal frame and the side windows shattered. An almost pyrotechnic explosion of red as the metal connected with Mikhail's head, obliterating everything in a wash of blood.

The moment ended abruptly when the airbags deployed, a slap in the face as the car spun out across the road. My foot found the brake and the car stopped. The impact left me stunned for a moment, but the sight that greeted me when the bags deflated left me stunned for quite a bit longer.

Mikhail's arms were thrashing around in wild spasms, like he was having a tantrum. I guess I would have been upset, too. I grabbed at his hands, trying to point the guns away from me. It wasn't until I had both hands pinned down and the muscle spasms stopped that I could assess the damage.

The tailgate had punched through the windshield, severed one of the pillars holding the roof onto the car, and smashed both passenger side windows and the rear windshield. But that was nothing compared to what it had done to Mikhail. His head was gone completely above the jaw. Chunks of it littered the back of the car—clumps of long hair covered with blood, shards of bloody bone. There didn't seem to be enough solids to make up the rest of his head, but there was more than enough blood. It seemed to cover every inch of the car's interior. My face was soaking wet with it, and even though my mouth had been closed, I spat anyway, just to be sure.

The headrest was in the way back, wedged under the remains of the rear window. When I saw an ear sitting next to it, my stomach lurched, and I scrambled to get out of the car. My fingers slipped on the bloody seat belt and the bloody door handle until I finally got the door open and fell out onto the road. My midsection heaved but nothing came out.

After a few seconds the spasms stopped. When I got to my feet, my head was ringing like a bell, but I paused to take in the situation.

The half of the windshield that remained was so badly shattered it was almost opaque. I yanked it the rest of the way out of its frame, so I'd be able to see. I didn't know what to do with it, but the back window was missing too, so I dumped it inside, covering the ear.

Across the street, the tailgate on Squirrel's Wagoneer was hanging off and smeared with bright red. As I walked over to it, I saw a clump of flesh snagged on the corner. I knew I couldn't just leave it there like that. The tailgate came off with a little twist. I dragged it back across the street and slid it through the back window, with the remains of the windshield. A foot and a half of it protruded from the back, but I didn't want to adjust Mikhail's seat to give it more room.

When I got back into the car, I saw Mikhail's hands still gripping the guns. I pried his fingers off them, trying to focus solely on the task despite the unsettling feeling that he was watching me. I left his gun on the floor between his feet and tucked mine into my waistband. The holster at my back was about the only thing not wet with blood, and the gun was going to need a good scrubbing before getting anywhere near it.

What was left of my car was already pointed in the right direction, so I put it in gear and headed toward home. I drove slowly at first, nervous about getting pulled over, but I quickly realized that between the semi-convertible roof, the headless passenger, the bright red interior, and the bloody tailgate sticking out the back window, it wasn't going to take a traffic violation to get me in trouble. I put my foot down and drove, the wind in my face and the roof bouncing up and down over my head, determined to get where I was going before anyone saw me.

I turned up the driveway without slowing down and the roof tapped me on the head, but I pulled right up to the garage and stopped hard. I got out and opened the garage door, and when I got back into the car, the way what was left of Mikhail's head was turned in my direction, I got the distinct and unnerving feeling that he wanted to say something to me.

I pulled into the garage and tried not to look at him as I gathered my phone charger and a few other things out of the glove compartment.

When I got out, I paused at the garage door and looked back. The front of the car was virtually untouched, but between the crumpled side and the demolished roof, I was pretty sure it was totaled. And even if it wasn't, I doubted I'd ever be able to forget the image of Mikhail in the passenger seat. As I closed the garage door, I thought maybe I just wasn't meant to have a nice car.

59

After ten minutes in a hot shower with a nail brush and a box of Boraxo, I was clean and so was my gun. I felt a certain attachment to my weapons, but showering with my gun felt like crossing a line.

Without a good dousing with gun oil, it would be a rusted mess in a few days. But at the rate I was going, I probably wouldn't be around to worry about it. I reassembled the gun and put it on top of the toilet. When it hit the porcelain, it made a loud clack—the sound of contact between two surfaces that weren't meant to touch.

My face was sore as hell from the airbag, and even more so after the scrubbing, but it didn't look too bad, and my nose wasn't broken. I closed my eyes as I was drying myself off, and saw a flash of Mikhail's headless body. I was thinking maybe I would try not closing my eyes for a while when I heard movement downstairs and I froze. Holding my breath and listening, I heard the sound again. The steps creaking. Someone was coming upstairs.

I wrapped myself in the towel and quietly scooped up the gun and slid in the clip. My heart picked up the pace, but just enough to keep up with the adrenaline flowing through my veins.

I heard another creak, and a couple of seconds later another. Then a louder one. The fourth step.

I timed the steps in my mind, rocking on my feet, getting into the rhythm, waiting for that ninth step. I didn't like it that the bathroom door opened inward, but I'd have surprise on my side and a superior position. When I heard the creak of the ninth step, I yanked open the door and sprang, leading with the gun.

"Freeze, motherfucker!" I yelled. I was looking for a gun, and if it was pointed anywhere near me, I was going to start shooting. But there was no gun, there was just Moose, holding a bag of cookies, wide-eyed and squealing in terror, stumbling backward down the steps.

I hurtled down the steps after him, tackling him at the bottom and clamping a hand over his mouth until recognition dawned in his eyes. I put a finger across my lips, waiting for him to nod his understanding before I removed the hand from his mouth.

"Are you okay?" I asked quietly.

He nodded. "You got to stop doing that. What the fuck is going on?"

"It's a long story. Short answer: I have no idea, but we need to get out of here, okay?"

"Why?"

"Trust me."

He looked at me for a moment. "Okay."

"You got your car?"

"I got Frank's pickup truck, yeah."

"Good. We're leaving now."

"Why?"

"I'll tell you later. Here, take this." I held out my gun to him, and his eyes went wide again. "I got to get some clothes on."

He shook his head. "I don't do guns."

"I hear you. But sometimes you have to."

"No. Not me. It's not a good idea anyway."

I took a breath and nodded. "Okay, but if you see anybody, you come get me."

He nodded, and I ran upstairs. I stuffed my bloody clothes in a bag and shoved the bag under my bed. I had just pulled on a fresh pair of jeans and some socks when I heard Moose at the bottom of the stairs, calling me in a loud whisper. "Doyle!"

I grabbed a shirt and a pair of boots and went to the top of the stairs.

"It's Pruitt," he said.

"Great." Whether he was there to ask me about my trip to the hospital for Narcan, or about Sydney Bricker, or about the headless Russian, his presence wasn't going to make my life any easier. "Tell him I'm not here. Tell him you haven't seen me."

Moose stared up at me and made a face to let me know he was not comfortable lying to Pruitt.

I ducked back behind the banister to make sure there was no chance of being seen from the door. "Just tell him you haven't seen me," I repeated.

Almost simultaneously, a terse knock sounded on the front door. *Bam-bam-bam!*

Even as stressed as I was, I smiled at the sound of Moose clearing his throat before he answered it.

"Hi, Chief Pruitt," he said cheerfully. "What can I do for you?"

"Where's Carrick?"

"Doyle? I don't know. Haven't seen him in a while. What's up?"

"Any idea where he is?"

"Not really. Might be at Branson's."

There was a pause, maybe Pruitt thinking about pushing it or asking to come inside for a look around. "All right," he said finally. "You see Carrick, you give me a call."

"I'll tell him you were looking for him."

"I didn't say that, dumbass. I said you give me a call. Can you remember that?"

I could hear Moose turning sullen. "Yes, sir."

When I heard the front door close, I cursed silently. It sounded like Pruitt was hoping to pin Bricker on me. He had probably checked her voice mail and heard my message saying I was coming to see her.

Creeping to the window at the end of the second floor hall, I watched Pruitt's car back out the driveway and speed off down Bayberry. When I turned away from the window, I saw Moose at the top of the stairs.

"That was not cool," he said, his voice shaking.

"Sorry. You did great."

"Bullshit. Now tell me what's going on."

"I'll tell you later."

"No, no, no. I just lied to a cop who already hates me. You tell me now."

"You know Sydney Bricker?"

"The lawyer? I've met her."

"She's dead. And the guys who killed her are trying to set me up."

"Oh my God! What? Why do you think that?"

"Because one of them told me so. Right before I killed him."

Moose's eyes were big again, and his mouth was open.

"Now, I need to get out of here so I can figure this out. You need to get out of here in case anyone comes to kill me and finds you here instead."

Moose was on his heels. I felt bad throwing this news at him, but I needed him to move quickly and I didn't have time to break it to him gently. I looked at my watch. "I need to go check on something. You got ten minutes to pack some clothes and anything you want to take with you. You could be gone a couple days." He could be gone a lot longer, but I didn't tell him that.

He nodded, a shocked, jittery movement that looked like it could easily go off the rails and turn into the shakes.

"Okay. I'll be back in five or ten minutes. I'll knock four times: two and then two. You don't let anybody else in. If I'm not back in twenty minutes, you go."

"Where?"

"Away. Anywhere. Go home to your folks' house, read about whatever happens here in the news."

He turned a shade paler, which was good. I wanted him to take this seriously.

Turning to go out the back door, I paused. "One last thing: Don't go in the garage."

60

I slipped out the back door and across the Christmas tree farm, running parallel to Bayberry Road for fifty yards before cutting across it and plunging into the thick screen of Siberian elm that lined the tall steel fence.

I paused inside the darkness of the brush. Then I jumped up onto the fence, climbing up and over and then halfway down before dropping to the ground on the other side. Keeping low to the ground, I took off at a fast, steady pace, over the rows of harvested corn. When I found the diagonal path I had followed before, I veered alongside it, losing it and finding it again several times as I rose and fell with the rolling hills.

When I came over a rise and saw the white tent, and two armed guards patrolling, I stopped and fell to the ground. They were thirty yards apart, and as soon as one of them disappeared around the corner of the tent, another appeared from around the other end. I'd seen all I needed to see. I had been hoping to pick an apple or two from over the fence and have them tested, but even from eighty yards away, I could see that the trees were gone. There weren't even any stumps, just a broad swath of freshly overturned soil.

The corn was gone. The trees were gone. Whatever they were up to, it felt like they were almost finished.

Having seen the armed patrols, I kept even lower as I returned the same way I had come.

Back at the house, I gave the agreed-upon knock, two and then two, and Moose opened the door for me. He looked pale and sweaty and very glad to see me, like his imagination had been hard at work while I was gone.

"You okay?" I asked.

He nodded.

I clapped him on the shoulder and told him to go out front and pull the truck around back. When he did, I squeezed into the tiny space behind the driver's seat and pulled a blanket over me.

Moose started up the truck and looked back over the seat at me. "Where are we going?"

"Shachterville."

"Shachterville?"

"That's where Nola is staying."

We rolled down the driveway, and he pulled out onto Bayberry. Five minutes later, I pulled the blanket off me.

"Okay," I said. "I got some questions for you."

"*You've* got questions?"

"You said Squirrel made his moonshine from apples, right?"

"It wasn't moonshine, it was squish. But yes, it was made from apples."

"And he stole the apples, right?"

"Well, that's one way of putting it, yes."

"Did he ever take apples from the mystery farm next to Nola's property?"

He thought for a moment. "I don't know, but he definitely might have. He said it was a hassle to get to, but wherever he was getting that last batch, I think he went back a few times. He said there was something special about that last batch."

"There was."

"Was what?"

"Something special."

"What do you mean?"

"I think the last batch had heroin in it."

Moose shook his head. "What, you think Squirrel spiked his all-natural nature booze with smack? No way."

"No. I think the apples he used already had the heroin inside." I told him about my experiences that afternoon.

"Jesus. But, why would they put heroin in the apples?"

"I don't think they put it there, I think they grew it there. Remember you were going on about genetically modified crops, and pharmaceuticals?"

"Whoa." He was quiet for a moment. "So that's how I ODed."

"Yeah, I guess so."

A sly smile spread across his lips. "Then I guess you owe me an apology."

I looked out the window. "I guess so." That was as much as he was going to get.

61

The house was dark when we pulled up, and I felt a brief panic that the bad guys had found Nola until I saw the dim blue flicker of television through the windows. On a sick day, even Miss Organic liked to veg out in front of the TV. Before we went up onto the porch, I grabbed Moose by the elbow. "I'm pretty sure she's feeling like crap, and I'm going to hit her with the whole Sydney Bricker thing," I told him. "So let's try to keep things as light as we can. I haven't told her about your overdose, so lets not mention that now."

"Okay."

I rapped twice on the front door, and then twice again.

Moose smirked. "What, you only know one secret knock?"

I waited a full minute, trying to keep my own imagination at bay. Then I repeated the knock.

"I'm coming, I'm coming," croaked a faint voice that sounded vaguely like my grandmother. Moose and I looked at each other as the keys scraped the other side of the door.

The figure that opened the door looked like my grandmother as well, right at the end. It was Nola, wrapped in a bathrobe. Her skin was a greenish gray, except her lips, which were white, and her eyelids and nose, which were bright red.

"You look like shit!" Moose blurted out. He gave me a look, like he thought it was my fault.

"What are you doing here?" she asked Moose.

"I don't know," he replied. "I'm just doing what I'm told."

She turned to me. "Doyle, what the hell is going on?"

"I'm still figuring it out. But something definitely is."

She gave me a dubious look, then turned to go back inside. "Take off your shoes before you come in."

Moose and I complied, then followed her inside.

The television cast a bluish light over the small living room. Nola coughed as she shuffled back to the armchair. She had a water glass and a couple of mugs of tea on the table next to her, a circle of crumpled up Kleenex surrounding the wastebasket on the floor. The chair faced the television, which was showing an infomercial with the sound off.

Moose fluffed her pillow and pulled the blanket over her, then headed into the kitchen and started tidying up. Nola looked up at me expectantly.

"Remember you told me the parcels behind your land kept changing hands? Well, a bunch of different companies owned the parcels, but Sydney Bricker was the agent for all of them. She, or whoever she was working for, bought each plot from the original owners at a premium price and sold them to Rothe, the developer, for a lot less."

"For less?"

I nodded. "Rothe told me other developers were trying to make a go of it, but they bailed and sold to him at a loss. It was a complicated deal, or a bunch of complicated deals. And there were lease-backs, so Rothe doesn't actually take possession for another month, even though he owns the land now. They completed the sales yesterday."

She looked at me, confused and bored, the way you would look if you felt like crap and someone was doing a bad job of explaining a complicated real-estate deal. Her eyes said one word: "So?"

"Today Sydney Bricker was murdered."

Her eyes widened.

I nodded. "Pruitt seems to think I did it, and I think it was set up to look that way."

"Why do you think that?"

"Mostly because some crazy Russian jumped me and told me so. Then he told me he was going to kill me and make it look like a suicide."

Nola's red eyes narrowed, and her faced pinched in anticipation. She seemed to be bracing herself for what was coming next. "Then what happened?" she whispered.

"I killed him."

Her eyes closed, and she exhaled quietly. She reached forward and squeezed my knee, then started coughing uncontrollably. The coughing went on and on, a deep, ragged, violent cough.

Moose came into the room, and we looked at each other.

"Sorry," she said when the coughing fit was finally over. "I feel like I'm dying from the inside out. I need to get home."

"Sorry," I said, squeezing her knee back. "You need to get to a hospital."

62

"No, Doyle," Nola said firmly. "I told you. No hospitals."

She said it with absolute conviction, and her jaw clenched, seemingly against any argument. But as her eyes bulged slightly and her face reddened, I realized she was clenching against the cough that was struggling to come out. When it erupted, it consumed her. She was doubled over and gagging. When she finally stopped, eyes streaming, she nodded and said, "Okay."

While she was getting ready, her fever seemed to spike, sweat dripping down her face even as she started to shiver. We wrapped her in a quilt and put her in the backseat of her car. Moose drove the car, and I followed in Frank's truck. He did better this time.

When we got to the hospital, Moose ran to get a wheelchair, but there were none available. As we helped Nola walk, she grabbed my sleeve and looked up at me, her eyes swimming with fear and anxiety. "I hate hospitals."

I squeezed her shoulder as I helped her along, and she reached up and held my hand.

"This is even worse than last time," she said in a strained voice. "I can't go through that again."

"You're going to be okay," I told her. I knew I had absolutely nothing to base that hope on, but it wasn't until the doors opened to let us in that the true hollowness of my words became apparent. The place was packed, more than before, with the sick and the injured milling around like a scene from a third-world country. But none of them looked as rough as Nola.

Moose looked around the room slowly. "What the hell is going on?"

"I don't know."

At least thirty people were between us and the admissions desk. I was trying to figure out how many of them were in line when I saw Janie Walters weaving through the crowd.

I called her name and she looked around, distracted. When she saw us, she came over.

"Hi, guys." She looked at us, concerned. "Are you two all right?"

"Yeah, we're fine."

"Okay, well, I'm very busy," she said, backing away. "The CDC is due any minute. . . ."

"This is Nola," I said, putting my hand on Nola's shoulder. "She's pretty sick."

Janie looked down as if noticing Nola for the first time. She had a dubious expression on her face, and I got the impression she was about to explain that "pretty sick" didn't buy you as much as usual on a day like this. But when she saw Nola, she stopped and looked closer. "Hi, Nola," she murmured, looking into Nola's eye, then taking out a little flashlight and looking again. "How long have you been feeling sick?"

Nola's red eyes looked sideways at us, questioning. "A couple of days, I guess."

"She thinks she might—" I started, but Moose and Nola both looked over at me. Moose gave his head a little shake.

Janie paused, waiting for me to finish.

". . . need a doctor," I said.

"Right," Janie said. Then she barked at Wanda to call Doctor McGee. "We've got her now," Janie said as she steered Nola through the swinging doors. As the doors closed, Janie looked back over her shoulder and held up a finger, asking me to wait.

I nodded, but I didn't like it. I had eluded Pruitt once here, and I felt like I was pushing my luck trying it again. I nudged Moose toward a spot in the corner, behind the soda machine, just in case.

"What was that about?" I asked Moose.

"Sorry. I thought you were going to say something about the multiple chemical sensitivity."

"I was."

He shook his head. "Not a good idea. A lot of doctors don't think it's real, and a lot of insurance companies won't pay for treatment of it, so it's best to be careful. Nola will tell them once they have her in the system for something else."

I nodded but didn't say anything.

"She's scared," Moose said, and I nodded again. "You never met her friend Cheryl. Nice lady, but really high maintenance. They met in a treatment facility, after Nola's second incident. Some kind of biodetoxification program or something."

"What's that, like, some kind of cure?"

"That was the plan, I guess."

"It didn't work?"

He shook his head. "Not for Cheryl. Couple months after they got out she had another attack, her third, and it was a bad one. Now Cheryl spends her life terrified she's going to have a reaction to this or that. The MCS, it controls her life, every part of it."

"What about Nola?"

He shrugged. "She's been lucky so far, but she's careful." He sighed and shook his head. "Nola's one of the strongest people I know, and there's not much she's afraid of, but she's afraid of that. Afraid she might lose her normal life and end up like Cheryl. Crazy stuff."

We were quiet for a moment after that, then I leaned my head close to his. "Speaking of crazy stuff, that crop duster the other night? Turns out it was spraying flour."

"Flour? What are you talking about?"

"Had it tested."

"What's up with that?"

I shrugged, and we were both quiet again.

Looking around the room, I spotted a face I recognized. Our eyes met and then he looked away. It was the guy who had been loading his U-Haul, the guy who'd seemed so bitter and desperate to get the hell out of Dunston. He looked like hell. Not as bad as Nola, maybe, but not far off. He looked scared, too, and I felt for him. I don't think a lot of breaks had gone his way, and it didn't look like his luck was getting any better. I saw the same expression in a lot of the faces around the room, as if the fear and desperation was as contagious as the mystery flu.

I turned back to look at Moose, hoping to avoid it. "So . . . Bruce, huh?"

He gave me the same withering look he had given Janie. "Don't call me that."

"You prefer Moose?"

"Anything is better than Bruce."

"Okay, then, I have to ask: Moose? How did that happen?"

He looked like he'd known this was coming and he'd been dreading it. "If I tell you, you never bring it up again. You swear?"

That little setup stoked my curiosity big time. I held up my hand. "I swear."

He sagged a little more after that, like he had been hoping I wouldn't go along.

"When I was younger, a few years ago, I used to be in a band. The girl I was seeing decided I needed to make more of an effort when I was onstage. You know how it is. She took me shopping and made me buy stuff I'd never buy—mesh shirts and leather pants, awful stuff."

He hadn't made me promise not to laugh, but I figured it would be a good idea to resist. "Go on," I said.

He sighed deeply. "She decided my hair was boring. So she got all this . . . product."

"Product."

"The other guys in the band thought it was hilarious. I'm not saying she was like Yoko or anything, but the band did break up a few months later."

"I don't get it."

"That's how I got the nickname." He closed his eyes. "Mousse, as in M-O-U-S-S-E. Or, more accurately, Bruce Mousse."

I smiled, and so did he. "So it's not 'Moose' as in antlers."

"Well, mousse is versatile stuff, and antlers are just one possibility, especially when you use as much as she did. But no, the name was not originally in reference to a large antler-bearing mammal."

I scrunched up my face, trying not to laugh. "Well, that does clear things up. A guy your size called Moose, I was wondering if you had suffered some horrendous shrink-ray accident."

"Well, how about Doyle? It's like you got two last names, like I can't tell if you're leaving or leaving."

I gave him a deadeye stare. "My dead father named me after his dead father."

Moose looked mortified, but then I smiled and then he did.

"Very funny," he said. "So where did it come from?"

I shook my head. "Actually, I've never put it like that, but that is where it came from."

"Oh."

We were quiet for a moment after that. As we sat there, I noticed the crowd was getting larger instead of smaller. The staff kept up an admirable pace, taking people back at a steady rate, but the stream of new patients coming in the front door more than made up for it.

My cell phone lit up, telling me two things: Danny Tennison was calling from his cell phone and my battery was almost dead.

As much as I didn't want to go outside and risk being spotted, I needed to plug my phone into the truck. I had a feeling this wasn't going to be the kind of conversation I would want overheard, anyway.

"Back in a second," I told Moose as I headed out through the ambulance entrance, past the glare from the EMERGENCY sign, and got in Frank's truck. I started the engine and plugged my phone into the car charger before I answered.

"Hey, Danny," I said.

"Doyle, what the fuck is going on up there? Have you lost your fucking mind?"

"I'm thinking I might have."

"Yeah, I'm thinking that, too. You know there's a warrant out for you, right?"

I sighed. "I was thinking there might be."

"It's murder this time, Doyle. Even Suarez isn't gloating about that. They have a stiff up there, and they're saying your fingerprints are all over the murder weapon."

"My fingerprints?" I pictured the pen protruding from Sydney Bricker's eye, and the pen she gave me to sign those papers she brought over. "Fuck."

"Did you kill someone up there?"

"I didn't kill Sydney Bricker. Is that what they're saying?"

This time he sighed. "That's what they're saying. So, did you kill someone else?"

"Danny, there's something big going on out here. I found out where the heroin was coming from, and it's apples."

He was quiet for a second, and I knew I was losing him. "Apples?"

"I swear to God. I think someone may have genetically altered apples to make them produce heroin."

"Apples. Jesus, listen to yourself, Doyle. You go for a week out in the country, and now you're seeing bad guys in your fruit."

"I know it sounds crazy, Danny—"

"No, Doyle. It doesn't sound crazy; it is crazy. If you didn't kill this Bricker woman, great. But you need to get yourself a good lawyer and straighten this out. You can even come back to the city to do it, so you're among friends."

I knew I wasn't going to get through to him, and he was right: What I was saying sounded crazy. He'd be crazy to believe me.

"Yeah, okay," I said. "You're probably right."

"Finally," he said. "Now, here's what we're going to do—" But that's when I ended the call.

As I came back inside, I saw Janie talking to Moose, but she was gone before I got there.

"What did she say?" I asked.

"They're admitting Nola. Going to run some tests. They'll let us know. Could be awhile, though."

He closed his eyes and leaned against the wall. I leaned in next to him and spoke quietly.

"So, you think this apple thing could be for real?" I asked. "With the gene splicing and the heroin?"

He opened his eyes and looked at me for a second, blinking.

"Hell, yeah, I think it's possible. They're doing the same basic thing all over—different drugs and different crops, but the same basic thing."

"So, how do they do it again?"

"The way I understand it, they use different enzymes to cut up the DNA at different places. You take these sections from this plant, mix them with cut-up DNA from something else, and there you go."

"Sounds simple."

"No, there's a lot more to it than that. But I know they're already doing stuff like that. You should go ask that Rupp guy, he'll tell you all about it."

"What, because he's a geneticist?"

"Well, yeah, but that's like, his specialty, GMO pharmaceutical crops. He's written papers about this stuff. I think he did his Ph.D. on it."

"Are you serious?"

"Yeah, I looked him up online after you and Nola went to see him. Interesting guy. He grew some corn that made like, penicillin or something like that. I didn't understand a lot of it. Apparently people already knew how to create proteins in crops, but he was working on other compounds as well. He developed some antifungal wonder drug, but it hit some snags with the FDA, never got approved. He's a bit of a hotshot, has all these papers and articles. You Google his name, all sorts of stuff turns up. He got stiffed for some award a couple years ago. I didn't find much about him after that."

"No shit." Rupp had said it couldn't be done. Didn't know anything about it.

Moose looked at my face. "What?"

I stood up. "I have to go check something out."

63

I called directory assistance as I drove, hunched over sideways because my charger cord was too short for Frank's truck. Jerry Simpkins was listed as living in a small, modern-looking condo a quarter mile from the college. It seemed nice enough, but even in the dark I could tell the construction was starting to sag and crack, even before the trees had fully grown in.

The lights were on in his unit, but they were on low. I gave the door my cop knock, and it opened a few seconds later, Simpkins's head poking out.

Through the doorway, I could hear a new agey wash of piano and synthesized strings. A mixture of incense and pot smoke wafted out.

Simpkins screwed up his brow as he looked down at me from two steps up. "Carrick?" He rolled his eyes. "Are you serious?"

"Hope I'm not interrupting anything." I totally hoped I was interrupting something.

"Actually, yes, you are."

"I have a few questions for you. Do you mind if I come in?"

"Actually, yes, I—"

"Is that marijuana smoke?"

He cocked his head to one side and gave me a look.

I smiled. "Or I could just come in, ask a few questions, and leave."

He took a deep breath and let it out, then started to step outside. "Okay, ask your questions."

I shook my head. "In there."

Simpkins's shoulders sagged, and he shook his head. "Whatever."

The reefer smell was a lot stronger inside, but that's not what I was there for. The girl with her feet tucked under her on the sofa looked barely eighteen, but that wasn't what I was there for, either. She wore a short denim skirt and one of those T-shirts with the spaghetti straps. The skin around her lips was flushed pink, and her eyes were bloodshot. When she saw me, she stiffened for an instant. Then she relaxed and gave me a smile.

"This is Maria," Simpkins said. "Maria, this is Detective Carrick. I'm helping him with an investigation."

She nodded her head, bobbing it up and down like a pigeon. "Cool."

"This will just take a second," he told her, looking at me to make sure I understood that as well.

I nodded.

Simpkins led me through the small living room and the dining area and into the kitchen. He filled a glass with water from the tap. "So what can I do for you?" he asked. Then he drank half the water.

"How do you know Jason Rupp?"

He smiled, maybe relieved at the question. "I met him at a party a few years ago. The head of my department at the time, Dennis Kovitch, it was his farewell party. He knew Jason from somewhere,

I don't know. I had a very interesting talk with Rupp that night. He has quite a mind, you know."

"How well do you know him?"

"Not well. Between what I told you before and what I've told you just now, you probably know as much about him as I do. Kovitch knew him better, I guess. I could get you his number."

"Call him."

"I'm not going to call him." He laughed. "It's almost midnight on a Saturday night. If you'd like I can—"

"Call him. Right now."

I put my hands on my hips and gave him one of my crazy nutjob looks.

"I don't even know where his number is."

"Call information."

He sighed, but he took out his phone and dialed 411. "San Diego, California," he said clearly, then "Dennis Kovitch," spelling it out. I didn't point out that it was only nine o'clock in San Diego.

"Dennis, hi, it's Jerry Simpkins. . . . No, Simpkins, from Pine Crest. Right . . . Yes, it's a surprise for me to be calling you. Look, I'm here with a Detective Carrick, I'm helping him with an investigation. . . . Yes, it is . . . Anyway, he has a few questions about Jason Rupp, and since you know him better than I do, I thought perhaps you could talk to him. . . ."

Simpkins handed me the phone. "He's delighted."

"Hello?"

"Who is this?" Kovitch demanded. He did not sound delighted.

"This is Detective Doyle Carrick, with the Philadelphia Police," I said, hoping my notoriety had not reached San Diego and mumbling my name just in case.

"Oh," he said, a little softer. I wondered if he hadn't believed Simpkins. "Well, what can I do for you?"

"I'm working on an investigation, and I have a few questions. Do you know Jason Rupp?"

"Not well, but enough to know I don't want to know him any better."

"Why's that?"

"Jason was a brilliant young scientist with a bright future, but he was lazy and sleazy and, I hate to say it, unethical."

"Unethical how?"

"Well . . . a lot of this is rumor, but when there's enough rumor, you know something is there. I know for a fact that he cut corners with his research; he was sloppy with his controls. He faked some data—that's what cost him his Gairdner Award. He's been *persona non grata* since then. I think he went into the pharmaceutical business."

"I heard he had been offered a teaching position at the University of Paris."

"The Sorbonne?" Kovitch laughed at that. "I hadn't heard that, but I would have a very hard time believing it. I was at a conference last summer with the head of the molecular biology department there. Rupp's name came up in conversation."

"Really?"

"He called Rupp a disgrace to the field, a delinquent, and . . . what was it?" Kovitch paused, remembering, then laughed. "Oh, yes, he called him a 'guttersnipe.'"

I laughed, too. "So, Simpkins said he met Rupp at your party. How did that happen?"

He grunted. "I had a research assistant, Liz Anne, I think her name was, something like that. Not very bright, or particularly attractive for that matter, but, well, I understand she had other attributes that made her popular. Rupp arrived with her." He laughed again. "Come to think of it, I don't think he left with her. Maybe she was brighter than I thought."

"Well, thanks for your help, Mr. Kovitch."

"*Doctor* Kovitch," he said. "You know it's a shame about Rupp. Apart from anything else, he was a brilliant young man, and he was doing some very impressive work, especially some of the work he was doing on corn."

"Corn?"

"Yes. I don't think he ever published it, because it was right when the business with the faked data blew up. But he was doing some very advanced work manipulating the corn genome to produce some very sophisticated results."

Son of a bitch. "He must have been an astonishing intellect."

Kovitch laughed awkwardly. "I guess you could say that."

I thanked him, and he said he was happy to help, but when he said I could call him if I had any other questions, it was obvious he was hoping I wouldn't.

I handed the phone back to Simpkins. "Thank you."

"So, are we done here?" Simpkins said, holding out his arm for me to walk toward the front door. My brain was humming with what Kovitch had just told me. I nodded and preceded him through the dining room and into the living room.

Maria was asleep on the sofa. Her head was back, one of her straps had fallen off her shoulder, and she had slumped down so that her skirt was riding up her thighs, showing a glimpse of pink satin underneath.

I glanced at Simpkins before he had a chance to erase his wolfish leer and look away from her. For a moment we stood there looking at each other. Then I stepped over and briskly patted the girl's cheek.

"Maria," I said loudly.

She stirred and looked up at me, her eyes slightly crossed.

"It was nice meeting you," I said.

She pulled her head back, rolling her eyes slightly, trying to get them aligned. "What?"

"I think you fell asleep," I said. "Do you want Jerry to give you a ride home?"

I could feel Simpkins's eyes stabbing me repeatedly in the back.

Maria put her hand on her forehead. "Um, yeah," she said, still groggy. She sat forward and grabbed her shoes, then stood up unsteadily.

When I turned around, Simpkins's expression was about what I expected. I gave him a nice big smile. "You leave now, you could be back before the end of *Saturday Night Live*."

64

Stan Bowers's voice mail picked up on the second ring. The bastard was screening me. I immediately hung up and called again, and the voice mail picked up on the first ring. On the fifth call, he picked up.

"Go away, Carrick," he said. "It's the middle of the night."

"Just a quick question—"

"No, Doyle. No. Not yet. Someday, maybe, looking back and laughing, but not now."

"I just need to know what kind of flour it was."

"What kind of . . . ? Are you fucking kidding me? It's past midnight. What are you, making a cake?"

"I just need to know, then I'll leave you alone."

"You are un-fucking-believable. How do you know I'm not asleep or banging my wife?" He sighed, then I heard him rustling paper. "Okay, here we go: 'Eighty micron, dry-milled, de-germinated, high-amylose white corn flour.' Okay?"

"Thanks."

He hung up without another word.

* * *

Rupp's Mustang wasn't in his driveway. I thought about breaking in and having a look around, but instead, I turned the car around and made a right at the intersection half a block away and parked so I could watch his driveway.

Then I waited. I tried to switch into stakeout-hibernation mode, but with limited success. Over the next several hours, my brain kept kicking on, either thinking about my mom and Frank, or thinking about the crazy, messed up little town of Dunston, with its meth fires and heroin busts and assholes with guns, its strange fields of genetically modified corn and disappearing apple trees. And its strange flu epidemic. Even my paranoid brain couldn't make them all fit together. It began to ache as it tried, and I felt great relief when Rupp finally arrived. I waited a couple of seconds, then started up the car and went after him, turning up his driveway and parking the Mustang.

Even in the dark, I could see that his tires were covered with mud.

He jumped when he saw me, but he recovered quickly, rolling his eyes. "You? Are you kidding me?" he said, without his accent. "Do you know what time it is?" He seemed younger, more vulnerable.

"Mind if I come in?"

He took a deep breath and stood up straighter. "Actually, you know what? Yes, I do." The accent was back. "I'm actually quite busy, and it's late. What do you want?"

"I just wanted to tell you, you were wrong about the apples."

"Really?" He laughed, and it sounded almost real, but not quite. "Wrong how?"

"Turns out someone figured out a way to do it. Apparently they were whatever you said, massive intellectuals or whatever."

"They must have been."

I leaned forward and lowered my voice. "Between you and me, a friend of mine in DEA said they tapped a bunch of phone lines. They're getting very close to putting it all together." I straightened up, backing off a step. "So, I just wanted to say thanks for your assistance. I'll make sure you get credit for your help in solving this."

"It was nothing," he said softly, gazing into the distance over my shoulder.

"No, you'd be surprised. A lot of people wouldn't have helped. So thanks."

I put out my hand for him to shake. When he did, his palm was clammy.

Back in my car, I pulled out of the driveway and made a right at the intersection half a block away. I drove up the block, turned off my headlights, then turned around and coasted back to the corner to wait.

Five minutes later, Rupp's Mustang backed out of the driveway and screeched off in the opposite direction. I gave him a few seconds to put some distance between us. Then I went after him—not too close, but keeping the Mustang's distinctive taillights ahead of me.

Luckily, I had a pretty good idea where we were going.

As we were getting close to Bayberry Road, I lost him for a moment. But then I caught sight of his taillights out of the corner of my eye, disappearing down a driveway behind a farmhouse on my left. It was one of the houses Nola and I had driven past the day we went to Hawk Mountain. She had said the family had kept the house but sold the land. I guess they sold the driveway, too.

As I watched, the taillights appeared again, much smaller, on the other side of a barn. Then they disappeared behind a gentle rise.

Across the street was the abandoned farm with the tax issues— the Denby place, Nola had called it. I pulled up into the driveway and parked in the back. Careful to look both ways, I darted across the street and kept running, across the fields, in the direction Rupp had driven.

My internal compass was spinning, as it had been since I'd come out to Dunston, but I knew we were heading east—toward the farm next to Nola's property, toward the big tent where I'd almost been shot two days earlier.

65

As I topped the rise behind the barn, I saw the Mustang's tail-lights, bouncing and jostling over the dirt road fifty yards ahead of me. Running low through the tall weeds, I stayed back from the road itself. The lights disappeared and reappeared several times as I chased them over the rolling landscape. I came up a small rise and saw Rupp stopped at a fence below. The fence extended as far as I could see, and I wondered if it was connected to the fence next to Nola's farm. As I dropped to the ground and watched, a large section of fence slowly rolled to the side. Rupp drove through, and I paused, watching longingly as it rolled back into place. I was getting really sick of climbing that damn fence, but I ran along it until it disappeared behind some trees, so I could climb it with some kind of cover.

Once inside, I crept along quietly, until I found myself looking down on the compound. The huge white tent extended off to the left, and the trailer sat at an angle next to it, extending off to the right: the area where the trees had been extended out from where the tent and the trailer met, like the third spoke of a three-spoked wheel.

The same two pickup trucks were sitting on the gravel. Parked next to them, Rupp's shiny Mustang looked as out of place as ever.

Two guys armed with assault rifles were standing at the foot of the steps to the trailer, on the side facing away from the tent. Rupp was talking to them, waving his hands in the air. I couldn't make out what he was saying, but I could hear the stress in his voice.

The guys with the rifles were at least a head taller than Rupp, and they stood close, looking down at him. Rupp made a move to go around them and up the steps to the trailer, but one of them stepped in front of him to block his way.

I could hear the guards laughing as Rupp protested. Then a guy with a shaved head appeared at the trailer door, and they stopped. I couldn't hear what he was saying either, but he barked and they snapped to attention. He waved Rupp up the steps, and together they retreated into the trailer.

I wanted to get behind that trailer and listen in on their conversation, but if I ran straight over there, they'd see me for sure. Instead, I took off in the opposite direction, circling all the way around the complex, around the far end of the tent. As I rounded the tent, I heard a noise and dropped into a crouch.

I had never felt the hairs on my neck stand up, but I felt like a Rhodesian Ridgeback as a guy in a full hazmat suit emerged from the tent, pausing under the spray of a hazmat shower. He must have been under there for a full minute; then the spray stopped and he stepped out. He shook off the excess and removed his hood as he disappeared around the far side of the tent.

I circled even farther out into the corn stubble so I wouldn't be seen. As I rounded the tent and the far side of the trailer came into view, I saw another hazmat shower, out past the edge of the gravel.

I waited another few seconds. Then I sprinted toward the trailer, creeping up to the middle of it, right about where the door and steps were on the other side. Standing in the middle of the angle formed by the tent and the trailer, I was very aware that if anyone discovered me, I would be cornered.

I could hear Rupp and the other guy going back and forth inside the trailer. The windows were too high to look in, but I found an old cinder block off to the side and I moved it over. Balancing on top of it, I was just high enough to look in the window and listen to what they were saying.

"Probably bullshit," the bald guy was saying, "but it don't matter, because we ain't changing shit without Levkov's say so. He's the boss."

Rupp looked insulted. "What do you mean, he's the boss? He's not *my* boss. We're both the boss." He seemed to be having a hard time maintaining his accent.

"Well, what can I tell you. He's *my* boss. Look, if you want, I can call him—"

"No, Leo, you dumbass! The phones are tapped. You can't call him."

"I guess we'll wait till he gets here, then."

"We can't wait, either. Carrick said the bust is imminent. We have to move things up."

"Look, if Levkov says we're moving it up, we'll move it up. But if not, what's the difference? Today, tomorrow, whatever."

"The difference, you idiot, is the difference between them showing up in the middle of the fucking release, or them finding a bunch of bulldozers building cheap houses."

Now the bald guy was stepping up close to Rupp, looking down at him just like the two guards had done. "Now, you look here, little dick. You watch how you fucking talk to me, okay?"

Rupp looked like he had something really smart to say. Maybe he figured it was even smarter not to say it, but I never found out, because the cinder block I was perched on suddenly crumbled. I pitched forward, my outstretched hands slamming against the side of the trailer. I heard a commotion inside the trailer, then the door banging open on the far side, followed by shouting.

Hemmed in by the trailer and the tent, my only escape was the open space off to my left. But even if I made it, a single burst from one of those assault rifles would cut me in half before I could hope to get away. At any second, gunmen were going to come streaming around the end of the trailer and probably around the tent as well. Frantically, I looked around for a place to hide. Ten yards away, up against the tent, was that big gas tank. It wasn't much of a hiding place, but it was the only shot I had.

I took off, trying to ignore the agonizing tingle up and down my back as I anticipated for a hail of bullets. I slid behind the tank, but the back of it was smooth and flat. There was nothing to hold on to, no way to pull up my feet. There was a hook holding the fuel hose, but it was too flimsy to support me and would have left my hand exposed. Other than that, the closest thing to a handhold was a ridge of peeling paint that came away in my hand as soon as I touched it. If there'd been a solid wall behind me, I could have braced myself between it and the tank, pulled up my legs and stayed hidden for a while. But with the tent, there was nothing to brace against.

They wouldn't take long to find me back here.

I could see a flicker of flashlight beams, and the voices grew louder as the gunmen got closer. I could picture them spreading out, creeping warily toward me. A couple of them might have gone out across the field, in case I had gotten enough of a head start to make it that far. But the others were coming toward me.

I took out my gun, but didn't risk the noise of cocking it. When they got close enough, I'd try to take them by surprise—maybe down one or two of them before the rest tore me to pieces, or until someone shot the gas tank and we all went up.

It was the closest thing to a plan I could come up with, but it sucked. Mikhail's description of my life notwithstanding, I didn't want to die. But it was looking more and more like that's what was going to happen.

The notion flashed through my mind that my entire family would then be gone: my mom, my dad, and me, all in the space of six weeks. A wave of memories washed over me, happy times, trips to the beach, sledding with my dad. Well, not my dad, but Frank.

I tried to picture my dad: playing catch with him, or hiking by the creek, sitting through a Star Wars triple feature. But all those memories were of Frank. I tried to conjure memories of my dad, but all I could come up with were images from photos, one Christmas morning, and now that restraining order. That and the hole he left behind. My eyes blurred, and I thought to myself, "Now?"

The voices were getting closer, and I knew if I let the gunmen get much nearer, they would shoot me down like a cow at slaughter.

Looking down at my feet lined up behind the stanchion holding up the tank, I made a deal with myself: The moment a flashlight beam played across my boots, that would be my cue to go down in a blaze of glory.

That was when I glanced at the tent and saw the patch over the jagged hole in the plastic sheeting from my previous escape. The image of the hazmat suit standing under the shower gave me another chill, but it was the only chance I had. I dropped to the ground, tore open the patch, and squeezed into the tent.

66

For a moment, I lay motionless between the potting table and the plastic, waiting for my eyes to adjust to the darkness and listening. But it was quiet.

Part of me wanted just to stay here, hidden and quiet. Eventually they'd find the hole, though, and then they would find me. If my plan was to hide and be quiet, it would have to be somewhere else.

The smell of the place was more intense than I remembered, and I could hear the hum of a fan. The air was warmer, and it tickled my nose, made me want to sneeze. As I rolled out from under the table, I could see dim light filtering down through the plastic ceiling. A haze hung in the air. It reminded me a little of the mist from the crop duster, but this had a heavier, denser feeling. Darker.

Through it, I could detect faint movement, a sensation of motion just out of sight. I looked down at the ground, squinting in the darkness, making sure I wasn't about to trip over anything as I stepped closer to the flowers growing on the rack closest to me.

Then I realized I wasn't looking at flowers. I was looking at butterflies. Dozens of them. Hundreds of them. Thousands of them.

Then the lights came on. Everything got brighter, but it remained as colorless as the darkness—a dull, ugly grayish green. The walls, the plants, the pots of flowers, everything. Including me. My hand and my arm were the same color as everything else.

Before I could move, a muffled voice said, "Hold it right there, fuckhead."

I turned to see one of the guys from outside, now wearing a white hazmat suit that looked blindingly bright compared to everything else in there. He approached with his assault rifle, maybe an M4, tucked under his arm and pointed at my middle.

Turning back, I saw Leo, the one Rupp had been arguing with in the trailer, approaching from the other direction in his own hazmat suit.

"Hands up," the first guy said.

I thought about making a move, but decided against it. As I complied, I rubbed my thumb and fingers together. The grayish green powder felt greasy between them. My shirt and my pants were covered with the same stuff.

Leo came up behind me, gave me a quick pat down. As he took my gun and tucked it into his utility belt, Rupp appeared at the end of the row.

"Carrick?" he said with a smug look on his face. He wasn't wearing a hazmat suit. He was holding a gun, maybe a .22. It looked heavy and unfamiliar in his hand. He laughed. "Jesus, look at you. You've got a dose on you that would kill an army."

He walked past me, giving me a wide berth, and stopped at the standpipe next to where I had come in. Stooping without taking his eyes off me, he disconnected the hose from the overhead sprinkler system and turned the faucet on. A thick stream of water spurted out from the hose.

"I don't know how many times I'm going to be able to keep saving your life," he said as he put his thumb over the end of the hose and started spraying me. "Now, hold still."

I recoiled when the cold water hit me, but I was relieved as well. I didn't know what the hell he was talking about, but the stuff he was rinsing off me had a bad vibe, and I was glad to be rid of it. For an instant I worried about my phone getting wet, but I remembered it was still in the truck, plugged in to the charger.

"We spend all this money on containment," Rupp continued. "The negative air pressure, the chemical shower that's ninety-nine point nine percent effective at killing the spores, all trying to make sure this stuff doesn't somehow get out, and you come in like an idiot and cut a hole in the tent."

The water running off me was cloudy and green.

Rupp lowered the hose. "Turn around."

When I did, I found myself looking at Leo's face through the faceplate of his hazmat suit. He had a sheen of sweat on his skin, and he seemed fidgety, like he was uncomfortable in the suit. I gave him a friendly smile as Rupp hosed off my back.

Leo kept his eyes on me but spoke out of the side of his mouth. "You know this guy?" he asked Rupp.

"Yes. He's a cop," Rupp replied.

Sometimes, when they find out you're a cop, they're a little scared, because they don't want to get busted, and they know that people who mess around with cops tend to get caught. Sometimes they don't care, because what they're up to is so bad that killing a cop on top of it won't make things much worse. Sometimes they're happy, because some crazy bastards really don't like cops, and they're always looking for a chance to hurt one. This guy smiled.

"In fact," Rupp continued, "this is the cop Mikhail was supposed to take out. You remember, when he didn't come back?"

Leo shot Rupp a look. Then he turned back to me and his eyes narrowed. He took a step back, and his suit rustled as he tightened his grip on his M4.

I had a feeling he'd like me even less if he found Mikhail's body.

"So, what brings you here, Carrick?" Rupp said, making a show of turning the hose off, cocky, like he was in control of the situation. "Just can't seem to not be a cop, huh? Even when you know it could cost you your job."

"I'd ask you the same thing, Rupp. Bit of a backwater for a hotshot like you." I was trying to sound smug, but it wasn't easy dripping wet. "Oh, that's right," I went on gamely. "You're on your way to Paris, right? Except the head of the molecular biology department said you were an embarrassment to the field, and, what was it? Oh right, a guttersnipe, whatever that is."

Rupp smiled, but his eyes were glaring at me.

"Yes, apparently, you're not such a hotshot after all, since you got caught making stuff up." I smiled. "Those award people *hate* that."

"Carrick, you're an idiot. Awards mean nothing to me. I do what I do for science."

"For science?"

He shrugged. "And for money."

"So, when I asked you about the apples, you said it would take an astonishing intellect. You were talking about yourself, right?"

He waved the comment away, modestly, as if I were the one saying it. "The apples are nothing. That was just for operating capital. And when you took out those degenerates, you were doing the world a favor."

I thought of a few more favors I could do for the world, but I kept that to myself. "So, if it's not about the apples, what's it all about? The corn?"

"Kind of. It's about Mycozene, a breakthrough in medicine. An antifungal cure for half a dozen minor plagues, and now one major one. The world should be grateful."

Leo was trying to scratch his neck through the hazmat suit, but he stopped and exchanged a look with the other guy as Rupp prattled on.

"So, you genetically modified the corn to produce some synthetic chemical?"

"It's not synthetic. It's totally natural, just tweaked a little bit."

"So, what's this stuff, then?" I gestured to the green powder that coated everything inside the tent.

Rupp smiled. "This stuff? This is the major one. A little something I cooked up. A rhizopus—like bread mold, but much, much nastier. You should be grateful; we saved you from it once already."

"Saved me, huh? And how did you do that?"

He smiled indulgently. "We dusted you after you broke in the first time."

"You mean with the crop duster. . . ."

"That's right. It sprayed you with the same stuff that's in these." He took out a small pill bottle and popped a capsule in his mouth. "Mycozene. It's best if you take it by mouth, but it works on contact. You can even absorb it through the skin."

When Pruitt had come to see me after the plane attack, I went outside in my bare feet. The next day my athlete's foot was gone. And when Nola pulled all that moldy food out of the refrigerator, the next day the mold was gone.

"We sprayed the whole damn area."

"And why would you do that?"

"Containment. We didn't want things getting underway ahead of schedule. And we didn't want things traced back to here. It's a good thing for you, too, because otherwise you'd be dead."

I looked around at the green powder coating everything. "So what's the angle? What are you after?"

He laughed and shook his head. "There's not much money in curing minor plagues. And geniuses have got to eat, too." He shrugged. "That's why I had to create a major plague. That's where the money is."

I think I could have gotten more out of him, and I was about to ask him what was up with the butterflies, but at that point they all turned to look toward the entrance.

67

He didn't recognize me at first. But I recognized him.

Even without a hazmat suit on, he stood several inches taller than the others, with an air of authority that left no doubt he was in charge. He had the same metal as before: a row of studs through one eyebrow, a series of small hoops in one ear, a diamond in his nose, and something else in his bottom lip. His eyes looked dangerous, or maybe that was just because I knew better now. Levkov.

Leo stopped fidgeting, and he and his partner both stood up straighter. Rupp's bravado evaporated, and he looked at the gun in his hand as though he had just been caught playing with his big brother's favorite toy.

For a moment, the only sound was the ventilation system and the water still dripping off me.

"Who the fuck is this?" Levkov asked, glancing at me, then looking back, recognition in his eyes and a slight smile stretching his mouth. He walked over to Rupp. "What's going on here?"

"That's Carrick," Rupp told him. "The cop. The one Mikhail was supposed to—"

Levkov's hand shot out and slapped Rupp across the face—not hard, but a bracing blow that rang throughout the tent. My own cheek tingled at the memory of a similar blow. Rupp froze, shocked. The butterflies responded to the sound, wings twitching and fluttering.

"Fuck you!" Rupp squealed. "You can't hit me. Don't forget whose operation this is. This is *my* operation."

Levkov snatched the gun out of Rupp's hand. "What have you told him?"

"I . . . I . . . nothing." Rupp put his hand up to his face. He closed his mouth.

Levkov looked over at Leo. "Was he talking?"

Leo nodded slightly, adjusting the hazmat hood so he could see Levkov better. "Just like with the fucking Mexicans."

Without hesitation, Levkov raised the gun a couple of inches and shot Rupp in the thigh.

A thick glob of blood spurted out of Rupp's leg and he screamed and stumbled backward, crashing against a large steel cabinet and collapsing onto a pile of sacks of potting soil. Several of the butterflies took flight.

Levkov pointed the gun at Rupp's chest, and two things went through my head: First, that if I didn't do something, Levkov would kill Rupp. And second, if Levkov killed Rupp, I was next.

While Leo was adjusting his hood again, I drove my elbow into his throat and ducked behind him. Even as I locked one arm around Leo's neck, Levkov and the other guy started firing. I could feel the bullets hitting Leo as I pulled him backward on his heels. My wet feet slipped on the floor, and I dragged Leo behind me for cover. The bullets from the handgun wouldn't penetrate the body, but I hoped the M4 wasn't firing jacketed rounds. Leo struggled at first, trying to get his feet under him, but after a few hits, he went slack. I found the trigger of Leo's rifle with my free hand and squeezed it blindly.

Butterflies filled the air with fluttering wings, thickening the gray-green haze of spores drifting in the fans' currents. By the time I reached the far end of the tent, the return fire had faltered. My feet skidded in the dust as I turned the corner, and I paused behind a row of tables, dropping Leo to the floor, dead. I pulled my gun out of his belt, and kept his, too. When I straightened up, I saw that Levkov had returned with reinforcements and a belt-fed machine gun, maybe an M60. I suppressed a shudder, thinking back to how he had handled me when he was unarmed. I reminded myself I wasn't scared of him.

At least four bad guys were in the tent now, not counting Rupp. Two of them were coming toward me down the row. I had to resist the urge to set the gun to automatic, but the memory of running out of bullets was fresh in my mind. I aimed carefully and squeezed off two shots—*boom, boom*—and took them both down. Then I started back down the row, toward the front of the tent. The air was so full of dust and butterflies, I almost tripped over one of the men I had just shot.

I had made it halfway to the front of the tent when two new gunmen appeared at the far end. Apparently, they were unconcerned about their ammunition supply, because they seemed to have no qualms about firing on automatic.

Bullets zipped through the air, tearing through the butterflies and sending bits and pieces of them floating to the ground like dirty snow. I dove into a gap in the row of tables and returned a few shots, first down one aisle, then down the other. The spores stuck to my damp skin. A plague, Rupp had called it. I tried not to think about it, but without much success. I wiped my hands on my wet jeans, leaving a grayish smudge.

During a lull in the shooting, I heard a quiet voice calling my name. "Carrick," it said faintly. It was Rupp, crumpled against the steel cabinet. His legs were splayed out in front of him, his feet sticking out into the aisle. I looked over at him but didn't reply.

"Am I dying?" he asked.

He sat in a pool of the blood that seeped from his thigh and from another hole that had appeared in his side.

"Looks like it, yeah."

"Fuck," he rasped.

I fired once again down each row. In response, I got two single shots from the two guys on one side and a sustained stream of mayhem from Levkov's gun. It shredded plants, tore through the wooden tables, and disintegrated countless butterflies.

Rupp touched a finger to the hole in his side. "I don't want to die."

I ducked down as another swarm of bullets screamed overhead. "Tell me what the fuck is going on here," I told him. "And I'll see what I can do for you."

I could tell just by looking what I could do for him: not much. But he didn't need to know that.

I glimpsed Levkov through the foliage, and I took a shot but missed. He returned fire with another barrage. The tip of Rupp's boot exploded into shreds. He whimpered, but it sounded like fear not pain. Seeing him cowering behind the steel cabinet, though, I realized his position was better than mine. I darted across the aisle to where he was sitting. Grabbing his pant leg, I pulled his feet out of the line of fire.

He reached into the outside pocket of his jacket, took out a bottle of pills, and shook a capsule into his hand. "Here," he said, holding it up to me.

I looked at it, then at him.

"Take it," he said. "Hosing you off isn't enough. Take the pill, and it'll protect you for two days. Otherwise, with the dose you got, you're a dead man."

When I hesitated still, he rolled his eye and took it himself. Then he shook out another one and held it up with one hand while the other hand returned the bottle to his jacket.

I didn't trust Rupp, but the green spores scared me more than any pill. My hands were still damp, and now they were coated in a thin layer of green. I wiped my finger off on Rupp's jacket before taking the capsule from him. As I swallowed it, I caught a glimpse of Levkov and took a few shots.

When it was quiet again, I could hear Rupp rambling on. I wasn't sure if he was talking to me or to himself. "You know, I grew up not far from here. An awkward adolescence." A brief wistful smile twisted into a grimace. Then his eyes turned dark. "I hate this fucking place, almost as much as I hate these fucking people."

After the next volley, Rupp called out again, weakly. "Carrick."

Tears had cut two paths through the thin film of dust that coated his face. I ignored him. The last thing I needed now was to be taking down the final words of the asshole who was responsible for whatever the hell was going on.

"Carrick, you've got to stop them."

Sure, I thought, now that he was on the outside.

"Carrick," he said quietly. "I'm sorry about your mother."

That stopped me. I looked over at him.

"That's why you're here, right?" he went on. "We tried to save her. We tried to dust her with Mycozene, from the plane, contain it like we did with you. But by the time we tracked her down, she was already in the hospital. She was dying anyway—you know that, right? That's why it got her so fast, because of the cancer, the chemo, her weakened immune system. . . . Once it spreads to the brain, it's too late."

"What are you talking about?"

"We put the test houses in the middle of nowhere to keep that from happening. But before we incinerated them, one of the Mexicans escaped. It's not contagious, you know, not person to person. But he must have had spores on him. That's how your mom got exposed." He shook his head, sadly. "Just bad luck. She brought the spores to the library. Not much we could do about that. Books can be so dangerous."

I stopped and looked down at him as half a dozen pieces clicked together. The gun was in my hand, and I closed my eyes and pictured myself placing the barrel against his head and pulling the trigger.

68

But that's not what I did. Instead, I grabbed him by the collar. "What the hell is going on here?"

"You've got to stop them, Carrick."

"Stop them from doing what?"

"It's all my fault."

"What? Stop them from doing what?"

"It starts out like the flu, kills in a couple of weeks." He snorted. "Unless you get a mega dose, like you got. Then it's a few days." He smiled weakly.

"The flu?" I immediately thought of Nola. It wasn't MCS at all, it was this crazy plague. Same with all those people swamping the emergency room. "Half the people in town are down with the flu. Are you saying they're dying?"

He raised a hand and tried to point at me. "They're sick because of you, Carrick. You and that Mexican. We tried to keep it contained, so no one would know where it came from. So much for that. Not with you tearing holes in the containment, tracking it all through town, shooting at the crop duster." He shook his head. "But it'll be released soon anyway, and then it won't matter." He stared at his hand as he rubbed his gray-green fingers together. "Once it's out in the environment, it can't be undone. It can be cured, but it can't be stopped."

"People are going to die."

He nodded and blew air through his lips. "A *lot* of people are going to die. But people always die, Carrick. That's what they do. And the rest of them, they're going to pay a fortune." His eyes turned sharp for a moment. "And that asshole out there is going to make billions."

"This was your plan?"

He smiled proudly for a second, like he was taking a compliment. But the smile faded. He coughed, and a bubble of blood formed on his lips. "That's how billions are made."

Once again, I fought the urge to shoot him. "So how were you going to release it?"

He reached up and grabbed my wet shirt, pulling me down to him with surprising strength. "It's going to be at dawn. As soon as it's light out. They'll have to move it up to today."

"How? How are they going to release it?"

He looked past me, up at the ceiling of the tent. Through the cloud of butterflies and the clear plastic roof, I could see the night sky. It was just starting to show the earliest hints of dawn.

"The monarchs," he said.

I looked back at him. "Butterflies? Are you fucking kidding me?"

He laughed with a wince. "I know, it's brilliant, right? They're cheap, they're quiet, and they cover a lot of territory. As they flutter down to Mexico and back, the spores will drift down onto half the states in the country and slowly start to grow and spread where they land. A few people will get it early, but it'll take a year or so before the epidemic begins. By then, this place will be long gone."

We heard a loud, metallic *sproing*, followed by the sound of something whipping through the air. Rupp flinched.

"What's that sound?" I asked.

"Roof cables. The top of the tent comes off. Levkov is letting them out." Rupp looked worried. "Once the sun comes up they'll take flight. Then it's too late."

The monarchs. I looked around me, at the thousands of butterflies fluttering around inside the massive tent. Their stripes and dots and colors were barely visible through the coating of gray-green spores.

Nola's words came back to me: *"An army on the move across two thirds of the country."* Within a couple of months, they would fly south down the Eastern Seaboard, across the Southeast, west to Texas, and down to Mexico.

"How do I stop it?" I asked Rupp.

He looked at me for a moment, his evil genius brain working hard. "I don't know. There's fungicide in the hazmat showers, but not enough. Heat doesn't kill most spores, but these ones, it does."

"Heat?"

"Yes, but it's got to be really hot, like three hundred degrees. That's their only weakness. That and the Mycozene."

"Where's the Mycozene?"

"This is all I have," he said. He held up the bottle and rattled the pills, then slipped it back into his jacket pocket.

"Where's the rest of it?"

"Don't know. Levkov handled transport."

"What about the corn?"

"Gone. Processed already."

"Where?"

Rupp shook his head, and his face fell.

There was another loud *sproing,* and at the far end of the tent, a corner of the roof came opened. "Carrick," Rupp said urgently. "You've got to stop him."

I couldn't even see Levkov, but I figured he was in the corner where the roof was opening. I fired a couple of shots in that direction to slow him down if nothing else. Levkov replied with another storm of bullets. The rack of plants next to us disintegrated. Then rounds started pelting the steel cabinet, making as much noise as the gun itself.

Cowering on the floor, I closed my eyes against the noise. Levkov was going to release this terrible plague, and people were going to die. A lot of people. Including Nola. And when Levkov was done, he was going to hunt me down with that big-ass gun.

I spotted a roll of duct tape hanging on a nail next to some gardening tools. It gave me an idea. An idea I really didn't like. Grabbing the duct tape, I started to tell Rupp to wait right there, but he wasn't going anywhere. I checked the clip and gave him the rifle instead.

He looked at me, confused. "What?"

"You count slowly to twenty, and shoot once in that direction," I told him, pointing to where Levkov had been. "Then count to twenty again and shoot again, every twenty seconds. And if anybody but me comes close, shoot him."

I'd seen Rupp handling a gun and I didn't think he'd do much good with it, but I didn't want Levkov to realize I was gone. The clip had about twenty bullets in it. I figured that gave me five minutes. I grabbed the duct tape and a trowel and clambered behind the table next to us.

Rupp looked panicked. "Carrick!" he called after me. "Wait! Where are you going?"

As I tore yet another hole in the plastic wall of the tent and slipped through it, I could hear him calling in a loud, frantic whisper, "Carrick! Don't leave me here!"

69

The cool night air on my wet clothes and skin was a shock to my system after the stuffiness inside the tent, like jumping into cold water. For an instant, I was stunned. Then I heard another *sproing*, and a silver cable snapped out overhead, lashing up into the paling sky. It was followed by a crumpling, billowing sound, like a tarp in the wind.

My shoes made squishing noises as I ran along the side of the tent, staying close to the ground. A light fog had formed, and in the darkness, I could see little shafts of light streaming through the bullet holes that speckled the tent: single ones here and there, and then broad swaths densely peppered by the automatics.

As I rounded the corner, I saw that one of the corner supports had been shot completely through, the shredded top of the pole suspended in the air in front of a tattered, gaping hole in the plastic. I slowed and came in close, peering around the edge, looking across the entrance to the tent. No one was out there. They were all inside.

I heard a couple of shots from inside the tent, and through the hole, I could see two of Levkov's men creeping toward Rupp. I had a decent shot at them, but didn't want to risk giving away my position. At the sound of a gunshot, they ducked back and a flowerpot exploded next to them. Maybe I hadn't given Rupp enough credit.

I hurried past the entrance to the tent, and as I rounded the other side, I saw what I was looking for. The gas tank.

I slid once more into the gap between the tent and the gas tank, and lifted the nozzle off its hook. Pulling the hose with me, I squeezed through the hole in the tent. Inside, I paused under the potting table with my back against the torn plastic, and I listened. Rupp fired off his regularly scheduled round from the far side of the tent, and Levkov's men returned fire. No one seemed to be standing near me. When I pulled the hose taut, it just reached the open space between the rows of tables.

Next came the tricky part—partly because I risked revealing myself, partly because I had serious doubts as to whether it would work, but mostly because the whole plan filled me with dread. The hose Rupp had used to wash me off was just a few feet away, one end connected to the water supply and the other end near the connection for the sprinkler system.

The intensity of the gunfire was growing, but I couldn't tell if Levkov and company were stepping it up or if Rupp was panicking and blowing through his ammunition.

I crept out onto the floor, across the aisle, and quietly picked up the loose end of the hose. Crouching flat against the table and as low as I could, I reconnected the hose and the sprinkler connector. Then I unscrewed the other end from the water supply. Water drained out as I pulled that end back under the potting table.

The nozzle on the fuel hose looked to be an inch and a quarter in diameter, and the sprinkler hose was an inch and a half—a closer match than I had expected. I held the nozzle flush to the sprinkler hose and wrapped the connection with duct tape as tightly as possible. Then I quickly covered it with another twenty layers. The gasoline would eat through the adhesive, but I hoped the time it took to get through twenty layers would be time enough for what I had in mind.

When I was done, the connection between the two hoses looked like a big silver ball. I squeezed the handle on the nozzle, and heard the pump kick on. The hose jumped in my hand as the gasoline coursed through it. I jammed the trowel through the handle and used the last of the duct tape to hold it in place.

The connection stayed dry, but I had to fight to stay focused as the fumes from the gasoline enveloped my head. I was having a hard time breathing, but I couldn't tell if it was from the vapors or from my subconscious skipping ahead to the next stage of the plan.

Climbing out from under the planting table, I looked up and saw the gasoline starting to mist down from the first sprinkler head. The sprinklers were set up in five rows, with a row of sprinklers over each row of tables. As I watched, the second sprinkler started misting, then the third.

In a matter of seconds, the fumes were almost overpowering. I tried to keep my head clear, tried not to picture what could happen to me if I screwed this up, or if I didn't get out in time. Staying low, I crossed the aisle and squeezed my way under the next planting table and out into the next aisle. I looked both ways before crossing, then climbed through the next table.

As the fumes got even stronger, I could hear the shouts growing inside the tent, the tone changing, becoming more frantic. I took off again, crossing another aisle, pushing through another table. I looked up and saw the sprinkler heads coming on, one by one, the spray of gasoline working its way up the center row toward me.

I heard another metal cable snapping overhead, and I looked up as it arced through a royal blue sky, glinting in the light from the rising sun. I started moving even faster. As the gasoline got closer, the shooting abruptly died out. The yells and screams grew louder and shriller, making it harder to ignore my own fears.

With the gasoline raining down from the overhead sprinkler system, the mixture of butterflies and green haze became even more bizarre and that much more surreal. One of Levkov's gunmen ran past me in a panic, wiping his faceplate. I got a clear glimpse of Levkov, just for an instant, loosening the next roof cable at the far end of the tent. He turned, and our eyes met. Before I could shoot, he was gone, back to the roof cables, and I was running again.

I pushed through the space under the fourth table just as the sprinkler over Rupp started spraying gasoline. He was already screaming, but at this, his screams became piercing. When I approached him, he swung the gun around at me, his eyes round with terror.

I took the gun from him and grabbed him by the collar. Then I pulled him under the last table, through the hole I had just made in the plastic, and back outside. He whimpered in pain as his leg banged against the ground, but I kept dragging him, all the way to the hazmat shower forty yards away. Then I turned and looked back.

The roof was halfway retracted now, butterflies already milling around in the air above it, illuminated from below by the pale fluorescent lights. As I watched, another roofing cable sprang loose, and the corner of the tent where the support post had been severed crumpled to the ground, leaving a large opening.

I could see Levkov jump up on one of the tables, M60 in hand. He climbed over racks and hurdled aisles, headed toward the hole left by the collapsed wall. He seemed to be staring right at me. Part of me hoped he would take a shot, because I was sure that would be enough to set off the gas fumes. But he didn't. He just kept coming toward us, jumping from one table to the next.

I fired once, and came close enough that he ducked down. But he kept coming, never taking his eyes off us. He was climbing over the final rack when I fired again. I had been aiming for a metal box near the uprights to the sprinkler system. I must have hit something electrical, because one moment, I saw Levkov launching himself toward the hole in the crumpled back wall, and then it went dark. For an instant, all I could see were butterflies, black silhouettes against the pink and blue dawn sky, and below them, in the darkened tent, a cascade of orange sparks bouncing on the ground before winking out.

Then the place went up.

I saw Levkov one last time, his dark form momentarily outlined against the flames. Then the fire swelled out around him. He was there, and then he was gone.

A wave of heat washed over me, penetrating the damp cold that had seeped into my bones.

The butterflies suddenly glowed a brilliant orange against a sky that seemed to have darkened back into night. The heat and the shock from the explosion pushed the butterflies high into the air. Then the fire rose up after them, consuming them one by one.

As the fireball died out, one last butterfly struggled to fly higher, its wings no longer fluttering but thrusting, pushing against the air as it inched higher into the sky. The ball of fire collapsed beneath it, releasing a last jagged shard of red orange flame, but that missed it, too. Even with everything that was at stake, part of me was pulling for that butterfly to escape. But while the fire didn't reach it, the heat apparently did. The butterfly lit up brightly for a moment; then the glow faded, and it drifted down into the inferno.

In the flickering orange light of the flames, I saw two of Levkov's men climbing unsteadily to their feet near the far side of the tent. When they spotted us, they started firing. I dropped to one knee and lined up a shot, but before I could pull the trigger, there was another blinding flash as the gas tank exploded on the other side of the tent. The concussion popped my ears and pulled the air out of my lungs, rolling me back like a candy wrapper in a strong wind.

Somehow I landed, stumbling, on my feet. A foot fell out of the sky and bounced on the ground next to me. I looked around and saw the rest of the two men scattered around me in little pieces. Rupp was moaning loudly, still leaning against the hazmat shower where I had left him.

My ears were filled with a noise like rushing water, but through it, I heard the sound of tortured metal and I looked up to see the remains of the gas tank, glowing a dull red and outlined in flames, slowly twisting high in the sky. It looked almost peaceful as it reached the top of its trajectory and started the return trip back to Earth. I'd never been particularly good at tracking pop flies, so I turned and ran, and I kept running until I heard a loud ringing thud and a clod of dirt hit my shoulder.

When I stopped and turned, I saw the crumpled metal tank half buried in a shallow crater where the hazmat shower had been. Right where I had left Rupp.

70

Rupp was dead and I wasn't sorry, but I was glad I wasn't the one who'd killed him. I don't know how long I stood there, dazed from the explosion, looking down at his legs sticking out from underneath the tank, like the Wicked Witch of the West under Dorothy's house. When I looked up, I noticed that the sun had fully risen. It looked like a nice day.

My ears were ringing from the explosion, a sound that seemed to echo in my skull, but through it I could hear the quiet lapping of the flames and birds chirping in the distance.

I knew I should be doing something else, but I couldn't seem to think of what. I couldn't tell if my wits had been addled by Rupp's pill or the explosions or the exhaustion, or if it was because I had no experience with any situation remotely like the one I found myself in.

A breeze brushed up against me, gently prodding me into action. Smoke was still billowing into the air as I started limping back to the truck. But then I remembered the doomsday spores that still covered me, and I doubled back.

The trailer was now burning wreckage, but it seemed to have absorbed the brunt of the explosion. The hazmat shower next to it was intact. I stripped off my damp clothes, turned on the shower, and got in.

I knew I'd be leaving the clothes behind. They were probably hopelessly contaminated. But I brought my car keys and my gun into the shower once again. I was keeping my gun.

The shower smelled reassuringly harsh, and it stung, like serious chemicals. As cold and unpleasant as it was, I stayed in there and did a thorough job.

When I was done I started off across the fields, back to my truck, dripping wet and naked, my gun in one hand, keys in the other. I gave a wide berth to the remnants of the tent, so I wouldn't pick up any more spores.

The walk back across the fields seemed a lot longer than when I had followed Rupp the previous night. As much as I tried to avoid it, the corn stubble scratched my legs and cut my bare feet.

When I came up against the fence, I took my time, especially at the top, making sure nothing got scraped, snagged, or torn. Neither Rupp and his plague nor Levkov and his belt-fed machine gun were as scary as climbing over the top of a chain link fence in the nude. After that, crossing the rest of the fields didn't seem so bad.

It was early enough in the morning that there was no traffic as I crossed the road to where I had left Frank's truck. I climbed in behind the wheel, grateful for the cloth seats.

In my rearview mirror I saw fire trucks already responding to the smoke cloud. Through the fog in my brain, I realized I needed to warn them off. I stared at my phone for a few seconds, thinking. Then I dialed 411 and got the number for Noreen Good, at home.

She answered on the first ring, and I knew I had made the right call.

I told her who was calling and she laughed nervously. "It's Sunday morning."

"I know. I'm sorry."

"You sure you don't want to talk to Chief Pruitt?" she asked. "He's been looking for you."

"I bet he has. Actually, Noreen, I was calling for you."

She laughed again, this time with no trace of nervousness. "Oh, were you now? What, you want me to go on the run with you?"

"That's not a half-bad idea," I replied. "Maybe some other time. Right now, there's a situation, and I need your help."

"Right."

"There's some fire engines responding to a call at a farm on Valley Road, just off Bayberry."

"Mm-hmm."

"Well, this is going to sound crazy, but you can't let them go in there. There's a dangerous disease in there, a plague, and if they go in there, they could all die."

She was quiet for a lot less time than I would have been. "A plague? Are you messing with me?"

"Noreen, you know who I am, you know where I'm from. You know how much shit I'll be in if I'm making this stuff up."

"Honey, you're already up to your neck in it. You're wanted for murder. You know that, right?"

"Yeah, but that's bullshit. Noreen, this is the same stuff that's been making half the town sick, only this will be much worse."

She gasped. "Oh my God. This is for real, isn't it?"

"Just get those firefighters away from there before they get hurt. I'll take care of the rest."

Stan Bowers had told me about an asshole he knew at Homeland

Security, a guy named Craig Sorenson. I called DHS and told the woman who answered that I needed to talk to Craig Sorenson. When she asked who was calling, I said, "Stan Bowers, over at DEA."

Special Agent Sorenson was not available, she told me. Before she could ask for my message, I told her it was an emergency, a biological weapons attack at Bayberry and Valley in Dunston, Berks County, Pennsylvania, some sort of fungal pathogen, and they needed to get a hazmat team and a fire suppression team over there right away. Then I hung up.

As I drove, I tried to think of what else I should be doing.

When I reached the house, I parked in the back and walked gingerly across the gravel, just me and my gun. My head was still ringing, but a warm breeze had picked up and it felt good on my skin. For a moment I felt like things might work out.

When I opened the back door and stepped inside, I saw Moose perched on a kitchen chair, hugging his knees and staring out the window. His face was as pale as a sheet of paper, and his thumbnail was wedged firmly between his teeth.

He looked at me—face, body, face—then back out the window.

In the quiet, I heard the coffee maker gurgle and hiss. Moose already had a cup, so I got one for myself.

"So, you went into the garage," I said, sipping the scalding coffee, very careful not to spill.

Moose glanced at me again, then looked away and nodded.

"I told you not to."

He nodded again, conceding that point.

"So that's the guy who killed the lawyer?" he asked without looking at me.

"Yeah," I said.

"What did you do to him?"

"He had a gun on me. Said he was going to make it look like a suicide. As we were driving, I drifted over, got him in the head with that broken tailgate sticking out from Squirrel's truck."

Moose winced and shuddered, but he stayed quiet

"It should be safe to stay here now."

"Good," he said quietly.

I set my cup down on the kitchen counter. "Guess I'll go put on some pants."

"Good idea."

Upstairs, I confronted a bit of a laundry problem. Between the clothes I had left at the hazmat shower and the bloody clothes in the bag, all I had left was my funeral suit.

I put it on and looked in the mirror. My face was haggard as hell. I looked like a guy who'd been up all night after a funeral. Actually, I looked like I could have been the guest of honor.

Sitting down on the bed to pull on my socks, I saw for the first time how badly my feet were torn to shreds. A large splinter of bloody corn stalk pierced the skin between my toes. As I pulled it out, I thought about Nola, farming in bare feet, and I winced. She was tougher than I gave her credit, I thought. Then I stood up.

Nola.

71

Perhaps with a little more sleep, a little less head trauma, or a few more IQ points, I would have thought of it earlier. With my foot on the floor, speeding down the country roads, I tried to focus on the task at hand instead of beating myself up for having forgotten the obvious.

Rupp told me I had been exposed to the spores the first time I went into the tent. He sent the crop duster to contain the outbreak; that's what kept me from getting sick. What did I do between exposure and treatment? I hugged Nola, kissed her, then forced her out of the treatment zone. Nola wasn't suffering from an attack of her Multiple Chemical Sensitivity; she had a deadly fungal plague, one that came from me.

As I drove up Valley Road, I called the hospital. They told me Nola was in room 308, but when they put me through, there was no answer.

Fire trucks were lined up on the side of the road. In front of them were a half-dozen black, government-issue SUVs. The smoke rising in the distance had thinned to a wispy white haze. Passing the fire engines, my heart fell at the sight of the cruiser with the seal of the Dunston Borough Police Chief.

I barely slowed at the driveway to the abandoned farm across the road, skidding as I cut a sharp right and pulled up into the back, behind the barn. I had three-quarters of a tank of gas in the truck, so I left the engine running. Either I'd be leaving soon and I'd be in a hurry, or else it just wouldn't matter.

The area was crawling with feds in dark suits, most wearing shades. They milled around in little clumps, separate from each other, like they were from different agencies or jurisdictions. Maybe Noreen had called the FBI or something, but I figured the confusion could be helpful. My vehicle may not have blended in, but from a distance, my funeral suit did.

Staying back from the road, I jogged about fifty yards, to a low point where I could cross unseen. On the other side of the road, I charged up a steep incline to an open, rolling field. A hundred yards in front of me was that ten-foot chain-link fence. To my right, I could see the gate Rupp had gone through the previous night, open but crawling with feds.

A couple of hundred yards to the left, the fence disappeared behind the trees, where I had climbed over the night before. I realized it was the endpoint of that screen of Siberian elm. I felt a small sense of satisfaction at seeing the end of that massive green curtain. Even though I'd been through it half a dozen times, seeing the end of it made it feel somehow less intimidating. Knowing that the bad guys with the guns were dead helped, too.

I took off at a brisk walk toward the Siberian elm and once again used it for cover as I climbed over the fence. I was really starting to hate this fence, but I was getting pretty good at crossing it, especially with clothes and shoes on.

Brushing myself off and flattening down my hair as best I could,

I started off in what I hoped was the direction of Jason Rupp. I tried to adopt the stoic, superior demeanor of most of the feds I had worked with, the ones that drove Stan Bowers nuts.

I knew I was getting closer when I smelled smoke and burnt plastic. I passed another cluster of suits. When they looked over at me, I ignored them, like I was more important than they were.

Up ahead, I could see half an acre cordoned off with red caution tape. Inside it, the feds weren't milling around in standard dark suits; they were milling around in white hazmat suits. At the center of it all was a huge blackened oval where the tent had been. Next to that was the overturned earth where the apple trees had been, the melted wreckage of the trailer, and the hazmat shower, still intact.

Strewn across the ground, I could make out the bits and pieces of Leo and his friends. Little yellow flags were planted in the ground next to each piece. There were a lot of them. It looked kind of festive.

The guys in the hazmat suits seemed to be doing a lot of standing around with their hands on their hips, like they were having a hard time making sense of it all. Good luck with that, I thought.

I'd help them later, but I wasn't going to risk spending hours in an interrogation room while Nola's infection killed her.

Off to the left, just inside the red tape, was the twisted, flattened metal hulk of the gasoline tank, standing straight up, maybe six feet high, plunged into the ground like a knife. None of the hazmat suits were anywhere near it, and there were no little yellow flags. They hadn't yet noticed Rupp's body pinned underneath. I had been worried about tracking around more of the spores, but the tank had come down some distance from the tent, and it had been engulfed in flames when it went up.

I walked along the outside of the perimeter, keeping my distance from the red tape until the tank was between me and the guys in the white suits. Then I ducked under the tape and hurried over to the tank, crouching down so I would not be seen.

Rupp's legs were still sticking out from under the gas tank. A piece of the trailer lay across his legs, but when I pulled it off, there he was, soaking wet and smelling strongly of the chemical decontaminant.

The way it was twisted, I couldn't tell if the bottom of the tank was three feet underground and, with it, the rest of Rupp's body, or if that part of it was resting lightly on top of him.

He had kept the pills in the outside pocket on his jacket. I was pretty sure it was the left side.

Reaching under the metal, I could feel the damp fabric of his jacket with the tips of my fingers, but the metal was firmly against his body. When I pushed against the tank with my shoulder, it rocked forward. A wet, sucking sound came out from underneath it, and I tried not to think about what it was doing to the remains of Jason Rupp. I pulled the fabric closer, but not enough to reach in the pocket. With my shoulder against the tank, I pushed with my legs and moved the tank back enough that I could reach in with one hand. I tried not to think about what would happen if my legs slipped out from under me, how the tank would rock back and crush my hand, trapping me there. My fingers found the pocket, and when they wrapped around the pill bottle I had to resist the urge to relax.

As I pulled the pill bottle out, however, I heard a groaning sound of twisting metal. The tank shifted slightly away from me. I held my breath as it seemed to settle into place for a moment. Then it pitched over, falling slowly away from me. It landed with a loud *whoomp* and reverberated with a bell-like hum.

The guys in the hazmat suits stopped and looked over at me, looking like a pack of prairie dogs. For a moment we just stared at each other. I snuck a peek at Rupp's remains, and immediately wished I hadn't. One of the prairie dogs pointed at me and took a step; then they all did, coming toward me in a slow wave of muffled shouts and awkward shuffles.

72

I angled away from most of the dark suits, but the ones nearby noticed something was up. They seemed conflicted at first; their natural instinct to chase whoever was being chased was mitigated by the fact that I was wearing a suit like theirs and the guys chasing me weren't. Eventually, one of the dark suits said, "Hey, hold on there. Stop!" Then the rest joined in the chase. They quickly outpaced the hazmat guys, but by then I had a decent lead.

When I got to the fence, I didn't slow down; springing as high as I could, I grabbed the links with my fingers and toes. When I reached the top, I had enough momentum to swing myself over. I think I beat Moose's time. When I came down on the outside, I could see a loose pack of six or eight feds in dark suits, close behind me, yelling "Stop," "Halt," or, most ominously, "Freeze!"

As I turned and sprinted off, I wondered what they thought was going on, and what I had to do with it. More to the point, I wondered if they'd feel justified shooting me in the back.

At the edge of the field, I jumped feet first, sliding down the

eight-foot incline and onto the road. I did not look both ways before I crossed, but halfway across, I did look one way, when the
sound of screeching brakes caught my attention.

I stopped and jumped back, and for a moment, Pruitt and I
stared at each other. Then I heard the rustle of dark suits approaching behind me, and I continued up the embankment on the other
side of the road. I looked back to see Pruitt, half out of his car,
looking on as a half-dozen federal agents crossed the road in front
of him like a small herd of dark-suited antelope. Then I cut left,
lowered my head, and concentrated on running.

My lungs were burning pretty good by the time I saw the truck,
still there, the engine still running. I vaulted in, put it in gear, and
sped down the driveway. Then I turned onto the road, only to see
Pruitt's car coming up fast behind me with its lights flashing. I put
down the pedal, trying to get as much as I could out of Frank's
truck. There were rules for police regarding high-speed chases, but
I knew that when it came down to it, Pruitt was about as concerned
with rules as I was.

I got it up to eighty, which was practically suicide on those
roads—not just because of the blind turns and the hidden drive-
ways but also the gut-wrenching lurches over each rolling hill.
Still, Pruitt stayed on me, and I wondered if he was going to start
shooting. When I pushed the needle up to ninety, he almost missed
a curve, spinning out on the side of the road in a cloud of dust. I
put some distance between us after that, and he fell behind even
more, apparently reluctant to try those speeds again.

Finally, the hospital appeared on my right. I swerved into the
entrance and parked right in front. A valet came up to me, then
stepped back. Whatever respectability the suit might have lent me
was now long gone; it was crumpled and sweaty, covered with grass
and dirt. He put up both hands, letting me know he wouldn't be
giving me any trouble.

If the truck was still there when all this was over, I'd make sure he got a nice tip.

The lobby was as crowded as the Emergency Room had been, but instead of the pale sweat of infection, these faces were stricken with fear and concern, in some cases despair. As I pushed through the murmuring crowd, trying not to make eye contact, I heard words like "plague" and "epidemic" and "quarantine."

I wondered if I was too late.

Nola's room was 308, on the third floor, but as tired as I was, I didn't want to risk the elevator. I took the steps two at a time and didn't slow down until I got there.

Then I stopped. The room was empty.

73

Standing in the doorway to the empty room, my thoughts were a jumbled mess, like they'd been smashed and shattered and swept into a single pile. At the sound of footsteps rushing behind me, I expected to be slammed against the wall and cuffed, read my rights if I was lucky. Instead it was a soft touch, and I turned to see Janie.

She read my face and shook her head. "No, she's still alive. They moved her to the ICU. But . . . nothing is working. We can't seem to help her."

"I need to see her. Now."

She shook her head. "She's in quarantine. They all are. "

"Take me there."

She stared at my face a moment longer. Then she said, "Come on."

I followed her down the hallway, my hand resting lightly on her back, making sure she didn't slow down. I kept an eye out, especially behind us, waiting at any moment for Pruitt or the feds to show up.

Through the glass doors of the isolation ward, I could see dozens of beds, patients covered with masks and tubes and wires. When I pushed the glass door, it didn't move.

"You can't go in there, but you can see her, third from the end on the left," Janie said. "She's in isolation. It's locked down."

"I need to get in there."

"You can't. We have to keep whatever it is isolated."

"Isolated? Have you seen the emergency room?"

She bit her lip, but shook her head. "You can't. Orders from the CDC."

I took the pill bottle out of my pocket and shook it. "This is the cure. I just took it off the body of the guy who created it, the guy who created the disease that's killing her. I need to go in there and give her one of these capsules before the infection spreads to her brain and she dies."

I felt bad for Janie. It was a tough spot to be in. But I didn't have time to wait for her to decide what to do.

When I tugged out my gun and pointed it at the glass door, she said, "Wait," and stepped forward to swipe her card through the electronic lock.

Nola was dying. Her face was gray except for an angry red around her eyes and nose. I needed to wake her up, but I was scared to touch her. She looked like she would break.

I took her hand between mine and kissed her forehead. Her skin felt cold and damp. When I brushed her hair away from her face, she opened her eyes.

"Hey," I said softly.

She looked at me, but she couldn't speak.

I opened the pill bottle. There were about two dozen capsules inside it. I shook one into my hand. "I need you to take this."

In the distance, I could hear raised voices.

Nola struggled to focus on the capsule. Then she looked back at me and gave her head a little shake.

"You've got to," I said.

"Can't," she rasped.

The voices were getting closer now. I could hear yelling.

I tried to put the capsule in her mouth, but she shook her head again. "Can't swallow."

I could hear footsteps now, running.

I twisted open the capsule and emptied the contents into her mouth, leaving a smudge of white powder on her lips.

She moved her tongue around in her mouth. Her lips were cracked. I dribbled just the tiniest bit of water in there from a cup on the table beside her bed. I waited a second, then dribbled some more.

"Careful," said Janie, behind me. "If that gets into her lungs . . ."

Nola coughed a little bit. She sounded like she wanted to cough more but didn't have the strength.

I didn't know how much of the Mycozene she was getting, but I knew she was in bad shape. I opened a second capsule and repeated the process. Then I sealed it with a kiss.

When I pulled back, Nola had tears in her eyes. "Scared," she said.

I gave her a smile with more confidence than I was feeling. "You'll be okay now."

I was holding her hand, and when I moved to go, she held it tight. "Don't go," she whispered.

"I'm not going anywhere."

Almost as soon as I said it, Pruitt came through the door with his gun two-handed out in front of him, swinging it around this way and that, covering the whole room. His face was a bright, even red, like a bad sunburn.

"*Get down, you piece of shit!*" he roared at me. He must have been ten feet away from me, and I still felt moisture land on my cheek.

As I turned around and raised my hands, I heard Pruitt grunt. Then I felt his gun come down hard on the side of my head.

74

I went dizzy for a moment, and the side of my head felt hot and wet. Janie was screaming.

Pruitt stuck his gun in my face, mumbling something about a right to an attorney as he grabbed me by the shirt and swung me off the bed and into a wheelchair. My head cleared as a small cluster of sweaty men in dark suits showed up, each flashing ID from a different agency, each trying to claim me as theirs.

Pruitt ignored them as he wheeled me toward the elevators. We all crowded onto the first one going down.

In the elevator, I could hear phrases like "jurisdiction" and "national security" and "global pandemic," but each time Pruitt would reply with, "*murder.*"

When the doors opened, Pruitt wheeled me out of the elevator and through the lobby, the entire gaggle of suits in tow. I had recovered enough that I could have put my foot down on the floor and brought the whole procession to a halt. But I figured resisting arrest in front of a lobby full of people would not help my already remote chances of professional rehabilitation. And going along for the ride probably wouldn't hurt my case if I ever decided to sue the bastard for brutality. I closed my eyes and struggled not to smile at that thought.

I heard the automatic doors whoosh open, and I felt the bump of wheels going over the threshold. But once we were outside, Pruitt ground to a halt. The chatter of the suits stopped as well.

When I opened my eyes, I saw a team of eight tactical agents in black combat outfits with Homeland Security insignias and "DHS" emblazoned across the front. They were aiming their laser-sighted M4s so that each of the suits had a red laser dot over his chest. Pruitt had one on his chest and one on his forehead. I looked down and saw one on my chest, too.

In the middle of the group was Danny Tennison, looking very smug. Next to him was an older guy who looked like he was in charge. Danny leaned over to him, gestured at me, and said, "That's him."

The older guy stepped forward and held up his ID. "Special Agent Craig Sorenson, Homeland Security." He looked down at me. "Doyle Carrick?"

I raised my hand, wondering if I was about to be disappeared. Once again, I regretted having brought up Danny's marriage.

One of the agents next to Sorenson stepped in and gave me a quick pat down before taking my cell phone out of my jacket. He tapped it a few times, then showed the display to Sorenson. Sorenson nodded, and the other guy stepped back out of the way. He kept my phone.

Sorenson looked down at me sideways, assessing the blood on the side of my head. "Can you walk?"

"Yeah."

He pointed to a large black van parked at the curb. "Then walk."

75

As it turned out, it wasn't just a van; it was a Mobile Intelligence Unit.

"Nice van," I said when we got inside.

"It's not a van," Sorenson replied. "It's a Mobile Intelligence Unit."

It was bigger than my college dorm room, and even with Sorenson, a doctor, and two agents named Lionel and Durand, it was less crowded. In the middle was a table with benches on either side and a chair at one end. It even had a bathroom.

Sorenson sat at the chair and took a deep, loud breath. "So what the hell is going on here?"

"You know, it's funny," I replied. "I've been wondering that myself."

Before we got started, I put the Mycozene pills on the table and told Sorenson what they were and where I got them.

He eyed them suspiciously. "This is what you gave the girl?"

I nodded. "I'm pretty sure whatever she has is the same thing that's filling up this hospital. This is the cure."

He gave the bottle a little shake, rattling around two dozen or so pills inside. "I don't think that's going to be enough."

I could see why Stan Bowers didn't like the guy. "I'm pretty sure the Dunston police have fifty kilos of the stuff in the evidence lock up. They thought it was heroin; then they thought it was flour. It's a drug called Mycozene, distilled from genetically engineered corn."

Sorenson gave Agent Lionel a nod that spun him on his heel and sent him from the van. Then Sorenson turned back to me and held up the pill bottle again. "And you're sure this stuff will cure this disease you're telling me about?"

"That's what the evil genius told me."

"You know, if it's not, you could be looking at another murder charge."

I laughed. "If it's not, my legal troubles will be the least of our worries."

For the next eight hours, we tried to piece it together.

I told Sorenson almost everything. When I finished, I asked him to check on Nola for me. He ignored that and asked me to tell the story again. When I finished the second time, he left for ten minutes. When he came back, he brought me a soda. Then he asked me to tell the entire story again.

I thanked him for the soda; then I told him I wasn't answering any more questions without an update on Nola's condition.

He looked at me like he was trying to decide which would be easier, breaking out the enhanced interrogation techniques or calling the hospital. He turned his back and mumbled into his phone. A moment later, he turned back to face me and said, "Critical but stable."

"Thanks," I said, sipping the soda. "I also need you to check on a kid named Carl Squires. Accidental death, drug overdose a couple of days ago. Pruitt found him under the Stony Creek Bridge. Looked like he got high and fell off the bridge. I think it might have been murder, and it might have been Levkov and company."

Sorenson raised an eyebrow, but he didn't say anything.

"I think they caught him stealing some of their magic apples and they killed him. Dosed him up and tossed him off the bridge. Pruitt said he had a lump on the side of his head and the back of his head was smashed in where he landed. I'm wondering if the pathologist can check the blood in the contusion on the side of his head, see if it has the same level of opioids as the rest of him."

Sorenson frowned. "Why?"

"Cause of death was the fall, but the theory was that he fell because of the drugs. If the contusion is clean, that means somebody thumped him, then dosed him and tossed him off the bridge."

Sorenson nodded to the other agent, Durand, and he slipped outside. Then Sorenson turned back to me. "One more time."

When I finished that time, Sorenson disappeared again. Twenty minutes later, he returned with a plate of meatloaf and mashed potatoes from Branson's. Moose was right; the meatloaf was good.

As I ate, Sorenson shared some information, on the condition that I not tell anyone else. They had found some of Rupp's notes and were still going through them, probably would be for years, but parts of the story had begun to emerge. I'd already figured a lot of it out, but I was impressed with how quickly Sorenson was able to fill in so many of the holes.

Rupp grew up just outside Dunston as Jason Gimble. Poor, fat, and socially awkward but very smart, he was a bully's dream classmate, and one of those bullies, coincidentally, was Dwight Cooney. Gimble took his grandfather's name, Rupp, when he left town. After his spectacular success and failure in academia, he tried legitimate business. He thought he had struck it rich when he created Mycozene,

but the FDA refused to approve his wonder drug for wide use, saying the minor risk of elevated liver enzyme levels were not justified
by the innocuous diseases it cured. Having failed to make his fortune
legitimately, Rupp tried a different approach. The opioid-producing
apples were his first attempt at making an illegal fortune. It was an
impressive scientific accomplishment, but not the world-changing
moneymaker he hoped it would be.

According to Rupp's notes, the apples were potent, but the trees
lacked vigor and required a lot of care. He couldn't just license
them, either, because the people who would be interested in licens-
ing them would also be interested in killing him and taking them.
That meant he had to be involved in production, and that meant he
had to deal with people like Levkov, who started out as his drug
middleman but quickly took over the operation.

Rupp probably could have made millions with those apples. But
he didn't want millions, he wanted billions.

Mycozene was a breakthrough cure for fungal diseases; what
Rupp needed was a fungal disease that was bad enough, deadly
enough, and common enough that the drug's health risks would be
overlooked. Mycozene was one hundred-percent effective against
common bread mold, which could become a deadly infection in
immuno-compromised patients. So Rupp altered the mold, creating
a designer rhizomycosis. Instead of affecting a handful of immuno-
compromised Americans every year, it would infect millions.

The outbreak in Dunston was not part of the plan; that was the
result of a failure in containment. Rupp had told me the same thing,
but I kept quiet when Sorenson mentioned that, because I wasn't
sure how much of that failure of containment was because of me.

Rupp's plan was to release the spores into the environment on the
wings of the Monarch butterflies. There would be a few cases right
off the bat, but not many. Rupp's rhizomycosis was like anthrax; it
was deadly, but it was not contagious, not from person to person. It

could only be contracted by exposure in the environment. Unlike anthrax, however, it could readily grow and spread in the environment, on wet leaves or garbage or other welcoming environments. It would take a while, but the spores from the butterflies would grow and spread in the environment, and after a year or two the cases would start to mount. By then it would be everywhere, and the world would come knocking, happy to accept slightly elevated liver enzyme levels and willing to pay any price for another chance at Rupp's wonder drug.

Levkov was bad news, but Rupp wasn't some absentminded professor going along for the ride. Rupp conceived of the entire plan, endangering hundreds of millions of innocent people. And while Levkov did the actual dirty work—imprisoning migrant workers, testing the pathogen on them to make sure it was lethal, and then incinerating them in staged meth lab fires—it was Rupp who came up with that testing regimen.

"It was a sick plan, but brilliant," Sorenson concluded. "It could have killed millions, and made billions. And it almost worked."

"What about Rothe? Do you see him as being in on it?"

"Rothe? Who's that?"

"The developer. He had some elaborate deal set up to buy all the land, to build a housing development on the land Rupp and Levkov were using."

"You mean the Redtail Properties guy? I don't think so. What do you think?"

"I don't think so either. He was an unwitting accomplice. They gave him a great price on the land, but part of the deal was he had to start construction right away. Rupp figured by the time the rhizomycosis became an issue, Redtail would have bulldozed and built over any evidence."

"Clever. And now the poor bastard is stuck owning a massive hazardous waste site."

"What about Bricker? The lawyer?"

"I can't say too much about that, because technically you're still a person of interest. I don't think she had any idea what Rupp and Levkov were up to, but let's say she was probably a little less innocent, and it ended a little worse for her. Still, she was more of a loose end than conspirator."

After Sorenson shared his information, he asked me to go over the whole thing one more time. As a cop, I knew there was a legitimate benefit to repeating a story, but it was a long story, and I had been through it several times.

"I don't know how much more of this I got in me," I told him.

"All right. One last question, though." He gave me a steely look. "Where are those apples?"

"I have no idea. Like I said, the shed was empty when I went back to test them. When I started to suspect there was something up with the apples, I asked Rupp about it. The trees disappeared right after that."

Sorenson grunted, eyeing me suspiciously for a moment. "A lot of money could be made with those apples," he said. "Drug cartels, pharmaceutical companies, they'd love to get their hands on them, and on the technology Rupp used to produce them. So would we."

I shrugged.

"You have any ideas, you let us know." He leaned in closer. "We might not be able to pay as much as the drug companies, but there'd definitely be a big reward. And it would be the right thing to do."

I nodded, and he seemed to let it go.

"I have a last question, too," I told him. "How did you guys get wind of this?"

"Levkov's been on our radar for some time. He was a major league asshole and we'd been looking for him, as have a half a dozen agencies around the world. When your friend Tennison ran a search on him, it got our attention, and we came looking. We had a file on Rupp, too, but we never expected anything like this."

I smiled. Danny might have told me to leave it alone, but he still did the search for me.

"All right," Sorenson said, standing up. "We'll pick this up later." He put a set of car keys on the table. "We're impounding your truck out there, but here's a loaner, parked out back, courtesy of the Federal government. We'll be sending someone over to your house to get the car out of your garage. I don't know if they'll give you a loaner for that. Go home and get some rest. Don't talk about any of this to anyone. Oh," he added as an afterthought, "and you can't leave town."

I smiled and nodded. "Yeah, I know the drill."

"No, I mean you can't leave town. Quarantine, a five-mile radius. If you try to leave, you'll be shot."

76

When I woke up the sky was light again, which totally confused me until I realized it was the next day. Moose had made coffee and, thankfully, had done laundry. After a quick shower, we were ready to go.

Getting to the hospital wasn't easy. The feds had set up a massive detour around the scene of the fire. A trio of black helicopters hovered over the field like dragonflies, motionless in the air. I used them as reference points as I navigated the back roads and eventually made my way to the hospital.

When we got there, the woman at the intake desk gave us Nola's new room number. But once again, it was empty.

"I'll go ask the nurse where she is," Moose said. I had already spotted Nola in the solarium at the end of the hall, but I let him go looking anyway.

She was sitting in a wheelchair, paler and thinner, gazing out the window. She turned and saw me and she started to stand, but I got there before she could. I wrapped my arms around her and squeezed. There was a frailty to her, but holding her tight, I could still feel the strength at her core. I held her close for a while, and then she pulled back and ran her fingers over the knot where Pruitt had hit me. "Are you okay?"

"I'm fine. You look great."

"Yeah, right."

She was wearing a hospital gown under a robe, and I slipped my hand into the robe, around to the back.

She let out a little gasp as my hand found the gap and the warm skin underneath it.

"You're bad," she said, pulling my hand up to her face.

"I'm trying to be," I told her.

"They treated the others," she said solemnly. "They're doing better, all of them."

"Good."

Her eyes welled up, and she squeezed my hand hard. "They told me what you did. I wouldn't have made it if it wasn't for you."

"Well, you wouldn't have been sick if it wasn't—"

She silenced me with a finger on my lips and said, "Thanks."

I knew I was supposed to say "You're welcome," but it didn't feel right. So I was relieved that Moose found us then. He gave Nola a long, teary-eyed embrace.

For the next half hour, I filled them in on some of what I knew. I told Nola about Cooney's little shrine to her, about the calls from his phone. She nodded quietly, and in her wet eyes I could see relief and fear and sorrow for Cooney's sad, lonely life. Moose seemed a little angry, and relieved Cooney was dead. I was with him on that, but we gave Nola a moment.

"But wait a second," Moose said. "If those calls weren't about trying to get her to sell, what about the text? Why did he torch Nola's crops?"

"That wasn't Cooney. I think that was Rupp's people. Nola told

Rupp she was getting pressured to sell when we brought him the corn that had been contaminated by his GMO corn. They used the hang-ups and the harassment as a cover to destroy Nola's tainted corn, erase their evidence. Then they harvested their own."

Nola's eyes welled up again at that, all her hard work, and how they destroyed it. I squeezed her hand, and after a minute I continued, telling them about my interrogation with Sorenson, and everything I'd learned about Rupp's plan, including the things I told Sorenson I wouldn't tell anybody.

By the time I was finished, Nola was visibly drained. We wheeled her back to her room, and Moose gave her a peck on the cheek. I helped her into bed, and I copped another feel when I did it.

As we got back in the loaner car, my phone went off. It was Sorenson.

"You were right about Squires," he said. "Contusion on the side of his head was inconsistent with the injuries from the fall. Coroner said he figured the kid had bumped his head on the railing or something, but you were right; the blood in it had traces of opiates, but nothing compared to the blood in his system. Looked like they hit him with a rifle butt. Good call."

He'd probably been consuming juice from those apples for a little while, so it was no surprise there were traces in his system.

"What was that?" Moose asked, staring at my face as I put away my phone.

"Squirrel," I said with a sad sigh. "I asked them to look into it. He was murdered."

Moose nodded like he already knew. Then he looked out the window and wiped his eyes.

When we got back to the house, Moose got out of the car, but I kept the engine running. I told him I had another stop to make.

The heart of town looked the same, but no one was walking on the street, and only a few cars were parked on the side of the road. The quiet didn't seem ominous like it did before; the town seemed tired, like it was resting. As I pulled open the door to Branson's, I wondered if this was the kind of catastrophe that could kill a town entirely, turn it into a ghost town, like Centralia with its underground fires.

The few people inside were mostly sitting by themselves, grim-faced, reading the newspaper. At some point, I'd have to read about it, too, learn the official story.

Two old guys were at the bar, but there was no sign of Bert Squires behind it. As I was turning to leave, one of the old guys reached over the bar for a bottle and I realized it was him.

He looked withered and old, his hand shaking as he filled his double shot glass. When I sat on the stool next to him, he turned and looked at me with hollow, red-rimmed eyes. He didn't say a word, but he reached over and grabbed another glass and poured me one, too.

We drank them down, and he refilled the glasses. Then he sighed and reached down the bar, refilling the other guy's glass as well.

"Thanks, Bert," the other guy rasped.

"So I guess you're stuck here for a while," Squires said. "What with the quarantine and everything."

"Yeah, I guess so," I told him. "But the place is kind of growing on me. Who knows, maybe I'll learn to love it as much as Frank did."

Bert laughed—a short, boozy cackle that couldn't sustain itself. "Are you kidding me? Frank hated it out here."

"What are you talking about?"

"Frank Menlow? Frank was a great guy, but he was a city boy, through and through. He missed the city, he missed his friends. He missed you."

I hadn't really thought about it, but it never quite made sense to me that Frank wanted to be out here. "Then why did he want to come out here?"

Bert swallowed his shot and shrugged. "Because of your mom. She loved it out here, and the thing that mattered most to Frank was making your mom happy."

He smiled and shook his head, thinking about it.

I blinked a few times, thinking about what he had said. Then I shook my head to clear it.

"Look, I don't know if this helps or not," I told him, "but I figured you'd want to know. Carl wasn't an overdose. He was murdered."

Bert turned and looked at me, trembling, with a look in his eyes like anger and sorrow had somehow combined into fear. "But they said he had enough drugs in him, he would've been dead even without the fall."

"They murdered him, Bert. They hit him over the head, and they put that stuff in him. Then they tossed him off the bridge. He never took any drugs, not intentionally."

He stared at me. "How do you know?"

"I know, Bert. Believe me. He saw something they didn't want him to see, and they murdered him."

"You sure?"

I nodded.

He stared at me for another second. Then I guess he decided he did believe me. "Who did it?"

"They're dead," I told him.

"Are you sure?"

"Yeah, Bert. I killed them."

His eyes got redder, and he put his hand on my arm. "Thanks, Doyle," he said. "Frank was right about you."

He gave my arm a firm squeeze as he stood up. Then he turned and hurried out of the bar.

It may have been the whiskey, or it could have been everything else, but by the time I got home I was ready to go back to bed. I figured it would be another twenty hours before I was ready to get up again. But when I pulled into the driveway, the Michelin man was sitting on my porch. For a moment, I thought one of the feds in the hazmat suits who had been chasing me finally caught up with me. But as I got out of the car, I saw it was actually Danny Tennison.

"Nice outfit," I said as I climbed the steps. "Very slimming."

He laughed. "Well, apparently, this town of yours has cooties. I had to go through decontamination before they let me leave the first time. Very *thorough* decontamination. I don't ever want to go through that again." He leaned forward and whispered loudly. "And some of us still have to go to work."

"You want some time off, I can tell you how to get it."

"That's okay. I said I was getting along better with the wife; I don't want to jeopardize that by actually being around her all the time."

"So that's your secret."

He smiled. "You're looking a little better. You get some rest?"

"A little. Another couple hundred hours and maybe I'll be caught up."

"Stan Bowers sends his regards. Wanted you to know he won't be pressing charges for impersonating a federal officer. You got anything to say about that?"

I had to say something, but I didn't want to incriminate myself. "Good?"

"You're goddamn right, good." Danny laughed, shaking his head. "Your buddy Pruitt's on unpaid leave, pending the outcome of an investigation into the way he handled your arrest."

I snorted. "Okay."

He craned his neck to see the lump on the side of my head. "Got you pretty good, didn't he?"

"If he'd gotten there a couple minutes earlier, my girlfriend would be dead."

"But he didn't, did he?"

"What are you getting at?"

"The Berks County D.A. wants me to ask if you're planning on pressing charges."

"Hadn't thought about that." I sighed. "The guy can be a pretty big asshole."

He nodded. "Yes, that does seem to be the case."

"And he was way out of line."

"Not the first cop to cross a line, though, is he?"

"No, but still, something needs to happen."

"Well, I think the D.A. wants this to go away. And he wants to know what it would take for you to let it."

I thought for a moment. Then it hit me. "Anger management training," I said. "*Mandatory* anger management training."

Danny laughed. We both did. "You're a real prick, you know that?"

"If I was a prick, I'd enroll in it alongside him, just so I could exercise my right to drop out." I smiled. "See? I am getting better."

He laughed again. "Well, thank God for that."

77

When I got inside, I started up the stairs, but looking down the hallway, I saw the mess of papers I had left on the floor in Frank's office. I smiled, thinking about all Frank's files and folders, everything exactly in its place. I thought about how, if I died, it would take a forensic accountant weeks to find the documents Frank had neatly filed away. And I'd never bought a house, or life insurance. I barely filed taxes.

I didn't want to find any more surprises, but leaving the room a mess felt disrespectful. So, before I went to bed, I started piling everything back into the boxes. As I did, one of the envelopes came open, and a sheaf of photos slid out across the floor. The ones on top were fairly recent, pictures of my mom on the front porch or in the garden, wearing the lilac print cardigan she always wore. Underneath were older photos of her when she was younger. Seeing them was sad, but they made me smile.

It struck me that I had never really appreciated how beautiful she was. I remembered some of the photos: the two of us on a roller coaster, at the top of a lighthouse.

They were happy photos, and I needed that. Frank was in some of them, staged shots of the three of us smiling awkwardly: Williamsburg, the Franklin Institute, a Phillies game. The rest were of my mom and me, playing, laughing, snuggling, just walking down the street.

There was one photo in particular that caught my eye, one that I remembered. The two of us laughing, eating ice-cream cones in front of Bredenbeck's ice-cream parlor, in Chestnut Hill. She's about to wipe my chin with a napkin. I'm about twelve years old, giving her this look, like I'm too old for her to be wiping my chin, and she's giving me this look like, no you're not. As I stared at the photo, I felt myself smiling, too, a bittersweet smile, along with the faces in the picture. Then I noticed Frank, reflected in the window behind us.

He was young, and I could see him laughing along with us as he took the picture.

I looked back at all the other photos of my mother and me, and I realized they were all taken by Frank. The only reason he wasn't in them was that he was the one taking them.

I spent the rest of the afternoon going through those boxes, looking through hundreds of pictures. In most of them, my mom is looking right at me, and I could see how much she loved me. But in many, she's looking right into the camera, and in those, I could see how much she loved Frank, too.

78

Dunston was declared quarantined for another two weeks, and that was fine with me. I had no place to go anyway. I wasn't even in much of a hurry to get back to work. Like I had told Bert Squires, the town was growing on me.

Nola got dramatically better over the next couple of days, and our visits got longer. Each time I visited her, the little sunroom was more populated, as more victims of Rupp's pathogen recovered. The doctors were concerned about the possibility of liver damage from the Mycozene, but so far everyone was fine.

At first, Nola was happy just to be alive, and to be with me. But after a couple of days, I noticed a melancholy setting in.

We were sitting in the sunroom, speaking in hushed tones since the room was now full. "My farm," she said, when I asked her what was wrong. "I put everything I had into it. Now it's gone. My little organic farm is a toxic waste site." When she sighed, it was deep and sad, but free of rasps or wheezing. "Maybe your friend Jordan Rothe will reconsider."

I didn't tell her that Jordan Rothe had probably lost everything and wouldn't be buying anything for a long, long time. Instead I put my arm around her and told her everything would be all right.

The next day, when I came to visit, she still seemed down. But I brought her a present. It was an apple, the one I had seen through the fence, half-buried in mud. It was bruised and withered, and Nola looked at me funny when I gave it to her.

"Thanks," she said, putting it aside. "I'll eat it later."

"No, you won't."

I told her about what Sorenson had said, about how they couldn't find Rupp's apples, and how badly they wanted to get hold of them. How badly the drug companies would want to get hold of them as well. How the feds would offer a big reward.

"And that?" she said.

I nodded. "There's ninety cases of them out there somewhere, and the trees themselves are out there, too. They're bound to turn up sooner or later. But this is the only one to turn up so far. It's up to you what you want to do with it. The pharmaceutical companies would probably make you pretty rich." I shrugged. "But Sorenson could probably come up with enough to pay off your mortgage and buy a few acres and a house in a town at least as nice as Dunston."

She smiled and picked up the apple. "And you're giving this to me?"

I nodded.

"You know, I . . . I don't really approve of profiting off genetically modified crops."

I put my hand on her knee. "Someone's going to find them, and someone is going to get paid. You might as well get paid first."

She thought about it for a moment. Then she smiled. "You're a heck of a guy, Doyle Carrick."

I smiled back. "I keep saying."

She put her arms around me and gave me the kind of long, lingering kiss that let me know she was feeling better.

She was released the next day with a clean bill of health. She was a little weak, but her color was back and she looked beautiful. I took her home, and I took good care of her until she got her strength back. And after that, she took care of me.